# Beneath *the* Frost

## USA *TODAY* BESTSELLING AUTHOR
## LENA HENDRIX

Developmental editing: Paula Dawn, Lilypad Lit

Copy editing: James Gallagher

Proofreading: Julia Griffis, The Romance Bibliophile

Model & Discreet cover design: TRC Designs by Cat

Model cover photography: Wander Aguiar

*To anyone who's ever wanted to teach **him** a thing or two . . . Wes Vaughn is eager for some extra credit. Class is in session.*

# LET'S CONNECT

When you sign up for my newsletter, you'll stay up to date with new releases, book news, giveaways, and new book recommendations! I promise not to spam you and only email when I have something fun & exciting to share!

Also, When you sign up, you'll also get a FREE copy of Choosing You (a very steamy Chikalu Falls novella)!

Sign up at my website at www.lenahendrix.com

# AUTHOR'S NOTE

This book contains mentions of a car accident, loss of a limb, depression, and isolation.

In addition to extensive research around above the knee, single-leg amputations, special care was taken when considering the extent of Wes's injuries and his recovery. Consultations with a prosthetic specialist, as well as amputees who have experienced similar trauma to him were conducted. My hope is that I handled this topic with the sensitivity and care it deserves.

To make things lighter (and hotter), I was sure to balance that heavy topic with sexy lessons (where SHE is the teacher), a grump with a filthy mouth, and lots of praise— I'm nothing if not a girl's girl, after all.

# BENEATH THE FROST

STAR HARBOR BOOK 3

LENA HENDRIX

# ABOUT THIS BOOK

Weston Vaughn has always been the most charming man in any room—until he saved my brother's life and the accident took his leg.

**Now he's a gruff recluse and my new roommate.**

After my life goes up in flames on my wedding day, I become my small town's favorite scandal. I want to lie low while the gossip dies down, but living with my parents feels impossible. Moving in with my brother's best friend is my best option.

He won't ask for help and I won't be dismissed. Trouble is, I like this gruff side of Wes, and despite his rules, I enjoy showing up for him. He's adjusting to his new life, and when he finally admits his confidence is shot, well . . . I know exactly what he needs.

**I'm a *hands-on* kind of caretaker.**

Tensions rise as our tentative arrangement melts into sexy, forbidden lessons aimed to rebuild the confidence he's lost. He thinks he's broken, but all I see is an irresistible man with a firm grip and a filthy mouth.

He's walled off his heart, but all it takes is a woman who's willing to see what lies beneath the frost.

# ONE

# CLARA

WELL, Phil was dead. Again.

There was something about staring at that pathetic little houseplant that made me want to burst into a fit of the giggles . . . or maybe it was tears. I couldn't quite tell.

*When was the last time I watered Phil?*

That could have been my first clue as to why I struggled to keep a houseplant alive . . . even the ones the tag claimed were unkillable.

January snow fell outside my window in thick, heavy clumps. This side of the apartment hadn't seen daylight in what felt like forever, so maybe it wasn't *all* my fault that the houseplant had kicked the bucket.

A soft knock at the bedroom door drew my attention away from poor Phil. "Come in."

My mother peeked from the doorway, looking me over as her eyes widened. "Sweetie, you aren't even dressed!" She stepped inside my bedroom and quietly closed the door behind her. "We need to leave for the church in five minutes."

I swallowed past the lump in my throat.

*Church.*

The word alone made my stomach swoop, like I'd missed a step on the stairs. It wasn't nerves, not really. It felt more like I was walking into a performance I wasn't sure why I had agreed to star in.

I nodded and moved toward the closet in my room. The expansive walk-in closet was exactly what had sold me on the apartment when Greg and I had decided to move in together. For my job, I needed the closet space, and there was something delightful about twirling in front of a floor-length mirror, ya know?

Standing in the doorway now, it didn't feel like my closet so much as a costume department. Racks of happily ever afters, none of which actually belonged to me.

With my mom behind me, I walked toward the open door. Rows and rows of wedding dresses hung there—all shades of white and cream and alabaster. There were dresses with tiered layers of tulle, sleek silky numbers that hugged my curves, and even one that was a smoky gray that almost matched my eye color.

The one I'd picked for today was hanging in the center, perfectly steamed and ready to go. It wasn't my favorite, but it had been Greg's mother's preference, and I didn't have it in me to argue with her.

Beside me, my mother's wistful sigh floated through the air. "Just gorgeous."

The lie pulsed in my throat. She was looking at her little girl like this was finally it—the moment I joined my sisters in the "happily ever after" club—and I couldn't even give her the courtesy of the truth.

I forced a smile at the lace atrocity.

It wasn't that the dress was horrible. None of them were. It was just that the dress I was going to be walking down the aisle in was the last one I ever would have picked for myself. Maybe that was why, when it came to today, I couldn't shake the overwhelming sense of dread.

"Give me a minute?" I smiled at Mom. "I'll call you in when I need to get zipped up."

My mother's eyes searched mine. I was sure she knew something was off, but my perfectly painted red lips pulled into a smile I thought she might believe. "Of course, honey. I'll be right outside when you need me."

She closed the closet door behind her, and I allowed myself to exhale. My fingertips dragged down the scratchy lace. I already knew it would rub and irritate me all day.

"Here goes nothing," I whispered with an exhale. "It's just another day."

You see, I'd been a bride before. One hundred thirty-two times to be exact. As a bridal model, I had been lucky enough to wear the world's most elite dresses, hot off fashion week runways. Most times designers would need them back, but sometimes I was told to keep the sample dresses that were sent.

Getting laced into a gown was nothing new.

Only this time, it was *real*. Well, real enough.

I slipped out of my robe and into the body-skimming dress before calling back to my mother. "I'm ready."

She stepped inside the closet and pressed a hand to her heart. "Oh . . ." Tears welled in her eyes and I looked away. I didn't have the heart to tell her the truth.

Mom zipped up the back of my dress and pressed her hands at my waist. "You haven't been eating. Are you nervous?"

I looked over my shoulder. "A little." It was the first honest thing I'd said to her all day.

Her phone vibrated, and she pulled it from her beaded purse. "The limo is here. All set?"

I smiled and nodded, unable to make myself move. With one last look around my overstuffed closet, I steeled myself for the day ahead of me.

It was supposed to be the happiest day of my life, and I felt like I was dying.

THE REST of the morning flew by in a blur. When I arrived at the cathedral-style church, the coordinator and photographer were already waiting. The air inside smelled like old wood, candle wax, and fresh flowers—a Pinterest board come to life. As soon as I saw the camera, my spine straightened and my chin tipped, like my body knew how to slide into bridal Clara whether I wanted to or not. I hit my best angles, pausing at the right moment to capture the slit in my dress as I stepped from the limo. If anything, the day felt like another day on the job. Flashing lights, gentle orders to lean my shoulders or tilt my chin.

Bridal modeling had never been the plan for me. Though, neither was marrying a man that I knew couldn't love me. Somewhere along the way, pretending had become my default. Pretend bride. Pretend college major. Pretend fiancée. I was starting to worry I wouldn't recognize *real* if it ever showed up.

When I went away to school, I'd just assumed I would find *something* that lit me up, but that particular muse turned out to be a fickle bitch.

Four major changes later, I was struggling to even graduate.

When I needed some quick cash, I'd answered an ad for

a bridal model with zero experience because *How hard can that be?*

Turns out, really fucking hard, but I fell in love with it. I fell in love with pulling all the pieces together and watching a vision come to life. It was the first time my "too much" energy actually had somewhere to go.

Initially I stayed in my lane as the model only, but the disorganized photo shoots got old quickly. I found I had a knack for finding hair and makeup experts, looking up dress designers online, researching florals and photographers. Mood boards were my specialty, and they never felt like work.

I eventually got a generic degree in "general studies," but if you asked me what that meant or what you could do with it, I couldn't tell you. So far, it meant that I would meet other wandering souls who also had no idea what they were doing.

Which is how I met my fiancé, Greg.

Greg had gone to school knowing he'd take over his father's tech company. His life path was set for him, but his father valued the experience of college. Greg's experiences mostly entailed partying and skipping class.

But he'd always made me laugh.

When we met, we became fast friends. He was as wide-eyed and enthusiastic as I was. If I got the wild idea to move across town or foster a rescue kitten or take up tap dancing, Greg was there to cheer me on.

Somewhere along the way, he'd become the man I agreed to marry.

Not because there'd been some sweeping, cinematic moment where everything clicked. Mostly because he was safe and familiar and already sitting next to me when the idea was floated. It felt less like a proposal and more like . . . forward momentum.

A creepy voice floated through the door of the bridal suite, where I was waiting for the ceremony to start. "Hello, Clarice."

My eyes rolled as I pulled the door open. "You're an idiot."

Greg stood with his silly grin, and I yanked him inside. "Your mom is going to freak out if she sees you and me talking before the ceremony. What's wrong with you?"

He scoffed and leaned against the counter, crossing one long leg over the other. A hand gestured between the two of us. "Please. She believed this schtick a long time ago."

A dry laugh escaped me. Shortly after meeting, Greg and I were hanging out, and I told him I had a crush on a guy in my math class. Turned out, Greg *also* had a crush on him.

The trouble was, Greg's parents were assholes, and his being openly gay wasn't an option if he wanted to take over the family business. He'd been hiding his true self nearly his entire life. I'd grown to feel oddly protective of him over the years. If I could stand between him and their disappointment—even for a little while—it felt like maybe I was good for something.

I suppose that was a major reason why I'd agreed to marry him in the first place. We had a great time together, liked the same food, and laughed all the time. We were great friends, even if he tended to be a little bit shallow and self-centered.

It also helped that Greg knew I dreamed of opening my own business. Bridal modeling barely paid the bills, but it was the planning that lit me up. A designer could come to me and say she needed four dresses to be captured, ten photos, and fifteen seconds of video per dress for their website and social media. I'd put together a quote that included a photographer, videographer, hair and makeup, and a florist. I could run the show and make sure the team was paid well and on time. All I needed to get my business off the ground was time and money to make it happen.

Greg's plan was simple—we'd pretend to be engaged and get his parents off his back. Then, when he finally took over the family business, he'd be my first investor.

He asked, and I said, *Why the hell not?*

The worst part was lying to my family, but I'd made a promise to my best friend. A huge part of me knew that when it came to the Darling family, any gossip would spread through our small town like wildfire. I was desperate to get my dreams off the ground, so I convinced myself that a little white lie would be worth it in the end.

Besides, what was a little lavender marriage between friends?

It wasn't hurting anyone. I genuinely cared for Greg. Sure, it wasn't the obsessive, heart-achingly passionate love my older sisters had found, but so what? I didn't need that.

I told myself that a steady partnership and a shared streaming platform were mature. Responsible. The way my chest ached thinking about my sisters slow dancing in their kitchens was just indigestion.

"You look hot." Greg smirked at me, a giddy laugh bubbling up his throat.

Compliments from Greg always landed like they were aimed at the version of me he needed me to be—polished, presentable, *believable*. A small, pathetic part of me still wanted someone to look at me and mean it like I was the only thing in the room worth staring at.

"Thank you." I blushed and dipped into a curtsy. "Though, I'm not going to lie. I hate this dress."

It was like wearing someone else's story. Someone quieter. Smaller. Someone who didn't mind shrinking herself to fit into lace her future mother-in-law approved of.

"You made Mom *very* happy. She thinks you look like she did on her wedding day, which—let's face it—you're twenty times prettier, and she hates that." Greg's leg was shaking with nerves as his words tumbled out.

"What is with you?" My eyes narrowed. "You're being weird." A prickle crawled up the back of my neck. My gut was trying to warn me of something, I just didn't know yet if it was about him . . . or me.

He stood to his full height, dragging a palm down his tuxedo pants. His palms went out. "Okay, so don't be mad."

I knew that face. My heart lurched. "What did you do?"

His expression twisted into a pout. "Nothing."

I pointed a finger toward him. "Don't *nothing* me. I know that look. You're about to tell me something I don't want to hear. Is the preacher drunk again?"

His lips rolled in like he was desperately trying to keep a serious face. "I told them."

I blinked, my mind not keeping up with what he was saying. "Told them? Told who *what*?"

Greg looked at me and rolled his eyes. "Well . . . my parents. About me. Us. That I'm not exactly, you know, straight as an arrow." He flattened his palm to emphasize his point.

"You came out to them? *Today*?" I couldn't believe it. A war of emotions rioted in my chest. This was huge—monumental, in fact. Greg had always told me that his parents would never accept him and that he felt safest keeping this part of himself a secret from them.

Pride swelled first—my ridiculous, brave friend finally saying the words out loud. Fear followed close behind, whispering, *Okay, but where does that leave you, idiot?*

"Wait a minute . . . so what does that mean? For us? For today?" I gestured down at my dress.

Greg folded his hands to calm his own nerves. "That's why I needed to talk to you right away."

"The wedding is off, isn't it?" Dread, thick as sludge, pooled in my gut. "You don't need me to pretend to be your wife, so the wedding doesn't need to happen?" My mind flew to the dozens of people waiting for me to walk down the aisle.

*What the hell was I supposed to tell my family?*

Greg's mouth curved into a sheepish grin. "That's the best part. My parents understand. Turns out they don't really care and only want to see me happy. Isn't that great?"

It was. It really, really was. I'd spent years imagining this exact scenario for him, begging the universe to soften his parents' hearts. I just hadn't pictured it happening on the one day where my entire life was balanced on the lie we'd sold them.

I shook my head. "Yeah, I mean . . . of course, but—"

"Slow down." A throb pierced behind my left eye, and I pinched it closed.

Greg exhaled, clearly irritated that I wasn't jumping for joy at his plan. "Look . . . Chris is already in a tux so . . . *we* are going to get married. You can be my best man!" Greg's smile wobbled as my brain short-circuited.

"Chris from the Tipsy Tiger? The bar hookup you said *had zero personality but the dick was a ten?*"

"I said that?" Greg's shotgun laugh startled me. "Well, we've been together for a while now."

I swear I could hear the dial-up internet noise from the

early 2000s as I tried to process the visual of me standing at the altar in a wedding gown while my fake fiancé married his very real boyfriend.

"What the hell, Greg!" He had always been a little reckless and wild, so it wasn't that I was shocked by his behavior. I was just . . . shocked. "You expect me to go out there *in a wedding dress* in front of my whole family and *not* get married while you marry your boyfriend and just expect that no one's going to notice?"

Greg pouted and crossed his arms. "I thought you'd be happy."

My ears started to ring as my mind raced. "I've lied to my parents. My sisters. It was a miracle to get my brother Hayes in a suit. I haven't been home in a year!"

The Star Harbor gossip grapevine would have a field day with this. My brother would go full overprotective caveman. My sisters would worry. My parents would quietly die inside. And I would be the girl who showed up in a wedding dress and left without a husband.

Greg's palms rose. "Hey, that was your choice. You're the one who didn't think you could play it cool in front of your family."

My armpits started sweating as I paced in the bridal suite. "This is unbelievable. What about a marriage license? It wouldn't even be legal."

Greg's shoulders bounced. "We'll have the party today —that's the important part—and figure out the details later."

I shook my head. "Greg . . . I can't, I—"

Greg's features hardened. "You had no problems using me for my money. I'm not asking for much here."

His words landed like a slap. I'd spent months bending myself into the shape of the perfect fiancée for him, for his parents, for the shareholders who'd never even meet me—and somehow I was still the one taking advantage.

Anger bubbled to the surface at his accusation. "Used you? You said you *wanted* to help me start the business. It was your idea to get married in the first place!"

Greg leaned forward and lowered his voice. "Will you please calm down? You're making a scene."

There it was. The old familiar verdict. Too loud. Too emotional. Too dramatic. I'd heard versions of it my whole life. I just never thought I'd get it while standing in a wedding dress that wasn't even meant for me.

Anger morphed into fury. "Calm down? *Calm down?* Do you have any idea how mortifying this is to me? How this looks?"

"You really are being dramatic about this whole thing." The boredom in Greg's voice sent me into a tailspin.

"Clara? Are you almost ready?" My little sister Kit's voice was muffled through the door.

*Oh, I'm being dramatic? I'll show him what being dramatic really looks like.*

I set my shoulders and whipped open the door. Kit's auburn hair floated with the gust of air, and her eyes went wide as they flicked from me to Greg.

Relief punched through me so hard my knees wobbled. If there was anyone on earth who wouldn't ask questions before helping me burn my life to the ground, it was my baby sister.

"Do you have your car?" I blurted without thinking.

Her mouth popped open, then snapped shut, mischief immediately sparking in her eyes. "Yes."

"Can you get me out of here?" I didn't have time to explain and knew Kit wouldn't ask questions.

All I could think to do was *run.*

Maybe it was cowardly. Maybe it was selfish. But for the first time in a long time, I wanted to choose me instead of the version of me that made everyone else comfortable.

"You bet." My little sister reached forward and grabbed my arm, pulling me past her. She looked right at Greg. "I don't know what you did to fuck this up, but you're an idiot." She looped her arm in mine and dragged me down the corridor before turning back. "Oh, and Clara told me about that weird thing with your . . . you know." Her eyes moved from Greg's face to his pants and back up again.

An unhinged cackle escaped me—Kit had definitely just made that insult up on the fly. We bolted down the hallway and pushed open the exit door. Sunlight spilled over my shoulders as the bite of cold air slapped me back. The train of my dress whipped around my legs, beads biting into my skin as I stumbled into the snow. My teeth chattered, adrenaline buzzing so loud in my ears I could barely hear the muffled music starting somewhere inside.

"Shit!" I couldn't stop laughing. It was uncontrollable now. "What did I just do?"

Kit grabbed my arm and tugged me closer to ward off the wind. "You set yourself free, babe. Let's get the fuck out of here before my tits freeze off."

I hugged her closer and we ran, our laughter shaking the snow from the trees.

# TWO

## WES

SNOWFALL COULD SUCK MY DICK.

The gray January sky peeked through my living room window, and all I could feel was dread. Well, dread and the white-hot poker of a limb that was no longer attached to me. With a frustrated breath, I closed my eyes and gritted my teeth.

It was the strangest thing to still be able to feel a limb that was gone. You didn't realize how much space a leg took up in your brain until it was gone and still refused to shut the hell up. The constant foot-asleep feeling dogged me, and even a five-minute break from it would have been a miracle. An electric zing of phantom pain coursed up my leg until I broke out into a sweat.

When it finally passed, all I wanted to do was roll over on the couch and pull the blanket back over my head. There were weeks where the farthest I traveled was from the couch to the bathroom and back. My whole life, shrunk down to twenty sad-ass steps.

The second I heard the bang on the front door, I knew that plan was fucked. I knew it was him. Nobody else knocked like that—like the building was on fire but he was trying really hard to sound casual about it.

I couldn't hide. Surely Hayes had seen my truck in the drive, and *where the fuck else would I be?* Despite my doctor's recommendation, just last week, I had fired yet another live-in care nurse. I hated having a stranger in my space and didn't need another person walking on eggshells around me. Hayes had taken it upon himself to slide into that role.

Every careful question, every soft voice, every "How are we feeling today?" made my skin crawl. I didn't want to be observed for a living. I just wanted to be left the fuck alone.

His fist banged again. "Open up, buddy. I've got coffee."

The tentative tone in his voice grated my nerves. I pushed myself up to a sitting position and looked down at my missing limb. Being an above-the-knee amputee was still jarring, even nearly six months later. My residual limb was covered with a shrinker—the stocking that helped shape what was left of my leg so it would fit into the prosthetic— but I knew beneath it was nothing but a scarred stump.

I swallowed past the rocks in my throat and looked away. I leaned forward to reach for my liner and prosthetic leg so I could answer the door before Hayes let himself in.

A key turned in the lock, and the front door pushed open. "Hey, it's me."

Of course he used the key. God forbid I get thirty seconds to strap my leg on without an audience. A frustrated breath pushed out my nose.

*All I needed was a fucking minute.*

My best friend Hayes let himself in, a sheepish smile plastered on his face. "Morning."

I grunted in his direction as I hastily attached my leg. We used to greet each other with insults and shit-talking about whatever game had been on the night before. Now it was this—him tiptoeing, me grunting like a feral animal.

I was rushing and the fit wasn't exactly right, but the faster I could get him out of my hair, the better.

Hayes's large frame loomed in the doorway as he stared at me, his dark eyebrows pinched down as he looked me over. I couldn't read his mind, but the careful way his gaze avoided my amputation told me everything I needed to know. I almost wished he'd just stare. At least then we'd be looking at the same ugly thing.

He set two coffee cups down on the entryway table and clapped his hands together. "It's cold as shit out there today."

I looked at him and nodded. That was what our relationship had become . . . discussions about the weather and him giving me *that look*. I missed arguing about nothing. Missed him calling me out when I deserved it. Missed feeling like his equal instead of his project.

I steadied myself and went to take a step when Hayes rushed forward. His hand reached out to support my elbow, but I jerked my arm away. "I got it."

His hands went up in defense at my shitty tone. "Sorry."

My molars ground together. The look of pity was back and I wanted to scream. "It's fine. I just didn't get much sleep last night. I'm in a shit mood." I walked toward the coffee and accepted the paper cup.

Hayes looked at the mess of blankets on the couch. "Still sleeping down here?"

I glanced at the rumpled sheets and offered a shrug. "Just fell asleep watching TV, that's all."

I didn't love outright lying to my friend, but I also wasn't going to admit that I hadn't slept upstairs in my own bedroom since my accident. Somewhere along the line I'd developed a fear that something would happen and I wouldn't be able to attach my leg in time to make it downstairs. The last thing I needed was there to be a house fire or something and get trapped.

Once the thought had taken root, I couldn't shake it. It sank in deep, wrapped itself around my ribs, and suddenly my own bedroom felt like a death trap instead of a place to sleep.

The coffee was hot, and at least that was something. "How was the wedding?"

Hayes froze. "You didn't hear?"

*Of course I didn't hear. I don't leave my fucking house.*

I just waited for Hayes to continue. "Clara bolted, man. Five minutes before the ceremony was supposed to start, she and Kit hightailed it out of there."

My brain unhelpfully supplied an image of Clara Darling in a white dress, running through the snow with her skirt fisted in her hands. I hadn't seen her in years, but even the memory version of her looked too alive for whatever shit show that wedding must've been.

"Damn." I shook my head. Hayes's little sister Clara hadn't really been around since she'd left for college, but I could imagine that whatever had made her run from her own wedding was pretty bad. "Cold feet?"

A pop of laughter erupted from Hayes, but just as quickly he looked down at my missing foot and used a cough to cover it. I had to stifle an eye roll. I would have loved to let the joke land, but the stricken look on Hayes's face killed the moment. That was our new normal—every half-decent joke detouring into a reminder that one of us didn't have both feet anymore.

"Actually," he continued, "the wedding still happened. The groom married the best man instead."

My eyes popped open. "Damn."

Hayes shrugged. "It's fucked up. She's moving in with my parents, but . . . I don't know how that's going to work out. Mom's already smothering her."

I stared at my friend. *Pot, meet kettle.*

"You ready to go? PT waits for no man." Hayes's eyes glossed over, and his smile thinned in that sad way it had since the accident.

I understood it—the guilt he felt. Hayes had called me when his car broke down on a dark and winding road. I was helping him out when a driver took a turn too fast, got spooked, and lost control. My instincts were sharp, and a moment before he hit us, I'd managed to push Hayes out of the way. I lost my leg, but he'd be dead if I hadn't been there.

The guilt sat between us like a third person in the truck. I hadn't figured out how to shut it up or kick it out. I only wish he'd go back to being my best friend instead of this mother hen who wouldn't leave me the fuck alone. I didn't shove him out of the way that night just to lose him to his own conscience.

"I need a minute to adjust." I lowered myself to sitting so I could take my time and reattach my prosthetic properly.

Hayes immediately moved into action, scooping up leftover dishes and empty cups to deposit them into the sink. It was pretty clear that watching me attach my leg still made him deeply uncomfortable.

Everyone in town thought Hayes was cursed with shitty luck, but in reality, I was the one who'd lost his leg.

Go figure.

When I was properly adjusted, I stood again. "Let's get this over with."

I had started to walk to get my winter coat from the closet when my eyes landed on a magazine on the console table. Hayes must have brought it in with him, because I sure as fuck hadn't put it there. It was a publication for people living with limb loss. I stared at the happy faces on the magazine cover—laughing and smiling with one another.

I picked it up and tossed it into the trash.

*What a crock of shit.*

I didn't want to join some shiny club of "brave survivors" smiling through the pain. I wanted my old life back. Failing that, I wanted to be left alone with my anger.

Hayes stayed silent as he opened the front door for me. The cold Michigan wind slapped against my cheeks. I looked down the porch steps and braced myself. Had I known I was going to have to navigate those steps with a fresh prosthetic, I would never have built the wraparound porch. I'd designed this place to be all charm and curb appeal. Now it felt like a level in some sadistic video game I hadn't signed up to play.

With a heavy sigh, I gripped the banister and slowly took one step down.

"Careful, man. It's icy today." Hayes hovered, not giving me a single inch.

"I've got it," I bit back.

I took another clunky step down and felt the wood beneath my sneaker. Hayes moved in next to me. "Here, let me—"

"I said I've got it." My arm jerked away as he tried to steady me, but the swift movement knocked me off-balance.

I stumbled forward, desperately trying to stay upright as I fumbled and grasped the air.

I face-planted in the snow with a grunt, my pride wounded more than anything else, though my back was none too happy about the fall. Snow packed into the collar of my shirt, icy and shocking. My prosthetic twisted at a weird angle, reminding me that even the fake part of me could screw up.

Hayes's hands immediately went to my waist, trying to haul me up.

Embarrassment and shame heated my cheeks as I fought back a swell of self-pitying tears. "Get the fuck off me! I said I've got it. Jesus Christ, man!"

The words were out before I could choke them back. Hayes reared away as I lashed out at him. Frustration bubbled to the surface as my sweatpants soaked in the snow and my palms pressed against the icy ground. I struggled but managed to get upright. My shirt was filthy, pants wet, and pride severely wounded. All I wanted to do was crawl into a hole and call it quits.

Instead, I brushed the grit from my hands and hobbled toward Hayes's truck. "Let's get this over with."

He was silent the entire ride, and I hated myself even more for it. Hayes didn't deserve my temper. The guy I used to be wouldn't have talked to his best friend like that. I wasn't sure I liked this new version of me very much.

LATER THAT NIGHT I was still stewing over what had happened. It wasn't the fact I'd fallen in front of my best friend. Hell, I'd done that drunk plenty of times. It was the heaviness Hayes carried in his shoulders the entire rest of the time we were together. I'd ripped his head off, and he'd just taken it.

*God, I was such an asshole.*

Holing up in my house wasn't just convenient—it kept everyone safe from the shitty person I had become. If I didn't go out, I couldn't snap at anyone. Couldn't watch their faces go careful and sad. Couldn't see that look that said they were glad it wasn't them.

I spent the rest of the day going through invoices. Vaughn Construction was busy, even in the winter months. Thankfully my construction company had grown enough that even after my accident I had plenty of guys on the crew to keep it up and running. We had projects all over town, and I had big plans come spring.

Despite my limitations, I couldn't stand to not work. Spreadsheets and blueprints didn't pity me. Lumber didn't look away. Houses didn't care how many legs I had as long as I built them right.

Sure the money was great, but a huge part of owning my own construction company was the ability to get in there and still do the work myself. I loved creating and building and giving my customers the home of their dreams. Trouble was, I couldn't do that if I was sitting at home feeling sorry for myself.

To burn off my stagnant energy, I dropped to the floor and started doing crunches. Sweat burned my eyes, my abs screamed, my shoulders shook, and still I pushed. I couldn't fix my leg, couldn't outrun the accident, but I sure as hell could make sure the rest of me didn't fall apart too.

After I was too sore to go on, I switched to biceps curls and shoulder work. I may only have one leg, but there was plenty I could do to stay focused and fit while I figured the rest of my shit out.

I was dripping sweat and finally tired enough to call it quits when my phone buzzed.

BRODY

Drinks at the Lantern. I'll pick you up in an hour. I'm not asking.

I STARED AT THE MESSAGE. The temptation to ignore it was strong, but a part of me liked that my friend Brody hadn't treated me differently after the accident. He also seemed to understand that I may need a little more advanced warning to be ready, but for some reason that felt okay. Maybe it was because he was a cop and his no-bullshit attitude followed him home. Maybe it was because he didn't carry the guilt Hayes did.

Whatever it was, the need to prove to myself that I wasn't a total hermit won out.

I can drive, you dick. I'll meet you there.

BRODY

Good. Then you can pick me up. See you in sixty.

BY THE TIME we got to the Lady's Lantern, the place was packed. The bar was equal parts watering hole and local legend. The wooden sign out front was carved in the shape of a lantern and cast a warm glow over the entrance. Inside the bar, it smelled like old wood and cheap whiskey. The walls were plastered with relics of the town's obsession with our local ghost, the Lady of the Dunes.

The owners had framed newspaper clippings of supposed sightings and grainy black-and-white photographs of the ghostly figure. In the far corner of the bar, they'd even made a glass case housing what was allegedly a piece of her original wedding veil. A dead bride haunting the dunes because her big day didn't go as planned. Seemed fitting, considering the town was probably still buzzing about our very own runaway Darling.

If it weren't for the local ghost story, I doubted anyone would have a reason to pass through Star Harbor.

Tension wound its way up my back and settled as a knot between my shoulders as we walked into the Lantern. Crowds meant unintentional bumps and curious eyes. Sure, I was wearing jeans, but my gait was still uneven enough to draw a few stares. Plus, in our small town, my accident was big news.

Brody took the lead, weaving through the crowd, and I walked behind him. When he made it to the table, he stepped aside and I nearly fell over. Standing in front of me was a woman with long, wavy blond hair and eyes that were the strangest shade. In the low lighting of the bar, they looked almost gray. Her smile was bright as she tapped a shot glass with Kit's and threw it back.

"Woo!" the woman shouted as her fist pumped the air.

I slid onto the chair at the high-top table and tried not to stare.

"Wes Vaughn, as I live and breathe!" Kit wound her arm around my shoulders, and a whisper of tequila wafted off her breath. "I'm drunk." Her forehead nearly collided with mine.

"I can see that." I offered a polite smile as my attention slid back to the blonde and I finally realized who she was.

I stared at Clara Darling. She looked nothing like the girl I'd remembered her to be. The last time I'd really clocked Clara Darling, she'd been all limbs and braces and too-big eyes, trailing after her older siblings.

She was all woman now. And absolutely, unequivocally off-limits. Hayes would cut my balls off and hang them from his rearview mirror.

*I miss eating pussy.*

The rogue thought jolted me, and I shifted in my seat to get comfortable and tamp down the sudden, unexpected surge of desire. Apparently my dick hadn't gotten the memo that we were in mourning.

Brody looked down at Kit, annoyance rippling across his features. "A little early for tequila, don't you think?"

Kit stuck her tongue out at him and turned toward the other woman. "We're celebrating!" She put her arm behind the woman and shoved her forward. "You remember Clara, right?"

*Not like this, I don't.*

Not laughing at a bar, hair loose around her shoulders, eyes clear and bright like the whole fake-wedding disaster had bounced right off her.

Her nose scrunched. "Hi, Wes."

I pressed my lips together and nodded. "Clara. What are you celebrating?"

Clara's blue-gray eyes stayed locked on mine, but Kit bumped into her. "Freedom! Liberty! And the pursuit of new dick!"

Clara laughed as Brody pinched the bridge of his nose and exhaled. "Jesus fucking Christ. I'm getting a drink." He turned and headed toward the bar in the back of the Lantern.

The music in the bar shifted to an upbeat country song. The crowd filled the dance floor, and they started moving in choreographed steps.

Kit was pulling Clara toward the dance floor when they stopped.

Clara turned to face me. "Want to dance?"

I stared at her. *Me? Dance? What the fuck?*

For half a second I almost said yes. My body leaned forward, eager, like it remembered the way hers had felt tucked under my arm at some long-ago family barbecue. Then reality snapped back—metal where flesh should be, a stumble where there used to be a sure step.

Maybe Clara had been gone long enough to not have heard about my accident, but that was unlikely. The way her eyes lacked any sort of pity made her offer very, very tempting. There was curiosity there, sure. A spark of mischief. But none of that soft, careful pity I'd started to hate. It made her offer feel like something dangerously close to normal.

Still, I knew it wasn't even a consideration, so I shook my head. "Have fun."

Without a glance back, Clara and Kit were folded into the crowd. Six months ago I might have taken her up on the offer. I'd been a decent dancer and knew my way around a woman. I would have charmed her, made her laugh and helped her forget about whatever dumbass had let her go. I would have respected the boundaries of my friendship with her brother Hayes and not let it go too far, but six months ago, I still would have flirted.

Six months ago I wouldn't have been thinking about how loving someone always cost a part of yourself.

## THREE

CLARA

A SLIVER of morning light filtered through the curtain, illuminating the diamond ring on my left hand. The brilliant round stone sent sparks flying across the ceiling, and I watched in awe at how the light danced when I moved my hand.

I wasn't exactly sure why I was still wearing it, but something about it represented the life I had been building. An uncertain adulthood of chasing a dream, an exciting life in the city, and not worrying about bills. That life had looked so good on paper—steady money, glossy social media stories, a built-in plus-one for every event. It was the kind of life my parents called *secure*, and I'd convinced myself it was enough.

It was a life I wasn't quite ready to let go of yet.

As the fire from my ring danced across the walls, I looked around at my childhood bedroom. Mom and Dad hadn't changed a thing since I left at eighteen. The bedsheets were still a dusty pink with tiny roses. My vanity was covered in old makeup and nail polish I was certain had long dried up. Pictures of high school friends were stuck to the corkboard. I'd kept in touch with a few of them, but there were others that had gone their separate ways and we'd never spoken again.

Nothing about the room felt like me anymore.

I'd tried on so many versions of myself since leaving this house—college Clara, model Clara, fake-fiancée Clara—that this old high school version felt like a costume I'd outgrown and stuffed in the back of the closet.

It was strange to feel relief that I no longer had to lie about my relationship anymore, but at the same time be consumed with uncertainty. I couldn't live with my parents forever but I'd taken Greg's financial generosity for granted, and now that I was left to figure things out by myself, I was just . . . lost.

Greg hadn't even reached out to talk, and I was still mad at him for how publicly our drama had played out. Online gossip columns made me the butt of many jokes, and it seemed like our mutual friends were all on Greg's side. Yes, I was happy he could openly love whomever he wanted to, but was getting a heads-up too much to ask?

It was like life had hit rewind and dropped me back at the starting line while everyone else kept running.

Burying my head in the sand was the most comforting option.

"Clara, breakfast!" my mother's voice called from down the hall.

I was thirty-one and living with my parents, but it came with free breakfast, so maybe it wasn't *all* bad.

When I didn't respond, Mom opened the door without knocking and waltzed right in. "Time to get up, lazy bones." She moved toward the window and jerked open the curtains, blinding me. The sunlight felt like an interrogation lamp, spotlighting my smeared mascara and the ring I still hadn't taken off.

My hand covered my eyes. "Jeez, Mom. A little warning next time."

She tsked and walked around the room, gathering my discarded clothes in her arms. "You didn't learn to be any tidier while you were away, I see." Her soft green eyes pinned me in place.

I offered a sheepish grin.

Mom patted my leg. "Let's go. The day's wasting."

I groaned and rolled over, pulling the blankets across my shoulders. Free breakfast wasn't quite worth moving yet.

"Morning, Clara." Dad's cheery voice floated across the room as he walked in. My dad was pretty fit for his age and often attributed his sunny disposition to early-morning runs. "Let's get a move on."

Frustrated, I sat up. "Can't a girl wallow for a while?"

Dad smiled but shook his head. "Our house, our rules."

My face twisted. My parents' rules had never been all that strict, but with five kids, we'd learned early that rules in Angela and Burt's house were what helped keep it a well-oiled machine. I never imagined those rules would still apply to me as an adult.

"Fiiine." I dragged out the word in hopes they'd feel my annoyance.

"Atta girl," Mom chirped. She continued infiltrating my space as I sat up, moving things over, and generally attempting to organize my chaos.

She plucked a thong from the ground and held it up with two fingers. "Now what in the world does *this* cover?"

I laughed and swiped it from her hands. "Not much. That's the point."

Scandalized, my mother shook her head. "I swear, I

don't understand young women today. Maybe that's why things didn't work out . . ."

There it was—the gentle, well-meaning insinuation that if I'd just been a little different, a little less, things might have gone another way.

She didn't mean any harm in her words, but defensiveness reared up anyway. "Greg and I didn't work out because he's gay, not because my underwear was too scandalous for you."

She shook her head and lifted her shoulders like maybe she didn't believe it. "I'm just saying is all . . ."

"Okay." I tossed the blankets aside and stood. "I'm up. Can this conversation please be over?"

Mom moved to the doorway, and before she left, tossed a wink over her shoulder. She had goaded me just enough to drag my sorry ass out of bed, and I'd fallen for it.

Downstairs, nostalgia hit me square in the chest. The air smelled of sweet pancakes and hearty bacon. It looked like my parents had already eaten, but left a stack just for me. I'd spent years chasing trendy brunch spots and overpriced oat milk lattes, but nothing touched a quiet kitchen and a plate someone made because they knew you were coming. I pulled one pancake off the top, placed a strip of bacon over it, and rolled the pancake up.

I took a bite and moaned.

"Gross. Make out with your breakfast somewhere else." My little sister Kit's voice had me turning. She shot me a grin before sticking out her tongue.

Simply because I could gross her out, I opened my mouth to show her my half-chewed food.

She laughed, throwing a tiny piece of bacon in my direction. "That's so hot."

I giggled and swallowed down the food. I looked over

her shoulder to make sure my parents were not within earshot. "Let me move in with you."

The words tumbled out before I could prettify them. I sounded desperate because I was. I loved my parents, but I was one "So, what's next?" away from a full mental breakdown.

Kit looked sympathetic but shook her head. "No can do. One-bedroom apartment. I'd rather keep warm with someone besides my sister. No offense."

I pouted but knew she was right. Though I hadn't seen it in person, her apartment seemed tiny, and we'd be practically on top of each other. I'd arranged for movers to clear out the apartment I'd shared with Greg, and the boxes were slated to arrive later in the week. I sighed.

*I already miss that closet.*

It wasn't just the hangers and square footage I missed. It was the version of me who'd stood in that closet and believed she was one good break away from making it.

"Get dressed. I'm going to the farm, and you can come with me," Kit said.

"Yes, I'm in." I shoved another bite of bacon pancake into my mouth and went to get myself ready.

Cal and my sister Elodie lived together. He owned the local inn, and together they were renovating the neighboring farm property. She'd turned it into a family-friendly destination, and they were even opening a restaurant on-site. I couldn't wait to see it in person.

As Kit drove past the Drifted Spirit Inn, I stared up at the beautifully peaked roofline of the old Victorian house. "Maybe Cal will rent me a room."

It came out half joke, half plea. Anything to avoid being the thirty-one-year-old cautionary tale living at home with her parents and a stack of moving boxes.

Kit's barking laugh shot out. "Good luck with that. Once Elodie revamped Star Harbor Family Farm, the inn's been booked solid. The waitlist is over a year long."

I was disappointed for myself, but happy for my sister. While my life was falling apart, hers was falling perfectly into place. Kit drove past the inn and toward the huge blue barn on the farm property. The once-overgrown farmland had been transformed into a family destination. A soft blanket of snow covered the pumpkin patch. In the distance, the dunes of Lake Michigan created a breathtaking view of the lake.

Old trees dotted the property, and immediately my mind went to a winter wedding with twinkle lights and an old chandelier hanging from the branches. I wondered whether Elodie had ever considered using the property for weddings. She'd make a killing.

I could already see it: velvet bridesmaid dresses, fur wraps, hot cocoa bar in the corner, the signature cocktails named something cute and romantic. My brain slipped into work mode without asking my permission.

Kit turned off the car engine, and we both climbed out. The huge blue barn was still under construction inside— together they were creating a farm-to-table restaurant, and the crew was still working on the interior.

As we walked in, cozy, warm lighting greeted us. "This is stunning."

The soft glow made the raw beams and unfinished edges feel intentional, like the whole place was mid-transformation. I felt a sharp, stupid pang of envy. The farm knew exactly what it was becoming.

I did not.

Kit grinned. "She really did it."

Warmth filled my chest as happiness for my sister spread through me. I could see her vision so clearly, but it was intermixed with my own thoughts of how gorgeous a wedding could be there.

From the restaurant side of the barn, my sister walked toward us. Her brown hair swung past her shoulders, and pure happiness made her green eyes glow. Being in love looked good on her.

"This is a nice surprise!" Elodie wiped her hands on a rag before she greeted us with hugs. "Sorry. I'm a mess. We're all dusty over there."

I smiled at her. "This is incredible. I can't believe what you've done with the old farm."

Her grin widened. "Isn't it great? Wes and his guys do some really impressive work."

When I had seen Wes at the Lantern, I was shocked at how handsome he still was. My brother's friend had always turned heads, but there was something about him now that had changed. His blond hair had darkened over time, but his eyes were the same icy blue.

The change in him was more than his accident. There was a broodiness to him that hadn't been there before—like a lost soul walking around in my brother's best friend's body. I was intrigued and more than a little turned on by his grumpy demeanor. Apparently my type was "emotionally unavailable with a tragic backstory."

*Fantastic.*

"I have so many ideas I can barely keep up," Elodie continued as we walked behind her. "Good thing I have Cal to keep me reined in."

Beside me, Kit snorted. "Please. That man has never told you no *once*."

Elodie blushed, and I assumed it was true. She turned to me. "How's life with Mom and Dad?"

I rolled my eyes. "Stifling."

"Aww, come on. They're the best," Kit said.

I shook my head. "Look, they're great. I know that. But I'm not a kid anymore, and living at home feels like I've become the biggest loser in Star Harbor. It's *embarrassing*."

I could practically hear the whispers already. *Poor Clara Darling. All that time in the city just to come home single, jobless, and sleeping under her high school stuff.*

"Oh please," Kit said, "you're not the biggest loser. That's still Peter Pilling."

Elodie's face twisted. "Peter from *third grade*? The one who dumped a container of chocolate milk down your back?"

Her eyes narrowed. "I still hate that kid."

Whatever else was a disaster, at least my sisters were still exactly who they'd always been—one ready to fight anyone who hurt me, the other building empires out of old barns.

I wrapped my arms around my little sister. "God, you've not changed at all. I love you." I turned toward Elodie. "Do you have time for a grand tour?"

Elodie nodded and she showed us everything in the barn and shared her and Cal's plans to continue to expand the farm. Romance and excitement laced through her words, and I caught myself feeling oddly jealous.

Her life was falling into place, everything coming together for her, and I was just . . . *stuck*.

In high school, I'd always assumed I'd be the one to leave and come back with stories and success. Elodie had been the homebody. Somewhere along the way we'd swapped roles, and I hadn't noticed until now.

Jobless, loveless, and living at home. One wrong move and I was *this close* to stealing Peter Pilling's loser crown for sure.

"You're going to start coming to the meetings, right?" Elodie asked, shaking me from my self-pity spiral.

"Meetings?" I asked.

Kit nodded. "The Keepers."

I looked between my sisters in disbelief. "Please don't tell me you guys bought into that."

They both looked shocked at my dismissive tone. "Bought into *what*?" Kit asked, clearly offended. "Hanging with the Star Harbor Historical Society is my favorite night of the week."

The Star Harbor Historical Society was a local women's group that had been around since the late eighteen hundreds. Our entire town revolved around the Lady of the Dunes, part silly ghost story, part local legend. The women of the historical society were informally known as the Keepers.

I raised my palms. "I thought it was just a bunch of bored old ladies gossiping. Clearly I've missed something."

Elodie shrugged. "That's what happens when you don't come home for over a year."

She wasn't wrong. I'd stayed gone on purpose, because it was easier to play the part of "city success story" from a distance than let anyone see the cracks up close.

Still, her words stung and my back went straight. "Damn, El. Back off a little."

Kit looped her arm in mine, trying to keep the peace. "*So much* has happened. While Elodie was building this place, they found an old trunk with letters from the Lady.

You know how the legend said she was haunting the town because she was waiting for her shipwrecked lost love?"

I nodded. Growing up, everyone knew about the Lady. Her story was a tragedy of lost love, and if you lived here long enough, you'd see her ghost with your own eyes. As kids, we used to dare each other to go out to the dunes at night and call for her, half hoping she'd appear, half terrified she actually would. The Lady had always been safely contained to spooky stories and barroom decorations. The idea of her being real—of her writing letters—made the hair on my arms stand up.

Kit shook her head. "She wasn't waiting for a sailor. Everything we know about the Lady is a lie. Her letters revealed that she was afraid. *Hiding*. Then Selene found a photograph of her, and someone had scratched X's over her eyes."

Our oldest sister, Selene, worked as an archivist and probably came across the photograph in her work. A chill ran up my spine. "That's unsettling."

There was something so violent about it—taking the time to scratch out someone's eyes. Like whoever did it wanted to erase her but couldn't quite manage it.

Kit moved in closer, as though she didn't want anyone— especially a ghost—to overhear. "The weirdest part . . . there was a man in the corner of the photograph, and I swear to you, he looks *exactly* like Hayes."

I reared back in disbelief. "What?"

Elodie and Kit nodded in unison. "Fucking weird, right?" Kit asked.

I don't know why, but my throat went dry and I tried to swallow. Everyone in Star Harbor knew of my brother's curse. I'd never wanted to believe it, but it was hard to deny that the man had the worst luck of anyone I'd ever met. The fact that there was some old-ass photograph with his face on it made the entire situation extra creepy.

And intriguing.

A tiny, reckless part of me wondered whether maybe the Darling family hadn't been telling itself ghost stories all these years, but warnings.

"Fine." I blew out a breath. "I'll go to *one* meeting, but if it's boring, you're buying drinks after."

Kit's grin bloomed. "Deal."

# FOUR

## WES

"I am the dungeon master. Welcome to the Horsemen."

I stared at Austin Calloway and wondered how the fuck this guy ever got laid.

Then again, the way his eyes lit up talking about made-up worlds and monsters, I kind of got it. Some people were just built for quests and happy endings. I used to think I was one of them.

Around Brody's kitchen table, I sat with Austin, Hayes, Brody, and Cal. Years ago we'd joined a men's softball team and continued the tradition of weekly meetings during the offseason. In the past we'd done poker or board games—anything that gave us an excuse to come together for a few beers and some laughs. Austin had suggested we try our hand at Dungeons & Dragons this time.

It was weird, but whatever. I gripped my thigh to ease the phantom pain. Besides, running bases really wasn't in the cards for me anymore, and it gave me an excuse to leave my house.

"So what is this again?" Cal asked with narrowed eyes.

Austin sighed. "It's called a campaign." His hand moved to his chest. "I'm the dungeon master." Brody and Cal snickered, but Austin kept explaining. "You are the players. I'll give you descriptions and information about the areas you're in, react to whatever you do, and tell a story while we do it. As the players, you go around interacting with everything—solving puzzles, exploring, engaging in combat—that kind of thing."

Austin talked with his hands like he was pitching a multimillion-dollar deal instead of a pretend elf problem. The guy had never half-assed anything in his life, which was why I had hired him in the first place.

"Oh," Cal chimed in. "So it's like a video game but without the console."

Austin grinned. "Exactly."

Brody bumped his half brother in the shoulder. "I think little Winnie's overactive imagination is rubbing off on you."

The tips of Austin's ears reddened. He and Selene Darling had gone from neighbors to lovers, and things seemed pretty serious. Selene's daughter was precocious, but a sweet kid. Despite Selene being older than him, Austin seemed to fit into their lives seamlessly. They made it look easy—like you could just slide into a ready-made family and know exactly where you fit.

Watching it made something in my chest twist.

Self-pity crept up my back. I had never given too much thought to having a family. I'd always assumed it would happen eventually. Now I was damaged and angry, and the prospect of becoming an actual recluse was feeling closer every day.

I could see it so clearly—me in ten years, yelling at kids to get off my lawn from behind a curtain, leg aching and beer gut hanging over my sweats.

*Hell of a retirement plan.*

"You okay?" Hayes leaned over to ask.

It was his new favorite question and my least favorite one to answer.

I bristled and hated myself for it. "I'm good." I focused my attention on what Austin was saying and not the worried look lingering on Hayes's face. "Are we going to start or what?"

Austin grinned and leaned forward to whisper. He was living for this. "You're all travelers in a distant land. A nefarious and mysterious noble has given you a quest. To aid you in your journey, he gives you each a horse and some weaponry. Brody, you're a fighter. Your horse is bright white and the nobleman has given you a bow. Cal . . . you are given a black horse and wear a magical ring."

Cal nodded and grinned, getting into it. "Badass."

Austin smirked as he continued: "Hayes, you are a Human Aasimar Cleric who provides guidance and leadership. Your horse is pale, like the moonlight. Your staff is the source of your celestial power."

Of course Hayes got the pale horse. In Star Harbor, the man couldn't trip over a curb without somebody muttering about curses and bad omens.

I swallowed thickly, unsure why I felt nervous as Austin's gaze tracked to me. "Wes, you will be our Warforged Paladin. You're a warrior, but also a healer. You carry a longsword and ride a red horse."

*A warrior.*

Flashes of my time as a Delta Force operator shook me. I *had* been a warrior, but that was a lifetime ago. Now I was a shell of that man. It was hard to even muster the enthusiasm to play one in Austin's stupid game.

My body remembered what it felt like to be that guy—

the one other men followed without question. My brain reminded me I couldn't even make it down my own porch steps without eating shit.

"As a unit, your armor is unrivaled," Austin continued, "and you carry your mission atop your mighty steed." Austin's gaze was steady and focused. "After this nobleman provides your weapon and horse, he gives you the collective mission to escape the dungeon."

*Must be nice . . . to have a clear quest and a way out.*

My real-life dungeon didn't come with maps or magic keys.

Austin's eyebrows bounced. "Let's roll."

I WASN'T ABOUT to admit it to anyone, but playing Dungeons & Dragons for four straight hours was the highlight of my week. When the night was over, we'd worked as a team to overcome obstacles, fight demons, and escape the dungeon. We argued, we screwed up, we rolled like shit, and still—we made it out. Together. Funny how that worked better in fantasy than it did in my actual life. Collectively, we mounted our horses and rode off toward the local village, where we'd continue the game next time.

It was nerdy and Brody, who was a High-Elf Fighter, kept breaking his magical bow, but hell—it was fun.

My house was dark by the time I got back. I pretended to not notice the headlights from Hayes's truck following me home. When I closed my front door, anxiety wound around my shoulders. The house was too quiet. Too dark. The place looked like a goddamn postcard for loneliness— no lights, no sound, just my reflection in the window and the ache in my leg for company.

It was nearly midnight, and instead of being able to collapse on my bed, I had to think about things like removing my prosthetic, checking for signs of irritation, and all the extra minutes it now took to get myself ready to do anything. Most people got to just fall face-first onto their mattress and call it a night. I got a checklist and a reminder that nothing in my life was simple anymore.

It was fucking exhausting.

Upstairs, my king-size bed was calling to me. I wanted nothing more than to sink into the mattress, pull the covers over my head, and ignore the world until morning. But it was no longer that easy for me.

My hips were sore, and my right foot was screaming for a break. Weary and exhausted, I lowered myself to the couch and exhaled. The upstairs bedroom might as well have been on another continent. The couch had become home base—close to the door, close to the bathroom, close to the version of me who didn't try too hard. I had started removing my prosthetic when a knock came at the door.

I glanced at the clock. It was way too late for unexpected visitors. My stomach dropped. There was only one person stubborn enough to show up at this hour and bang on my door like he paid the mortgage.

"Wes, open up. It's me." Hayes's voice boomed through the door.

I gritted my teeth and wanted to ram my fist into the wall. It found the couch cushion instead.

I knew he wasn't going anywhere, so I blew out a breath. "Use your key and come in."

When he did, Hayes's frame filled the entryway.

"What?" I snapped. I heard the bite in my own voice and hated how automatic it had become with him.

Hayes lifted his chin and took my lashing out like he

deserved it. "Just making sure you got settled in okay. I didn't see the light go on upstairs, so I just wanted to make sure you didn't need anything."

Irritation ground into my jaw like a kernel. "Checking up on me? What the fuck, dude." I used all my strength to stand, balancing on one leg. "Did you check up on Austin or Cal when they left? I don't need you to babysit me. I don't need you following me home or lurking outside or looking at me with that fucking look on your face." My arm flipped in his direction to emphasize my point.

"I didn't suddenly turn into a fragile antique just because I've got fewer parts," I added, the words scraping my throat on the way out.

Pain flicked over his features. "I'm just—"

I registered the hurt in his eyes and still couldn't stop myself.

Anger and frustration bubbled over. "You just *what*, Hayes? Just need to come here and coddle me and somehow make up for calling me that night? You want to come over and wipe my ass too? Goddamn it, man. Leave me the fuck alone!"

My harsh words landed with a tough blow. Regret and shame coursed through me as I watched my best friend take the verbal assault without flinching.

Hayes only nodded as his jaw worked. "Understood, man." He turned, his hand landing on the knob of the door. "I can see that you can take care of yourself. But for the record?" He turned and his eyes pinned me in place. "Even if you did need someone to wipe your ass, I'd be there. Not because I felt guilty—which I do, by the way—but because I love you."

The words hit harder than any punch I'd ever taken. I wanted to tell him to fuck off. I wanted to grab him and beg him not to leave. Instead, I just stood there, one-legged and silent, watching him leave.

Without another glance back, Hayes walked out. The front door rattled as it slammed closed. Hurt, confusion, and self-loathing coursed through me. I wanted to scream or cry or beat the shit out of something. The only thing nearby was a half-empty glass of water on the console table.

With a yell, I swiped it hard enough to send it careening through the air until it hit a wall and smashed into a thousand pieces. Water streaked down the paint in crooked lines, tiny shards glittering in the lamplight. I stared at the mess, chest heaving, knowing I'd just broken something a hell of a lot more important than a glass.

I barely recognized myself anymore. Six months ago I'd been happy and would never have dreamed of speaking to my best friend that way. I hated the man I'd become since the accident.

I hated myself, and nothing could fix that.

## FIVE

## CLARA

BEING an outsider in your childhood home was something I hadn't expected. All week I'd been trying to make the best out of being a grown woman living at home, but everything felt off. I didn't understand the inside jokes. I caught the looks my parents passed one another when my presence messed with their established routines. I wanted to shake them and scream, "Hey, I don't want to be here either!"

Instead, I did what I'd been doing since I came back—I swallowed it down and tried to fold myself into a life that had kept moving without me.

I grumbled as I folded my body into a stretch.

"Relax your jaw and your forehead." My yoga teacher instructed the class. My muscles did as they were told. My brain, however, was still scrolling through unpaid bills, my parents' worried looks, and the diamond ring still on my finger.

"Very good. Let's hang here and breathe. In . . ."

The yoga studio in town was busy in the evenings, but midday, it was practically a ghost town. During the height of the tourist season, I was certain classes would be packed, but in the dead of winter it was just me and the geriatric crowd.

As a class, we transitioned to lying on our backs and focusing our breath. I was busy counting ceiling tiles. When my phone buzzed beside me, I sat up.

When my brother's name flashed across the screen, I grabbed it and whispered, "Yeah?"

"Hey, it's me. You busy?"

I earned a stern look from my yoga instructor, so I quickly scrambled to my feet and cupped my hand over my mouth as I walked toward the locker room. "No, what's up?"

Frustration oozed from Hayes's voice. "I need a ride."

My brows scrunched. "Where's your truck?"

He let out an exasperated breath. "Well, that's the question of the hour. I have no idea. I think it got towed."

A snort tickled my nose. "Still cursed by the Lady, I take it?"

Hayes growled on the other end. "It's not funny."

I thought it was hilarious. And ridiculous. For as long as I could remember, Hayes had suffered from impressively bad luck. Nothing huge, just minor inconveniences that made small moments in his life infuriating.

I glanced back at the studio as the class started rolling up their mats. "I need five minutes and then I'll be there. Where are you?"

I tried to sound annoyed and put out, but the truth was, it felt good that out of everyone he could've called, he'd picked me.

Hayes wasn't far, so I agreed to meet him. After wiping down my mat and rolling it up, I gathered the rest of my things and headed off to find him. At the opposite end of town, I saw him sitting on a bench near the sidewalk. His shoulders were hunched against the cold, jaw tight, expression pure murder.

I slowed the car and rolled down the passenger window. "Hey, stranger. Need a ride?"

Hayes rolled his eyes and stood. When he went to open the passenger door, I quickly hit the lock button.

"Come on. Open up." He was annoyed and I was tickled.

"Dance for me." I tried to contain my giggles as my eyebrows bounced.

"What?" he demanded, pulling on the door handle again. "Come on, Clara. Open it."

"You heard me. If you want in, you gotta dance for it." I leaned forward and turned up the radio as I grinned at him.

My brother's jaw worked and his nostrils flared, but I wasn't giving in. "Come on . . ." I shimmied my shoulders in encouragement.

After a moment, Hayes rolled his eyes and started dancing along with the music, right in the middle of downtown. It was mostly angry shoulder shimmies and a half-hearted hip twist, but he did it. I dissolved into a fit of giggles.

"There." His hands went out. "Happy?"

I laughed again and unlocked the door. "Yes. Very. Smooth moves."

Hayes folded himself into the front seat. "You're so annoying."

I beamed at him. "Thank you." If I could keep him dancing and rolling his eyes instead of stewing in guilt, I'd happily play the clown.

Hayes rubbed his palms across his pant legs.

"Where to?" I asked.

Hayes directed me out of town in the direction of the

junkyard where he assumed his truck might be. It was a short drive, but I hummed along to the radio. When curiosity got the best of me, I glanced at my brother. "Why me?"

He hummed something that sounded like *huh?*

"Why did you call *me?*" I clarified. I wasn't sure what answer I was fishing for. Maybe something like, *Because I missed you. Because you're my favorite.* Definitely not what actually came out of his mouth.

My big brother eyed me as though he was choosing his words carefully. "You're the only one without a job."

My face twisted. "Damn. Okay. Thanks, bro." I tried not to let his words hurt me, but it stung anyway. I *did* have a job. Sure, I didn't have any modeling prospects on the current horizon, but that was because I wasn't looking for them. I could have something lined up tomorrow if I wanted to.

Probably.

Maybe.

*Fuck.*

"Sorry. I'm just in a mood," Hayes said.

I glanced at his rigid posture. "I can see that."

Hayes ignored my poking. We pulled into the tow lot and sure enough, his truck was there. Before he climbed out, he looked at me. "Thanks for the ride. See you at dinner?"

I pressed my lips together. "Yep."

Mom had informed me that morning that she and Dad wanted everyone over for dinner "now that the family was all home." A tiny pang of guilt poked my ribs at the thought that my absence had meant no family dinners for them either.

If only they knew it had been because I couldn't bring myself to lie to them about my relationship with Greg.

Once I saw Hayes was fine to pick up his truck, I swung the car around and headed back toward town to do a little shopping before dinner. Picking up a few things for Mom felt like the least I could do to help out. If I couldn't contribute rent or a clear life plan, I could at least show up with groceries and pretty flowers.

I took my time in the little grocery store, wandering the aisles and adding a few snacks into the cart in addition to the things Mom needed. The front display had gorgeous flowers you could bundle to make your own bouquet. I started plucking stems to create something pretty to bring to my mom. I hummed as I worked, arranging the flowers in a beautiful arrangement. My hands knew what to do without thinking—balance the colors, vary the textures, tuck in a sprig of greenery here, a pop of something unexpected there. It was the same quiet thrill I got on set, making something ordinary look like magic.

Movement caught my eye, and I looked down the aisle to see Wes Vaughn. His back was to me, but there was no mistaking him. The sweatshirt he wore did nothing to hide his broad shoulders and muscular build. Even in a grocery store under terrible fluorescent lighting, he looked like he'd been cut from some rugged, broody-hero catalog.

It was deeply unfair.

I took one last look at the bouquet, and once I was satisfied, I wrapped it in paper and placed it in my cart. Then I wheeled off in Wes's direction. Every sensible cell in my body screamed *Don't do it*. The rest of me—apparently in charge—steered straight toward him anyway.

As I got closer, I could spot the hitch in his gait. There was something about him that drew me in. I wanted to talk to him, but he was giving off serious *don't fucking talk to me* vibes.

Undeterred, I sidled my cart next to his. He paused, and I could feel his eyes on me. I ignored him and reached high on the top shelf for something. I pretended to struggle, and when he made no move to help me, I turned his way.

"Hey." I smiled at him.

Wes looked confused. "Hi, Clara."

I batted my lashes. "Can you help me grab that? I can't quite reach it."

His eyes were skeptical, but he moved in so close I could smell the spice of his bodywash on his skin. Heat prickled up my spine. I didn't move as he leaned in and stretched to reach the box on the top shelf. The world shrank down to the clean, warm scent of him and the way his arm brushed mine as he reached. I was suddenly acutely aware of every inch of my own body.

Wes handed it to me and I smiled again. "Thanks. You're my hero."

He gave a disbelieving grunt, and the rumble settled low in my belly. Heat danced across my neck.

Wes's attention drifted over my shopping cart and landed on the bouquet of flowers.

"My parents are having everyone over for dinner tonight. Mom needed a few things, and I thought *every woman deserves pretty flowers*." I twirled the bouquet, fully aware that I was having a one-sided conversation and rambling. "Cute, right?"

Wes's eyes settled back on me, and the intensity of his stare rattled me. "Gorgeous."

I told myself he meant the bouquet. My stupid, traitorous body decided to believe otherwise. Flustered, I swiped a hair from my face and glanced at his near-empty cart. "Looks like you've got more shopping to do. I'll let you hop to it."

Wes's blue eyes bore into me.

"Hop to it. Get it?" I swallowed hard and a nervous giggle bubbled up. "Because of your . . ." Panic and embarrassment gripped me. The second the words left my mouth, horror detonated in my chest.

*Who makes a hop joke to a man with a prosthetic?*

A swift exit was my only option. "Okay, bye."

Mortified that I'd made a joke about his injury, I quickly wheeled my cart away, banging it into a display and nearly knocking it over. Heat clawed up my neck, and I wanted the earth to open up and swallow me whole.

Just as I was about to die of embarrassment, Wes's deep chuckle rattled behind me. I slowly turned to find him with a hand pressed to his chest and laughing.

"Hop to it." He shook his head. "That's pretty good."

I offered a sheepish smile as relief washed over me. "Sorry." I pointed to my mouth. "No filter."

His smile softened. "That's the first time anyone's had the balls to tease me since it happened."

My shoulders lifted. "That's me. Big Balls Clara." *What the fuck am I saying right now?* "Okay, I'm going to go die now. Goodbye."

Without a second glance back, I shoved my cart forward. I was too mortified to bother getting the rest of the groceries. Instead, I abandoned my cart and made a beeline for the exit. There was a supermarket in the next town over, and I could get what I needed without shoving my foot in my mouth. I left behind everything—the snacks, the flowers, whatever dignity I had left—parked neatly in the frozen food aisle.

I wasn't used to being so flustered, but there was something about the intensity in Wes's stare that knocked me off-kilter. I had no idea what it was, but I also had zero intention of finding out.

~

MY PARENTS' house was a quaint little Cape Cod on the outskirts of Star Harbor. Once all my siblings, plus their partners, showed up, it was downright small. Selene and her daughter, Winnie, were getting settled while Selene's boyfriend, Austin, shook hands with my dad. The two of them, plus Hayes, started talking about sports. Elodie showed up with Cal and his teenage son, Levi. Kit was solo and sitting on top of the counter—like she always did—as my mom stirred the pot on the stove.

Everyone seemed to slot into place like puzzle pieces—partners, kids, routines. The only piece that didn't quite fit anywhere was me.

The house was loud and chaotic, but something about seeing everyone together made my chest feel too tight. There was barely enough room at the table as we all sat elbow to elbow, talking over one another and passing food around.

I loved them. God, I loved them. But squeezed between all that happiness and forward momentum, I felt like I was slowly disappearing.

I mostly stayed quiet, soaking in the chatter and feeling like an outsider. It was so clear that everyone's lives were moving forward and I was living at home with my parents without a clue as to how I was going to afford to go out on my own.

When a knock sounded at the door, we all quieted and turned. My dad stood, walking toward the entrance and pulling the door open. My mouth popped open when I saw

Wes standing outside the door with a bouquet of flowers in his hand.

*My bouquet.*

The air whooshed out of my lungs. Of all the people to show up holding the evidence of my grocery store meltdown, it had to be him.

"Well," my dad said. "This is a surprise. Come in."

Hayes stood, eyeballing his best friend.

Wes took a step inside. "I didn't mean to interrupt. I happened to see Clara at the store today, and she left these." His eyes flicked to mine, and I could feel the heat rising on my cheeks. There was something unreadable in his gaze—amusement, maybe, or curiosity. Whatever it was, it saw straight through me.

His attention moved to my mother. "I believe they're for you, Mrs. Darling."

"Oh, well . . ." Mom fussed as she stood and crossed the room to meet him. "Thank you, Weston."

His lips pressed together and he nodded. "I didn't mean to interrupt. I'll be going."

"Wait." Hayes hesitated. "Stay." My brother's voice held that rough edge of concern I'd been hearing more and more lately whenever he talked about Wes.

Wes's jaw clenched as the curious eyes of my family tracked him. "You have a good night."

Before any of us could interject, Wes was gone. The door closed behind him, and the house seemed to exhale, noise slowly filling the space he'd left. I couldn't stop staring at the spot where he'd been.

My mother was still swooning over the flowers when she returned to the table. "Such a shame." She sighed. I wasn't sure if she meant the accident, his loneliness, or the fact that he'd just walked out of a Darling family dinner like the walls were closing in.

"That's the first time I've seen Wes in weeks," Elodie noted.

Austin nodded. "He hasn't been on the jobsite at all lately. I'm really worried about him."

Our eyes moved to Hayes as though he held the answers to his best friend's finicky temperament. "Don't look at me," he grumbled. "He's been a prick lately."

"Don't say that!" my mother chided. "He's been through a lot. That man has lost so much. He's *suffering*."

The pity laced into her words didn't sit right with me. Sure, Wes had been through the wringer, but he was more than capable. He'd been an elite soldier, for fuck's sake. Turning him into some tragic cautionary tale felt wrong. Wes Vaughn was a lot of things, but helpless wasn't one of them.

"He's refusing care," Hayes said. "Doesn't want it, but he needs help. He's been missing appointments and not taking care of himself. I don't know if it's depression or spite." Hayes dragged a hand through his hair. "Whatever it is, he doesn't want my help. But whether he likes it or not, he does need someone. At least for the time being. He's fired the last three live-in care nurses, so the company doesn't want to send another. All the research I've done says this is normal, but . . . I'm just really worried about him."

The raw fear in my big brother's voice did something to me. I knew that tone. It was the same way I'd sounded talking about my career to my friends—half frustrated, half terrified. Completely unsure of what to do.

I straightened in my chair. "I'll do it."

All eyes turned to me, but I ignored the stares.

If there was one thing I knew how to do, it was step into

chaos and make it look beautiful. I couldn't fix my own life, but maybe I could help steady his.

"What?" I shrugged, desperately trying to hide my nerves. "I've known Wes my entire life . . . it'll be fine." My pulse was drumming hard enough that I could feel it in my ears. *Fine* was doing a lot of heavy lifting in that sentence.

Selene, ever the voice of reason, looked around the table. "Doesn't Wes have to agree to this? He's a grown man."

"It could be nice, though." My mother tried, and failed, to hide the glee in her voice at the prospect of not having me in the house. "Clara could help him get back on his feet—foot—oh, you know what I mean."

"I can talk to him." Cal's confident voice helped calm my nerves. "Reason with him and explain that it's only temporary. Healing takes time, and I think Clara would be a perfect fit."

*Temporary.* Such an easy word to say when it wasn't your entire life currently stuck on pause. Cal's reassuring smile did nothing to ease the tightness in my stomach.

I'd just agreed to move in with my brother's best friend . . . and he had no idea it was coming. Somewhere between a grocery store aisle and my parents' dining room table, I'd gone and upended both our lives. And there was no graceful way to back out now.

SIX

WES

I STARED at the sketch in my lap and grumbled. Something was off. Drafting used to be the one place my brain went quiet, where lines and measurements snapped into place like they'd been waiting on me to notice them. Now everything felt . . . crooked. Like I was trying to draw with the wrong hand. Ever since my accident, I found even my favorite part of the job mentally taxing. Now I couldn't escape the questions swirling in my mind.

*What if the homeowner suddenly loses a limb?*

*Is this accessible?*

*How will the shower accommodate someone with special needs?*

*Is that corner too tight for someone in a wheelchair?*

I couldn't stop redesigning every room in my head—widening hallways, lowering counters, shaving off inches that used to feel like nothing. I used to chase open-concept kitchens. Now I was chasing the version of a house that wouldn't turn on you the second your body did.

Private residences weren't required to accommodate physical differences. It was something I never gave much thought to until I became someone whose own home was a challenge. There were a million *what-ifs* and lately they stalled me every time I went to draft a concept.

Hell, I couldn't even get my own bathroom to stop feeling like a damn obstacle course. The house I'd poured myself into before the accident had turned into a daily reminder of everything I hadn't planned for.

I built houses other people were proud to come home to. Mine had turned into a place I endured.

With a huff, I tossed my notebook aside and dragged a hand down my face. My palms rasped against the days' old stubble. I'm not sure how long I'd been parked on the couch, but my ass was numb. My leg throbbed in that familiar, furious way—pain where there wasn't even a limb.

Phantom bullshit, my physical therapist called it. I called it a cosmic joke.

I lifted my shirt to sniff.

*Oh, fuck.*

I used to come home from twelve-hour days on-site and still have enough left in the tank to hit the gym and grab a beer. Now the idea of dragging myself into a shower felt like summiting Everest. The fall from "guy who could handle anything" to "guy who can't manage basic hygiene" had been fast and brutal.

I needed a shower and a shave, but every time I gathered the gumption, I easily talked myself out of it. For most people, they didn't have to think about the dozens of steps it took to simply take care of yourself. For me, every task seemed daunting.

When my doorbell rang, I paused. The sound sliced through the quiet, sharp enough to make me flinch. Nobody rang the bell anymore unless they wanted something—from me or for me. It was midday, so Hayes should be at work, unless it was another casserole from the town's unofficial pity committee. I already had a freezer full of lasagnas from people who barely knew my last name but knew I was the guy who lost his leg.

The bell rang again, and I lost all hope of the visitor leaving on their own.

I walked toward the door and paused when I looked through the peephole and saw Clara Darling standing on my front porch. Her blond hair fell in waves down her back, and her foot was tapping like she was nervous. Sunlight caught in her hair, turning it almost white at the ends, and I forgot how to breathe. Clara Darling did not belong on my sad excuse for a porch, not with her restless energy and that always-moving mouth.

She had always looked like trouble. Today she looked like trouble with a suitcase full of feelings I didn't have the bandwidth for.

Intrigued, I opened the door.

"Hi, Wes." Her smile bloomed and heat crawled up my neck. I hadn't seen that smile up close since our run-in at the grocery store. Once again, it hit hard—right in the space between my ribs and all the shit I hadn't dealt with.

She was also the only person in six months who'd had the balls to tease me about my leg and not immediately fall all over herself apologizing. I wasn't sure if that made her brave or reckless.

I frowned. "Clara."

Her eyes moved over me until her face twisted. "You look like shit."

The worst part was she wasn't wrong. If anything, she was being generous. I scrubbed a hand across the back of my neck, trying not to laugh. "Thanks?"

Flustered, she let out a nervous chuckle. "Sorry. That was rude. Can I come in?"

"Sure." I stepped back to allow room for her to enter. "Come on in."

"Thanks," she said, and as she slid past, her perfume wafted with her. It smelled woody and feminine, like flowers wrapped in spice. It didn't belong in my stale, take-out-and-muscle-rub air. It made the place feel smaller, like the walls had shifted closer just because she was present.

When Clara walked into my house, she spun in a slow circle, taking in the haphazard blanket crumpled on the couch and Chinese food containers scattered on the coffee table.

Embarrassment heated my skin.

"I wasn't expecting company." I tried to move quickly to pick up some of the mess, but I stumbled and had to recenter myself.

Heat scorched up my neck. I hated that she'd seen that —how awkward and slow I was now. Before, I could carry a sheet of drywall up a staircase without breaking a sweat. Now walking around my own damn coffee table required concentration.

Frustrated, I turned to her. "What do you need?" I meant for the words to come out bored, but they landed closer to defensive. I was so goddamn tired of being someone's project. Their penance. Their proof they were a good person.

Clara's shoulders straightened. "It's not about what I need, but what *you* need." Her face brightened as a hand went to her chest. "Me."

Of course. The universe had a sick sense of humor. Out of all the people to show up and offer themselves as a solution, it had to be the one woman I was not allowed to want.

My brows scrunched. "You?"

She nodded. "Yes. Me."

I let out an exasperated breath. "I'm not following. Why are you here?"

Clara's gray-blue eyes narrowed as her finger swirled around my living room. "You need someone to help with . . . all this. I need to get the hell out of my parents' house. I help you. You help me. We live happily ever after." Her eyes rolled as a pink blush stained her cheeks. "Temporarily, of course."

I tried to process exactly what Clara was proposing but came up short. "You want to . . . move in with me?"

She nodded, eyes bright. "Yes. We'll be roommates. I can help you with whatever you need. I'm a fantastic roommate."

This insane plan had *Hayes* written all over it. I shook my head. "No. Absolutely not."

There was no way in hell I was letting a walking sex dream move in with me. Not when she was Hayes's little sister and I was barely holding my shit together as it was. I had no business thinking about her mouth when I could barely make it into my own shower.

Clara's grin widened. "It's happening."

My arms folded. "No. It's not."

Clara popped one hand on her hip and lifted her shoulder. "Okay. I'll let Hayes handle you. He was chomping at the bit over the idea of him rooming with you while I took over his house."

A muscle jumped in my jaw. The image of Hayes moving his crap into my spare room, hovering and clamping me on the shoulder with that earnest, apologetic face, made my skin crawl. I loved the guy, but I didn't want him watching me struggle to put on a sock.

My hackles rose. "Whoa. Wait a minute. What the hell are you talking about?"

Clara pressed her lips into a slim smile. "My overzealous brother is ready and eager to make amends . . . and that included being your live-in helper."

*Fucking Hayes and his Boy Scout honor code.*

He was only trying to make up for the way things had gone down. For the fact that I'd only been on that dark, winding road because of him. Guilt sat between us like a third person in every room, and the last thing I needed was it sleeping down the hall.

"I do not need your brother, or anyone else for that matter, moving in with me. I'm *fine*." The words tasted like a lie even as I said them. Fine men didn't have take-out containers for decor and a permanent dent in their couch.

Clara's brows rose as she dramatically looked over my disheveled house. "Clearly." She blinked her eyes at me and scrunched her nose. "When's the last time you showered, Wes? I can smell you from here."

Humiliation pricked hot under my skin. It was one thing to know I'd let myself go. It was another to have Clara fucking Darling wrinkle her nose at me like I was something she'd stepped in.

"I just worked out," I deflected. I adjusted my stance, ignoring the sparks of pain that shot down my leg. "This plan is actually insane."

Clara shook her head. "It's not that crazy. You don't have family around to help you get all"—she waved a hand in front of me—"this figured out. I'm here to help, but I'll stay out of your way. I promise."

My molars ground together. I couldn't believe I was even considering it, but if Clara was even half as stubborn as her brother, I had a hell of a fight on my hands. "What's in it for you?"

Nobody did anything for free. Not for me, not anymore. There was always a string attached—pity, obligation, guilt. I searched her face for it, and all I saw was exhaustion and something that looked a lot like my own brand of lost.

Clara lit up like she'd been dying for me to ask. She ticked off each item on her fingers. "One, like I said, you'd be getting me out of my parents' house. Two, you'd be upping my cosmic karma points, since running out of a wedding was not my finest moment. And three, you'd eat up the free time I'd otherwise be spending wallowing in self-pity." Her arms folded over her chest. "So really you're doing *me* the favor here."

I'd heard whispers of her wedding-day drama as Hayes filled the silence between us and ranted about how small towns loved to gossip. Seeing her now—cheeks pink, chin tipped up like she dared me to agree with them—I realized how wrong they'd gotten her. She wasn't unhinged. She was untethered.

Her logic made absolutely no sense, but I couldn't quite muster the energy to come up with a rebuttal. To be honest, the prospect of having someone who looked like her around while simultaneously getting Hayes off my ass was tempting. Even in the months since my accident, daily tasks were a lot more complicated.

I sighed and pinched the bridge of my nose. "I think this is a terrible idea."

Terrible ideas had never looked so appealing. A warm body in the house. Someone to nag me into showering. Someone who wasn't paid to see me at my lowest.

"It's me or another stranger moving in. Besides, I

wouldn't have to be here if you'd stop firing your helpers." Clara's simple logic annoyed the fuck out of me.

"They weren't *helpers*," I growled. "They were licensed nurses with experience aiding recent amputees. Everyday tasks get harder when you don't have someone helping at home." Hearing my physical therapist's words in my own voice was jarring.

The hired nurses had also looked at me like I was their good deed for the year. I didn't want to be anyone's inspiration. I just wanted to be a guy who could make it through a shower without supervision.

"Then what was the problem?" she asked.

Exhausted, I sighed. "They were also little old ladies who shuffled around my house and tried to give me sponge baths."

Clara's eyes widened as they raked down my body.

Heat licked up the back of my neck.

Fantastic. Now I was picturing her hands on me instead of the nurse's, which was a whole different problem.

"That's not a requirement of the position." I stumbled over the words, scrambling to get this strange conversation back on track.

Her lips pursed. "Shame."

Before I could respond, she whipped her head around and walked back out the front door. Moments later, Clara dragged two huge suitcases plus a shoulder bag over the threshold. She muscled them inside and looked at me with a huff.

"So . . . are we doing this or what?"

## SEVEN

WES STARED at me with heavy brows as my heart thudded in my chest. With my shoulders squared, I didn't move. If it was a battle of wills, Wes had never seen Clara Darling's stubborn streak.

Finally, his shoulders dropped and he exhaled. "Fine."

A giddy zip ripped through me.

*Holy shit. He said yes.*

My offer to help Wes had come from a genuine place. Anyone could see that he was suffering and too stubborn for his own good. All he needed was a little help getting on his feet—metaphorically, of course—and he'd be back to his old charming self.

It made sense to me why he wouldn't want strange nurses living at his house. Not only was he trying to get his life back, but walking on eggshells around a stranger in your own home had to have been maddening.

Sure, I was only one degree away from being a stranger, but I'd technically known Wes all my life.

We were friends . . . sort of.

He gripped the door and stepped aside to make room

for me, leaving a wedge of cold air slicing between us. We just . . . stood there. Me with my overstuffed luggage and manic smile, him with his exhausted eyes and *What the hell have I done?* energy.

The silence made me itchy. "So . . . Do I sign a lease or just pay you in homemade dinners and witty banter?"

One of his brows lifted up. "No lease. No banter." His voice was flat and rough around the edges. "Just . . . come in."

It wasn't exactly the charmed, warm welcome I was used to. I told myself not to take it personally, but I still felt the sting anyway.

I reached for the first suitcase and dragged it across the threshold. He had moved to close the door when I stopped him with a hand to the wood.

"Hang on. There are a few more." Heat crept up my cheeks as I scrambled back out to grab the other two over-stuffed suitcases and muscled them into his house. By the time I got the third one over the lip of the doorway, I was breathless and sweating in my coat.

Wes's eyes narrowed at how the zippers of my luggage bulged and strained to stay closed. "You said temporary, right?"

I blew a stray piece of hair out of my face with a huff. "Yeah. Of course."

His wary gaze stayed locked on my overpacked suitcases.

"Oh . . . that." A nervous chuckle bubbled up. "A lot of this is for work. I model wedding dresses. There are only a few of my favorites here. The rest are still at my fiancé—*ex*-fiancé's apartment. I haven't gotten them yet but couldn't leave without these . . . I'm going to style a few to add to my portfolio and—"

Wes stood silent, his eyebrows dangerously close to his hairline.

"I'm rambling. I'm sorry." A lump lodged in my throat.

This was supposed to be a hypothetical offer. A "sure, I'll help" that never made it off the dining room table. Now my suitcases were in his foyer, and my stomach was doing Olympic-level backflips.

I cleared my throat. "Where can I put these?"

Wes shook his head. "Come on," he said, the words coming out more like a sigh than an invitation.

I wrapped my fingers around the suitcase handles and followed him.

The door clicked shut behind us, and the quiet hit me first. Star Harbor's main drag was only a few miles away, but out here, on the outskirts of town, it felt like we were in our own little world. No traffic, no chatter, just the faint sigh of wind through trees and the soft creak of his house settling.

I'd seen the place from the road, but stepping inside was something else entirely.

The living room opened right up into the kitchen, all warm wood and clean lines. Vaulted ceilings with exposed beams drew my eyes up, and built-in shelves flanked a stone fireplace like something out of a magazine. The kind where the family wears coordinated sweaters and drinks cocoa without spilling.

Except instead of cocoa there were empty Chinese take-out containers, a couple of crumpled napkins, and what might once have been a sock now fossilized under the coffee table.

Beyond the living room, big windows lined the back wall. Through them, I caught a glimpse of the pine forest hugging the edge of his property, dark green against the winter sky. There was a narrow break between the trees—a sandy, worn path I would've bet money led straight to the dunes and down to the beach.

Of course his house backed up to a postcard.

My brain, ever the opportunist, immediately slapped a wedding over the top of the scene—white chairs lining the path, twinkle lights strung through the branches, a small wooden arch at the tree line, Lake Michigan glittering in the distance. I could practically see the caption: Evergreen Dunes Elopement.

"Your house is . . ." I searched for the right word and landed somewhere between *Architectural Digest* and *sad bachelor den*. "Beautiful," I settled on, because it was. Even under the mess.

Wes made a low sound that might have been a scoff. "It's just a house."

I took in the custom trim, the way the kitchen island was perfectly proportioned to the room, the little reading nook tucked under a window with built-in drawers beneath. This wasn't just a house. This was someone's dream. His dream.

I whispered under my breath, "No, it's definitely not."

You didn't get details like that by accident.

I could see him in every choice—practical and solid, but with these flashes of softness he probably didn't even realize he had. The deep farmhouse sink. The way the outlets were perfectly placed, like he'd thought through how a person would actually live here. The warm pendant lights over the island that made even the stacks of mail and abandoned coffee mugs look almost intentional.

It was gorgeous craftsmanship at war with clutter and neglect.

Kind of like the man standing in the middle of it, pretending not to notice.

As I dragged my suitcases farther in, I started to see the places where the house didn't quite match the man living in it anymore.

There was a small lip where the tile met the hardwood leading into the hallway—nothing I would've clocked before, but suddenly it looked like a trip wire. The hallway in the back was narrow.

And the couch . . . *sheesh.*

The couch was clearly command central. Blankets piled at one end, a dent in the cushions exactly where his body would fit. The coffee table was a graveyard of take-out containers, pill bottles, and half-tangled charging cords. Everything he might need was within arm's reach, like he'd built himself a little bunker and never bothered to come out.

This house was clearly designed for the old Wes—the one who could sprint up and down stairs and haul lumber without thinking. The space hadn't gotten the memo that everything had changed.

A sharp, surprising thread of protectiveness tugged in my chest. I'd never looked at a man's house and thought, *Okay, how do we make this less of an obstacle course for his life?*

But I was thinking it now.

"Upstairs," Wes said, breaking into my thoughts. He nodded toward the staircase at the back of the house and reached for the handle of the nearest suitcase.

He stopped at the base of the stairs, and something like fear swept across his face. It was gone almost as quickly as it came, replaced by that familiar, closed-off blankness.

Before I could offer to help, his hand wrapped around

the suitcase handle. With his other, he gripped the banister and started up. The movement wasn't smooth—it took effort, deliberate and careful—but he did it. One step, then another.

My heart lodged somewhere in my throat.

I hovered a few feet behind him with the other two suitcases, every instinct screaming at me to stay close in case he slipped, but not so close that I turned into another person smothering him. Hayes's voice echoed in my head—*He doesn't want my help*—and I forced myself to let Wes set the pace.

By the time we reached the top, I was panting and sweaty, my arms burning from hauling my wardrobe and emotional baggage up his stairs. Wes adjusted his stance like the climb had cost him more than he wanted me to see.

"There are three empty bedrooms," he said, nodding down the short hallway. "You can take your pick." His chin jerked toward the first open door. "This one is mine, but the rest are free."

I peeked past his shoulder into the primary bedroom.

It was beautiful. A king-size bed centered against the far wall, flanked by matching nightstands. A big window with that same view of the pines and a sliver of sand path. An en suite bathroom beyond an open doorway, all sleek tile and glass.

And absolutely no sign that anyone actually lived there.

The bedspread was smooth and unwrinkled, the pillows perfectly fluffed. No kicked-off jeans on the floor, no boots by the door, no half-empty glass of water sweating on the nightstand.

Nothing.

It felt wrong that I was the one moving into the room next door while he was downstairs wearing grooves into his couch.

I swallowed, suddenly lightheaded.

"I, uh . . . I'll take one of the guest rooms," I said, my voice softer than I meant it to be. I tore my gaze away from the life he'd stopped claiming and forced a smile. "Wherever you want me."

His jaw ticced at that, something unreadable flickering over his face. Then he turned and nodded toward a door across from the primary. "This one's empty."

The guest room Wes pointed to was as neutral as they came—soft gray walls, simple dresser, a bed made up in plain white sheets and a navy comforter. A single lonely hanger swung in the otherwise empty closet. No art on the walls, no rug, no personality. Just a room waiting for a story.

Apparently, for now, that story was mine.

I rolled one suitcase over the threshold and set it by the dresser. The other two waited in the hall, and so did Wes, his hand still braced on the handle of the one he'd carried up.

Hayes's voice from dinner floated back to me. *He's refusing care. Missing appointments. Firing the last three live-in nurses . . . I'm just really worried about him.*

Standing here, next to an empty room and an untouched primary suite, I finally understood why the care company didn't want to send anyone else. Wes wasn't a broken faucet you could fix with the right wrench. He was . . . complicated. Hurting. And I'd just volunteered to be in the front row for all of it.

A sliver of doubt slid under my rib cage. I was good with chaos—fashion shoots, late photographers, demanding designers. I knew how to step into a disaster and make it look intentional. This, though? This was someone's actual life.

*What if I wasn't enough?*

*What if I made it worse?*

I glanced back at Wes, and the way he was standing just slightly off-balance, like his body still wasn't entirely his. Then I recognized the feeling creeping over me—the same one I always got on set when everything was teetering: that moment right before I took charge.

"Well," I said, forcing some lightness into my voice, "I guess we should lay down some ground rules. I promise not to reorganize your entire life . . . on the first day."

One corner of his mouth twitched. It wasn't a full smile, but it was something. "That supposed to make me feel better?" he asked, dry as dust.

A tiny spark of satisfaction flared in my chest. "Also, for the record, there is absolutely a no-sponge-bath clause in my contract."

This time, I got a low huff that might have been a laugh. It vanished almost as quickly as it came, but I caught it.

"Noted," he said.

Wes stepped into the room without asking and lifted my second suitcase like it weighed nothing. Muscles flexed in his forearm, the movement automatic despite everything his body had been through. He set it down by the closet, then nodded toward the last one still in the hall.

"I'll grab that one, and then I'll get out of your hair," he said. "You can . . . settle in."

For half a second, something like amusement flickered over his face. It was gone almost as quickly as it came, but I saw it.

There he was—the man who used to give Hayes endless shit and flirt with half the women at the Lantern.

Buried, but not gone.

That tiny glimmer was enough to keep my feet planted

instead of bolting down the stairs and pretending this had all been a very elaborate joke.

"Thanks, roommate," I said softly.

He paused in the doorway, his shoulders going tight at the word. "Yeah," he murmured, not quite looking at me. "Roommate."

Then he was gone, his uneven footsteps retreating down the hall, the house swallowing him back up.

Silence rushed in behind him.

I sat on the edge of the bed and looked around at my new, featureless little kingdom. Luggage busting at the seams. Four blank walls. A closed door across the hall leading to a bedroom he refused to sleep in.

Scared wasn't a strong enough word for what I felt.

I was scared of failing him. Scared of saying the wrong thing and watching him shut down even further. Scared that this was just another way I was putting my life on hold for someone else's.

But there was something else too. Stubbornness. The same streak that had grabbed Kit's hand and run out of a church in a wedding dress. The part of me that refused to let his house—or his life—feel this empty if I could help it.

I lay back on the too-perfect bed and stared at the ceiling. I'd moved in with my brother's best friend. Maybe I was out of my mind. Or maybe—for once—I was exactly where I was supposed to be.

Somewhere downstairs, a floorboard creaked, and I pictured him settling onto that damn couch again.

"Okay, Wes Vaughn," I whispered to the empty room. "Let's see if we can get you back into your own life."

## EIGHT

I woke up to the sound of humming.

For a second, still halfway in a dream where I had two working legs and a life that made sense, I couldn't place it. It threaded through the house—light and aimless, drifting under doorways and across the ceiling. A cabinet door thumped shut. Something clinked against the counter.

Not my TV. Not the furnace.

*Her.*

I blinked my eyes open. My neck ached like I'd slept on a pile of rocks instead of the couch I'd once been proud to own. My residual limb throbbed in that familiar, pissed-off way, the shrinker twisted halfway down. A ridge from the cushion dug into my spine.

For months, the only sounds in this house had been mine—my uneven steps, the creak of the couch, the occasional food delivery at the door.

Now there was humming in my kitchen.

I wasn't sure what pissed me off more—that the sound grated on my nerves, or that it didn't entirely.

I scrubbed a hand over my face and stared at the ceiling

fan. I had said yes. I'd stood in my own doorway yesterday and told Clara Darling she could move in.

*Idiot.*

Somewhere beyond the living room, water ran. A drawer slid shut. The house didn't feel empty this morning, and I didn't know what to do with that.

I shifted, biting back a groan as my back popped. The stale smell of sweat and takeout hit my nose, and I swore under my breath.

Perfect. Exactly how a man wanted to smell with a woman in the next room.

I'd gone months without giving a single shit what I looked like. Now, with one stubborn runaway bride under my roof, I was suddenly aware of everything—the mess on the coffee table, the dent in the couch, the fact that I hadn't shaved in days.

I hated that. Hated that I cared. Hated that there was someone here to care for.

This was my house. My space. I'd built damn near every inch of it with my own two hands, and yet lying there on the couch, listening to her move around, I felt like an intruder in my own life.

I forced myself upright, every muscle in my back protesting. The shrinker had twisted in my sleep, digging into skin that already felt flayed. I reached for my liner and prosthetic, hands clumsy with sleep and irritation.

Putting the leg on was second nature by now, but it still wasn't fast. Roll the liner. Adjust. Lock in. Check the fit. I'd done it in under a minute in PT before, but lying on my couch with someone else in my kitchen, it felt like trying to assemble myself under a timer.

Any second she could walk in and find me half put together. The thought made my jaw grind.

When everything was finally attached and as comfortable as it was going to get, I pushed to standing. The room tilted for a heartbeat, then settled. I grabbed the back of the couch until my balance caught up with me and then made my slow, uneven way toward the kitchen.

Clara was there, of course.

She stood barefoot at the counter, tiny pajama shorts showing a ridiculous amount of toned leg, a loose T-shirt hanging off one shoulder. The T-shirt was thin enough that her nipples were on full display, hard points against worn cotton.

Her hair twisted up in a knot. No makeup. No armor. Just soft skin and sleep-warm curves and absolutely no awareness of what she looked like in my kitchen. My body woke up and took notice, heat sparking low and unwelcome.

"Good morning," she said, glancing over her shoulder. Her voice was easy, like we'd been doing this for years.

"Morning." The word came out stiff, like I'd forgotten how to use it.

A coffee maker gurgled on the counter between us. She turned back to it, poured herself a mug, then hesitated for half a second before grabbing another and filling that one too. She didn't look at me as she set it on the opposite side of the counter.

"There's some if you want it," she said, like it was an afterthought. Not an offer. Not caretaking. Just information.

I hated how much I wanted it. Hated how the smell alone made something in my chest unknot a fraction.

"Thanks," I muttered, the word scraping my throat on the way out.

She gave a quick little nod, like that settled that, and didn't push. No questions about how I'd slept. No comment about the leg. No bright, chirpy monologue to fill the silence.

Instead, she took her own mug and flitted right past me, out of the kitchen, like it was the most natural thing in the world to leave a grumpy man alone with his thoughts and fresh coffee.

I was left standing there in my own house, blinking at the spot she'd just vacated, feeling weirdly exposed in a room where nothing had actually happened.

Great.

Now I was stewing over coffee and a "good morning" like a goddamn teenager. I wrapped my hand around the mug and took a careful sip. It was strong and hot and exactly how I liked it, which irritated me on principle.

My phone buzzed on the counter.

I ignored it at first, expecting another check-in text from Hayes or some automated email about a bill. It buzzed again, this time with the sharp little chime I'd never bothered to change on my calendar app. The screen illuminated where it lay face up by the knife block.

**PT—10:00 a.m.**

I'd forgotten I'd even left that alert on. I had already planned to call and cancel later. I could blame the weather or a scheduling conflict or anything except the truth—that I didn't feel like being poked, prodded, and measured like a science project today.

The buzzing stopped, but the banner stayed on the screen, glaring at me.

Of course that was the moment Clara drifted back in, mug in hand. She crossed to the sink, rinsed out the last of her coffee, and set the cup upside down on the drying mat. The whole time, I willed my phone to go dark again.

It didn't.

Her gaze flicked down as she turned from the sink. Just a quick glance, the way anyone's eyes would catch on a lit screen. She didn't lean in, didn't pick it up, didn't act like she'd been caught snooping.

"Do you need to be somewhere this morning?" she asked, reaching for a towel to wipe a ring of water off the counter. Her tone was light. Neutral.

"I'm fine," I said automatically.

"That's not what I asked." She nodded toward the phone without really looking at it. "You've got an appointment?"

The muscles in my neck went tight. "I'm not a child, Clara. I don't need a keeper."

She stilled, the dish towel in her hand. I braced for a lecture—some combo of guilt and my therapist's pep talks.

Instead, she just shrugged, folding the towel back over the oven handle. "Okay. I can drive you, or you can call and cancel. It's your leg. Your choice."

No pity. No lecture. Just that.

Somehow that pissed me off more. If she'd nagged, I could've dug in my heels and blamed her for being overbearing. If she'd begged, I could've felt righteous turning her down.

But this—this dropped the decision squarely in my lap. If I skipped, it wasn't because the roads were bad or I couldn't get there. It was because I'd chosen not to try.

"I was going to reschedule," I muttered.

She nodded, unbothered. "Then reschedule." She turned toward the doorway like the conversation was already over. "I'll be around if you change your mind."

I stared at the back of her head, at the messy knot of blond hair and the way it bounced slightly as she walked away.

I hated the idea of her driving me. Hated the image of myself hobbling out of her car under the fluorescent lights of the PT clinic, of her watching me wobble and sweat through exercises that used to be nothing.

But I hated the idea of calling and canceling more.

"Be ready in twenty," I said, the words out of my mouth before I'd fully decided on them.

She paused halfway up the stairs and glanced back with a small, unreadable smile. "You got it."

When she disappeared again, I stared down at my coffee and at the appointment reminder still glowing on my phone.

*This was my decision. My life. My rehab.*

So why did it feel like I'd just been maneuvered into doing the right thing by someone who'd barely said ten words to me before breakfast?

Getting showered and out the door was a whole damn operation.

I shrugged on my coat with more effort than I wanted to admit, wrestling my arm through the second sleeve while my balance adjusted. Then the boots—one easy, one not. I hated putting them on while sitting down, but there wasn't really another option unless I wanted to risk face-planting before we even hit the porch.

By the time I made it to the front door, my residual limb was already starting to complain, and the cold never helped.

Clara was waiting by the entryway, keys in hand, a chunky knit hat pulled low over her ears. She glanced at me, then reached past to open the door. The blast of Michigan winter slapped me in the face.

"Watch the top step," she said, and then—nothing. No reaching. No hovering. She stepped out ahead of me, moving to the side so I had a clear shot at the stairs.

I gripped the banister and took the first step down, slow and careful. Snow clung to the edges of the boards, the kind that packed into a slick film over the wood. Anyone else would have had a hand clamped around my arm by now, breathing down my neck.

Clara just walked ahead of me, boots crunching on the path as she hit the bottom and veered toward the car. My truck, for once, stayed where it was. Today, she was driving.

By the time I reached the last step, she'd already unlocked the passenger side and was sitting in the driver's seat, fiddling with the radio or the vents, pointedly not looking at me.

I made my way across the yard, leg heavy, focusing on each placement of my foot. No gasp of panic when I slipped slightly on a patch of ice, no startled movement in my peripheral vision. She stayed bent over the console until she heard the door close.

The silence in the car was thick enough to chew on. She buckled her seat belt, then reached for the ignition. The engine turned over, heater roaring to life.

"Seat warmers work," she said, flicking a switch on my side. "In case you were wondering."

"Great." The word was flat.

We pulled out of the drive and headed toward town, the wipers squeaking across the windshield. Snowbanks rose on either side of the road, the sky that familiar, oppressive gray.

After a minute, she tried again. "Star Harbor looks different," she said, mostly to the windshield. "When did we get so many people? And a second stoplight?"

"Summer," I said.

"Is that because of the farm?" Her mouth curved faintly. "Elodie won't shut up about the restaurant. She said your crew did the heavy lifting."

My shoulder rose. "Some of it."

"Did you design it?"

"Parts."

My clipped answers dropped between us like cinder blocks.

She huffed out a little breath that wasn't quite a laugh. "You know most people would turn that into a humble-brag." She lowered her voice to sound like a man. "'Yeah, I built half this town, no big deal.'"

I almost laughed. "Most people like talking more than I do."

A short burst of laughter huffed out of her nose. "Noted."

For a while, Clara filled the space with small observations—how her favorite bakery wasn't around anymore, how the Lady's Lantern sign had been repainted, how the lake still managed to look both beautiful and scary in winter. It was mostly one-sided, her voice a low hum under the grind of the tires on packed snow.

I stared out the window, watching the familiar streets slide by.

She wasn't treating me like glass. She wasn't talking to me like I might break. She was just driving a man to his appointment and occasionally tossing words into the void to see if any would stick.

I didn't know what to do with that any more than I knew what to do with pity. Both made me feel off-balance, like the ground under my feet had shifted and I was the last to know.

The clinic came into view all at once—brick, glass, too much light. Clara pulled into a spot and shifted into park.

Her fingers drummed the steering wheel once. "You want to go in," she said, "or you want me to turn around? We can make a break for it. It would be very on brand for me."

My mouth twisted into something resembling a smile.

"Let's go," I said before I could talk myself out of it.

## NINE

WES

THE PT CLINIC smelled like disinfectant and rubber mats. Bright overhead lights bounced off every metal surface, making the place feel more exposed than it already was.

Clara checked us in at the front desk like this was any other appointment and then drifted toward the seating area while I made my slow way to the back.

Gone were the tiny pajama shorts and soft T-shirt. Clara had pulled on dark jeans that hugged her legs, a fitted sweater that did nothing to hide the curve of her waist, and a pair of ankle boots that added just enough height to make her look like she belonged in one of those lifestyle shoots I used to flip past in magazines. Her hair was down now, falling in loose waves around her shoulders, and there was the faintest sheen on her lips that hadn't been there earlier this morning.

"Wes." My therapist, Jess, spotted me the second I came around the corner. Her dark ponytail swung as she crossed the room, tablet in hand. "Good to see you back."

I grunted something that might have been hello.

Her eyes did a quick sweep from my face to my gait, a mental checklist I'd grown to recognize.

Weight-bearing: good.

Range of motion: needs improvement.

Attitude: surly.

"You brought company," she said, nodding past my shoulder.

I didn't have to turn to know she meant Clara.

"She's just my ride," I said. "It's nothing."

Jess's mouth tipped into the slightest smirk. "Support systems aren't nothing. They're important."

My skin crawled. "Can we just . . . do the thing?"

"Always so charming," she muttered, but she stepped aside and waved me toward the parallel bars.

I glanced back as I moved into position. Clara had picked a chair against the far wall, near a rack of outdated magazines. She'd already sat, one leg crossed over the other, her phone in her hand.

She wasn't staring at me.

For some reason, that annoyed me.

"Okay," Jess said, bringing my focus back. "Let's start with walking the bars. Nice and easy. I want to see where we're at today."

We were at "tired and cranky," but I knew that wasn't what she meant.

I wrapped my hands around the cool metal and took a breath. Step, shift, step. The prosthetic did what it was supposed to do, mostly, but every movement still felt like doing algebra with muscles that only knew basic math.

"Lengthen your stride a little on the left," Jess said. "You're babying it."

"It's trying to kill me," I grunted.

"That's why you're here."

We went through the motions. Walking drills. Balance work. A sadistic exercise with a foam pad that made my residual limb work twice as hard just to keep me upright. Sweat slid down my spine, my T-shirt sticking to my back.

Every few reps, my eyes flicked to Clara.

She was scrolling with her thumb, her expression neutral. At one point she set her phone aside and picked up a magazine, flipping through pages without really looking at them. She shifted in her chair, uncrossed and recrossed her legs.

Not once did I catch her openly watching me.

I wasn't sure what pissed me off more—that she wasn't hovering and fussing like everyone else, or that I kind of wanted her to look up and see that I wasn't completely useless.

"Again," Jess said when I stumbled. "You're capable of better than that."

I clenched my jaw and went again. Harder this time. Pushed through the burn in my hip, the electric zing of phantom pain. Focused on the bar in front of me instead of the woman pretending to be utterly uninterested in my progress.

"Better," Jess murmured. "There he is."

By the time she moved me over to the step platform, my leg shook with fatigue. She nudged the riser up a notch anyway.

"You're not made of glass, Vaughn."

"Tell that to everyone else," I muttered.

She raised an eyebrow. "You letting them treat you like you're going to break, or are you just assuming that's what they're thinking?"

I didn't answer. I was too busy not falling on my ass.

Out of the corner of my eye, I saw Clara stand and walk

to the water cooler, refill a paper cup, then go back to her seat. Her gaze skimmed past me once, quick as a blink, before she sat down again and pulled her knees up, the magazine balanced on her thighs.

It shouldn't have mattered. I was here for me. For my leg. For the life I wasn't sure I wanted but apparently hadn't given up on, because I was voluntarily sweating under fluorescent lights while a woman half my size told me to lift my knee higher.

Still, every time I stuck a landing or didn't wobble on a turn, a small, stupid part of me wondered whether Clara had seen it.

Jess finally released me with a clap on the shoulder and a "Same time next week, Vaughn," like I hadn't just done an hour in her personal torture chamber.

By the time I made it back to the front, my leg felt like it was made of wet cement. The world had that sharp, too-bright edge it got when I was past my limit and pretending I wasn't.

With Clara at my side, the clinic doors whooshed open, and cold air knifed in. There was a short concrete ramp down to the parking lot, dusted with a fresh layer of snow that some half-assed plow job hadn't quite cleared.

I paused at the top, jaw tight.

Clara stepped through ahead of me, letting the door close gently behind. She didn't reach for me. Didn't rush to block the ramp with her body like a guardrail. She just shifted a little closer to the side and bent her arm at the elbow, hand hanging loose between us. Not touching. Just . . . there.

An offer, not an order.

I told myself I didn't need it and took one careful step down. The prosthetic hit a slick patch and skidded a fraction sideways, the kind of slide that would have sent me sprawling a month ago. My muscles seized.

Before I could overthink it, my hand shot out and caught her forearm.

Warm. Solid.

The world steadied.

We stood like that for half a breath—her arm under my grip, her body a grounded line next to mine—before I realized what I was doing and let go like she'd burned me.

"I've got it," I muttered.

"I know." Her tone stayed mild. She tucked her hands back into her coat pockets. "The car's right there."

It was easier, that was the worst part. The ramp, the snow, the whole thing. Having her arm within reach had made it easier, and I hated that so much I could feel my teeth grinding as I eased myself into the passenger seat.

I spent the ride home stewing in it.

Stewing in the fact that PT had gone better than the last time. Stewing in the fact that I'd pushed harder with her in the room. Stewing in the fact that borrowing her arm for two seconds had saved me from eating pavement.

Clara seemed to pick up on my mood, because she didn't bother with small talk this time. The car filled with the low murmur of the heater and the thrum of tires over packed snow. Every so often she tapped the steering wheel in time with a song only she could hear.

By the time we pulled back into my driveway, the knot between my shoulders felt like it had its own pulse.

Inside, I went straight for the couch. The cushions welcomed me like an old, shitty friend. I dropped down with a grunt, leg screaming, hip throbbing in time with my heartbeat.

Clara didn't hover. She just moved through the living room like a quiet storm.

She picked up the empty pill bottles and half-full ones, set the current prescriptions into a small ceramic dish she'd grabbed from the kitchen, and left the expired ones in a separate pile. She gathered two clearly fossilized take-out containers, popped them open just enough to confirm their level of horror, then snapped them shut again and carried them to the trash.

She didn't sigh. Didn't make a face. Didn't give me the "this isn't healthy" talk I could practically recite from memory.

She just . . . triaged.

A glass appeared on the coffee table within reach—clean, full of water, the condensation already beading on the side. She didn't say *drink this*. She didn't say anything at all.

To her, it was probably just basic living. Clearing surfaces. Making sure I wouldn't accidentally poison myself with bad lo mein.

To me, it felt like she was rearranging my failure. Putting it into neater piles so it looked a little less pathetic.

My house had been my cave. My evidence. The mess, the bottles, the couch groove—they all told the story of a guy who'd earned the right to be left alone. Watching her quietly dismantle that story one crusty container at a time made my skin itch.

"Clara," I said, sharper than I meant to.

She glanced over from inside the kitchen, where she was rinsing out one of the containers. "Yeah?"

Before I could decide what I wanted to say, she disappeared down the hall. I heard her door open, then close.

Good. Fine. I could breathe better with her out of sight.

I let my head tip back against the couch and stared at the ceiling. The house was quiet again, minus the hum of the fridge and the occasional creak of old wood. I tried to let the familiar emptiness settle over me. Tried to sink back into the numbness that had carried me through the last few months.

It didn't take.

A few minutes later, her door opened again.

I looked up without meaning to.

She grabbed her coat off the hook and shrugged into it, fingers working the buttons.

"You heading out?" I asked, the words out before I could stop them.

"Yeah." She didn't look at me as she dug in her bag for her keys. "Meeting Kit in town."

Kit. Right. It could've been true. Might have been a date. Might have been anything.

The fact that I cared at all sent a hot, ugly spike of something through my chest.

*Jealousy.*

There was no other name for it, and I hated it.

I had no right to it. She was my best friend's little sister and, more importantly, a grown woman doing me a favor I'd made as unpleasant as possible. She could go out with whomever she wanted. Fill her nights with drinks and laughter and men who didn't need a prosthetic to get up a flight of stairs.

Still, the idea of some guy I didn't know being brought back here—to this house, this couch, this tiny, fragile routine we'd barely started—made my hackles rise.

"We need some rules," I said.

Clara paused mid-zip, her brows lifting as she turned to face me fully. Hands went to her hips, a spark of defiance in her gray-blue eyes. "Fine," she said. "Let's hear them."

*Shit.*

I hadn't actually thought that far ahead. I just knew the sight of her all put together and ready to walk out of my front door had flipped some switch I hadn't known was there.

*Don't say anything about the pajamas. Don't say anything about the nipples. Don't say anything that makes you sound like a possessive asshole.*

"The first one," I said slowly, "is no random guys in my house."

Her head tilted. "Excuse me?"

"If you're going to date, fine." The word caught in my throat, bitter. "Just . . . not in my living room. Okay?"

For a beat, I thought she might fight me on it. Demand to know why I thought I had any say over her life. Call me out for being a hypocrite, or an idiot, or both.

Instead, she laughed.

Not a big, wild laugh. Just a low, disbelieving huff that did nothing to reassure me. She shook her head, amusement curving her mouth, and didn't bother giving me an answer at all.

She just slipped her keys into her coat pocket, opened the door, and stepped out into the cold, leaving my rule hanging in the air like an unanswered question.

Somehow that made me even more pissed off.

TEN

CLARA

KIT HAD ALREADY CLAIMED the corner table when I walked into the café, a half-empty latte in front of her and her boots kicked out like she owned the place. The bell over the door jingled, and she glanced up, eyes brightening when she saw me.

"You're late," she said, even though I very clearly was not.

"I'm exactly on time." I shrugged out of my coat and draped it over the back of the chair. "You're just dramatic."

"Runs in the family," she shot back, but there was a flash in her eyes that told me exactly where her brain had gone—wedding, runaway bride, big small-town gossip.

I pretended not to see it and busied myself with the menu board like I hadn't already memorized it in high school. The server took our drink orders with a nod before giving us time to decide on our food.

Across the table, Kit was watching me like a cat who'd spotted a bug.

"Don't," I warned, palming my latte as soon as it arrived. "I can feel you about to pounce."

She widened her eyes innocently. "What? I'm just spending time with my favorite black-sheep sister. Can't a girl enjoy brunch without ulterior motives?"

"Please." I teasingly kicked her boot. "You don't even know what 'ulterior' means."

"Rude," she said, but she grinned around the rim of her mug.

Kit mentioned Mom had already started "reclaiming the house" now that I wasn't camped out in my old room—more dinners out with Dad, fewer big grocery runs, talk of finally repainting the hallway.

It was all perfectly normal empty-nester stuff, but it still landed a little sideways. I'd barely moved my suitcases into Wes's house, and it already felt like my parents were quietly resetting back to life without me. Elodie was neck-deep in farm renovations and restaurant plans, Selene was buried in archives and old paper, and Hayes was . . . Hayes. He'd apparently managed to lock himself out of his truck at the gas station while it was still running, which felt right on brand for the most cursed man in Star Harbor.

We traded a few more low-stakes updates, but I could feel the real conversation pulsing under the table, waiting. My move into Wes's house sat between us like a third cup of coffee neither of us wanted to acknowledge yet.

"So," she said, drawing the word out. "There is a Keepers meeting coming up. We're learning how to knit."

I blinked. That was not the topic I'd expected. "Wow, okay. Hard left."

Her eyebrows bounced. "Seriously, though . . . you're coming to the next meeting, right? Selene has more stuff about the Lady. She actually squealed on the phone, and Sel never squeals."

"Obviously I know the basics," I hedged, not really sure

where Kit was going with it. "Lady of the Dunes, tragic love story, cursed town." My eyes sliced to her. "Cursed *brother*," I mumbled low enough for only her to hear.

Kit scoffed. "That was the Disney version. This is the messed-up version."

I couldn't help it—I leaned in. "Messed up how?"

She glanced around like someone might be eavesdropping, then lowered her voice anyway. "So they found her letters."

"Afraid, hiding, not waiting for some shipwrecked sailor but running from someone," I recited.

"Right," Kit said, eyes lighting. "Well, Selene's found even more references to this man. The one in the photograph."

I shivered, remembering the way my sisters had described it. The grainy black-and-white picture, the Lady's eyes scratched out, and the eerie figure in the corner who looked like he could've walked right out of our century and into theirs wearing Hayes's face.

"The guy who looks like our brother," I said.

"Exactly." Her voice dropped into something reverent and gleeful. "We still don't know who he is. We've checked the obvious stuff—marriage records, death notices, land deeds—but nothing concrete yet. Selene thinks he might've worked on the Barker family land. A farmhand, maybe. Someone who slipped through the cracks."

The Barkers were the old-money family tied to the Lady's legend, the ones whose property stretched from the dunes to half the town. If there was a place for secrets, it was their land.

I frowned at my mug. "Maybe she was knocked up," I said, half joking, half not. "Terrified and pregnant. That would've been about as scandalous as it gets back then."

Kit froze, her eyes going huge. Then she slapped the table. "Oh my god, can you imagine? Secret baby? Town scandal? This is exactly the kind of thing the Keepers live for."

A couple at the next table glanced over. Kit dropped her voice a notch and leaned in. "No, seriously. If there was some guy tied to the Barkers—farmhand, overseer, whatever —there'd be records somewhere. Pay ledgers, work rosters. Selene probably hasn't gotten through all the boxes yet. We could actually—"

"Help?" I finished, a reluctant smile tugging at my lips. "Join the coven and solve a hundred-year-old teen pregnancy?"

"Precisely." She sat back, smug. "Tell me that doesn't sound more fun than moping around Star Harbor."

"I'm not moping," I pouted. But Kit had a point.

My life felt like it had stalled out in my childhood bedroom and on Wes's sagging couch. The idea of focusing on someone else's mess—a dead woman's secrets instead of my own—had an undeniable appeal.

"Fine," I said slowly. "If there was some mystery man hanging around the Barker farm, and if he was the one she was hiding from or hiding with . . . there might be a paper trail."

Kit's grin turned feral. "That's my girl. We'll pitch it to Selene. She'll pretend not to be thrilled and then stay up all night reading microfiche or whatever archivists do for fun."

I laughed, the sound loosening something in my chest. For a minute it felt like old times—me and Kit in some diner booth or crappy bar, spinning stories out of nothing and daring each other to go one step further.

Except this time, there was a ghost, a cursed town, and our brother's face in a photograph that shouldn't exist.

I took a long sip of my latte, letting the warmth slide down. "Okay," I said. "I'm in. On the condition that if we accidentally raise the Lady from the dead, you're the one who explains it to Mom."

Kit snorted. "Deal. I've survived Dad's lectures about responsible life choices. I can handle one homicidal ghost."

The joke landed, but as I set my cup down, a little shiver walked up my spine anyway.

Maybe it was the thought of the Lady, or her scratched-out eyes. Maybe it was the eerie, unexplained resemblance to Hayes. Maybe it was the idea of some scared, pregnant young woman hiding in the dunes and nobody listening.

Or maybe it was just that digging into someone else's haunting sounded a hell of a lot easier than dealing with my own.

Kit's eyes slid back to me, sharpening in that way it did when she smelled fresh gossip.

"So," she said slowly, sipping the last of her latte.

I groaned. "Don't."

She ignored me completely, and her grin turned wicked. "How's life with Mr. Sunshine? Have you two learned to coexist, or is it mostly aggressive glaring?"

Heat crawled up my neck. I suddenly found the latte foam very interesting. "It's fine," I said, too quickly. "Awkward. He's . . . Wes, but different."

Kit's brows rose. "That was a lot of syllables to say nothing. Hayes made it sound like he's one bad day away from becoming a full-time hermit." She leaned in. "Is he really that bad? Missing appointments, shutting people out, refusing help, all that?"

Images flickered through my mind, uninvited—the dent in his couch where he clearly slept more than his bed, the lip into the bathroom that caught his prosthetic every time, the way he'd gripped the parallel bars this morning, jaw clenched as sweat slid down his spine. The stubborn line of his mouth when Jess pushed him, the raw humiliation in his eyes when he'd stumbled.

I forced my shoulders to relax. "He's doing better than Hayes thinks," I lied. "He's stubborn, but he's . . . trying. You know how dramatic big brothers can be."

Kit frowned into her drink. "Hayes isn't dramatic, he's—"

"Protective," I cut in, softening it. "I get it. I just don't think treating Wes like a lost cause is helping."

Kit frowned again. "I never said 'lost cause.'"

"You were thinking it," I said lightly, then immediately regretted the sharpness in my tone.

Her eyes narrowed. "Okay, what's that about?"

I tapped a fingernail against the ceramic mug. "Nothing. I just . . . he's not a project. That's all."

A small voice in my head grated on my nerves. *Since when do you care?*

Since he let me move in and I saw what it costs him just to get through a day, apparently. Since I watched him work his ass off at PT so nobody could accuse him of not trying. Since I've seen enough of the man he used to be to know he's still in there somewhere.

Kit's mouth tugged into a smirk. "Wow. Listen to you, defending Wes Vaughn. Is there something there?"

"Shut up," I muttered, but there wasn't much heat behind it.

What I didn't add was that hearing Wes reduced to a problem to manage or a list of failures made something twist in my chest. I didn't like him being picked apart when he wasn't here to defend himself.

For reasons I really didn't want to examine, it suddenly

felt like my job to make sure nobody else got to write his story for him.

"So what's it actually like?" she pressed. "Living with him."

I hesitated, then gave her the sanitized version. "He gave me rules."

That got her full attention. "Rules? Like . . . chore chart rules?"

"Well it was only one," I said, rolling my eyes. "A very specific one about no random guys in the house."

Kit barked out a laugh. "Oh my god. Of course he did. Did he at least write it down? Please tell me he wrote it down."

I thought of the way his jaw had clenched when he'd said it, the way something had flashed in his eyes. "No. Just grumpy landlord vibes."

"You should absolutely poke at that," Kit said, wicked delight sparking again. "Make your own list. Hang it on the fridge. 'Tenant Rule Number One: Landlord must smile and stop being a broody asshole.'"

Despite myself, I laughed. The idea lodged itself in my brain and refused to budge.

"Seriously," she went on. "He wants to play house-rule dictator? Fine. Give him something to look at besides his own misery. Make him mad. Maybe he needs to be mad more than he needs to be sad."

I wasn't sure that was sound psychological advice, but I couldn't deny the tiny, reckless thrill the thought gave me.

I took another sip of my latte, letting it linger on my tongue. "We'll see," I said.

Kit's phone buzzed and she glanced down, nose wrinkling. "Ugh. I've got to go or Elodie's going to fire me from my unpaid labor position at the farm."

She stood, leaned over to kiss my cheek, and squeezed my shoulder a little harder than necessary. "Text me if he drives you nuts," she said. "Or if you find any secret ghost babies."

"I'll keep my eyes peeled," I promised.

When she left, the café felt oddly louder. Conversations rose and fell around me, the hiss of the espresso machine punctuating the quiet at my little corner table. I sat there for another minute, hands wrapped around my empty cup like it could anchor me.

Eventually, I pushed to my feet and took the mug back to the counter.

"Have a good one, miss," the older woman at the register said as she passed, patting my arm.

I blinked. I had known the woman my entire life. "Ms. Fitzsimmons, it's me, Clara Darling."

She paused, squinting at my face. "Oh! Right. The middle one. I forgot about you."

She laughed like it was harmless and moved on before I could do more than force my lips into something resembling a smile.

Forgot about you.

*Awesome. Love that for me.*

Outside, the air was cold enough to sting my nose. I tugged my coat tighter and started walking toward my car. Star Harbor had always been prettier on foot anyway.

Main Street was a postcard—the kind of place city brides begged me to recreate in styled shoots. Brick storefronts with hand-painted signs, strings of white twinkle lights still up from Christmas because nobody had the heart to take them down yet, the distant glint of Lake Michigan at the end of the road. A few tourists in puffy coats wandered in and out of the bakery, but mostly it was locals ducking their heads against the wind.

My boots clicked along the sidewalk as I passed the Lady's Lantern, its carved wooden sign swinging gently in the breeze. Across the street, the historical society building hunkered like it was keeping its secrets to itself. Beyond that, if I squinted, I could see the faint rise of the dunes and the dark slash of pine trees against the gray sky.

A pregnant Lady of the Dunes. Possibly a homicidal farmhand. Hayes's cursed face in an old photo.

*Sure, why not.*

I pulled my phone from my pocket and thumbed out a quick text to our oldest sister.

> Have you checked old Barker ledgers for mysteriously handsome farmhands who disappeared? Asking for a ghost.

Three dots popped up almost immediately but then disappeared again. I smiled to myself. That meant Selene was already thinking about it, probably mentally rearranging her entire afternoon around the idea.

I slipped my phone away and kept walking, letting the cold air clear my head.

It was a strange feeling, being back in the town where everyone knew the Darling kids by name . . . and having to reintroduce myself. Being the sister who'd left and stayed gone long enough that people forgot about me.

Now I was back, half jobless, living with my parents one week and in my brother's best friend's house the next. No husband. No grand plan. Just a complicated living situation and a talent for making wedding dresses look good.

And on top of that, I'd somehow appointed myself the

emotional goalie for a man who barely wanted to look me in the eye most days.

By the time I looped back toward my car, my brain had run through every bad decision I'd made since college twice. Back at his house, the pine trees behind his place stood tall and dark, a solid wall between his backyard and the dunes beyond. Smoke curled lazily from a nearby chimney, and the faint swell of the lake carried on the wind.

I paused at the bottom of his front steps, eyeing the porch and the front door and the life I'd stepped into without really thinking it through.

*He wanted rules?*

A smile tugged at my mouth. *Maybe it was time the fridge got an official list.*

# ELEVEN

## CLARA

When I stepped inside, the house was warm and dim, the late afternoon already starting to bleed into evening. I toed off my boots by the door and listened.

The TV was on low in the living room—some sports channel, the soft murmur of commentators drifting down the hall—but Wes didn't say anything, and I didn't call out. We were still in that weird phase where every interaction felt like opening a door you weren't sure you had permission to touch.

I hung my coat on the hook and headed for the kitchen, refusing to look in his direction. The fridge hummed quietly, the same old magnet from the hardware store clinging to its side like it had been there since the dawn of time. The counters were less chaotic than when I'd first arrived, but only because I'd taken a pass through that morning while he pretended not to notice.

*No random guys in my house.*

The memory of his voice—tight, annoyed, and a little too pointed—made something in me flare. Not hurt, exactly. More like . . . *challenge accepted.*

Kit's words from earlier echoed in my head: *Make him mad. Maybe he needs to be mad more than he needs to be sad.*

"Okay, landlord," I muttered under my breath. "Let's play."

I rummaged in the junk drawer until I found a pad of legal paper, its sheets a sickly shade of yellow. There was a thick black marker rolling around in there, too, probably from a jobsite. I snagged both and slapped the pad down on the counter.

In big, looping letters, I wrote at the top:
**HOUSE RULES**
Underneath, I added:


**Rule #1: No pity parties.**
**Rule #2: No sponge baths.**
**Rule #3: No random guys in the house (per the landlord).**
**Rule #4: Landlord must attend his own PT.**
**Rule #5: Tenant reserves the right to eat ice cream for dinner without judgment.**


I capped the marker and leaned back to admire my work. It was ridiculous. Petty. Absolutely designed to get under his skin.

It also made me weirdly giddy.

This was my tiny way of reclaiming a little territory in a house that still didn't feel like mine. If he got to lay down rules, so did I. If he was going to act like my presence was some huge imposition, then he could at least be forced to look at his own reflection in cheap neon stationery.

I peeled the page off the pad and walked over to the

fridge. With a small, satisfying smack, I used the magnet to stick it dead center, right at eye level.

"Perfect," I whispered, a smug little laugh slipping out. I could practically see his face when he spotted it—jaw tightening, eyes narrowing, that muscle in his cheek ticcing.

Affection tugged at the edges of my irritation. I didn't want to humiliate him. I just wanted him to engage. To do something other than sink into the couch and disappear.

From the living room, the volume on the TV nudged up a notch, like he was flipping channels.

"Anytime now," I told the note, giving it one last pat. "Go rile up the beast."

I left the note to do its evil work and climbed the stairs toward my room, scrolling absently through my phone. Kit had already texted a string of dagger emojis and a GIF of someone rubbing their hands together, which made me snort.

"Operation Poke the Bear is underway," I typed back, then tossed my phone onto the bed.

I dug in a drawer for pajamas and pulled out the softest sleep shorts I owned. Across the hall in the primary bedroom, I could hear the shower kick on and the low rush of water through the walls.

Normal house sounds. Background noise.

I shimmied into my shorts and was halfway through tugging my T-shirt over my head when a sharp thud echoed through the quiet.

I froze.

For a heartbeat there was nothing—no curse, no follow-up noise, just the steady rush of water.

My stomach dropped.

*He slipped. He hit his head. He's bleeding out on the floor and he can't get up.*

The thought hit so fast it stole my air. Before I could talk myself out of it, I was in the hall, bare feet slapping against the wood. The door to Wes's room was closed, soft light peeking out from the crack where it met the jamb.

I knocked hard on the wood. "Wes?" My voice came out too high. "You okay?"

Nothing. Just the faint sound of running water from the en suite bathroom.

Panic spiked. I pushed the door open and stepped into his room, the warm, humid air wrapped around me. The bathroom door was only half-shut, light peeking from the gaps. I crossed the room in three strides and knocked on the door, louder this time.

"Wes, I'm coming in, okay?" I waited a heartbeat for him to yell at me, but could only hear running water. My heart rate doubled. "Wes? If you don't answer, I'm coming in."

Still nothing.

I gripped the handle.

"Oh please," I whispered, and shoved the door all the way open. "Don't be dead."

A wall of steam hit me first, fogging the mirror and blurring the edges of the tile. The shower was on full blast, water pattering against stone. Through the haze, the glass door was a fogged-up rectangle—and inside it, a very large, very naked man.

Wes was braced against the tile with one hand, the other arm bent, jaw tight, chest heaving. He was standing, but only just, his weight clearly shifted to his good leg. The residual limb on the other side was bare and stark, his skin an angry mix of pinks and whites. Muscles trembled under the strain of holding himself steady.

For a split second my gaze dropped—taking in the solid

line of his thigh, the dark hair at the base of his stomach, and, yes, the very real, very unmissable view of his dick, water and soap sliding over every inch of him.

"Oh my god—sorry!" I sucked in a breath and slapped a hand over my eyes, spinning so fast I nearly slipped. "I thought you fell. I heard—I thought—are you okay?"

Behind me, there was a wet scrape and the squeak of skin against glass as he shifted, trying to cover himself with absolutely nowhere to go.

"Jesus, Clara," he snapped, his voice rough and way too close. "Ever heard of knocking?"

"I did knock!" My heart was pounding so hard it felt like it might punch right through my ribs. "Twice! You didn't answer. I thought you cracked your skull open or something."

His breathing stayed uneven, like maybe he *had* slipped a little, and maybe it had scared him too.

"I'm fine," he snapped. "Get out!"

I kept my face turned toward the steamed-up mirror, eyes pinned forward, but my peripheral vision was apparently an asshole, because I still caught another flash of him when I risked a tiny sideways glance.

This time, the shock of nakedness took a back seat to everything else. The way his hand splayed across the tile. The way his muscled shoulders glistened under the spray. The way the scarred limb ended abruptly. How his thigh quivered where it worked twice as hard to keep him upright.

Wes didn't look fine. He looked like a man standing on the edge of a cliff, pretending the view didn't terrify him.

"You don't . . . look fine," I said quietly, keeping my back to him.

That hit something raw.

"Well, I'm not dead," he snapped. "So congratulations, the wellness check worked. Now get the fuck out."

The bite in his tone should have pissed me off. It did, a little. But under the anger, all I heard was humiliation.

"Fine." My cheeks burned so hot I was amazed the steam didn't sizzle. "Next time I'll let you bleed out, then," I muttered, even though we both knew I wouldn't.

I backed out of the bathroom, fumbling for the handle without turning around, and pulled the door shut behind me. My pulse was still racing when I crossed back through his bedroom and out into the cooler hallway, slamming that door, too, for good measure.

Only when I was in my own room with the door firmly closed did I sag against it, pressing the heels of my hands to my flaming face.

*Fantastic. Less than a week into our roommate experiment and I'd already seen my landlord's dick.*

And no matter how hard I tried to scrub the image from my brain, what stuck with me more was the look on his face —pain, stubbornness, and the kind of vulnerability that made my chest ache.

I slid down the back of my bedroom door until I hit the floor, knees bent, heart still thundering like I'd sprinted the length of the dunes.

I pressed my palms over my face and tried to breathe.

He was not just Hayes's grumpy best friend anymore. Not just the surly, former Delta Force operator who'd glared at me across bar tables and grocery aisles. Now my brain had a full-color, high-definition image of him—scarred and solid and so very, very male—filed under *Do Not Think About This Ever Again*, which of course meant it was the *only* thing I could think about.

But it wasn't just the naked part.

Every time I closed my eyes, I saw the way he'd been braced against the tile, muscles shaking, jaw locked. The way his hand had white-knuckled the wall like letting go wasn't an option. The way that residual limb ended too soon, skin stretched and angry, working twice as hard to keep up.

The unfairness of it punched through me all over again. That someone could go from running jobsites and creating beautiful homes to nearly wiping out in his own shower because the floor was slick and he was too stubborn to sit. That a man who'd probably walked into firefights without flinching now had to plan his every step in a goddamn bathroom.

My mind replayed his body, but it lingered longer on the limb than on his dick. On the ugly-beautiful mix of what he'd survived and what it cost him every day. On the panic in my own chest at the idea of him going down and no one finding him in time.

Sorrow twisted through the attraction until I couldn't tell where one ended and the other began. I'd barged in. I'd seen more than I was supposed to. I'd made an already humiliating moment worse, then snapped back at him like I hadn't just walked straight into his worst nightmare.

And under all that, coiled tight and hot, was the part I really didn't want to look at too closely: I'd *liked* what I saw.

Not the pain. Not the fear. But the rest of it.

The broad shoulders, the carved lines of muscle, the way his body still looked capable and strong even when he was off-balance. The way just being near him in that tiny, steam-drenched room had lit me up like a live wire.

I dropped my hands to my lap and stared at the wall, my pulse finally starting to slow.

Living with Wes Vaughn had already been complicated

when he was just a grumpy landlord with a broken hero complex.

Now I'd seen exactly how stubborn he really was and exactly how dangerous he could be to my peace of mind.

Across the hall, his bedroom door opened and shut, and footsteps moved slowly back toward the stairs. I held my breath without meaning to, listening to the creak of the floorboards as he passed.

This was supposed to be temporary. A favor. A little cosmic karma cleanup.

Instead, it felt like I'd just stepped into the deep end without checking how far the bottom went.

And for the first time since I'd dragged my suitcases over his threshold, one thought cut through the noise, sharp and clear:

*I am in way, way over my head.*

## TWELVE

WES

I sank onto the couch like gravity had doubled in the last five minutes.

My muscles still held the heat of the shower, my skin prickling with that trapped, overheated feeling you got when adrenaline refused to burn off even after the danger was gone. My hair dripped onto the collar of my T-shirt, the damp cotton clinging to my chest. The TV played something mindless—sports highlights, a commentator's upbeat voice bouncing off the walls—but it might as well have been static. I wasn't seeing any of it.

All I could see was steam.

The bathroom door swinging open.

Clara's sharp inhale.

That split second where her eyes had snagged on me like I was a wreck she couldn't look away from, even if she wanted to.

My stomach turned hard.

Humiliation sat in my throat like a fist. It had been months since I'd let anyone see me without the armor of clothes, without the clean lines of a prosthetic, without the carefully arranged illusion that I was handling this. The nurses had been professionals, and even then I'd hated it.

Clara wasn't a professional. Clara was . . . Clara. The girl I'd watched grow up, the one I'd scowled at in high school when she got too close to the guys, the one who'd glittered through Star Harbor like she belonged to a different world. Hayes's little sister. Off-limits. Loud. Bright.

Now she'd seen me naked, half wrecked, and braced against tile.

My jaw clenched so tight my molars ached.

It wasn't even the nudity that pissed me off most. It was the moment right before it—right before the door—when I'd been trying to prove something to myself like a goddamn idiot.

I'd been stubbornly standing under the spray when I should've been sitting on the built-in ledge like my physical therapist had told me a hundred times.

*Sit when you're tired, Vaughn. Sit before you slip. Sit before your body reminds you it's not the same body it used to be.*

I'd ignored all of it.

The water had been too hot, the tile too slick, my balance a little off because my mind had been elsewhere. For one stupid moment, my foot had skidded and my gut had dropped out. I'd pitched sideways and landed hard on the built-in seat with a jarring smack that shot pain up my spine.

It wasn't a catastrophic fall. It wasn't blood or broken bones. It was worse.

It was a reminder.

It was the fact that I'd been standing there in my own shower—my own house—and I still couldn't trust myself not to fall.

Anger had flared hot enough to sting. I'd forced myself upright again, hands splayed on the tile, water hammering my shoulders, just to prove I could. Just to prove the slip didn't own me. Just to prove I wasn't . . .

Weak.

That was when Clara had come in.

That was what she'd seen.

Not just my body, not just scars and skin and everything I'd rather keep hidden. She had seen the way I'd hauled myself back to standing out of nothing but spite.

She had seen me losing to my own damn bathroom and trying to pretend I wasn't.

My fingers curled into the couch cushion. The fabric strained under my grip.

I could still hear her voice—too sharp with panic, too close to fear.

I swallowed, my throat rough.

She'd come running. Not hovering like Hayes, not the pity committee with casseroles and sad eyes. Clara had come running because she'd heard a thud and her brain had leaped straight to cracked skull and blood on tile.

The thought landed in my chest like a weight. Annoying, inconvenient warmth tried to spread behind my ribs.

It made me angrier.

I didn't want warmth. I didn't want soft edges. Soft was how you started needing people. Soft was how you let them into places they didn't belong. Soft was how you ended up with someone seeing you in your worst moment and then acting like you owed them gratitude for it.

Clara didn't have any business seeing me like that. She didn't have any business being in this house at all, no matter what my exhausted, poorly functioning brain had agreed to earlier.

My gaze drifted to the hallway, waiting for movement. Waiting for the creak of stairs, the sound of her coming down with one of her jokes or that stubborn chin tipped up like she dared me to be a jerk about it.

Nothing.

The house sat heavy and quiet, the only sounds the TV and the heater kicking on and off.

Clara wasn't coming down.

She'd retreated. Probably mortified. Probably telling herself this was a mistake. Probably texting her family a play-by-play while she laughed her ass off.

The image should've satisfied me. It should've been a clean, easy reaction.

Instead, my mind played the scene again, slower, crueler. I couldn't shake the feeling that there was something more there.

The way her hand had flown up, but not before the look in her eyes shifted. Shock, yes. Panic, yes. Then something else that flickered so quickly I couldn't name it without wanting to put my head through the wall.

It hadn't been disgust.

She hadn't looked at my residual limb and flinched away like it was something grotesque.

For the smallest moment, it almost looked like *desire*.

I cut the thought off hard, but my body reacted anyway. My chest tightened, my skin still humming with leftover heat. I hated the part of me that was cataloging her reaction like evidence. I hated that my brain wouldn't let the moment die. It circled it, poked at it, kept turning it over like it could find the answer to a question I wasn't ready to ask.

Clara was not anything I could afford to want. Wanting felt like the first step toward losing something. Wanting was a debt you paid later with interest.

I stared at the dark ceiling above the living room, the TV flashing reflected light in the corner of my eye. My hands loosened slowly from the cushion. My body felt heavy, used up, as if the shower had taken the last fight out of me.

Somewhere upstairs, a floorboard creaked.

My whole body went still.

I closed my eyes and exhaled through my nose, tasting anger, embarrassment, and something dangerously close to relief.

Tomorrow was going to be awkward as hell, and the worst part was that I'd done it to myself.

I shifted on the couch, trying to find a position that didn't make my hips ache, and my body answered the movement with a cruel, immediate reminder that it had its own opinions about tonight.

I was hard.

Not a flicker. Not a passing thought I could ignore. Full and unmistakable, pressing against the seam of my sweatpants like I'd been sitting here watching porn instead of replaying the most humiliating five minutes of my life.

A sharp laugh scraped out of my throat, humorless and bitter. "Really?" I muttered to my dick. "That's your takeaway?"

My pulse kicked again, like my body wanted to argue.

Heat curled low in my gut, the kind that didn't care about pride or guilt or the fact that I'd been braced against tile two seconds away from eating shit in my own shower. It didn't care that Clara was off-limits, that she was Hayes's little sister, that she was upstairs right now probably wishing she could bleach her eyeballs.

All it cared about was the curve of her waist in those

sleep shorts earlier, soft and bare and too damn casual for a house that had been mine alone.

The way she'd rushed toward the bathroom with panic in her voice, like I mattered.

The split second in the steam when her eyes had landed on me—quick, accidental, human—and something in her gaze had caught.

My hand flexed on the couch cushion again, knuckles whitening.

*No.*

I wasn't doing this. I wasn't going to use Clara Darling like she was a fantasy I could indulge and then tuck away when I was done.

I tried to breathe through it, tried to pretend this was just another flare-up—like phantom pain or the nightmares that dragged me under. Something you rode out. Something you survived without giving it more power.

I lay back and stared at the ceiling, jaw clenched, fists tight at my sides.

The erection didn't care.

It lingered, heavy and insistent, a physical betrayal on top of everything else. My skin still held the memory of hot water and steam, my brain still stuck on the flash of her silhouette in the doorway, cheeks flushed, voice trembling with adrenaline.

The worst part was how easy it would be to give in.

To wrap my hand around myself and chase the quick, mindless relief that would erase her voice for sixty seconds. To pretend I was still the kind of man who could take what he wanted and not pay for it later.

My throat worked. Shame crawled up my spine, hot and mean.

I wasn't that man anymore.

I couldn't even be alone on a couch without wanting something I had no right to want.

I shut my eyes hard, hoping the darkness could smother the image of her and the ache in my body at the same time, and I let the self-loathing settle where it always did—thick and familiar, layered over the need, over the humiliation, until I couldn't tell which one made me feel worse.

I listened for her.

For the soft click of her bedroom door, for the cautious creak of the stairs, for the sound of her like she hadn't just seen me naked and trembling under the spray of water. Part of me dreaded it—the forced eye contact, the apology, the inevitable joke she'd use as a shield.

Another part of me waited anyway, wired and restless, as if her footsteps could undo what had already happened.

Nothing came.

My hand slid down my stomach before I could stop it. One brief, stupid drag over the front of my sweatpants, palming myself like I might find some kind of answer there. My cock twitched, aching hard and hot, and my chest tightened with a sharp, ugly mix of want and rage.

"At least one thing isn't broken." Bitterness hit so fast it tasted like blood.

Disgust flared. I yanked my hand away like the skin had burned me.

Clara was upstairs. In my house.

The need lingered anyway, pulsing and stubborn, as if my body didn't give a damn about any of the reasons I had to stay away.

I rolled onto my side with a grunt, shifting until the pressure eased enough to breathe. My shoulder sank into the cushion I'd worn into a permanent groove. My eyes locked on the dark wall across the room. The words came quietly, certain as a verdict.

Letting her move in was a terrible idea.

Letting her see me like this.

Letting her see me at all.

Somewhere upstairs the house gave a tiny settling creak, like it was laughing at me, and I lay there in the quiet with my jaw clenched and my heart still racing—waiting for a door that didn't open.

THE NEXT FEW days Clara and I barely made eye contact. My house was filled with awkward hellos and noncommittal grunts, like we were speaking a language made entirely of avoidance. The neon House Rules she'd slapped on my fridge stayed there like a hostage note. I told myself I was leaving it up out of spite—because taking it down would mean she'd gotten under my skin.

*Well, two can play that game.*

I pulled a pen from the drawer and scrawled at the bottom:

**Rule #6: Knock like you mean it.**

I stared at the paper a second longer, then added:

**Rule #7: No hostile workplace signage.**

I scoffed like the whole thing was stupid, like I didn't feel dangerously close to smiling. Then I grabbed my keys. I needed to get the hell out of there, and a night with the guys was the perfect excuse.

Brody's kitchen smelled like beer, fried food, and whatever candle he'd convinced himself to buy to make the place feel less like a bachelor pad. It didn't work. Not with the empty bottles lined up on the counter and the chip bags crinkling every time someone reached across the table.

The Horsemen were all here—crowded around Brody's kitchen table like we were planning a heist instead of rolling dice and pretending we were fearless men with magical weapons and intact knees.

Austin sat at the head of the table, elbows planted, a screen propped up like a shield so no one could cheat and read his plans. His eyes shone with the enthusiasm of a man living his best life. He had maps. He had miniature figurines. He had a whole damn binder of notes.

Hayes sat across from me, but I could barely look him in the eyes—not after I'd pictured his little sister on her knees for me. Brody flicked a chip crumb off his character sheet. Cal was grinning like he'd actually gotten into this stupid game.

Me? I was there because, for a few hours, the only thing I had to manage was a set of dice.

It helped. More than I wanted to admit.

"All right," Austin said, dropping his voice into that dramatic storyteller cadence he'd perfected. "You enter the village at dusk. Smoke curls from chimneys. Lanterns glow along a muddy road. The townspeople are . . . nervous." He leaned forward, eyes glittering over the top of his screen. "Because something is hunting in the woods."

Brody snorted. "Something is always hunting in the woods."

Austin ignored him. "You hear a scream. A shape darts between the trees—too fast, too low to the ground." He tapped the map with a pencil. "Wes, you're the closest. What do you do?"

My fingers closed around my d20 dice. The tiny plastic edges bit into my skin. "Fine," I said flatly. "I go after it."

Hayes's brows lifted. "You're going alone?"

"Warrior," I reminded him, pointing at my chest. "Not babysitter."

Brody laughed and clinked his bottle against mine. "That's my guy."

Austin held up a hand. "Roll initiative."

The dice clattered across the table, bouncing off character sheets and empty beer caps. I watched the numbers tumble like it mattered.

It shouldn't have, but it did anyway.

"Okay," Austin said, scanning his notes. "The creature lunges from the underbrush. It's got a jaw like a bear trap and eyes like—"

"A Darling woman," Brody supplied, clearly needling Hayes.

Cal choked on his beer. Hayes shot Brody a look that could've cut steel. I didn't smile. I didn't do anything except reach for my longsword figurine and push it forward on the map without laughing.

"Your warrior takes the hit," Austin continued, unfazed. He pointed at me with his pencil. "The claws rake your thigh—deep. Your leg screams, but you push off anyway, launching yourself forward."

The words landed like a fist to the ribs.

My jaw tightened. The kitchen blurred around the edges, and all I could feel was the phantom flare of pain, hot and electrical, like my body had heard Austin and decided to join the game.

I grunted, the sound low and involuntary.

Austin blinked. "Too soon?" he asked, suddenly uncertain.

"No." The word came out sharp, clipped. I forced my mouth into something that almost passed for a smirk. "He's fine. He's a warrior."

Brody waggled his brows. "Big tough guy."

I rolled the dice again, harder than necessary. It bounced and hit my beer bottle with a dull thunk.

"Twenty," I said when it landed, not bothering to hide the satisfaction.

Austin's face lit up like he'd just been handed Christmas. "Critical hit! Describe it."

"Uh . . ." I stared at the map, at the little creature mini. I didn't want to describe it. I didn't want to think about bodies and damage and pushing through pain.

But the table was waiting, so I did it anyway.

"My warrior doesn't hesitate," I said, keeping my voice even. "He takes the hit and keeps moving. Drives the blade straight through the thing before it can get away."

Austin nodded solemnly, like this was sacred. "The creature collapses. The village is safe. For now."

For a few minutes after that, it worked—the game. The stupid quest. The dice. The trash talk between friends who had known me before and after and didn't ask me to explain myself.

It gave me a place to put my focus that wasn't my body.

For a few hours, I could be a warrior again.

Even if it was only on paper.

We'd been at it long enough that the kitchen had shifted into that comfortable, lived-in chaos—empty bottles, scattered dice, chip dust ground into the grain of Brody's table. Austin had paused to flip through his notes with the inten sity of a man decoding ancient scripture while Cal stood to refresh his drink.

The lull should've been a relief. A breath between battles.

Instead, it turned into a target.

Cal dropped back into his chair and looked at me like he'd been holding the question in his mouth for twenty minutes. "So," he said casually, like he wasn't poking a bruise, "how's it going with your new roommate?"

My stomach tightened.

Tiny sleep shorts.

Bare legs.

The shape of her in my kitchen like she belonged there.

The way my body had reacted to her like it hadn't gotten the memo that I was supposed to be dead inside.

I clenched my jaw and forced the thoughts back into the same locked room I shoved everything else into.

"Fine," I said, which was a lie by omission. Then I added, sharper, because that was easier: "She barged into my life the same way she barged into my house."

Hayes's gaze flicked up fast, but I ignored it.

"It's temporary," I continued, like saying it enough times might make it true. "She's . . . loud. And bossy. And thinks it's funny to post house rules on my fridge."

Brody leaned back in his chair, the legs creaking, and snorted. "That's the Darling effect right there," he said. "Those women are irresistible. They just . . . get in your head."

The table went dead quiet for half a beat.

Austin froze mid–page turn, eyebrow lifting slowly.

Cal's stare slid between Brody and Hayes like he was watching a tennis match and didn't know which side he'd bet on. His mouth twitched, but he didn't laugh.

Hayes went still, the muscles in his jaw tightening like a loaded spring.

Brody blinked, the confidence on his face flickering—like he'd just realized he'd said that with a little too much truth in it. He cleared his throat and coughed into his fist, trying to patch the moment.

"I mean," he hurried on, waving a hand like he could physically bat the words away, "you know what I'm saying. The whole family's intense. Big personalities. They sort of . . . take over a room."

His save didn't quite land.

Not with Hayes watching him like that.

Not with Austin still staring.

Not with my chest tight and my pulse suddenly too loud in my ears.

Because Brody wasn't wrong, and that was the problem.

Clara Darling had taken over my house in less than a week, and I couldn't tell which part of me hated it more—the part that wanted my space back or the part that was already bracing for what it would feel like when she eventually left.

Hayes's stare cut first to Brody—sharp and warning, the kind of look that he used to shut down anyone who dared glance at his beloved sisters. Then his attention swung to me, and somehow it was worse.

Because with Brody, it was older brother annoyance, but with me, it was history.

All the shit we didn't say out loud. The phone call on that dark road. The way his guilt sat between us like an extra chair at every table. The way he'd hovered since the accident like he could rewrite the ending if he just tried hard enough.

And now Clara was in the mix.

Hayes leaned back in his chair, casual on the surface, but his eyes stayed locked on me like he was bracing for impact. He kept his voice light, like he was asking about the weather.

"Something I should know about you living with Clara?"

My spine went rigid.

I felt the question like a hand closing around my throat. It wasn't even what he said—it was everything underneath it. The protectiveness stitched into him where his sisters were concerned. The suspicion that came with any man in their orbit. The automatic need to make sure they were safe, even when they were grown women who could handle themselves.

He didn't want to think about Clara in my house.

He sure as hell didn't want to think about Clara in my house with *me*.

My mind flashed, unhelpfully, to steam and glass and tiny sleep shorts.

My stomach dropped.

I swallowed hard and snapped the answer out too fast, too sharp, like if I cut it clean enough it would stop the conversation from bleeding. "No," I said. "It's nothing."

Hayes didn't move. He didn't blink. He just stared at me, the way he used to when we were out together and he could tell I'd made up my mind to do something stupid.

"It's temporary," I added, because apparently I couldn't leave well enough alone. The words came out with an edge, as if saying them harder would make them truer. "She needed a place. I needed . . . someone who isn't a nurse."

I could feel the pin in place inside my chest, the needle of my pulse in my throat. The more I insisted it was nothing, the more the lie took up space. Too loud. Too obvious.

Because if it was really nothing, I wouldn't have been so damn defensive.

If it was really nothing, I wouldn't have pictured her beneath me as I sank into her and stretched her open.

If it was really nothing, my body wouldn't have betrayed me the second I was alone on my couch.

Hayes held my stare for another beat, then looked away like he'd filed the moment in a drawer he planned to open later.

Austin cleared his throat awkwardly and flipped through his binder like it could save us. "Okay," he said, too cheerful. "Back to the campaign. You've made it to the edge of the woods—"

But the air had already shifted.

The game pieces were still on the table. The dice still sat waiting to be rolled.

And yet it felt like we'd wandered into a different kind of dungeon altogether.

## THIRTEEN

CLARA

Morning came in thin and gray, the kind of winter light that made everything in Wes Vaughn's house look a little softer and a lot more haunted.

I lay there for a beat with my eyes open, letting my brain catch up to the fact that I lived here now—across the hall from Wes Vaughn—and no amount of pretending otherwise was going to change that.

Unfortunately, neither was pretending I hadn't seen him naked.

Across the hall, there was a door that should have belonged to a man sleeping in his own bed. A man who brushed his teeth in the bathroom attached to that bedroom. A man who had a glass shower door and a talent for turning my brain into soup.

I stared at the ceiling and waited for the house to make sense.

The upstairs was dead quiet.

Not the peaceful kind of quiet either. The kind that felt like a decision.

His door across the hall never opened. It sat there like a

sealed-off part of the house—like the upstairs belonged to the man he used to be, and the man who lived here now had been exiled downstairs with the couch and the ghosts of his former life.

I swallowed and rolled onto my side, blinking hard until the memory of steam and tile and *oh my god, that is his actual penis* stopped flashing behind my eyelids.

It didn't help. Not really.

*It's fine. I'm a grown woman. I could be an adult about this. I could exist in a house with a man I'd accidentally seen naked without combusting.*

All I needed was coffee.

I slid out of bed as quietly as possible, tugging at the hem of my pajama shorts and straightening my mismatched top. It was chilly so I tugged a tossed-aside zip-up sweatshirt from the chair and pulled it on. I walked to the doorway and cracked it open, peeking into the hallway.

Still silent.

I took one step out, then another, moving with the careful precision of someone attempting a museum heist—except my prize was caffeine and my security system was a grumpy, traumatized construction god with a bad attitude and an even worse talent for making me feel twelve kinds of flustered.

Halfway to the stairs, the house gave a faint creak beneath my foot.

I froze.

Held my breath.

Waited for any sign of Wes.

Nothing.

*Okay. Great. Good job, Clara. Stealthy. Professional. Totally not losing your mind in your brother's best friend's hallway.*

I made it down the stairs and slipped into the kitchen, where the cold morning light streamed through the big windows at the back of the house. Beyond them, the pines stood shoulder to shoulder like a wall, dark and dense, the property line hugged by forest. In the distance there was a sliver of sandy path cutting between the trees toward the dunes—barely visible unless you knew to look for it.

It was so peaceful out there it made my chest ache.

I turned toward the fridge—and stopped.

The House Rules page was still smack in the middle of it.

Not ripped down.

Not balled up.

Not set on fire.

If anything, it looked . . . slightly repositioned. Straighter. Like some part of Wes couldn't help himself.

My eyes tracked down the list, already knowing what I'd written, until they snagged on two new lines at the bottom in harsh, masculine handwriting.

**Rule #6: Knock like you mean it.**
**Rule #7: No hostile workplace signage.**

Heat rushed up my neck so fast I felt it behind my ears.

"Oh my god," I whispered, even though nobody was there to hear me.

He didn't tear it down.

He'd answered.

A laugh bubbled in my throat before I could stop it. I clamped my lips together, but it still escaped as a quiet huff as I leaned closer to read it again.

*No hostile workplace signage* was so petty it bordered

on charming, which was unacceptable for early-morning hours.

I smiled, then wiped it off my face like it was evidence.

*Get coffee. Leave. Pretend you never saw it. Pretend you didn't just feel a weird, stupid spark of triumph because Wes Vaughn had engaged in stationery warfare with you.*

I turned toward the counter, moving too quickly, too eager, as if the coffee maker was a getaway car. I reached for a mug, fumbled it, caught it at the last second, and let out a silent curse that would have earned me a lecture from my mother and a high five from Kit.

The coffee was already made, which prompted something in my chest to tilt—annoying and soft all at once. Even in his misery, Wes Vaughn wasn't the kind of man who skipped caffeine.

I poured myself a mug and took a cautious sip.

A soft sound came from behind me.

Heavy, measured footsteps.

My spine went straight.

Wes walked into the kitchen in gray sweatpants and a dark T-shirt, hair damp like he'd washed his face and run a hand through it without looking in a mirror. His eyes were tired. His jaw was shadowed in a way that made him look rough around the edges, like sleep had fought him and won.

His gaze dropped.

Not to my face, but to *me*.

My pajama shorts. My bare legs. Beneath the sweatshirt my oversize tee that—oh, god—probably clung in all the wrong places. I suddenly remembered with a hot, sick swoop that I wasn't wearing a bra.

I crossed my arms over my chest so fast I nearly sloshed coffee down my front.

Wes's eyes flicked up for half a second—caught mine—then moved away like he'd burned his hand.

The air between us felt too warm. I couldn't tell if it was the heater or my shame.

"Good morning," I said, and it came out wrong. Too bright. Too careful.

"Morning." One word. Flat. Gravelly.

I lifted my mug like it explained why I was standing in his kitchen in basically nothing. "Coffee's good."

"Okay."

I nodded like that was a complete exchange and not two robots trying to pass as humans. "Okay."

My gaze betrayed me with one quick, stupid dip—because my brain had apparently decided to torture me—catching the line of his sweatpants before I yanked my attention away.

His eyes narrowed slightly, like he'd clocked the movement even if he didn't know why.

Both of us looked away too fast.

I turned toward the counter and grabbed a paper towel, wiping the already-clean surface because my hands needed a job. My heart hammered like I'd done something worse than exist in pajamas.

Behind me, Wes poured himself a mug without a word. A beat passed where it felt like he might say something—anything—and then he didn't.

He left the kitchen like it was hostile territory and disappeared toward the living room.

The quiet that followed was somehow louder than the quiet before.

I stared at the fridge again—at my loud, obnoxious list and his controlled, cutting add-ons—feeling that ridiculous, reluctant spark of amusement flicker again.

Proof of life, whether he wanted it to be or not.

Back upstairs I busied myself by getting ready for the day.

I took another sip of coffee and tried not to wonder why he kept choosing that couch—why he kept choosing discomfort—over the bed he should have been sleeping in.

I didn't want to wonder what he was afraid of up there . . . or what he thought would happen if he let anyone see him live like a person again.

Instead, I chose to get lost in my work.

My coffee went cold on the bedside table an hour ago, but I kept sipping it anyway. In my room, the house felt far away and too close at the same time. The upstairs remained quiet in that loaded way it had been all morning, and I could still hear Wes moving downstairs if I listened hard enough—the soft creak of the couch, the muted clink of a mug, the occasional thud like he was setting something down with more force than necessary.

We hadn't spoken since the kitchen. If you could even call that speaking.

In reality it was two robots, one awkward note on the fridge, and a whole lot of pretending our living situation wasn't completely messed up.

I sat cross-legged on the bed with my laptop open, phone in hand, and made myself do the only thing that ever steadied me when my life felt like it was slipping out from under my feet.

Work.

I'd spent the morning reaching out to designers whom I'd worked with in the past, a couple of photographers who actually delivered on what they promised, and one florist who understood that "winter bridal" did not mean sad white roses and baby's breath.

My Sent folder was a graveyard of carefully worded professionalism.

Outside the snow fell in fat flakes that almost looked fake. I smiled to myself and let the image of a winter bridal shoot consume me. Using Wes's secluded backyard as inspiration, I wrote down my ideas, saved images to mood boards, and considered price ranges.

Every message I sent felt like tossing a little line into the dark and waiting for something to tug back.

It didn't take long for my producer brain to snap online, and I found my groove. Timelines, a photo shot list, deliverables, pricing—things you could measure and control.

Things that didn't involve standing in a hallway trying not to picture Wes Vaughn naked.

I opened a blank doc and started listing what I needed like it was survival:

- Location: accessible, visually striking, winter friendly
- Wardrobe: 3–5 gowns, 2 "styled looks," 1 statement veil
- Hair and makeup: 1 artist, travel fee included
- Video: 15 seconds per dress for socials
- Lighting: natural + supplemental, bring battery packs
- Backup plan: indoor options if the snow turned into freezing rain

My fingers moved faster once I got going, the familiar rush of building something from nothing. It didn't erase the awkwardness downstairs, but it gave me something else to obsess over.

A notification popped up.

KIT

Whatcha doing??

*Oh you know, hitting roadblocks at every turn and trying not to obsess over the fact that I saw the hottest man alive without any clothes on.*

I stared at my phone, thumb hovering over Kit's name.

I could already hear her voice in my head, big and gleeful and incapable of subtlety. I dropped my hand.

I didn't want that to be the first nugget I gave her. A part of me didn't want her picturing him naked either. I also didn't want Wes to become a family group project where everyone passed notes about his moods and watched him like he was a storm system on the radar.

He was difficult. He was hurting. He was . . . Wes. Not a bulletin board.

I decided mild deflection was the best course of action until I could get my bearings.

Living my best life. Call you later?

KIT

You better. I'm going to the knitting store to get supplies to make a knitted eggplant.

An eggplant?

It's cute and phallic and will be perfect for my bookshelf.

> Maybe grab what I need to make a scarf or something. Something EASY.

BORING.

> Thanks. Love you.

I LAUGHED at my phone and shook my head. My stomach growled, and I realized I hadn't consumed anything besides coffee all morning. I pressed a hand to my empty belly and groaned. Going downstairs to get a snack meant coming face-to-face with my surly roommate. I stretched my neck and looked out the window. The snow had finally stopped, and everything looked cold and still. Peaceful.

I needed to get out of this room.

I shoved my laptop closed, grabbed my keys off the dresser, and tugged on jeans with the kind of urgency that suggested I was fleeing an active crime scene. I added a sweater, boots, and a scarf, and in the mirror I looked like a woman who had her life together.

I almost believed it.

With a smile plastered on my face, I looped my laptop bag over my shoulder and headed for the front door. Downstairs, Wes was on the couch, his shoulders hunched like he was holding himself in place. The TV was on, but he wasn't watching it. His gaze was fixed somewhere ahead, unfocused, jaw tight, a mug cooling on the coffee table.

He looked up when he felt me there. For a second neither of us said anything.

I held my chin high without so much as a glance toward Wes. At the door, I paused with my hand on the knob.

*I could leave without saying anything. Wes wouldn't care. He probably preferred it.*

I'd been in his space for less than a week, and already I could feel how hard he clung to whatever control he still had left. But then I thought about Hayes's face at the table. The way he genuinely worried about his best friend. He'd said *missing appointments* and *refusing care* like he was listing symptoms.

I had agreed to help, no matter how awkward my intrusion had made things.

I thought about the thump. The silence. The way my heart had lurched into my throat because for a split second I had been sure something was wrong.

Wes wasn't broken, he was simply a man who'd built his entire life around being capable, and now even the shower had turned into an obstacle course.

I could feel the house breathing around me, waiting to see what I'd do. The air in the house was too warm, too thick.

I swallowed, tried to sound normal, tried not to sound like a girl asking a boy for permission to leave the house.

"I'm going to head to the farm," I said. My voice came out steadier than I felt. "I'm meeting Elodie."

His eyes narrowed slightly, studying me like he didn't know why that mattered. Like he didn't know what to do with information that wasn't a problem to solve.

My fingers tightened around my keys. "Call if you need anything."

The words hung there, but so did his silence.

I braced myself for a grunt. Maybe an eye roll or a dismissive flick of his hand. Something that told me I was overstepping again.

Instead, Wes just stared at me, his expression unreadable, like the idea of calling someone—anyone—was a language he'd forgotten.

Then his throat worked, and he gave me a firm nod.

A nod that was almost . . . grateful. Like he hadn't expected me to offer that. Maybe Wes didn't know what to do with help that didn't come wrapped in pity.

My chest tightened.

I didn't let myself linger long enough to name it. I turned on my heel and bolted, because I was braver in motion than I was standing still.

Outside, the cold air slapped my cheeks back into my body. I inhaled until my lungs burned, started the car, and drove toward Star Harbor Family Farm as snow-covered dunes flew past the car window.

The farther I got from Wes's house, the easier it was to breathe.

The closer I got to the farm, the more I could feel myself coming back online.

STAR HARBOR FAMILY Farm looked like a postcard in winter.

In the distance, the big blue barn wore a soft cap of snow. The peaked roofline stood out against the pale sky, and smoke drifted from somewhere behind it—someone burning something, someone warm inside while the world stayed cold. Twinkle lights were strung along the front, and even in daylight they glowed faintly, like stubborn little stars.

When I stepped inside the barn, warmth wrapped around me. The air smelled like fresh-cut wood and coffee and the faint tang of paint. It was the comforting chaos of a place in progress.

Elodie was near the restaurant side of the barn with her sleeves pushed up and hair pulled back. Her cheeks were pink from work. She had a rag in her hands and a look on her face like she'd been built for this—like she'd found the exact shape of her happiness and decided to live inside it.

"Clara!" Her bright smile hit me right in the ribs. "Hi. What are you doing here?"

The question wasn't suspicious. It was delighted.

I realized how much I'd missed that.

"I needed to get out of the house," I admitted, and then, because I wasn't ready to unpack anything else, I lifted my chin and added, "I have an idea. You busy?"

Elodie's eyes lit. "I'm always busy." Her eyebrows bounced. "What's the idea?"

I laughed—real laughter, the kind that didn't have shame clinging to its edges—and followed her deeper into the barn, where the warm light made everything look softer. Finished and unfinished living side by side. The space had beautiful bones. A dream mid-build.

"This place is unreal," I said, meaning it. "You guys really did this."

"We're doing it," she corrected, but her grin widened. "Okay. Tell me the idea."

I pulled my phone out and flipped to the notes app where I'd already started drafting bullet points. My lips pulled in as I considered where to start. "Um . . . so I never really shared this, but I've been doing a bit of bridal modeling—organizing photo shoots, that kind of thing."

Elodie's eyes widened. "Um, are you kidding?"

Heat bloomed across my cheeks. I hadn't shared my passion with anyone outside of Greg and the small friend group I had in the city. It only took one of his colleagues mocking me to solidify the fact that my job wasn't something people understood.

I set my shoulders, ready to defend myself to my sister. "It's a real job and takes significant amounts of work for what I do. It's actually—"

"Really fucking cool!"

I stared at my sister as her grin grew wider. I blinked.

"Clara!" She bumped me in the shoulder. "Why didn't you say anything? Do you keep the dresses? Have you met anyone famous? I have so many questions. Have you been in a magazine?"

The heat was back in my cheeks, and I shifted my weight. "I've been in lots of magazines, actually."

Elodie squealed. "Shut. Up."

My gaze dropped to my boots as I laughed. "So that's why I popped over today. I want to do a winter bridal shoot."

Elodie's face shifted from curiosity to immediate interest. "Here?"

"Here," I said, heart kicking. "Twinkle lights. Snowy dunes. Barn warmth. Pine trees. The inn. All of it." I gestured around us like I could scoop the whole place up and package it. "It's romantic. It's cozy. It's . . . exactly the vibe."

Elodie didn't even hesitate. "Yes."

The word hit me so fast it stole my breath.

"Wait. Really?" I blinked at her, not quite believing it was that easy. "Just . . . yes?"

Elodie laughed. "Of course. Use it. All of it. The barn, the porch, the tree line. It's an awesome idea. It's a family farm, you goose. I want you to feel like you belong here."

*Belong.*

The word landed with a dull ache.

I looked away under the guise of clearing my throat. "Okay," I said, like it was nothing, like my eyes didn't suddenly feel hot. "Okay. Great. So—practical stuff. I'll need a date and a time window. I'm thinking late afternoon for light; then we'll shift inside when it gets dark. I'm getting a photographer and—"

"El," a voice cut in. Levi stepped out from behind a half wall, tall and lanky in that teenage way, hair falling into his eyes, carrying a box like he'd been assigned manual labor and decided to endure it with quiet sarcasm.

With her rag, Elodie gestured for him to come over. "Levi. What's up, kiddo?"

"The knobs on the cabinets are swapped out," he said, then turned his attention to me. His expression softened just slightly. "Hi."

"Hi," I said, smiling. It was still strange to see Elodie in a mother's role, but it suited her perfectly. "Your timing is perfect, actually. Have you ever done any modeling?"

"What?" He looked wary, and an embarrassed chuckle escaped. "Are you serious?"

"Possibly," I admitted.

He sighed like the weight of the world was on his shoulders, then shrugged. "I guess I would consider it."

Elodie snorted. "Believe it or not, that's his enthusiastic face."

Levi shot her a playful look before moving toward the barn door. I laughed again and let the heady excitement of a plan coming together flow through me.

Elodie turned back to me, all business now. "Okay. Date. How soon?"

"As soon as I can get a team," I said. "Photographer, makeup, maybe someone to help with the video. I can model the bridal looks myself if I need to, but I'd rather bring in one other model so it doesn't feel like a solo show. Levi's a little young, so I'll keep my eyes out."

Elodie nodded, already tracking. "And you'll need indoor shots, too, in case the weather turns."

"Exactly. That's why this is perfect," I said, looking around the newly renovated farm-to-table restaurant. "It gives me options."

She leaned in, lowering her voice like we were conspiring. "If you can get some extra lifestyle shots while you're at it—maybe Levi and his friends by the firepit, hot cocoa, the restaurant space when it's done—I'll buy a package. We need content for socials and website stuff. The more professional, the better."

Momentum slid into my chest, warm and steady.

Income. A plan. Something all mine.

Pride prickled at the back of my eyes, and I blinked it away, because I refused to cry in a barn like in a sappy movie.

"That would . . . help a lot," I admitted.

Elodie's gaze softened. "Then it's done."

Levi, still hovering nearby, shifted the box in his arms and arched a brow. "Does being in a photo shoot mean I'm getting paid?"

"No," Elodie and I said in unison.

He scoffed instantly and headed out the door as we chuckled. I smiled and leaned in. "Of course he'll be paid."

I pulled my phone back out, already opening a calendar, already making lists. The world narrowed down into controllable pieces again—dates and people and deliverables.

It was a version of myself I barely recognized. A version I was falling for.

## FOURTEEN

## CLARA

THE LATE-AFTERNOON DUSK turned Wes's house into a postcard—winter light fading soft and blue over the pines, the snow outside smoothing everything into something almost peaceful.

Almost.

I came into the house with my arms full. A grocery bag cutting into my fingers, another bumping my hip, a cheap string of twinkle lights looped around my wrist like an afterthought I refused to overthink.

I was choosing—actively choosing—to be in a good mood.

The farm had lit something back up in me. Options. Momentum. Elodie's immediate yes. A plan that belonged to me. I carried that feeling into the house like it was a coat I could shrug on and off whenever the air got too heavy.

My keys hit the bowl on the console table with a clack.

Somewhere deeper in the house, I heard movement.

Not the quiet shuffling I'd come to associate with Wes these past few days. This was rhythmic. Controlled. A low exhale that sounded like effort. A muted grunt.

Curious without meaning to be, I stepped forward and angled my head toward the living room.

Wes was on the floor in front of the couch, a mat beneath him, his shirt darkened with sweat at the collar and down his back. The tight tee clung to him like it had given up the fight, putting his body on full display in the most unfair, casual way—hard lines of muscle and broad shoulders and those ridged, stupid abs pressing through fabric every time his torso lifted.

Crunch. Exhale.

Crunch. Grunt.

His face was turned slightly away, jaw clenched, brows heavy like he was taking it out on the air itself. He didn't look up. He didn't acknowledge me.

Relief should've been the first thing I felt.

It wasn't.

Heat climbed my throat, fast and unwanted, and I tightened my grip on the grocery bags like that could anchor me to something normal. My pulse did this stupid little quickstep in my wrist.

*Get it together, Clara.*

My gaze dropped to my left hand as I stepped toward the kitchen, as if I needed proof I was still myself. The ring was still there, bright and ridiculous against my knuckle. Greg's idea of what my future was supposed to look like. A shitty plan that had already cracked apart.

I flexed my fingers once, and the diamond caught the dying light, throwing it back like it was mocking me.

I rolled my eyes at myself. *Jesus, not now.*

I shoved the thought into the same box as the shower incident and the upstairs silence and the fact that Wes was making my brain short-circuit with nothing but sit-ups.

Cooking was my escape hatch.

I set the bags on the counter and started unpacking like I was hosting a cooking show for an audience of one. Onion. Garlic. A package of ground beef. Pasta. A jar of marinara as backup in case I chickened out of making sauce from scratch. A loaf of crusty bread. Parmesan. Butter.

I wanted comfort food. Something that smelled like effort. Something that made a house feel lived in, even when the people inside it were determined to haunt it.

A pot hit the stove. Water turned on. I peeled an onion and chopped it fast, the knife thudding against the cutting board with the kind of purpose that steadied me.

The first sizzle when it met the pan put a giddy pep in my step. I checked the recipe twice and followed every step perfectly.

I let myself hum under my breath as I stirred, the sound quiet enough not to announce itself, just a thread of noise that made the kitchen feel less like a mausoleum.

From the living room, Wes grunted again. A harder sound this time, like he was pushing past a limit.

Too curious for my own good, I leaned back and sneaked a peek.

He was still on the mat, sweaty hair damp at his temples now, shoulders flexing as he braced. His arms looked carved. His mouth tightened with effort.

My stomach flipped.

I grabbed a dish towel and fanned myself once, pretending it was the heat from the stove and not the fact that my roommate looked like a sin with a pulse and a bad attitude.

I refocused on dinner and lifted my shirt away from my neck.

The onions softened, sweetening in the pan. Garlic

followed. The smell rolled through the kitchen like warmth you could taste.

I forced my attention back to the cutting board and kept moving. Chopped. Stirred. Salted. Tasted. Adjusted.

A pot lid clinked. A spoon scraped. The small, ordinary sounds piled up until the house started to feel . . . less empty. Less sharp around the edges.

My phone buzzed with an email reply from a photographer, and that rush came back—professional excitement, the clean hit of progress.

Work mode, my brain purred. Safe. Familiar.

Another grunt pulled my attention sideways again.

I risked one more glance.

Wes had switched exercises, seated now, shoulders hunched as he worked dumbbells with deliberate control—biceps curls, slow and punishing. Sweat glistened along his forearms. His hands tightened around the weights like they'd offended him personally.

My pulse tripped again as my throat went bone dry.

I turned away so fast I nearly flung garlic across the room.

"Focus," I whispered to the food like it could hear me and rechecked the recipe.

The kitchen smelled like butter and heat and something that wanted to be called home. I leaned into it. I let the rhythm of cooking pull me forward—one step, another, then another—until the awkwardness I had felt became background noise instead of the soundtrack.

Somewhere behind me, the mat shifted. A soft thud. The unmistakable sound of weights being set down.

A pause.

Then heavier footsteps, moving off the rug.

Not toward the stairs or the bathroom, but toward the kitchen.

Wes's footsteps stopped at the edge of the kitchen like he'd hit an invisible line.

I kept stirring until the sauce thickened and steam curled up into my face—because if I looked at him too directly, I was going to think of him in a way I didn't have the bandwidth for.

Unfortunately, my body did not care about my bandwidth.

Sweat had darkened the collar of his T-shirt. A sheen caught along his forearms and throat, and the heat of him— fresh from working out, all muscle and effort—rolled into the room like another element. My stomach dipped. A spark low in my belly fluttered, hot and intense.

I focused harder on the pot.

He didn't say anything. He just stood there, filling the doorway with that heavy, silent presence that made the kitchen feel smaller.

I glanced up anyway.

His eyes were on me. Not skimming past. Not politely avoiding, but *looking*.

My pulse stuttered like it had tripped over its own feet.

I cleared my throat, because I refused to be the only one acting weird. "I had a taste for spaghetti," I said, gesturing at the stove like it was no big deal, like I wasn't acutely aware of the way his gaze made my skin feel too tight. "There's enough if you're hungry."

For a beat, he didn't answer. His eyes stayed on my face, intent enough to make my grip on the spoon go a little too firm.

Then his jaw worked once, like he was swallowing words he didn't want to give me.

"I'm going to shower," he said.

And then he turned and walked away like the kitchen was on fire.

I stood there with my spoon hovering over the sauce, staring at the space he'd just left, and tried—really tried—not to imagine the word shower attached to Wes Vaughn.

Steam. Tile. Water. A body I hadn't asked to see but couldn't unsee.

I blinked hard and forced myself back to the stove.

"Get it together," I muttered to the garlic.

The rest of dinner came together on muscle memory. Pasta draining in the sink. Sauce simmering. Bread warming in the oven. I smiled at the stove. I couldn't remember the last time I'd successfully cooked a meal from scratch.

Still, my brain kept snagging on the fact that Wes had looked at me. Really looked.

I plated two servings without thinking—two twirls of pasta, two ladles of sauce, Parmesan falling like snow—then froze with the second plate in my hand.

*What was I doing?*

I could leave his portion on the counter, covered with foil, like it was an offering he could pretend didn't come with any expectation. I could take mine and eat in my room and let him do whatever he always did—rot on the couch with TV and silence.

I stared at the plates and felt that familiar tug between stubborn and scared.

Finally, I set both at the table anyway.

If he wanted to take his plate to the couch, then fine. At least I wouldn't be forced to carry a steaming plate across the living room like some kind of anxious waitress in my own temporary home.

I focused on slicing the bread.

The house made small sounds around me—the oven ticking as it cooled, the distant hush of his footsteps above me.

My shoulders lifted with every creak, every footstep, until the moment I heard him again.

Wes came in quietly, like he didn't want to be noticed. Like he could move through his own home without taking up too much space.

His hair was damp, darker at the roots. His face was clean-shaven, his jaw sharp, his skin flushed from heat. He smelled . . . good. Not cologne. Just soap and clean skin and something faintly woodsy that made my mind go annoyingly blank for half a second.

He paused when he saw the plates.

His gaze shifted from the table to the living room like he was already mapping his default route back to the couch.

My heart did that hopeful, traitorous thing.

He reached for the plate.

I braced myself for him to take it and leave.

Instead, he pulled out the chair and sat down.

I kept my face neutral through sheer willpower, even as something inside me loosened like it had been waiting for proof that he wasn't completely gone.

I sat across from him, and we ate in silence for a few minutes. My fork scraped against the plate. A swallow. The soft push of winter wind against the windows.

I couldn't stand it.

"Is this okay?" I finally asked, nodding toward his plate like I was asking about the pasta and not the entire fragile dynamic between us.

Wes chewed and swallowed. Then, after a beat, he nodded. "Yeah," he said. His voice was rough, like he hadn't used it much today. His eyes dropped to his plate, then lifted. "It's really fucking good."

My chest warmed and a happy grin split my face.

"Well," I teased, "don't get used to it." I swirled noodles and lifted my shoulders. "This is about the only thing I know how to cook, and I still need to look up the recipe every time."

A soft sound left him—barely there. Not a laugh. Not really. More like a huff that had the shape of amusement if you listened for it.

"Noted," he said.

He took another bite and made a low, involuntary sound in the back of his throat—gravelly and unguarded—and my entire body reacted like it recognized it as something else entirely.

Heat chased up my neck. I reached for my water too quickly and nearly knocked it over.

Wes didn't seem to notice. After a moment, he cleared his throat and said, quieter, "Thank you."

The words were simple, but their effect was not.

Something in me glowed—warm and proud—like I'd been starving for any proof that I could do something right in this house.

I stared down at my plate so he wouldn't see it on my face.

"So, uh . . . what were you up to today?" Wes's question was quiet, like he didn't have the right to ask, but was curious anyway.

"Oh . . ." I twirled a noodle just to give my fingers something to do. "I went out to the farm. Talked to Elodie. I think we're going to do a winter bridal shoot out there. Use the barn, the dunes . . . it should be pretty."

Across from me, Wes's fork slowed. His gaze lifted from

his plate, really lifted, like he was seeing me instead of just the food. "Yeah?" His voice dropped a notch. "Like a photo shoot?"

A knot formed low in my belly. This was the part where people either politely shifted the subject or tried to hide a smirk.

"I, um . . . never really talked about it much," I said, hearing the defensive edge creep in even though I tried to keep it light. "In the city, I did bridal modeling. Styled shoots. Helped put them together—locations, vendors, all of it. It's . . . a whole thing," I added, bracing for the laugh, the *oh, that's cute*, or the subtle dismissal I'd heard before.

None of that came. His eyes stayed on me, steady and sharper than I expected. "You do that for a living?"

My laugh came out thinner than I intended. "I did. In the city. Before everything went sideways." I shrugged, trying to make my voice match the casual flick of my shoulder. "I sort of fell into it and found I had a knack."

Wes's eyes moved over me, slow and thoughtful, like he was lining up the idea of me in a gown against the mental picture of my sister's farm. His jaw worked once, and butterflies erupted in my belly at his achingly slow assessment.

"Yeah." His voice was low and rough. "I can see that."

The words simmered low and hot, tangled up with the way his eyes were on me—on my face, my shoulders, the neckline of my sweater, like he was picturing me in one of those gowns and absolutely not hating the view.

*Oh.*

My pulse kicked hard enough that I had to look back down at my plate before I did something stupid. Like preen. Or blush harder. Or climb into his lap.

"I've been in magazines," I heard myself say, chasing the

flicker of confidence his tone sparked. "Campaigns. Catalogs. I just . . . never really talked about it here."

"Why not?" he asked.

I nudged a noodle through sauce, watching the red smear across white porcelain. "People don't always get it. And now after everything that happened . . ." A laugh escaped me. "Being a bride was my literal *job*, and I ran."

Wes was quiet for a beat, chewing and shaking his head as he looked down. "He didn't deserve you."

I stared across the table, stumbling to make sense of what he'd just said.

Wes cleared his throat. "Setting up at the farm's a smart move. It's a good backdrop. You'll crush it."

My throat was thick, and I hummed a response. Warmth spread under my skin, slow and syrupy. I took a sip of water so I wouldn't say thank you in a way that sounded too much like *please keep talking to me like that.*

I set my fork down and let my hands move as I talked. "The goal is to capture a winter bride. Think twinkle lights, falling snow, the blue barn, maybe some stylized shots on the porch at the inn. I'm talking to a photographer, maybe a videographer. Elodie wants a few extra lifestyle shots for the farm too—kids at the firepit, the restaurant when it's done. She said she'd buy a package."

His gaze stayed on me, intent and steady. It should have unnerved me. Instead, heat slid under my skin in slow, dangerous ribbons.

"Sounds smart," he said. "She'll get free advertising. You'll get paid. The town gets to show off a little bit." He tipped his chin. "You doing the modeling too?"

I swallowed, suddenly too aware of my own body. "Yes. I mean, I'll try to snag a groom if I can, so it's not all me, but . . . yeah."

His eyes dragged over my face in a way that felt less like appraisal and more like confirmation as he chuffed a laugh. "That shouldn't be hard."

The words landed low in my stomach, hot and heavy. Old Wes was right there in that sentence—the one who used to charm women without trying, who knew exactly how to make her feel seen without making it gross. His tone wasn't sleazy. Just . . . confident. Flirtatious and certain.

My pulse tripped. "Is that your professional opinion?"

His mouth curved, slow and wicked, a flash of the man who'd existed before the world took a piece of him. "Professional. Personal." His shoulders lifted in a small shrug. "You in a pretty dress on that property? They'd be idiots not to pay for it."

Heat climbed my throat until I was sure it showed. I took a quick sip of water to cover the way my tongue suddenly felt too big in my mouth.

"Wow," I managed. "Careful. If you keep complimenting me like that, I might start to think you don't hate having me here."

His gaze held mine for a beat that felt longer than it probably was. Something flickered in his eyes—something warm and wary. "I don't hate having you here," he said, voice low. "I just haven't figured out what to do with you yet."

Every nerve ending I owned stood at attention.

I broke eye contact first, because self-preservation was still a thing I pretended to care about. My fingers tightened around my fork, knuckles white.

Outside, the snow fell harder, filling the dark with white. Inside, Wes Vaughn sat at his own table, eating my food, breathing the same air as me.

Wes pushed back from the table and cleared his throat. "I think we should add a rule."

I blinked. "What?"

"The one who cooks doesn't do dishes," he said, reaching for my plate before I could argue. "Now tell me you've got something sweet for me."

FIFTEEN

WES

*T*ELL *me you've got something sweet for me.*

My words hung between us, thick as steam off the pot and just as hard to pretend away. I'd be a liar if I said they had been completely innocent.

Clara blinked once, slow, like her brain had to buffer before it could decide what to do with that sentence. Her fork hovered over her plate, the prongs catching the warm overhead light. A beat passed where the only sounds were the heater ticking and the faint hush of snow sliding down the window outside.

My throat tightened.

*Oh god, did I lick my lip? What the fuck.*

Heat crawled up the back of my neck as my brain started scrambling for a version of that sentence I could live with. A joke. A roommate thing. A harmless comment about dessert.

My body didn't seem interested in harmless.

Clara stared up at me in an oversize sweater that swallowed her shoulders and made her look smaller than she was, sleeves shoved up like she'd been cooking with both hands and zero hesitation. Her legs were tucked under the chair, the denim just tight enough to show off the curve of her ass, and the sight of them did something stupid to my gut. Her hair fell loose around her face, softened from the heat of the kitchen, a few strands curling near her jaw.

She looked . . . pretty. Too pretty for my table. Too alive for the man I'd been lately. They were details I had no business cataloging.

The curve where the sweater dipped at her collarbone.

The way her fingers worried the edge of her napkin like she needed something to do with her hands.

The steady rise and fall of her chest when she breathed.

I hated that I noticed any of it. I hated that the noticing came first, and the self-control had to sprint to catch up after, but for the briefest moment, I'd felt like *me* again. Somewhere our conversation reminded me of the guy I used to be—the one who liked to flirt and was damn good at it.

Clara's gaze flicked down, one quick dart to my hand on her plate, then back up to my face. Her cheeks colored just slightly, the kind of flush that made my pulse jump in a way I hadn't felt in months. Her expression shifted—shock fading into something more careful, more assessing, like she was deciding whether to pretend she hadn't heard the double meaning or call me on it.

My eyes had stayed on her mouth for half a second too long. My brain had supplied an image of her lips parting—again—only this time not to take a bite of spaghetti. The thought hit fast and hot, a flicker of lust that made no sense in my chest, because I wasn't a man who got to want things right now. Wanting was for people who had their shit together. Wanting was for men who didn't sleep on couches and flinch at the sound of footsteps in their own hallway.

My stomach tightened as I turned.

Allowing her in my house had been a mistake.

Wanting her at my table felt like something else entirely.

Clara cleared her throat, the sound small and careful. "You're . . ." She started, stopped, then tried again like she was choosing her tone on purpose. "You're really doing the dishes?"

The question was simple, but the way she asked it wasn't. There was something tentative under it, as if she didn't trust me not to snap if she moved the wrong way.

My jaw clenched as I barely glanced over my shoulder. I forced my eyes to stay on her face and not dip, not betray me, not do the thing they kept trying to do—trace the line of her legs, the softness of that sweater, the way she looked too damn good in my kitchen.

"I said the cook doesn't do dishes," I replied, but the words came out too clipped, too defensive, like I was arguing with someone who hadn't attacked me. "I meant it, Duchess."

Her eyes went wide. "Duchess?"

I smirked, feeling the glimmers of the old me poking through again. "Well, you're too hardheaded and wild to be princess."

Clara's mouth twitched into a half smile. She lifted her shoulder. "Okay."

My pulse stuttered as I busied my hands with the dishes.

Her eyes held mine for a second longer than necessary, then glanced toward the freezer like she needed an escape route. "If you're looking for something sweet . . ." Clara licked her lips, and my dick twitched. "We might have ice cream."

*What the hell was happening?*

It had been ages since I'd flirted with a woman, let alone had one flirt back. *Is that what we were doing here?*

I swallowed, plate still in my hand, and forced a nod. "Yeah?"

She slid her chair back and stood, sweater falling into place over her hips, the hem skimming her thighs in a way that made my attention snag and my patience with my own body evaporate. She moved with that unthinking confidence of someone who didn't have to plan every step, every pivot, every reach. She gathered the rest of the dishes as if it were nothing—just a normal night, in a normal kitchen, and a normal man sharing a meal with her.

I gestured toward the glasses in her hand. "I'll do those too."

Clara glanced up, a beat of surprise passing over her face before she masked it. "Oh, I know. You already made the rule." Her eyes flashed with playful amusement.

I shook my head.

*New rule: Stop imagining your friend's sister naked, you fuckwad.*

I focused on rinsing the dishes and stacking them into the dishwasher, keeping my movements careful, my expression neutral, my mind locked on the mechanics of the task.

Clara joined me at the sink anyway, shoulder to shoulder, close enough that the warmth of her bled through the air between us. The faucet roared to life, hot water steaming up. Plates clinked softly, a domestic sound that hadn't been heard in my house in a long time. The scent of her perfume cut through the lingering garlic and meat sauce. Winter light pressed against the windows, dim and slate-colored, snow drifting past the pines like the world was being erased one flake at a time.

Clara slid a dish under the stream and hummed under

her breath—quiet, absent, like she couldn't help it—before passing it to me to stack in the dishwasher.

I grabbed a towel from the drawer, snapping it once like that could shake the tension off my skin. "I've got it," I muttered.

Her eyes cut to me. "I'm not trying to steal your job, Wes."

The way she said my name—flat, matter of fact, no pity tucked inside it—hit harder than it should have. Clara Darling had a mouth that knew how to turn words into trouble. Tonight, I was trying to keep them from doing exactly that.

Her eyebrows rose as she handed me a freshly rinsed glass.

Our hands grazed.

It wasn't even a full touch, just skin against skin—my fingers brushing the side of hers for the smallest fraction of a second—but my entire body reacted like she'd pressed her palm to my chest. Heat climbed, fast and sharp. My stomach tightened. Somewhere lower, something hungry shifted.

Clara's breath caught, quiet and unmistakable, and her fingers lingered that half heartbeat too long before she pulled back. Her gaze flicked to my face, then away, quick as a blink. A flush rose along her cheeks. The focus she suddenly found in the dish she was rinsing did not help.

The air in the kitchen thickened until it felt hard to breathe.

My brain reached for the easiest place to put the blame.

Proximity. That was all this was. A normal reaction to a beautiful woman in my space.

My body disagreed, loud and immediate.

It remembered things it had no business remembering.

The weight of a woman straddling my lap and moaning when I stretched her open. The slide of bare skin under my hands. The way my mouth could make her forget she was anything but alive.

I'd been a damn good lover, and I missed the way a woman could use my body while I used hers. I missed the casual fun of a good fuck. Nothing about Clara Darling could ever be casual. She was the kind of woman you changed your plans for.

Now my body was nothing but a problem I carried around—something to manage, compensate for, apologize for without ever saying the words.

Clara's fingers moved with quick efficiency, bringing a pan to the sink and making the kitchen look like it belonged to someone who lived there instead of someone who survived there. Her shoulder bumped mine lightly as she reached past me for another plate. The contact was accidental and small.

It still hit me like a shove.

I shifted my stance, cursing under my breath as phantom pain flared, my nerves firing in a place that no longer existed. My jaw clenched. My breath went shallow.

Clara's head turned, a question rising in her eyes.

I stiffened before she could ask it. "I'm fine," I said sharply, like it was an answer to something. Like it would stop her from seeing what she saw.

Clara blinked, then dipped her chin. "Okay."

She didn't press. She didn't hover. She didn't offer help I hadn't asked for.

The restraint should have been a relief, but it wasn't. It made me want to reach for her and yank her into me and prove I was more than this broken shell of a man.

My hand tightened around the towel until my knuckles went white.

She stepped to the side to put the clean pan away, and I needed to get past her to the cabinet. The kitchen narrowed in that moment—tight space, two bodies, nowhere to look but at her.

My brain said, *Go around.*

My body said, *Move her.*

My hand landed at her lower back, a brief, instinctive press meant to guide her out of my way.

The contact was light. Nothing. The kind of touch a man used without thinking.

My skin registered it like a brand.

Clara's spine straightened under my palm. Her muscles there went taut, like she'd been braced for impact and wasn't sure whether to lean into it or run.

My hand lifted immediately, yanked back like I'd burned myself.

Clara turned her head slightly, eyes wide for a beat before her lashes lowered. She swallowed. Her voice came out careful when she spoke.

"Sorry," she said, even though she'd done nothing.

The apology gutted me in a way I didn't expect.

"I didn't—" The words jammed in my throat. I didn't know what I was trying to say. *I didn't touch you like that. I didn't mean it. I did mean it.*

I cleared my throat hard enough to scrape it raw. "Cabinet," I managed, like that explained everything.

Clara nodded and stepped aside. "Right."

The dishes were done within minutes after that, both of us moving too fast, as if finishing the task would drain the tension out of the room.

Soon the sink was empty. The counters were wiped. The kitchen looked . . . normal.

I dried my hands on the towel and turned, expecting space.

She was closer than I thought.

Clara had stepped sideways and ended up right in front of me, half boxed in by the counter and the cabinet. We were barely a foot apart. Close enough that I could see a faint smudge at the curve of her jaw. Close enough that the steam from the sink hadn't quite left her hair, loose strands curling at her temple.

I should have stepped back. Given her room. Done the smart, safe, gentlemanly thing.

My body stayed put.

Her eyes lifted, catching on mine. The air between us shifted, tight and charged, like the whole house was holding its breath.

"Uh . . . you have something." My voice came out low and gravelly.

Her brows knit in confusion. "Where?"

I reached up, fingers brushing the side of her face as I swiped my thumb over the spot near her cheekbone. Warm skin. Soft. The barest hint of a tremble under my touch.

Clara went still.

Her breath hitched, just enough that I felt it against my wrist. Her pupils blew wide, the gray blue of her eyes darkening as they flicked from my eyes to my mouth and back again like she was fighting herself every inch of the way. Heat punched low in my gut. My pulse kicked hard. My dick stirred, thick and insistent, like it remembered things my life had no room for anymore.

The world narrowed to the space between us.

Her hand came up like she might catch my wrist, then

stopped halfway, hanging there in the air between us. I could feel the heat rolling off her and whatever perfume she wore that made my head go loose and my restraint feel flimsy. My thumb stayed at her cheekbone a second too long, rough pad against smooth skin.

I leaned in.

Not much. Just enough that I could feel the ghost of her breath against my lips, just enough that if either of us moved another fraction, our mouths would meet and there would be no taking any of this back. My hips edged closer on pure instinct, the front of my jeans brushing the hem of her sweater, my heart pounding so hard it felt like it lived in my throat. Every remembered version of myself—the man who used to kiss women against walls and make them forget their names—came roaring up like he'd just been waiting for an opening.

Clara didn't move away.

Her lips parted, the smallest sound catching in her throat, a soft, helpless little inhale that lit every fuse I had left. Her gaze dropped to my mouth again, slow and deliberate this time, like she was giving herself away on purpose.

Hayes's face flashed in my mind. Clara with a diamond on her finger. Our stupid rule list on the fridge. Every reason this was a terrible idea lined up in a neat, brutal row.

I forced myself back a few inches, enough to break the gravity that had been pulling us together. The loss of warmth hit first, then the hollow feel of air sliding between us again.

"Wes . . ." she whispered, my name barely there, more exhale than sound.

Shame crashed in on the heels of want. Best friend's little sister. Roommate. Woman who had walked in on me at my lowest and still moved into my house anyway. I wasn't a man who got to put his hands on her and pretend it was simple.

"Sorry," I muttered, though I wasn't entirely sure what I was apologizing for. Almost kissing her. Not kissing her. Hell, all of it.

Clara swallowed, throat bobbing. Her gaze skated away, finding refuge in the safest thing in the room—a damn cabinet door. "It's . . . fine," she said too quickly. Her fingers fumbled for the pan handle like she needed something to hold on to that wasn't me.

I cleared my throat, the sound too loud in the small kitchen. "You want to . . . watch something?"

The second the words left my mouth, I wanted to drag them back. It sounded weak and obvious, like a teenager trying to translate almost-kiss into couch time.

Her eyes flicked to the living room entrance, and the reality of what she'd see out there landed in my gut like a stone.

Then her gaze came back to me, and I watched all of it cross her face—the memory of my hand on her cheek, the way I'd leaned in, the space I'd put back between us. Something in her softened, then shuddered. Maybe she remembered who I was to her.

Her voice was barely above normal, but I heard the wobble under it. "I can't," she said. "I need to send a few emails. If I don't do it tonight, I'll talk myself out of it tomorrow."

Of course she did. It seemed Clara Darling ran on momentum. Plans. Anything that kept her from standing still long enough to feel how close we'd just come to crossing a line.

I nodded once, trying to make my face something

neutral instead of the prickling embarrassment clawing at my throat. "Yeah." I tried to sound casual. "Do your thing."

Clara hesitated at the edge of the kitchen, like part of her was tethered there and the rest was already halfway up the stairs. Her lashes lifted in my direction.

"Dinner was really nice, Wes," she said, and the quiet emphasis on my name made my chest tighten. "Thank you."

Before I could respond—before I could say out loud what was almost eating me alive—she turned and headed upstairs, her footsteps light but quick, each a reminder of everything I avoided and everything I'd almost done.

I stayed in the kitchen long after she disappeared, staring at the clean sink, the warm light, the empty chair across from mine.

My body still felt like it was humming.

My mouth still felt like it had been inches from hers.

My house felt too quiet again.

My chest felt like it had been cracked open a fraction, and I didn't know whether to curse or breathe.

I turned toward the living room and took two steps before I saw it the way she probably did.

Not the way I saw it, from the inside, as a place I'd made do. A place where I could keep my leg within reach and my panic contained. A place where I didn't have to climb anything, face anything, or admit anything.

The couch was a nest. Chargers coiled like vines. A half-empty bottle of water. Pill bottles clustered near the remote like they belonged on display. A blanket I'd been sleeping under for months, bunched up in the corner with a permanent dent in the cushion where my body had trained it to hold me.

The room looked . . . tired.

Like I'd moved my whole life down here and let it shrink to the width of one piece of furniture.

Heat pulsed low in my gut, equal parts irritation and something close to shame. Clara hadn't said a word about it, which was almost worse. She'd just looked toward the living room with that careful, too-gentle expression, then excused herself like sitting next to me on that couch would've been more dangerous than standing with me in the kitchen.

*Dinner was really nice, Wes.*

Nice.

I dragged a hand down my face and crossed the room in short, irritated strides, like I could outwork whatever was crawling under my skin.

The first thing I did was grab an empty wrapper off the coffee table and shove it into the trash. Then another. Then a stack of mail I'd been ignoring because opening it required feeling responsible for something again. I straightened a throw pillow that didn't need straightening, folded the blanket with sharp, impatient snaps, and lined the pill bottles into a neater row like organization could erase what they represented.

My movements came in bursts, the way my brain did things lately—go until the energy ran out and stop before the thoughts caught up.

The quiet in the house pressed closer.

I stood in the center of the living room, staring at the couch like it was evidence of my fall from grace.

It wasn't that I couldn't go upstairs.

My body could climb stairs. It had climbed them plenty of times in PT, under fluorescent lights and other people's eyes, with a therapist counting my steps like each one was a victory. I could do it.

My brain was a different story.

Upstairs meant distance. Upstairs meant being far from the front door, far from the exit, far from the ground level where I could get out if something went wrong. Upstairs meant that stupid fear I'd never told anyone about—the irrational, humiliating certainty that if there was a fire, if something happened, if I woke in the dark and couldn't get my leg on fast enough, I'd be trapped.

It was ridiculous, but it was real and had taken root.

The couch had become my compromise. My surrender. My safety net.

Tonight, after almost kissing Clara in my kitchen like every rule we hadn't said out loud didn't exist, it felt like a spotlight.

My gaze drifted, uninvited, toward the staircase at the back of the house.

The banister caught the dim light. The steps rose clean and steep, the wood polished and beautiful—the kind of staircase I used to take pride in. I had designed it. Built it. Lived in it like a man who never thought his own home could become an obstacle course.

Clara had walked through this house and seen the way I lived now. Had stood in my kitchen and almost let me kiss her, even knowing all of it. She'd been quiet about what she thought, which only made it louder in my head.

He should be sleeping upstairs.

His bedroom is right there.

He's choosing this.

A soft sound came from above—something settling, a floorboard giving under weight, a reminder that Clara was up there, alive and moving in the room across from mine. The woman I'd almost kissed. The woman I had absolutely no business wanting.

My lungs tightened.

This was what she'd moved into. A house where the upstairs belonged to a ghost, and the man downstairs pretended he didn't notice.

I took a slow breath and walked to the bottom of the stairs.

My hand slid onto the banister. The wood was smooth under my palm, familiar in a way that should have steadied me. My prosthetic felt secure tonight, the liner fitted right, the subtle pressure at my residual limb a reminder that my body was doing what it could. Phantom pain fizzed in the background like static, never gone, but quieter than usual.

I stared up.

The hallway light upstairs was off. The landing was dim, lit only by the faint spill from Clara's room.

My mouth went dry.

The fear rose in the same place it always did—under my ribs, tight and irrational, as if my body didn't trust my own house anymore. My brain started listing risks like it always did.

Trip. Fall. Fire. Stuck.

Add to that the fresh memory of nearly backing her against a cabinet and kissing her like I hadn't lost anything at all. The idea of crashing down these stairs—or crashing headfirst into whatever that was between us—made my stomach drop in the same ugly way.

My jaw clenched hard enough to ache.

No.

I wasn't doing this for her. I wasn't proving anything. I wasn't trying to be some version of myself she could admire or justify almost kissing in her head later.

I was just . . . tired of living like I'd already lost. Tired of being the guy who slept on a couch and pretended wanting things was above his pay grade now.

My fingers tightened around the banister until the tendons in my hand stood out.

*This isn't a big deal. We've gone up before, and we can always come back down. Stop making this more than it is.*

I lifted my foot and set it on the first stair. The house creaked softly, the sound almost like a sigh. My pulse thundered in my ears as I shifted my weight forward, testing. The prosthetic held. My knee locked. My balance caught.

A breath left my lungs in a shaky exhale.

I climbed another step. Then another.

By the time I reached the landing, my thigh was burning, my shoulders were tight, and my skin was damp at the back of my neck like I'd been hauling lumber instead of climbing the staircase in my own damn house.

My bedroom door waited at the end of the hall, half shadowed, quiet, and closed.

It looked like a stranger's room.

I stepped toward it, slower now, each movement deliberate and controlled. The air up here was cooler, less lived in, smelling faintly of cedar and clean sheets and something I used to think meant comfort.

My hand lifted.

My palm settled against the doorknob of my bedroom, the metal cool beneath my skin.

My chest rose and fell, too fast, my heart kicking like it didn't trust what I was about to do.

Across the hall, another floorboard shifted—soft and small, like someone had moved in bed or stood up.

My fingers tightened on the knob anyway.

It turned beneath my grip.

The primary bedroom greeted me like a place I'd built for someone else, the bed made too neatly, the comforter smoothed flat, the pillows stacked and untouched as if nobody had ever laid a head there. Moonlight leaked through the curtains in pale strips, painting the floor and the edge of the dresser in winter gray.

I stepped inside and shut the door behind me, the sound soft, controlled, like I could keep everything contained if I moved carefully enough.

My prosthetic felt heavier the second I crossed the threshold, my body suddenly hyperaware of what it would cost me to get out of this room quickly if I had to. My throat tightened with the familiar irrational panic, that ugly certainty my brain liked to feed me in the dark.

Fire. Smoke. Stairs. Clara's mouth, inches from mine.

My jaw clenched as I crossed to the bed anyway, refusing to let the fear—of upstairs or of wanting her—decide for me tonight.

I lowered myself onto the edge of the mattress with a slow exhale, the springs shifting under my weight in a way that felt almost shocking after months of couch cushions and half sleep and the constant readiness to move. The bed was soft and generous. It cradled me and welcomed me to stay.

My hands went to my thigh on instinct, fingers pressing through fabric as if I could anchor myself to something solid. The phantom pain flickered, a low static in the background, and my shoulders tightened like my body thought it was still braced for impact.

Across the hall, there was the faintest sound—wood settling, a quiet footstep, the house remembering there was another person inside it.

Clara.

The thought hit me in the chest, warm and unwanted, tangled up with the memory of her at my table, her hands in my sink, her breath catching when I'd leaned in close enough to taste it.

My stomach tightened as I tipped back, letting myself fall onto the mattress fully clothed, staring up at the ceiling I hadn't looked at from this angle in months.

The plaster above me was smooth and unremarkable, the kind of ceiling you never notice when your life was normal.

My heartbeat thudded too loud in my ears, my body waiting for the old fear to surge and chase me back downstairs, my mind waiting for the house—or my conscience—to prove I was right to avoid sleeping there.

Instead, I lay there and let the quiet wrap around me, pretending I didn't feel like a man trespassing in his own bed . . . or on the edge of wanting something he had no right to touch.

CLARA

Morning came in slow and hazy, seeping through the thin curtains in a pale wash of light that turned my ceiling into a watercolor.

For a few seconds I didn't know why my chest felt tight or why my body already buzzed like I'd woken mid-fall.

Then my brain caught up.

Wes's hand on my cheek. The rough drag of his thumb at my face. His breath, warm and close. The half inch between us that never quite disappeared, even after we did.

My eyes slammed shut again.

*Oh god.*

Heat rolled through me so fast it was almost dizzying. Every place he'd almost touched felt lit up in neon. My skin remembered the way his body had leaned in, how he'd braced one hand on the counter behind me and crowded my space like something in him had snapped.

We hadn't actually kissed, but that didn't seem to matter to the rest of me.

My nipples tightened under the thin cotton of my sleep shirt, pebbling hard enough that the fabric rasped when I shifted. My hand moved, palm flattening over my breast like I could smooth the feeling away. A sharp pulse of pleasure shot through me instead, low and insistent.

"Jesus," I muttered into my pillow.

The sound came out more like a broken sigh than a prayer.

I tried to breathe past it and reroute my thoughts to literally anything else. Grocery lists. Shot lists. Bridal gowns. A million other lists that didn't involve the way Wes Vaughn had looked at my mouth like he was starving.

My body wasn't interested in grocery lists.

It replayed last night in jerky little flashes, like an old film stuttering on a projector.

His fingers brushing mine at the sink. The way his touch had branded the small of my back. The heat in his eyes when he'd murmured, *I meant it, Duchess*. His thumb on my cheekbone, careful and somehow reverent.

My thighs pressed together, chasing pressure. I curled onto my side, dragging a pillow between my knees, trying to ease the ache and only making it worse. A tiny, helpless sound slipped out of me before I could catch it, halfway between a moan and a curse.

I shoved my face deeper into the pillow to smother it.

*This is ridiculous.*

Wes Vaughn had nearly kissed me in his kitchen, with my brother's name in both of our histories and an engagement ring still glittering on my finger.

I almost let him.

My hand slipped lower on autopilot, not quite touching anything I was willing to name, just skimming my ribs, gliding over my stomach, fingertips tucking into the waistband of my shorts before I yanked them back like the elastic had burned me.

"Absolutely not," I whispered into the pillow, as if my body would listen if I made it a rule. "Nope. We are not . . . doing this."

My pulse thudded between my legs anyway, steady and traitorous.

He was your brother's best friend.

He almost kissed you.

You almost *begged* him to.

My mind tried to rebrand it as nothing. It was proximity, that was all. Too much shared air, too much awkwardness, too much relief that he'd sat at the table instead of disappearing back into the couch. Two lonely people in a quiet house with a decent meal between them and way too many unspoken things.

My body called bullshit.

It remembered the way his eyes had gone dark when he watched my mouth. The way his voice had dipped when he'd said, *I don't hate having you here. I just haven't figured out what to do with you yet.*

Heat surged again, hot enough that I kicked one leg out of the covers just to cool off, then immediately dragged it back under because the air felt too cold without something holding me together.

Embarrassment crawled up the back of my neck as the reality of it settled in.

I wanted him to kiss me.

Not in some vague, flattering way. Not in a wouldn't-that-be-nice-if-I-lived-a-different-life way. In a very real, very here, very *now* kind of way.

*He's your brother's best friend.*

The thought snapped across my mind like a rubber band.

Hayes, with his protective big-brother glare and his

tendency to treat me like a slightly defective egg. Hayes, who already carried more than his share of guilt when it came to Wes.

My stomach flipped.

I rolled onto my back and stared at the ceiling, chest rising and falling too fast, the sheets twisted around my legs like I'd been wrestling myself all night.

"Get it together," I told the cracks in the paint. "He didn't even kiss you."

The protest felt flimsy, even to me.

The not-kiss had felt like more than most actual kisses I'd had. All that tension, all that almost, stretched tight and humming between us. It had lived in the fraction of space separating his mouth from mine, in the way he'd apologized like it hurt to pull back. In the way his name had left my lips without permission—*Wes*—as if my body already knew the shape of him in that context.

A tiny, stubborn thrill flickered to life under the embarrassment.

*He wanted to kiss me.*

It wasn't just me inventing a moment and pinning it to the wall. He'd leaned in. He'd reached for me. His thumb had brushed my cheek like he'd needed to touch me more than he needed to do the smart thing.

My gaze slid sideways to the closed bedroom door, to the stretch of quiet hallway beyond it, and the memory of last night shifted in my mind, making room for something new.

The soft creak of floorboards. The low thud of weight moving around. The almost-impossible realization that Wes had climbed the stairs.

My heart tripped over itself as I pushed the covers back and swung my legs over the side of the bed, palms braced on the mattress while my head sorted through want and worry and whatever this new feeling was.

Somewhere in all that messy, charged space between what we'd nearly done and what we hadn't, something had shifted.

I pressed my lips together, my pulse still a frantic flutter beneath my skin, and stood.

I walked to the door and cracked it open, cold air licking at my bare legs as I stepped into the hallway.

I just stood there, listening.

Wes's bedroom door was open a few inches, just enough that I could see inside as I passed. The bed was made, but not in that untouched, catalog way I'd first seen it. The comforter had the faintest line down the middle where a body had been. One pillow sat a little flatter than the other, like someone had slept there and then tried to smooth the evidence away.

Something in my chest pulled tight.

He'd come upstairs. He'd slept in his own bed. Not on the couch. Not in arm's reach of the front door. Up here, where the man he used to be had lived.

I shouldn't have felt proud. It wasn't my victory. I hadn't done anything but almost kiss him and then run away like a coward.

Still, a quiet, stupid swell of warmth rose under my ribs.

He was trying, not just surviving.

"Okay," I whispered to no one, fingers brushing the doorframe as I moved past. "Progress."

The smell of coffee drifted up from downstairs—a rich, dark promise that there was a world beyond my own spiraling thoughts. My stomach growled on cue.

I hesitated for half a second, then ducked back into my room instead of following it, shutting the door with a soft click. If I was going to face Wes Vaughn and the ghost of an almost-kiss, I could at least do it wearing a bra.

Leggings, thick socks, a soft sweater. I ran my fingers through my hair until it looked less like I'd been rolling around thinking about his mouth and more like a person who had it moderately together. A swipe of mascara. Chap-Stick. Nothing dramatic. Just a little light feminine armor.

Unfortunately, none of it did a thing to quiet the low hum under my skin.

When the scent of coffee finally proved stronger than my nerves, I wrapped my hand around the banister and headed downstairs, following it toward the kitchen—and whatever version of Wes Vaughn was waiting for me there.

~

Downstairs looked . . . different.

I hit the bottom step and blinked, trying to make sense of it. The living room usually greeted me like a cautionary tale—blanket heap, empty cups, a scatter of mail and wrappers.

This morning, it looked almost like a living space again.

The blanket was folded over the arm of the couch instead of lying in a defeated tangle. The coffee table was mostly clear—no wrappers, no empty bottles, just a small stack of mail squared off and the remote lined up like it belonged there. The dent in the cushion where Wes slept was still there, but it looked less like a crater and more like proof of use, not surrender.

Something in my chest loosened a fraction.

The smell of coffee pulled me toward the kitchen—rich and dark with a stripe of sweetness running through it.

Wes sat at the table with his forearms braced on either

side of a small white plate. Two cinnamon rolls sat in the middle, steam feathering up from under a crooked drizzle of icing. A mug waited at the place across from him, already poured.

He looked up when I stepped into the doorway.

My brain didn't supply words, just impressions. His jaw was clean-shaven, the sharp line of it at odds with the softness around his eyes. His hair was still mussed from sleep, sticking up a little like he'd towel dried it and given up halfway through. The shadows under his eyes weren't as deep. He looked . . . rested. Less hollowed out.

My body responded before my thoughts caught up—heat sliding low in my belly, a quick, traitorous flutter as last night's almost-kiss replayed in high definition.

His hand on my cheek. His breath. The space that hadn't stayed space for very long.

"Hey," he said, voice rough and low in a way that did not help. The corner of his mouth twitched, like his face hadn't quite remembered how to commit to a smile but was considering it. "Coffee's there. The cinnamon rolls might be questionable."

My throat went tight. "You made these?"

"'Made' is overstating it." He glanced down at the plate, then back at me. "Came in a can. I twisted. The oven did the rest."

"It still counts." My lips curved. "They look good. They're exactly how my mom used to make them."

His gaze tracked the movement of my mouth. Heat crept up my neck, and I pretended to be extremely interested in the chair.

"I saved you the center one. It's always the best." Wes was staring at his plate as my grin widened.

I stacked three cinnamon rolls onto a plate and slid into

the seat across from him. The mug was warm in my hands, the first sip of coffee hitting my system like permission to breathe. The cinnamon roll was soft when I tore off a piece, still warm in the middle. I popped it into my mouth and had to fight a frankly obscene sound trying to crawl up my throat.

"They okay?" Wes asked, a hint of something wry in his tone.

"Dangerously okay," I said once I'd swallowed. "I fear if you don't act fast, I'll eat them all myself."

One side of his mouth kicked up, quick and fleeting, but it was there. "They're all yours."

The quiet that settled after that wasn't the same brittle silence that used to fill this house. It felt fuller somehow. My heart was still doing that nervous tap dance, but there was a thread of something else woven through it now. Something that felt suspiciously like hope.

Last night we'd stood in the kitchen breathing the same charged air, half a second away from making a very bad decision.

This morning he'd slept in his own bed, cleaned his living room, and was feeding me breakfast from a can like it was the most natural thing in the world.

I finished my breakfast slower than I needed to, stalling without admitting that was what I was doing. When my plate was empty and my mug mostly drained, the old instinct kicked in—take yourself upstairs, retreat, hide away in logistics and to-do lists.

My legs didn't get the memo.

"Thanks for this," I said, fingers brushing the rim of my mug. "Seriously. It's nice not eating cereal over my laptop for once."

His gaze flicked to my face, steady in a way that made my chest feel too tight. "You're welcome," he said simply.

I stood, expecting him to do the same and vanish into whatever routine he'd built for himself here. Instead, he reached for the plates, carrying them to the sink with a casualness that felt like its own kind of miracle.

"Hey, I thought the rule was if you cook, you don't clean."

Wes paused and turned, gesturing to the list still hanging on the fridge. "I don't see that rule up there."

I playfully rolled my eyes, moving to the junk drawer to pull out a pen.

"Besides," Wes added with his back to me. "Sometimes I like to break the rules."

A delicious and slow tingle wove its way up my back as I suppressed a grin and wrote our new rule at the bottom.

## Rule #8: The one who cooks doesn't do the dishes.

I stood back and smiled at our silly little list.

"I think I'm going to hang out down here for a bit," I heard myself say, the words already escaping before I could chicken out. I tipped my head toward the living room. "If that's okay. I promise not to rearrange anything important."

Wes glanced back at me from the sink, water running, sleeves pushed up his forearms. "You're fine," he said. "I was just going to read."

A ridiculous warmth bloomed in my chest in a way that was almost embarrassing.

The armchair by the window welcomed me—the one piece of furniture that didn't feel claimed by his insomnia. I grabbed my knitting bag from the corner and dropped into the chair, the strap thumping against the floor beside me. Kit had left it by the door with a note that said: *For your boring old lady scarf.*

Footsteps sounded a second later. I kept my eyes on the tangled ball of yarn in my lap, pretending not to track the way Wes crossed the room, hesitated for half a beat like he wasn't sure he was allowed to relax in front of me, and then lowered himself onto the couch with a quiet exhale. By the time I risked a glance, he was stretched out, long and solid, with an open book.

I dug into my bag until my fingers closed around two mismatched knitting needles, clacking together like they were mocking me.

Knitting was supposed to be soothing. So far, mine looked less like a scarf and more like a cry for help.

I adjusted the yarn into my lap and tried not to feel ridiculously aware of the fact that Wes had a clear line of sight to everything I was doing. He wasn't staring. He wasn't hovering. He was just there, in my peripheral vision, silently taking up space.

My imagination filled in the rest.

I slid the first few stitches onto the needle, tongue caught between my teeth in concentration, the yarn snagging at all the wrong points. By the fourth attempt the whole thing looked like it had been through a bar fight.

*It's you and me, yarn. Let's try not to humiliate ourselves in front of the hot roommate.*

A page turned on the couch, the soft whisper of paper scraping paper. I could practically feel Wes's amusement, even if he didn't make a sound.

Staying downstairs meant he was right there. In my space. In my line of sight.

It also meant I got to be in his.

## SEVENTEEN

CLARA

I EXAMINED the half-mangled attempt at a scarf and the ball of yarn that had somehow developed a knotty, vengeful personality. My phone went on the armrest, a tutorial video already queued up and chirping in a soothing British voice about casting on like it was no big deal.

A few minutes in, I was ready to fight her.

The stitches on my needle looked nothing like the neat little row on the screen. Mine were crooked and tight in some places, sagging and loose in others, like I was drunk and had tried to build a fence out of spaghetti. The yarn snagged around my fingers, the strand cutting across my palm in a way that made my hand cramp. Every time I tried to fix one loop, three others went rogue.

Outside, the snow had brightened the whole room. Light bounced off the drifts and poured through the windows, crisp and cold. It made the pines at the edge of the property glow dark and sharp. It made the inside of Wes's house feel like a snow globe—quiet, contained, full of things swirling that pretended to be still.

Across from me, Wes shifted on the couch.

He'd grabbed a book from the stack on the side table, stretched out, and angled himself toward the corner cushion —the same spot he always claimed, like his body didn't know how to sit anywhere else.

I pretended not to notice as he settled deeper into the cushions—a long, solid line, ankle propped on his knee, one arm slung along the back like he had no idea what he was doing to the air molecules between us. The spine of the book was already worn, the cover catching a bit of the winter light.

He reached over, picked up a pair of glasses, and slid them on.

Something low and traitorous fluttered in my stomach.

They were plain black frames, nothing flashy, just practical and solid. On his face, they turned into a whole situation. They sharpened his eyes, framed his cheekbones, made his mouth look fuller when he frowned at the page. The whole effect screamed hot professor who growls across the desk and knows exactly what to do with his hands.

Slutty little glasses.

My stomach dipped like I'd missed a step on the stairs. Heat fluttered low in my belly, ridiculous and insistent.

I yanked my attention back to the yarn before he could look up and catch me ogling him like a creep. On my phone, the woman's soothing voice chirped, "If your tension is uneven, don't worry, that's completely normal as you—"

"Why is this so freaking hard?" I hissed at the yarn, stabbing the needle through a loop that might have been correct three steps ago.

A beat passed.

"You're strangling it," Wes said, voice low, without looking up from his book.

My head snapped toward him. "Excuse me?"

The corner of his mouth kicked, the closest thing I'd seen to a smile this early in the day. His gaze stayed on the page. "The yarn. You're pulling it like it owes you money."

"I am not," I said automatically, glancing down and realizing he was one hundred percent correct. The yarn was pulled so tight between stitches it looked like a tiny, angry fence.

I glared at it. "Know-it-all."

Wes made a quiet sound that might have been a laugh and finally lifted his eyes.

It was stupid how much that small shift affected me. One second, he was a guy on a couch. The next, his attention was on me—glasses catching a sliver of light, irises a deep, complicated blue behind them, amusement softening the usual hard line of his mouth.

His gaze dropped to my hands, taking in the needles, the uneven row, the loop of yarn tangled awkwardly around one finger.

"Newfound hobby?" he asked.

"Yes," I gritted out. "I'm decompressing. Coming offline. *Relaxing.*"

His brows lifted. "How's that working out for you?"

"*So* relaxed." I huffed and nudged my phone with the back of my knuckles. "The tutorial says this is 'an easy beginner pattern' and that anyone can do it. Which is a lie, by the way."

The corner of his mouth tugged again. "New hobbies take time. You'll get there."

I narrowed my eyes at him, even as my chest did that stupid warming thing again. "You're very confident for someone hiding behind a book."

His thumb flattened against the page, marking his place. "I'm not hiding."

"Mm-hmm." I squinted at the cover. A dragon curled around a sword in the center, flames and storm clouds, and, unless I was mistaken, a woman in armor who had absolutely no business having that much cleavage.

"Is that . . . ?" I leaned forward, trying to make out the title. "Oh my god. Is that the one with the dragon riders and the horny queen?"

A beat of silence.

His jaw ticced. "It has dragons," he said slowly, like that explained everything.

A bubble of laughter burst out of me before I could stop it. "Wes. That book is, like, ten percent battle scenes and ninety percent very creative use of castle walls."

A faint flush touched his cheeks. "It was on a list," he muttered. "Someone at PT said it was good."

"Don't get me wrong, it *is* good. I read it in a day. But don't kid yourself—you're reading angst and smut disguised as fantasy," I said, delighted. "I did not have that on my Wes Vaughn bingo card."

He shifted, the faintest hint of embarrassment slipping under the gruff. "It's well written."

"It is." I nodded solemnly. "Structure. World-building. *Penetration.*"

He choked on nothing, coughing once. "Jesus, Clara."

"What?" I tried to look innocent. Failed. "I'm just saying, I wouldn't have pegged you for a 'pining warriors and morally gray queens' kind of guy."

His gaze snagged mine over the top of the book, something flickering there that hadn't been there a few weeks ago. "You been thinking about what I'm into lately, Duchess?"

My throat went dry.

The kitchen flashed in my mind—his hand on my

cheek, the millimeter of space between our mouths, the way my entire body had leaned toward him on instinct. Heat crept up the back of my neck.

"Absolutely not," I said lightly, twisting the yarn tighter than I meant to around my finger.

The air between us shifted, going quiet in a different way. Not empty, but dense.

His eyes held mine, the edge of his glasses glinting, that forced neutrality slipping in the corners. He knew what I wasn't saying. I knew what he wasn't saying. The almost-kiss pressed against the edges of the room like a secret trying to get out.

My pussy fluttered at the thought of what *could* have happened.

I glanced back at my lap before I could drown in the look on his face. "So," I said, wrestling the needles into something that vaguely resembled a stitch. "If you're going to silently judge my tension, you could at least be useful and tell me what I'm doing wrong."

"Besides abusing the yarn?" he said with a smirk.

I shot him a look.

His mouth twitched; then he set the book face down on his chest and tipped his head, studying my hands. The focus in his gaze made my pulse jump. It was the same look he probably used on blueprints and beams—calculating, precise, already fixing things in his mind before anyone else saw the problem.

"You have it in a chokehold," he said. "Loosen your grip."

One sculpted eyebrow rose higher. "My grip is fine."

Red splotches crawled up his neck, and he cleared his throat. "You don't need to white-knuckle it, that's all. Let it slide a little."

I snorted softly. "Story of my life."

He huffed out a laugh that sounded way too close to pleased. "Try wrapping it . . . here."

He leaned forward, reaching out, and my brain didn't process anything but the fact that his hand was moving toward mine, that the space between us was going to shrink again, that his fingers were going to be on my skin.

He stopped just short of touching me.

"May I?" he asked.

The simple courtesy shouldn't have done what it did to me.

My chest tightened. "Yeah," I said, and my voice came out lower than I meant it to. "Show me."

His fingers brushed mine as he adjusted the yarn, guiding it more loosely through my grip, knuckles grazing the inside of my wrist. The contact was brief, impersonal if anyone else had been looking. No one else was.

My breath stuck.

His scent cut through the faint clean smell of the house —soap, skin, that woodsy note from earlier. The memory of him leaning in last night flooded my body with heat, pooling low and insistent. My nipples tightened under my sweater, traitorous and very aware of the fact that there was a man within touching distance who knew exactly what to do with a woman's body and had almost done it to mine.

"There," he murmured, concentrating on the yarn. "Less death grip, more . . . guiding."

"You're awfully confident for someone reading about horny queens," I managed.

His lips twitched. His thumb brushed the side of my finger as he pulled back, slow and unhurried, like he had no idea what he was doing to me.

"Someone's got to maintain standards around here," he said. "Can't have you starting a fight with a sweater."

The warmth that rolled through me at the teasing was bigger than it had any right to be. Comfortable. Dangerous.

"How the hell do you know how to knit?" I asked, adjusting my grip and trying again.

Wes leaned back against the couch, his book open. "My grandmother taught us—Mary and me—when we were kids."

Mary was his little sister—Cal's wife, before the car accident that took her life. He'd never mentioned her before, and a tiny spark ignited inside of me. There was something trusting and reverent about Wes opening up . . . even if it was to casually mention his sister.

"I remember her—your sister. She was older than me, and I remember how pretty she was. She had great hair." I tried not to look too hard at Wes as I brought up his sister.

His lips pressed together as if he could picture her too.

"You guys were close?" I asked.

Wes nodded, his voice thick. "Yeah. For sure when we were kids. More so when I got back from overseas and she and Cal got together. We did a lot as a unit."

By then I had already started a new life in the city and was barely back in Star Harbor. I wished I could have known her, but it felt too risky admitting that aloud to Wes. Instead, I sneaked a glance at him, catching the way his eyes softened as he watched me attempt another row. His expression was less guarded. Less hollow.

We were just two people in a living room. Knitting. Reading. Trading barbs over fantasy porn. Sharing tiny shards of our souls and pretending like it was no big deal.

We were also two people who'd almost kissed in a

kitchen, who'd both leaned in, who both knew exactly what they were doing when they didn't mention it now.

My body knew which version of the story it believed.

My heartbeat ticked up. I focused on the yarn, on the small satisfaction of a stitch that actually looked right, and told myself I was just sitting here because the lighting was good.

Not because I liked the way Wes Vaughn looked in his slutty little glasses, sprawled across his couch, book in hand, eyes occasionally flicking up to check on me like I was something worth watching.

Over the back of the armchair, the world outside was blinding and soft. Overnight, more snow had fallen, smoothing out yesterday's footprints, filling in every dip and rut until the backyard looked spotless. The gentle slope behind the house rolled down toward the line of pines, the kind of hill kids would take one look at and immediately weaponize with plastic sleds and no sense of self-preservation.

The sky was a bright, hard blue. Sunlight shattered off the drifts, making the whole yard look like it had been hit with a glitter bomb.

A weird little fizz of energy went through me. Fresh snow always felt like a do-over. No tracks. No evidence. Just possibility.

"We should go sledding." The words left my mouth before my brain had a chance to dress them up as a suggestion and not a declaration.

Wes's head snapped up. "What?"

I nodded toward the window, feigning nonchalance as I poked the needle through another stitch. "Sledding. You know, sit on something questionably safe, hurl yourself down a hill, pray you don't die. It's very therapeutic."

His brows climbed like they were trying to escape his forehead. "You're not serious."

"Dead serious."

He shifted in his seat. "That's kid shit, Clara."

"Kids have the right idea," I said. "They fling themselves at fun with zero dignity. We should all be so brave."

He stared at me like I'd suggested we go run a marathon barefoot on broken glass. "Absolutely not."

"No sled?" I asked lightly. "Because I bet there's one in the garage. If there isn't, we improvise. Trash can lid, cardboard, plastic storage bin. I am nothing if not versatile."

"It's icy." His voice went flatter, edged with something that wasn't just annoyance. "I'm not breaking my neck so you can relive your childhood."

My chest squeezed. There it was, under the gruff—the pulse of fear he would never admit out loud.

"We'll pick a small hill," I said, keeping my tone calm, practical. "Nothing wild. You set the pace. We stop when you say stop."

His jaw flexed. "That's not the point."

"Sure it is." I slid another stitch off the needle, my hands steady even though my heart had kicked up a notch. "You need some fresh air. I need an excuse to justify the number of cinnamon rolls I just ate. It's a win-win."

He huffed out a humorless sound. "You say that like it's already happening."

I let my gaze flick over him—broad shoulders, strong arms, a body that could absolutely handle a half–baby hill in the backyard no matter what his brain told him—and then met his eyes again.

"I'm simply suggesting it." I held his gaze and shrugged. "You're the one deciding whether we chicken out."

His eyes narrowed, heat and something sharper sparking there. "I'm not afraid of a damn hill."

Wes had walked right into my challenge and couldn't back down. "I know. That's why we should go."

The quiet around us hummed and Wes considered my offer. Outside, the sunlight caught the slope behind the house and made it glow. Inside, Wes Vaughn glared at me like he wanted to say no on principle . . . and some traitorous part of him was already picturing the snow.

We stood at the top of the little hill behind Wes's house, breath puffing white, bundled within an inch of our lives. The yard dipped in a slow, steady slope toward the pines, the trees standing in a dark, watchful line. Beyond them, the narrow path cut toward the dunes and the water—a pale suggestion of the lake through the branches, gray blue and endless.

Getting out here had taken longer than I'd expected. Wes moved carefully on the snow, testing each step like the ground might give way. His boot would go down, then there'd be a subtle shift of his weight, his jaw working as he recalibrated. It was cautious, measured. Not timid. Just a man familiar with what happened when your footing betrayed you.

We'd found two sleds hanging in the garage rafters—one red, one blue, both a little scuffed but still solid. The blue one sat on the packed snow now, pointed downhill. Wes stood beside it like it had personally offended him.

"This is stupid," he muttered.

I flipped my scarf back over my shoulder. "You've said that three times."

"Because it's stupid three times."

His shoulders were tight beneath his coat, muscles bunched around his neck like his body was braced for impact before he'd even sat down. His gloved hand flexed on the rope at the front of the sled, testing it, then dropping it, then picking it up again.

"If I eat shit," he added, "I'm suing you."

His mouth twitched, like he wanted to be annoyed but the corner of it hadn't gotten the memo. He swallowed it down, eyes tracking the hill instead. My boots crunched as I stepped around him, checking the way the sled rested on the snow.

Up close, I could see the nerves he thought he was hiding. The way his thigh tightened when he shifted his weight. The faint hitch in his breath when he looked down the slope and then away.

I crouched beside the sled and straightened it out, nudging the runners into a cleaner line. "Sit," I said.

He shot me a look. "Don't talk to me like I'm the dog."

"Then stop acting like one," I said lightly. "Come on. It's a baby hill. If I rolled you down it in a sleeping bag, you'd just look cozy."

He huffed, but after a second he accepted my arm as he lowered himself down, movements stiff and careful. His hands went to either side of the sled, fingers pressing into the edges like he was anchoring himself.

I moved in front of him, boots on either side of the sled's nose, blocking his view of the drop so he had to look at me.

wHis eyes lifted, hood shadowing the top of his face. The wind had put color in his cheeks, making him look more alive than I'd seen him in weeks.

"This is a terrible idea," he said.

"It's a tiny hill and fresh powder."

"Things go wrong on tiny hills too."

"True," I said. "But I am very dedicated to not having to explain to my mother that I killed her favorite contractor in a low-impact sledding incident."

"Real comforting, Duchess."

"You're the one who's acting like a princess. Ready?"

He opened his mouth, about to start another argument or give an excuse to cover the fear I could feel coming off him in waves. "I still think this is a terrible idea."

"That's small-dick behavior, Vaughn." My eyebrows bounced as I lowered my gaze to meet his. "And I've seen it, so . . ."

The words hung there, suspended between us in the cold, white air.

His eyes went wide.

He just stared at me like I'd hauled off and slapped him across the face. Shock hit first, cracking through his expression so fast I almost bit my tongue to keep from laughing. Then it shifted—slow, dark, molten—into something else entirely.

Heat.

His gaze dropped, rapid and automatic, a flicker down my face, my coat, like he was replaying the memory whether he wanted to or not.

"Jesus, Clara." His voice came out rough. He stopped, swallowed, and tried again. "You can't just—"

"Name the thing we're both thinking about?" I lifted a shoulder. "Too late."

Something flickered in his eyes—half outrage, half arousal, full of things we had no business opening up out here in the snow.

"That is absolutely a violation of the roommate code,"

he said, trying for unaffected but landing somewhere closer to wrecked. "Weaponizing . . . that."

"Relax." I stood to my full height. "It was a compliment."

I had definitely crossed a line, but there was no taking it back. He knew I'd liked what I saw. I knew he knew. The truth of it sat there, hot and dangerous, right next to the fear he kept trying to dress up as irritation.

He opened his mouth, maybe to regain control again, maybe to throw another excuse on the fire.

I didn't let him.

"You're not afraid of this hill." I planted my hands on my hips. "You're scared of what happens if you trust your body and it lets you down again."

His jaw clenched so hard I could see the muscle jump. I thought he might actually tell me to go to hell and haul himself back up the slope.

The wind tugged at the ends of my scarf. Snow glittered around us, bright and indifferent.

"News flash, Vaughn," I said softly. "You already lived through the worst thing. This?" I motioned down the hill. "This is just gravity and bad decisions. It's choosing *fun*."

His gaze searched my face, something raw and aching in it.

I smiled, sharp and bright, letting the wicked edge slide back in. "Besides," I added, "if you bail now, I'm telling everyone in town you backed out after I complimented your dick."

He huffed out a startled sound that was almost a laugh, eyes squeezing shut for half a second like he couldn't believe me.

When they opened again, that hot, dark spark was still there.

"You're insane," he muttered.

"Yup," I said. "Ready?"

"No."

"Good enough."

Before he could protest, I planted both hands on the back of the sled and shoved.

It jerked forward, then launched, plastic scraping over packed snow before catching and flying. Wes's shout punched the air—half curse, half wild, startled sound that ricocheted off the trees and slid down my spine like a live current.

He shot down the hill in a spray of powder, shoulders hunched, hands gripping, the blue sled cutting a clean path through untouched white.

For one suspended heartbeat, he looked less like a man braced for disaster and more like someone who'd been yanked headfirst into something terrifying and maybe, just maybe, a little bit fun.

A laugh ripped out of me, bright and breathless.

I watched him hurtle toward the pines, my pulse racing to keep up, and knew with bone-deep certainty that whatever waited at the bottom of that hill, for both of us, there was no shoving this back uphill.

EIGHTEEN

WES

Snow screamed past my ears.

Cold air knifed down my throat, my eyes watered, and the sled beneath me rattled like it had a death wish. The ground fell away faster than my brain could catch up, the hill dropping out from under the runners in a long, slick rush that felt like falling and flying at the same time.

A shout scraped out of my chest, sharp and ripped bare. Half furious, half something a lot closer to exhilarated.

*Clara had shoved me.*

No warning. No countdown. Just that wicked little glint in her eyes, her mittened hands braced, and a hard push that sent me and the sled tipping over the edge before I could finish telling her what a bad idea this was.

The first second was nothing but panic.

Too fast. Too much. Snow a blur, the slope tilting wrong, my stomach lurching in my ribs. My brain went straight to the worst-case scenario, the way it did now without asking permission.

If I wiped out, if the sled slipped from under me, if my leg caught wrong, if I twisted—

The prosthetic thudded against the packed snow through the thin plastic, every vibration a reminder of what could go sideways. My hands clenched around the rope until my knuckles ached. My shoulders locked. Every muscle in my torso braced like I was waiting for impact.

The hill didn't care. It kept on dropping.

My body remembered anyway.

My weight shifted with the sled. My core tightened and leaned into the curve as the ground dipped. Snow sprayed at the sides in a cold arc when I hit a little rut, the runners bumping and skittering for half a heartbeat before finding their track again.

The leg held.

The strap bit into my residual limb, solid and familiar. My balance wobbled, but it didn't go out. The hill under me was steep enough to feel, but not steep enough to kill me. Wind tore at my eyes. My chest burned. The world narrowed to the hiss of snow, the pull of gravity, the drag of the rope in my fists.

Something in my ribs loosened.

A laugh punched out of me, raw and startled, like my body had gone ahead and decided before my brain.

The sound shocked me more than the ride.

I couldn't remember the last time anything had just . . . yanked a laugh out of me. No warning. No effort. Just that hot, wild sting of adrenaline hitting joy and sparking to life.

The sled hit the flat at the bottom with a jolt, skidding sideways as it lost momentum. Snow sprayed up over my boots and onto my jeans, freezing through the denim. The runners scraped and shuddered and then finally gave up, the whole thing jerking to a crooked stop in a shallow drift.

Silence rushed in, huge and bright, broken only by my own breathing.

My heart hammered against my ribs like it was trying to get free. The cold bit at my cheeks, my ears, even my teeth. My ass felt like I had just ridden over twenty land mines. The hand I'd wrapped around the rope was numb and burning at the same time.

I sat there anyway.

Alive. Upright. In one piece.

My mind did a quick inventory, automatic and practiced.

Leg? Still attached. No extra pull, no sharp twist, no screaming protest from the stump. Just the usual deep ache where bone met socket and the faint ghost buzz of a calf that wasn't there.

Back? Fine.

Head? Clear, aside from the left-behind echo of the shout that had ripped out of me.

I had not eaten shit on the way down the hill. I had not face-planted. I had not toppled sideways into some humiliating tangle of limbs and carbon fiber and sled.

The hill, from down here, looked . . . small. Manageable. The kind of slope I wouldn't have given a second thought a year ago. Now it felt like I'd just summited something in my own backyard.

Snow glowed around me, bright and untouched except for the track I'd carved through it. The pines stood sentry on either side, branches heavy with white, framing the cut of the path that led toward the dunes and the water beyond. The air had that sharp, clean bite that came only after fresh snowfall, like the world had been scrubbed down and reset.

A breath left me on a shaky, disbelieving exhale.

From the top of the hill, Clara whooped.

The sound knifed through the cold—bright and sharp

and so full of delight it made my chest jolt. I tipped my head back.

She was a small, bundled shape against the pale sky, hat crooked, scarf flapping, one mittened fist punched into the air like she'd just won something.

"You're alive!" she shouted. "I was only, like, eighty percent sure that would work out."

My laugh came out rough and still half breathless.

She just grinned wider, practically vibrating. Then she dropped onto her own sled with the easy confidence of someone who'd never had to think about how her body moved through space.

"Move over, old man," she shouted. "I'm coming for you."

Before I could tell her not to call me that, she pushed off.

Her sled didn't launch as hard as mine had. The plastic eased over the edge, then picked up speed, sliding down the track I'd carved. Snow kicked up past the runners. Clara shrieked, a high, delighted sound that broke into laughter halfway down. Her scarf streamed out behind her, hair spilling loose from under her hat, cheeks flushed bright pink from the cold and the rush.

The sight did something disorienting to my insides.

She wasn't careful. She wasn't calculating. She just . . . let go. She fully trusted the hill and the sled and the moment.

She also trusted me, by extension, because I was the idiot sitting at the bottom without a plan if she wiped out.

"Lean left!" I shouted when her sled started to drift toward the edge of the track.

She did, laughing the whole time, and the sled straightened, coasting the last few feet in a sideways skid that brought her right toward me.

The speed bled off fast on the flat. By the time she reached me, the sled was more drift than bullet, sliding in slow motion across the snow.

Reflex beat panic to the finish line.

My hand shot out and caught the front rope, fingers digging into the cold nylon as I hauled the sled to a stop. The plastic bumped my boot, and her knee knocked lightly against my shin.

We rocked once and settled.

Her breath came in frantic little puffs, fogging the air between us. A laugh still clung to her mouth, turning the corners up, but her eyes went straight to my leg.

"Holy shit," she breathed, the words spilling out on one exhale. "Your leg. Does it hurt?"

The question staggered me more than the ride.

My body did another quick systems check. Residual limb? Achy, yeah. Not screaming. Prosthetic? Secure. No hot spike of pain, no warning flare, just the usual background buzz of nerves that didn't know when to quit.

Shockingly okay.

Snow clung to the cuff of my jeans. My ass was numb. My heart was trying out for a rock band.

I snorted, still half laughing because I didn't know what else to do with the adrenaline. "No," I said, breath puffing white. "But you about gave me a heart attack. Christ, woman."

Clara's shoulders sagged with relief, then shimmied with leftover energy. She whooped into the sky—real and wild, head tipping back, the sound rolling out of her like it had been pressurized.

"I told you it would be fine," she said, giddy, eyes

sparkling. "Look at you. Sledding. Like a functioning human."

"Big talk from the menace who committed attempted murder via a plastic tray," I muttered, but it didn't have any teeth.

She grinned at me, so close now I could see individual snowflakes caught in the ends of her hair, melting against the knit of her hat. Her cheeks were bright, lips flushed, eyes blown wide with excitement and something that looked a hell of a lot like triumph.

She hadn't just wanted to drag me outside.

She'd wanted this. Proof. That I could still do something stupid and fun and not break.

The realization hit harder than the hill.

Clara shifted on the sled, boots digging into the snow so she could turn toward me. The movement brought her knee up against my thigh, a solid, casual press that my body treated like a live wire. She was close enough that her breath brushed my cheek when she laughed again, softer this time, still edged with adrenaline.

"You screamed," she said, eyes bright with mischief. "Just for the record."

"I did not scream," I grumbled.

Her grin sharpened. "There was definitely a suspiciously high-pitched noise."

"It was a perfectly reasonable exhale," I said. "Caused by you shoving a one-legged man off a hill."

"Oh, please." She rolled her eyes, the movement tugging her scarf askew and exposing the shallow curve of her throat above her collar. "If I'd waited for you to push off on your own, we'd still be at the top arguing about incline angles."

I snorted, even as my pulse picked up. "I guess you're not wrong."

Her sled had drifted crooked, so she planted one boot in the snow and scooted closer to brace herself, fingers catching on my jacket. Her gloved hand landed on my chest, palm flat over my sternum, just long enough to steady her balance.

The contact was light, fabric to fabric. My body didn't know the difference.

Heat punched through me, fast and hot, settling low between my thighs. My heartbeat kicked under her hand, thudding against my ribs hard enough I was half convinced she could feel it through the layers.

She must have, because her eyes flicked down to where her hand rested, then back up to my face. Some of the wild, delighted chaos in her expression shifted into something hotter, more focused.

"See?" she said quietly, fingers curling slightly in my jacket. "Still here. Fully functional."

My dick twitched at the way she said *fully functional*, the words slipping right under my skin like they belonged there. Every inch of me went too aware—of the damp chill seeping into my jeans, of the weight of the prosthetic anchored in the snow, of the warm, soft woman in front of me who had absolutely no business touching me like this and yet felt exactly right doing it.

Her mouth twitched. "Even if you did . . . *exhale* . . . in a cute little shrill."

"You keep talking like that, Duchess," I said, my voice coming out lower than I intended, "and hauling your ass back up this hill is going to count as PT."

She laughed, breath ghosting across my face. "Oh no," she gasped, mock dramatic. "Cardio and core strength? How will I ever survive?"

Her hand slid up a little as she pushed herself off the

sled, palm dragging up my chest to my shoulder in a way that was definitely not necessary for balance. Snow clung to my jacket where her fingers had been. My skin burned underneath.

She got her feet under her and straightened, then leaned over me to flick at my hat, knocking loose a clump of snow that had landed there during my uncontrolled descent.

"Hold still," she murmured.

Gloved fingers moved through my hair, brushing away the remaining flakes. The touch was quick, half practical, half an excuse, but it sent a sharp electric line straight down my spine. Her face was inches from mine—eyes intent, lips parted, cheeks flushed with cold and something that was no longer just victory.

I didn't lean away.

Couldn't.

My gaze dropped to her mouth, helpless. Pink and a little chapped from the wind, curved in a grin she was trying to tame and failing miserably. She smelled like cold air and sugar from breakfast, like my kitchen and my house and something that had started to feel dangerously close to home.

"Snow," she said, flicking one last bit off my shoulder. "You were starting to look like a lawn ornament."

"Rude," I muttered, but the word came out rough, the edge dulled by the way her hand lingered that extra heartbeat before dropping back to her side.

Her knee stayed pressed against my thigh. My glove brushed her boot where it rested in the snow. Tiny points of contact, stupidly small, each one dragging my focus back to the fact that we were alone and flushed and buzzing with too much energy that had nowhere to go.

Clara sank down to kneel in the snow beside me, jeans darkening where they touched the powder. She looked at me the way she had at the bottom of the hill—like I'd done something more impressive than gravity and plastic could account for.

"You did good, Vaughn," she said softly.

The praise hit with embarrassing force.

My throat went tight. "You assaulted me with recreational equipment," I replied, aiming for dry and landing somewhere closer to fondness. "Minimal property damage, though. I'll send you a bill."

Her smile turned slow, satisfied, like she heard everything I wasn't saying. "Pretty sure you owe me for that ride," she countered. "Consider it exposure therapy."

"Exposure therapy usually doesn't involve attempted homicide."

She tipped her head, eyes sliding over my face like she was trying to memorize something. "You're laughing," she said. "I'll accept the charges."

I hadn't realized I was. A low raw sound still lived in my chest, an echo of the one that had ripped out of me on the way down. It felt foreign and familiar all at once.

Her gaze fell briefly to my mouth, then jerked back up. The move was quick. It still sliced a hot line through me.

Clara Darling had dragged me down a hill and straight into a reality I'd been avoiding for months.

I was still capable of joy. I was still capable of wanting.

And right now both of those things were sitting in the snow in front of me, cheeks flushed, eyes bright, looking at me like I'd just done something that mattered.

## NINETEEN

"Up for another ride?"

Her words slid straight past my brain and landed in my dick. There was a whole different kind of ride I wanted her to take, and none of it involved a plastic sled.

"I just smoked you down this hill," I said, aiming for gruff but missing. "You really want a rematch already?"

Clara's laugh broke through the crisp air as she stood. We climbed back up the hill in a slow, clumsy truce with the snow—her boots punching neat prints, mine dragging a little wider, the sled rope gripped tight in my hand. My thigh burned halfway up. The socket pinched. None of it mattered as much as it would have yesterday.

I was alive in a way I hadn't been in a long time. Breathless, yes. Off-balance, sure. But alive.

At the top, Clara turned to face me, her breath puffing white between us. Snow clung to the ends of her hair where it stuck out from beneath her hat, melting into dark, damp strands against her cheeks. Her eyes were clear and wicked.

Her eyebrows wiggled as she lifted her chin. "Wanna race?"

"You really want to lose twice in one day?" I asked.

She snorted. "Please. You screamed the whole way down."

"I made a tactical noise," I said evenly. "Also, you pushed me."

"That sounds like an excuse, Vaughn." Her mouth curved, pure trouble. "On three?"

I rolled my eyes and dragged my sled into position beside hers, both noses aimed at the same cut in the snow where we'd carved a path.

My heart kicked harder.

Clara held my sled steady as I lowered myself down, careful with my leg, feeling for the right angle and the right weight distribution. The plastic flexed and groaned under me. I planted my boots in the snow ahead, ready to push off.

Clara dropped onto her own sled with a graceless plop that made me huff out a laugh. She wriggled to get comfortable, cheeks pink, hat slightly crooked, scarf askew. She looked like every winter afternoon I'd ever wanted and never thought I'd get again—messy and laughing and not careful with me in a way that felt like oxygen.

She glanced over, eyes skating down the line of my body like she was checking my posture . . . and maybe a little more. Heat slid under my skin.

"Ready?" she asked, voice breathless.

Not even close.

"Yep," I lied.

She wiggled her ass again as she stared down the hill. "Three . . . two . . . one—"

We pushed off at the same time.

Snow rushed beneath us in a hiss. The sleds lunged forward. The cold wind knifed at my ears, my eyes watering as the world narrowed to white and motion. My stomach dropped again, but the edge of panic that had nearly choked me the first time was dulled now—still there, still sharp, but layered with something else.

Clara's laughter cut through the air, bright and wild, riding just ahead of me. "Woo!"

Her sled shot slightly faster than mine, angled a little crooked as we barreled down. She twisted to look back over her shoulder at me, eyes dancing, mouth open in a grin that punched straight through my gut. The shift in her weight made the front of her sled wobble.

"Eyes forward," I yelled, even as a laugh tore out of me. "Drive, Duchess."

"Relax, old man," she called back. "I've got this—"

The sled hit a shallow drift and skipped sideways. She went weightless, momentum jerking her off the smooth track, her body pitching toward the softer snow at the edge of our carved path.

Instinct hit before thought.

I dug in my heel as best as I could, yanked my sled toward hers, and reached out. Our sleds collided with a hollow crack of plastic. Her sled spun, twirling sideways. Clara let out a startled shriek that dissolved into laughter even as she tipped.

My good leg braced. My prosthetic held. My arm hooked around her waist on pure muscle memory.

We toppled over.

Snow exploded around us in a spray of white. My back hit the drift first, the impact cushioned by a thick layer of powder. Cold shot up my spine. The plastic sled dug into my side. A grunt punched out of me as my lungs tried to catch up.

Then there was weight.

Clara landed half on top of me, half against my chest, all

warm limbs and cold gear and the familiar clatter of cheap plastic sleds knocking together. Her knee slotted between my thighs. Her gloved hands fumbled against my jacket, fingers bunching in the fabric. The world shuddered, then stilled, everything going oddly quiet under the thick winter air.

My arm was still around her waist, holding her tight to me from where I'd grabbed her. Her body fit along mine, soft and solid in all the ways that rewrote my understanding of gravity. Snow dusted her hat and the curve of her cheekbone, a few flakes caught in her lashes like glitter that hadn't finished falling.

She blinked down at me, breath puffing against my mouth, our noses almost brushing.

"Jesus," I breathed, pulse slamming so hard it felt like it shook the snow beneath us.

Her thighs tightened around my hip as she caught herself. The shift dragged her over the hard line pressing against my fly, and a flash of helpless arousal shot through me so fast it stole my breath. Every nerve I had zeroed in on where her body pressed into mine, cataloging heat and weight and the impossible fact that she was here, on top of me, laughing and alive and not flinching.

Her gaze flicked down, catching on my mouth for one raw, naked second.

The temperature between us changed.

The laughter in her eyes went molten, something darker and softer bleeding in at the edges. Her hand on my chest tightened, glove creaking as she fisted the front of my jacket like she wasn't sure whether she meant to push me away or pull me closer.

The snow around us seemed to fall quieter. The whole

world narrowed to the four inches of air between our mouths.

I could feel her breath ghost against my lower lip—warm and quick. Her nose brushed mine on a tiny exhale, an accidental nudge that knocked something loose in my chest.

We went utterly still.

Her face was right there, framed in light and snow and flushed skin, her lips parted on a breath she hadn't finished taking. My fingers flexed at her waist, thumb digging into the thick fabric of her coat, like I needed to convince myself she was real and not something my lonely, broken brain had conjured up on a hill.

There was nowhere to look but at her.

Nowhere to go but forward.

I didn't move. I couldn't breathe.

We just stared, both of us breathing hard, the slope and the pines and the whole frozen world dropping away until there was nothing but her face hovering over mine.

Her mouth curved, breathless and bright. "You didn't die or lose another limb," she said with a laugh, voice soft and shaky. "Congrats."

"Yet," I managed, but it came out rough, more gravel than a joke.

She huffed another laugh, shoulders shaking. Then, before my brain could catch up, she leaned in and pressed a kiss to my cheek.

It was quick, clumsy—half a peck and half a victory stamp. Her lips were hot against my cold skin, soft and sure, the press lingering just long enough to burn.

My lungs forgot how to function.

She pulled back an inch, eyes wide like she'd surprised herself too. We were still close enough that her breath slid over my mouth, warm in the freezing air. Something low inside me snapped the fragile leash I'd been holding on myself since the day she walked through my front door with her suitcases and that damn diamond ring.

My hand moved before my good sense could.

Fingers slid up into the loose hair at the nape of her neck, the glove rough against silk-soft strands. I felt the small, startled shiver run through her when my palm settled there, thumb brushing the warm line of her skin just under the edge of her hat.

She froze—then didn't move away.

Her gaze locked onto mine, pupils blown wide, the gray blue of her irises eaten up by black. Every version of *What the hell are you doing, man?* screamed in my head at once.

Hayes's face. Clara's ring. Our deal. Every line I wasn't supposed to cross.

"Fuck it." I tightened my grip and drew her down the rest of the way, closing that last impossible distance.

Our mouths met like they'd been headed there from the first second she walked into my house. The first brush of her lips against mine was soft, almost questioning. Then she made a sound—a tiny, helpless whimper right into my mouth—and whatever restraint I thought I had went up in flames.

I kissed her like a starving man.

My other hand found her hip and hauled her the last few inches onto me, dragging her fully into my body. Her chest pressed against my chest, thighs slotting over mine, the weight of her settling exactly where my body wanted her. Her mouth parted under mine, giving, opening, inviting.

I took the invitation.

My tongue slid against hers, slow at first, relearning the shape of a kiss after too damn long without one. She tasted like cold air and cinnamon sugar, sweet and sharp. Her fingers curled into my coat, clenching in the fabric over my shoulders like she needed something to hold on to while I devoured her.

Heat roared through me, hot enough to make the winter air feel irrelevant.

She shifted to get closer, and her hip rolled right over my cock, hard and pressing against the fly of my jeans. The drag of her body over mine sent a white-hot bolt straight through my spine. A groan tore out of my chest before I could swallow it.

Her answering whimper shot straight to my dick.

Clara leaned into me instead of away, kissing me back with a kind of hungry relief that had my head spinning. She met every stroke of my tongue with her own, matched every angle, like we'd been doing this for years instead of dancing around it for days.

Snow crunched under us as we moved, coats rasping, sleds shifting. My hand at her hip tightened, dragging her even closer, anchoring her there so she could feel exactly what she was doing to me. My thumb slipped under the edge of her jacket, found the warm curve of her waist through her sweater, the heat of her bleeding into my palm.

She shivered like I'd touched bare skin.

"Wes," she breathed against my mouth, my name breaking on the syllable, half moan, half laugh, the sound tipping something over inside me.

I angled my head and deepened the kiss, taking more, giving more, letting myself want without throttling it for the first time in months. She met me there, mouth fierce and greedy, like she'd been holding back, too, and had finally decided she was done.

Everything narrowed to her.

Not the sled. Not the snow. Not the leg, or the hill, or the thousand ways this could go wrong.

Just Clara's mouth under mine.

Clara's body pressing me into the snow like she was staking a claim.

Clara's breath mixing with mine, her hands sliding up to bracket my jaw through my hood, holding my face like she was just as terrified to let go.

A rush of emotion punched through the heat—sharp and terrifying in its own right.

Relief, bone deep and staggering, that I could still do this. That my body was good for more than pain and maintenance and getting from point A to point B without falling.

Gratitude, ugly and bright, that she'd pushed me, that she'd dragged me out here and told me my fear was small-dick behavior and meant it in the exact way I needed to hear.

Hope, the most dangerous of all, curling low and stubborn in my chest at the feel of her kissing me like she'd wanted this just as badly.

For the first time since the accident, I didn't feel like a man managing symptoms or surviving another day.

Kissing Clara Darling in the snow, with her body pressed tight to mine and her mouth wrecking me in the best possible way, I felt alive.

TWENTY

CLARA

COLD AIR BURNED in my lungs, each breath a sharp drag, but everywhere else was heat—wild and disorganized, pulsing under my skin like I'd swallowed a live wire. Snow prickled along the back of my neck, sneaking under my coat and melting down my spine. I barely registered it.

All my nerve endings had narrowed to two points.

His hand on my hip.

His palm at the back of my neck.

Wes's fingers were still there, heavy and warm through my coat, holding me like he hadn't decided yet whether to let go. His body was solid beneath me, the sled buried somewhere under the tangle of our limbs, his chest rising hard against mine as we tried to remember how to breathe.

The first coherent thought that made it through the static was not *What did I just do?*

It was *Oh my god, I want more.*

Heat throbbed low in my core, deep and insistent. My thighs pressed tight around his like they were trying to keep him there, my muscles aware of every inch of him in a way my brain absolutely could not handle. I could feel the imprint of his mouth on mine, the echo of his tongue against mine, the way he'd groaned into the kiss like I'd given him back a piece of himself.

My fingers were still fisted in the front of his coat, knuckles buried in the thick fabric like I'd gone down with the ship and taken him with me.

*This is bad. This is so, so bad.*

"So that was . . ." My voice came out high and breathless, too bright, like I was narrating someone else's choices. "Probably a terrible idea."

It sounded like a joke, but I used it like armor.

Under me, Wes's chest expanded with a harsh inhale. His hand didn't immediately leave my hip. His fingers flexed once like he was testing his own grip on reality, and then loosened.

"Yeah." His breath puffed white between us, the word rough, humorless. "Definitely . . . not smart."

The speed of his agreement hit my ribs like a small, mean punch.

I nodded so quickly I probably looked like a bobble-head. "Right. Of course. Adrenaline." My laugh came out thin and skittered off into the open air. "Post-sledding brain malfunction."

My body had the audacity to disagree.

Heat pulsed between my legs, sharp and rhythmic, like my nerves were frayed. My nipples dragged against the inside of my bra, tight and aching, every part of me cataloging the solid weight of him beneath me, the way his thigh was still slotted between mine, the way his mouth had felt like a problem I wanted to have again.

His thumb dragged once at my waist, a tiny, traitorous stroke I might've imagined if my heartbeat wasn't pounding in my ears at the exact same time.

On the surface, we were two adults acknowledging a mistake.

Inside, I knew that wasn't what any of that had been.

I pried my hands free of his coat one finger at a time and pushed up, snow squeaking under my knee. The world tilted as I scrambled off his lap, boots slipping before they caught, heart still trying to climb out of my throat.

"Okay," I blurted, brushing at my sleeves like that would erase the last sixty seconds. Snowflakes scattered off my coat and onto his chest. "Well. You're alive. Sledding achievement unlocked."

*Shut up, Clara.*

I swiped at the snow clinging to my legs, dusting it off a little too hard, like I could scrub away the way my body was still buzzing. My pulse hadn't gotten the memo that we were going back to being reasonable human beings.

Behind me, I felt more than saw him sit up. I heard the low rustle of his coat and the faint scrape of the sled against packed snow.

I didn't look at his mouth.

I didn't look at his hands.

I fixed my eyes on the hill instead—the track we'd carved through the untouched white, the faint groove where the sled had flown, the path that had led directly to me doing the exact thing I'd promised myself I would not do.

"Come on," I said, voice wobbling only a little as I grabbed the sled rope. "Let's get back before we freeze to death."

*Or do anything else incredibly stupid.*

My heart thudded hard and hot against my ribs.

I turned up the hill, snow crunching under my boots, trying to move like we'd just survived a minor collision and nothing else—like my mouth hadn't belonged to his a few seconds ago, like I wasn't already wondering how I was supposed to live in the same house as a man whose kiss felt like the first good decision I'd made in a long time.

Every step back up the hill felt like trying to walk a straight line after spinning in circles.

The sled rope bit into my glove where I'd wrapped it around my hand, the plastic dragging over the packed track we'd carved. My thighs burned from the climb. My lungs stung from the cold and from the fact that my heart had not calmed the hell down.

My lips tingled. My mouth tasted like him. Every time my brain relaxed for half a second, the kiss replayed in high definition.

His hand on my neck, fingers spread, holding me like he meant it.

The rough drag of his mouth over mine, hungry and sure and nothing like an accident.

The way his body had pressed up into mine, like his restraint had finally snapped and I'd been standing on the fault line.

Beside me, Wes tromped up the hill in stubborn, measured strides. His sled rope looped around his hand too. His breath came out in steady, controlled exhales, fogging in front of his face. His jaw was set, the line of his mouth back to neutral like he hadn't just kissed me so thoroughly I was going to be mentally revisiting it in the nursing home.

We crested the slope and hit the flatter stretch of yard. The house glowed at the far end of the property—big windows lit warm, roof shouldering a fresh cap of snow, smoke ghosting from the chimney. The path we'd trudged out was already softening, edges blurring as flakes drifted down again.

The warmth of the house hit me like a wall.

The door shut behind us with a soft thud, swallowing the bright white world and replacing it with heat and the faint smell of breakfast that had sunk into the walls.

I kicked my boots against the mat, snow thudding off in clumps. Mittens went into my pocket. My fingers felt clumsy, half frozen, half fried from everything else.

My mouth still tingled.

Wes stepped in behind me, crowding the narrow mudroom with big shoulders and cold air, the whisper of his breath brushing the back of my neck as he reached past to shove the door all the way closed. His coat rustled. Snow slid off his sleeves and hit the floor with soft, wet plops.

We were both suddenly very interested in the practical business of having bodies.

I peeled my hat off, static making my hair lift and cling in a chaotic halo. A chunk fell into my eyes and I shoved it back, fingers trembling just enough that I hoped it looked like cold instead of kissing-your-brother's-best-friend-on-a-hill shakes.

Across from me, Wes's movements were slower than usual as he worked his coat off his shoulders. Controlled. Deliberate. I watched the way his jaw tightened when he tugged his sleeve free, like his muscles were protesting the extra work.

He was steady, though.

Solid, even as he shifted his weight to toe his boots off. The prosthetic thudded lightly on the mat. No flinch. No wince. A small, stupid coil of pride unfurled in my chest.

We both bent to wrestle with laces at the same time and nearly knocked heads.

"Sorry," I blurted, jerking back.

"You're fine," he said, and his hand bumped my shoulder in the tight space as he straightened.

Every brush, every contact in the cramped mudroom felt magnified. His arm along mine when he reached for the hook. My hip grazing his when I stepped sideways. The ghost of his mouth still imprinting heat on my lips while the air around us tried to pretend nothing had happened.

Instinct screamed at me to bolt.

Up the stairs. Into the safety of my room. Pull the covers over my head and pretend the kiss had been a weird, hyper-specific hallucination brought on by cold exposure and sled-related near-death experiences.

Greg's face surfaced for a heartbeat—not as some great lost love, but as the friend I'd almost married, knowing he wanted a different kind of life and a different kind of love than I could ever give him. I'd called it helping, called it practical, while I smiled and said I was fine and let us both hide behind a lie until it had nearly swallowed me whole.

All those truths I'd been too scared to say—*this isn't the life I want, this isn't the right kind of love for either of us*—had burned the back of my throat for months. I refused to make myself that small ever again.

My heart hammered, but I squared my shoulders anyway.

If we left this hanging with nothing labeled, I was going to implode in on myself like a star.

"So," I said finally, pitching my voice a little too loud, a little too bright, the way you do when you're trying to sound casual and land somewhere near deranged instead. "We're good to blame adrenaline, right? Near-death sledding. Temporary lapse in judgment."

I winced at my own phrasing.

*Lapse in judgment. Great. Nothing sexier than calling a man's mouth a mistake.*

Snow squeaked under my boots as we walked. I thought

maybe he wouldn't answer, that he'd just let it hang there in the air like a weird-shaped balloon and pretend he hadn't heard me.

Then Wes huffed out a breath that sounded suspiciously like a humorless laugh.

"Pretty sure we were nowhere near death," he said, avoiding my eyes. "But yeah. Adrenaline works. We don't have to make it a thing."

It was absurd how much those words managed to sting.

My body had absolutely made it a thing. My pulse, my mouth, the way every nerve ending had sat up and taken notes the second his tongue slid against mine—they'd all voted unanimously. This was very much a thing.

"Look, I just—" The words tangled, my tongue tripping over all the versions I couldn't say. *I kissed you because I wanted to. I kissed you because you laughed and it broke me open. I kissed you because I haven't wanted anything this much in a long time and that scared the shit out of me.*

His mouth twitched like he wanted to smile and didn't trust himself with it. He shrugged out of his coat the rest of the way and hung it on a hook, shoulders tightening under the motion.

"I just mean," he said, looking past me at the kitchen doorway, "we don't have to overcomplicate it. It happened. Adrenaline. Snow. Whatever."

There was that word again. *Whatever.* Like this wasn't currently rearranging my internal organs.

I cleared my throat and tried again. "The last thing I want is to screw up your friendship with my brother."

There it was. The safe excuse. The shield I could hold between us and pretend it wasn't welded to my own fear.

Hayes's face flashed across my mind—protective, tired, carrying his own stack of guilt about Wes that he never quite put down. The idea of being the reason things got weird between them made my stomach flip in a way that had nothing to do with the sled.

If I wrecked this, I didn't just lose a kiss.

I risked Wes retreating right back into his house-ghost version. I risked Hayes looking at me like I'd broken something fragile he'd trusted me with. I risked this tiny, flickering version of progress we'd somehow stumbled into.

Wes's jaw flexed, a muscle jumping near his ear. He finally glanced over, his gaze skimming my face quick, like a touch he didn't trust himself to hold.

"You're not going to screw up my friendship with Hayes," he said. "I've done a decent job of that all on my own."

The words landed heavier than he probably meant them to.

"If this blows up," I said quietly, "I'm the one who lit the match. Again." The last word slipped out before I could stuff it back down where it belonged, somewhere under bad memories and broken engagements.

Wes looked at me then.

Really looked.

His eyes were darker in the hallway's weak light, the color deep behind the sweep of his lashes. I thought I saw something soften there, something almost tender.

"Hey," he said, brow furrowing. "You didn't do anything wrong."

I huffed out a brittle laugh. "We definitely did something."

He exhaled, a humorless little breath. "Yeah. We did."

His hand went to the back of his neck, fingers digging in like he needed the anchor. "I'm just saying . . . if anyone's a bad idea here, it's me."

Something in my chest pinched.

"Don't," I said automatically. "Don't do that."

"Do what?" He leaned a shoulder against the door-frame, looking suddenly, unbearably tired. "Tell the truth?"

He flicked a glance toward the window, where the hill was just visible through the glass—our carved tracks already filling back in with white.

He exhaled through his nose, a white cloud dissipating. "Besides," he added, tone shifting into something drier, something with an edge. "You just dragged a half-functional contractor down a hill. That is not anyone's dream rebound."

The word *rebound* hit like a tiny hammer—knocking into Greg's ghost and that ugly, lingering belief that maybe that was all I'd ever be good for. The girl who looked good on someone's arm until she didn't. The girl who didn't see the cracks of her misjudgment until she was standing in the rubble.

I snorted, because humor was easier than bleeding. "Wow. Okay. Rude to both of us."

His mouth twitched, like he hadn't expected that answer. A tiny flash of apology crossed his face. "That's not what I meant."

"I know what you meant," I said, sighing. "I just . . . for the record, I'm not looking for a rebound."

His jaw worked, like there were words he wanted to say and didn't trust. "Good," he said finally. "You shouldn't be."

He scrubbed a hand over his face. When he dropped it, his expression had settled back into something wry and self-directed.

"I'm still figuring out how to walk down a hill without doing the splits," he said quietly. "I don't have any business figuring out *you*."

The honesty in it hit me harder than the self-deprecation.

It wasn't just that he thought he was a bad bet. He believed it. Deep down at the marrow level.

I wanted to argue and tell him he'd handled that hill just fine. To tell him I'd seen him laugh and felt something in me unclench like it had been waiting months for that exact sound.

I didn't trust my voice not to crack open with too much.

So I nodded slowly instead, chewing the inside of my cheek.

"Okay," I said finally. The word felt like walking barefoot over gravel. "So. We blame adrenaline. Snow. A temporary . . . brain malfunction."

His mouth curved, just barely, like the phrase amused him in spite of everything. "Sure," he said. "One-time post-sledding brain malfunction."

"We're adults," I added, hearing the faint hysterical edge under my own voice and hating it. "We can be . . . roommates. Normal. Friends."

*Friends* tasted complicated on my tongue. Too small for what my body wanted. Too big for what my fear would allow.

Wes's throat bobbed. His gaze flicked to my mouth for a fraction of a second before he caught himself. "Yeah," he said, voice low. "Friends."

The word landed between us like a stone in fresh snow. Soft on the surface. Heavy underneath.

Silence stretched, thick and humming.

I needed to cut it before it swallowed me whole.

"New rule," I said, dredging up a smile and pointing it at the counter like I was issuing a decree to the kitchen instead of the man who'd just kissed me senseless. "No making out in the snow."

One corner of his mouth tugged higher. The House Rules list on the fridge flashed in my mind—his handwriting under mine. A weird, paper-thin truce.

"Probably for the best," he said. "Snow's cold as hell anyway."

Heat flashed over my skin at the memory of his mouth. The way nothing about that kiss had felt cold.

"Total drawback," I managed. "Very impractical."

His eyes crinkled, the ghost of a real smile haunting the edges. For half a second, we were standing there in the hallway with a shared joke instead of a shared disaster, and it almost felt easy again.

Almost.

I took a step back, my heel brushing the first stair. "I'm gonna, um . . . change," I said, gesturing vaguely upstairs. "Get warm."

"Yeah," he said, pushing off the doorframe. "I'll make coffee."

We moved at the same time and had to do that awkward little shuffle to get past each other in the narrow space. His shoulder brushed mine. The side of my hip clipped his thigh. The contact was quick and fully clothed and somehow still made my stomach swoop.

I didn't look at him as I climbed, but I could feel his gaze on my back, hot and questioning and careful, like he was trying to memorize the distance we'd just agreed to put between us.

At the top of the stairs, I paused, fingers curving around the banister for a second longer than necessary.

My lips still felt swollen. My body still thrummed with the echo of his hands.

*Friends,* I reminded myself.

Right.

My heart rolled its eyes and continued doing cartwheels as I walked down the hall, careful like the floor might crack if I stepped wrong.

I shut my bedroom door with more force than necessary and pressed my back to it, like I needed the solid wood to keep me from sliding straight down to the floor.

The house was quiet again. No sleds. No shouting. No wild, reckless laughter ripped out of Wes Vaughn like the sun finally remembered how to rise. Just my heartbeat thudding in my ears and the echo of his mouth still humming under my skin.

I pushed off the door and crossed to the bed on autopilot, dropping face-first onto the covers. The comforter smelled like laundry detergent and the faintest hint of hay from Elodie's farm, familiar and safe in a way my body absolutely did not feel. I flipped onto my back and stared up at the ceiling, trying very hard not to replay the last hour and failing almost immediately.

Snow spraying up around us. His laugh cracking open the cold. The weight of him beneath me, solid and unyielding. The way his hand had fisted in my coat and dragged me down without hesitation. The low, wrecked sound he'd made into my mouth like kissing me was both a relief and a problem.

Heat curled low in my belly. My thighs ached in a way that had very little to do with climbing the hill. I pressed the heels of my hands over my face and a soft, helpless noise escaped into my palms anyway.

"I told him it was a terrible idea while I was still tasting him," I muttered, disgusted and a little impressed with myself.

Hayes's face flickered in my mind—how he looked at Wes, the way he carried his guilt like it was welded to his bones. The thought of being the reason something cracked there made my stomach flip. I thought of Greg too—his quiet judgment, his colleagues' mocking comments about my work, the way I'd ignored every red flag until they were the only color left. One failed engagement under my belt and here I was, catching feelings for a man who was healing from the kind of trauma that rewrote a person.

Every time I tried to focus on the reasons this was a bad idea—Hayes, the accident, Wes's recovery, the fact that I lived across the hall from him like some walking temptation—my brain cut back to the feeling of his tongue sliding against mine. His hand on my neck.

We'd made an agreement. We'd been very mature and rational in the mudroom. Adrenaline. One-off. Brain malfunction. Roommates. Friends.

I rolled onto my side, then onto my back again, the word *friends* rattling around in my chest like it had no idea where to land.

*Friends*, I told myself again.

Friends weren't supposed to feel like that.

## TWENTY-ONE

WES

THE HOUSE FELT wrong the second Clara walked away.

I stood there in silence, snow melting in small, dark circles on the mat, breathing like I'd just run a mile instead of walked across the yard. Frigid air still clung to my clothes. My lungs burned in that sharp, clean way from laughing too hard in the cold.

My lower lip was tender, skin stretched tight, like it remembered the exact shape of hers and was insulted we'd stopped. Every time I swallowed, I tasted winter air and Clara Darling, the faint ghost of her breath and the mint on her tongue.

My dick hadn't gotten the memo that we were *friends* now either. It sat there at half-mast in my pants, heavy and stubborn, throbbing in time with the mental highlight reel my brain insisted on playing.

Her weight settling on top of me.

Her fingers in my coat.

The way she'd whimpered when I dragged her closer, like she'd been waiting for me to lose control.

It was adrenaline. A one-off. Roommates. Friends.

I repeated the words in my head like a script I'd been handed and told to memorize.

*Terrible idea. Adrenaline. Roommates. Friends.*

My body's answer was simple and obscene.

*Let's do it again.*

I huffed out a frustrated breath, dragging a hand over my face, and turned toward the kitchen like movement alone could burn it off.

Evidence of her was everywhere.

Her wet boot prints tracked across the tile—small, messy, toes pointed a little inward at the doorway where she'd paused. A single wavy hair clung to the shoulder of my coat, catching the light when I shifted. Her knitting shit still occupied the armchair—yarn a tangled, angry ball, needles stabbed through it like she'd tried to pin it into submission and walked away mid-fight.

I checked the clock on the stove—PT in forty minutes.

For weeks, maybe months now, the idea of leaving the house at all had been a fight. Today, the thought of staying in it—with Clara upstairs, flushed from sledding and still tasting like the best part of my life—felt like the real danger.

I needed some distance. Neutral ground. Fluorescent lights and ugly rubber flooring and someone telling me what to do with my traitorous body.

I shrugged the rest of the way into my coat, fingers clumsy on the zipper. I was tired, but my leg felt good—too good. The residual ache was low, manageable, more of a hum than a scream. My balance still buzzed with the memory of the hill, the way the sled had carried me and my body had remembered how to trust movement instead of bracing for impact.

She'd done that. Clara had shoved me down a hill and kissed me like it was the most natural thing in the world.

The thought made my chest tighten and my cock twitch, which was exactly why I needed to get the hell out of here.

I jammed my keys into my pocket and moved toward the stairs, my prosthetic ticking faintly against the hardwood. Halfway there I hesitated, my hand braced on the newel post.

*I could just leave.*

She'd figure it out when she heard the truck. Less conversation. Less room to say something I couldn't take back. I shook my head. That was a coward's move and exactly the kind of thing that would put that kicked-puppy look in her eyes the next time she saw me.

*Adrenaline. One-off. Roommates. Friends.*

Friends didn't sneak out like teenagers after getting caught.

My jaw flexed. I tilted my head up toward the second floor.

"Clara?" My voice boomed up the staircase.

There was a beat of silence, then the thud of hurried footsteps. Her door opened, hinges soft. "Yeah?" she called back, closer now.

She appeared at the top of the stairs a moment later, one hand on the railing, hair pulled into a ponytail that was already working pieces free. Her cheeks were still pink from the cold. Her mouth looked a little swollen, like mine.

My stomach dropped straight through the floor.

*Focus.*

"I've got PT," I said, clearing my throat. "I'm gonna head out."

A small line formed between her brows. "Oh." She came down two steps, socked feet careful on the wood. "Let me grab my shoes. I can—"

"I've got it," I cut in, faster than I meant to. Her eyes flicked up, surprised. I forced my shoulders into a shrug that felt like it belonged to someone else. "They've got parallel bars and ugly carpet. I think I can manage the parking lot."

The joke landed flat between us.

Clara paused on the stair, fingers tightening around the banister. The shift in her face was tiny—just the barest dimming of something bright, a shadow that crossed her eyes before she caught it and smoothed it away.

"Oh," she said again, lighter this time. "Sure. Yeah. Of course."

She tried for a smile and it almost worked.

Guilt punched me square in the chest.

She was reading it exactly the way I'd earned—the guy who'd kissed her like a starving man, then agreed it was a bad idea, then made sure he didn't have to be trapped in a car with her.

Self-preservation tasted an awful lot like cowardice.

I hooked my fingers tighter around my keys so I wouldn't reach for her. "I'll be back in a couple of hours," I said. "Try not to strangle the yarn while I'm gone."

Her mouth twitched, a flicker of real amusement slipping through. "No promises."

For half a second we just looked at each other—her on the stairs, me at the bottom, a whole house and one very stupid rule between us.

*Roommates. Friends.*

I turned before I could wreck it any more than I already had.

The front door clicked shut behind me, the cold outside hitting my face like a reprimand, and I walked to the truck, telling myself distance was the right call.

My body throbbed with a different opinion all the way down the driveway.

The drive into town was only fifteen minutes, but it felt like an hour.

My hand sat at ten and two on the steering wheel, knuckles pale, jaw locked so tight my molars ached. The heater hummed, blowing warm air at my face. Outside, the world was all white and gray—plowed banks along the road, bare trees, the occasional smear of lake effect hanging low over the fields.

Inside my head, it was Clara.

Clara on the hill, cheeks flushed, laugh breaking open the air.

Clara in my lap, snow in her hair, mouth hot and eager on mine.

The soft, desperate little sound she'd made when I dragged her down against me, the way her whole body had gone pliant and hungry at the same time. The snap of control I'd felt when she opened for me like she'd been waiting.

My dick had not mellowed in the intervening drive time.

It had settled into a steady, sullen throb that made every bump in the road a reminder. The memory played on a loop, high definition and unhelpful—her taste, her fingers in my coat, the exact grind of her hips when she'd tried to get closer.

I adjusted myself once, muttering a curse, and focused on the double yellow lines.

*Absolutely not.*

There was wanting, and then there was jerking off to your best friend's sister, then having to look her in the eye over coffee and pretend you hadn't. I'd already checked off the first two, and I was barely holding the line on the third.

By the time I pulled into the PT lot, my shoulders were so tight it felt like my traps were welded to my neck. I killed the engine, sat there with my hands still clamped on the wheel, and took one slow breath.

Inside, the clinic smelled like disinfectant and a weird mix of lemon cleaner and burned beans. Country radio murmured from a wall speaker. Jess looked up from her tablet when I came in, purple sneakers, dark hair in a messy knot, eyebrows lifting in a way that said she was cataloging every inch of my posture already.

"Well, look who it is," she said. "You're early. Feeling ambitious or just sick of your own house?"

"Little column A, little column B," I muttered, signing myself in.

She gave me a look that hit more than muscle and bones. "Good. Let's take advantage before you remember you hate me."

The routine was familiar by now. Parallel bars. Warm-up laps. Stretch, then strength. I moved through it the way I always did—mechanical at first, then a little looser once my body remembered it knew how.

Only today something was . . . different.

When Jess sent me toward the ramp—a gentle incline up to a platform, the kind of thing that had felt like Everest the first few weeks I'd been here—my stomach didn't imme-diately seize.

"Same as last time," she said, stepping back. "Up and down. Focus on the step-through. Don't stare at your feet."

I set my prosthetic on the ramp, weight shifting forward. That old spike of fear flashed, quick and automatic, like a faulty alarm.

Steep. Slippery. Lose your footing, and you eat shit in front of everyone.

Except it wasn't steep. The rubber was tacky. My knee locked the way it was supposed to, the microprocessor in the joint doing its quiet, expensive job.

My body remembered the hill. The drop. The speed.

And the part where I hadn't fallen.

I exhaled and took another step. Then another.

I pivoted carefully and came back down, focusing on the smooth roll of heel to toe, the way my weight transferred. There was a small wobble near the bottom, a tiny hitch where old panic tried to claw its way back in, but my core caught it, the rest of my muscles stepping up and doing what they were supposed to do.

Jess's voice came from my left. "Your balance and confidence are up across the board today. Whatever you've been doing?" she said, sounding annoyingly satisfied. "Keep doing it."

Clara's laugh exploded in my head. Her hand on my chest when she shoved me. The world dropping away. The sled flying. Her straddling me in the snow ten seconds later.

*Yeah. About that.*

"Guess I'm just . . . getting used to it." My voice came out rough as I stepped off the ramp, flexing my foot to shake out the phantom fizz. "The leg's having a good day."

"Your leg," she said, crossing her arms, "is doing exactly what you ask it to do when you trust it. That's you, not the hardware."

Out of the corner of my eye, I saw some guy on the bike glance over like he wished we'd lower our voices before the breakthrough therapy hit him by association.

Jess ignored him. "You've seemed more engaged the last few sessions," she added, tapping something into her tablet.

"Less staring at the ceiling like you're making a grocery list while I talk. Are you getting out more? Seeing people?"

I cleared my throat, fighting the heat crawling up the back of my neck. I didn't want to lie to Jess. "Just . . . winter chores," I said. "Stuff around the house."

Jess's mouth twitched like she'd heard exactly how full of shit that was. "Well, whatever 'stuff' is, it's working. Your gait's smoother. Your reflexes on the balance board were better than last time. You even talked more than five words today."

"Careful," I said. "You're going to ruin your hard-ass reputation if you start complimenting people."

She snorted. "Oh, don't worry. I'm about to kick your ass on the stairs. Then you'll remember you hate me."

She wasn't wrong—the stairs sucked.

The problem was simple.

What I'd been doing was letting Clara Darling into my house and my head and my hands. Letting her drag me down hills and kissing her breathless in the snow.

The last thing I needed was permission to want more of that.

I MADE it almost all the way back through town before the universe decided to pile on.

Snow flurried lazily across the windshield as I rolled past the hardware store and the coffee place, heading for the turn that would take me back to the house. My leg ached in that used way Jess would've been proud of. My brain still hummed with Clara.

Which was exactly when I saw Hayes.

He was in front of the coffee shop, standing by his truck

with his arms spread, coat half unzipped, shirt absolutely drenched down the front. Steam rose off the splatter on the snow at his boots. His truck door was hanging open, cab light on, keys nowhere in sight.

*Of course.*

I slowed automatically, taking in the picture—Hayes glowering at the sky like it had personally wronged him, coffee dripping off the brim of his hat, one glove in the slush at his feet.

I rolled the window down. "You lose a fight with a latte?"

He cut me a look, his scowl deep. "Black ice. The cup went flying. Took the hit like a champ." He glanced down at himself. "My dignity did not."

A laugh punched out of me, quick and unplanned. "Are you planning to stand here and steam until spring?"

He sighed, long suffering, and kicked at the snow like it had started it. "Keys slid under the truck somewhere. I'm gonna be late to my meeting." He jerked his chin toward my passenger door. "You offering or just heckling?"

"Get in, dumbass."

He rounded the front of the truck, boots sliding once on the packed snow, hands pinwheeling before he caught himself on my hood.

There was a sweatshirt crumpled on the back seat. "There's a clean one back there," I said as he climbed in, already peeling his wet jacket off.

He twisted, grabbed the sweatshirt, and hauled it over his head, shucking the soaked shirt in the process. The cab filled with the familiar scent of coffee and sawdust and the guy who'd had my back since we were two idiots with learner's permits.

"Appreciate it," he muttered, dragging the hem down

and raking a hand through his hair. "It's been a shit morning."

"Shocking," I deadpanned, pulling away from the curb. Everything Hayes touched turned to chaos. "Should've seen it coming when you left the house."

He huffed, the edge of a grin tugging at his mouth. "Speaking of leaving the house . . ." His tone shifted. "How's she doing? Clara. She settled in okay?"

My grip on the wheel tightened.

*You mean: How's the little sister I had my tongue in two hours ago while pretending it's me doing her the favor?*

"She's fine," I said too quickly. I forced my shoulders to loosen, eyes on the road. "Already reorganized my kitchen and put marching orders on the fridge."

He snorted. "Sounds about right."

I needed a way out of this conversation—and fast. "She, uh . . . has some photo shoot thing she's planning at the farm. A bridal something-or-other. Looks like she's got it handled."

Hayes nodded, jaw working once like something in that eased a knot I couldn't see. "Yeah. That tracks. She always lands on her feet." He stared out at the snow-slick road, then blew out a breath. "I'm really glad she's with you, man."

The words settled like cement in the cab.

"I trust you," he added.

My stomach dropped.

He didn't say it like a big thing. No dramatic pause or meaningful stare. Just a simple fact tossed into the air between us, like it weighed nothing. Like it wasn't currently lodging in my gut like shrapnel.

*I trust you. To keep her safe. To give her a soft place to land. To not drag her into the wreckage.*

"She needed somewhere solid after . . . everything." He shrugged, eyes cutting over to me. "And you're solid."

I swallowed once, hard, the lie of that scraping all the way down.

I'd kissed his sister in the snow and wanted to do it again so badly my hands shook.

I'd pressed her down into me like she belonged there.

I was currently thinking more about the way she'd whimpered into my mouth than thirty years of friendship.

"Yeah," I said, voice rough. "I know."

For a few beats the only sound was the engine and the hiss of tires on packed snow. Hayes settled back in the seat, oblivious, trusting, already scrolling through his phone to text whomever he was late meeting.

I stared straight ahead, jaw tight, a decision slotting into place like a beam locking into a frame.

Whatever this thing was with Clara—whatever it could be—I didn't get to lean into it. Not with him sitting next to me saying he trusted me. Not with her still getting her feet under her. Not when my own life was one bad day away from unraveling.

I cleared my throat, forcing my voice into something that sounded almost normal. "Where to?"

## TWENTY-TWO

THE BACK ROOM of the Crooked Spine bookstore looked like a cozy witch's cottage.

Mismatched candles lined every flat surface. Teacups and saucers were scattered on end tables. There were books stacked in leaning towers, a basket in the middle of the room overflowing with yarn, and a cluster of women already half settled into armchairs and mismatched dining chairs, all of them with needles flashing in their hands like this was some kind of secret coven.

Which, maybe, it kind of was.

"Clara!" Mom waved me in with the bossy warmth of a woman who had run a household full of rowdy kids and never really stopped. "You're late."

"You're early," Kit countered, one leg slung over the arm of her chair, purple yarn tangling around her wrist. "Time is fake. Look at this thing, Mom. I'm knitting *sin*."

The *thing* in question was her eggplant.

Not a tasteful, abstract interpretation of one. A very large, aggressively anatomical knitted eggplant.

A laugh sputtered between my lips. "Oh my god."

Mom groaned. "Katherine Elizabeth Darling, can you please make something that does not make me question my parenting choices?"

"It's to adorn my smutty bookshelf," Kit said, unbothered. "I'm providing joy and art. Also, the pattern called for worsted weight. I only had bulky. Now it's . . . delightfully large."

Selene's mouth curved as she lifted her own knitting, the picture of calm competence in black leggings and a cardigan the color of moss. Her stitches were even and perfect as a row of soldiers. "That is not bulky. That is a weapon."

"It's bigger than my forearm," Elodie said from the corner, where she was attempting something cable-knit and already making it look annoyingly easy. "I'm not sure there's a real-life man who can live up to whatever you're manifesting there."

Kit's eyes slid to me, wicked and sharp. "A girl can dream."

Heat slammed into my face so fast I nearly choked on my own tongue.

Mom's gaze sharpened. "Kit."

"What?" Kit blinked innocently, but failed.

"Come on, Kit. Stop giving Mom a heart attack." Elodie's voice held the warning of an older sister who had seen this shit show before.

I busied myself while images flashed across my brain with no respect for my sanity—Wes in the snow, Wes under me, Wes's mouth on mine, Wes's hand on my neck. Wes in the kitchen, damp hair, clean jaw, a whole lot of him I had absolutely no business remembering in such vivid detail.

I focused hard on my tote bag and pulled out my knitting.

The lumpy, half-mangled scarf sagged between my needles like it knew it was a disappointment.

"I genuinely don't know what this is going to be yet," I said, dropping into the empty chair between Selene and Elodie. "Could be a scarf. Could be a cry for help."

Helen, the unofficial leader of the Keepers, snorted. She leaned forward to get a better look, her tight gray curls pinned back, readers perched on the end of her nose. "Oh, it's not that bad," she said kindly. "You only mangled . . . this first half."

"Encouraging," I muttered.

Wes's voice slid into my head, low and annoyingly sure, from earlier that morning on the couch.

*You're strangling it.*

My fingers flexed around the yarn, remembering the way he'd adjusted my grip. I tried to remember I needed less of a death grip and more gentle guiding. The thought of his big hands unexpectedly careful as they'd brushed mine sent a tingle down my spine. He had sat there on his couch, glasses on, telling me his grandmother had taught him and Mary when they were kids, like it was nothing. Like mentioning his sister wasn't opening a door he usually kept bolted shut.

It was a simple thing. A soft thing. A piece of himself he'd handed over without making a big deal about it.

My chest did that quiet, traitorous ache.

"Your tension is wild," Selene observed mildly, leaning over to eye my stitches. "I can see the trauma from here."

"I'm working on it," I grumbled. "Apparently I'm strangling it."

Elodie's brows rose. "Apparently?"

I cleared my throat. "Wes, uh . . . gave me some pointers."

Four sets of eyes snapped to me, synchronized as a firing squad.

"Wes Vaughn taught you to knit?" Kit asked, delighted. "I thought his hobbies were brooding and avoiding sunlight."

"He said his grandma taught him. And Mary," I added, softer.

The mood shifted, just the tiniest degree. Mom's knitting paused for half a second, the needles held in midair.

Selene's smile gentled. "Wes Vaughn: fiber arts instructor," she said, tipping her mug toward me. "That is not on my bingo card, but I am thrilled to be wrong."

My cheeks warmed again. "He just . . . showed me how to loosen my grip. Guide the yarn. Apparently choking it isn't the goal."

"Choking is usually not the goal," Kit said solemnly, then lifted the mutant eggplant with both hands and wiggling eyebrows. "Unless it is."

A shocked sound escaped Mom as she put a hand to her forehead. "Katherine."

"It's a metaphor, Mom."

"It is not and you know it."

Laughter rolled through the circle, easy and bright, and some of the new-girl tightness in my shoulders eased. I was still the latest addition, the one who had lied to them all for years about a picture-perfect engagement while she stayed away, the one who had shattered that illusion on their doorstep. They had every reason to keep me on the outer edge.

Instead, they handed me tea and knitting and a seat in the circle like there had always been space saved.

Selene set her project in her lap and gave her needles a little tap against her mug. The sound cut through the low buzz of conversation. "All right, Keepers," she said, a glint lighting her eyes. "I have news."

A ripple went around the group. Kit sat up straighter, eggplant drooping over her knee. Elodie leaned in. Everyone's attention sharpened.

Selene reached into the big canvas tote at her feet and pulled out a manila folder, the edges soft and worn like she'd been thumbing it all day.

"So," she said, turning her gaze on me. "Remember when you joked that Alma Barker was hiding because she was knocked up?"

I winced, my eyes slicing toward Kit. "I, um. Vaguely."

Kit grinned. "Some of us remember it fondly."

"Well." Selene slid a paper out and smoothed it on her knee. "Turns out your throwaway theory had legs. Or, I guess, a birth certificate."

The room leaned closer in unison.

My pulse picked up.

"There was a gap in Alma's paper trail," Selene continued. "We knew that already. She goes quiet here, then reappears a county over briefly, then suddenly she's back in Star Harbor with an engagement announcement to William Lovell." She tapped the paper. "I started digging in the other county. Hospital records. Church logs. Midwives."

Mom made an approving noise as she bumped against Cora's arm. "That's my girl."

Selene smiled, quick and sharp, then sobered. "I found this. A birth record for an A. Barker. No first name spelled out, just the initial. No father listed. The date . . ." She glanced down again, then back up. "The date falls right in the middle of Alma's missing timeline."

The room went quiet.

I stared at the black-and-white copy as it made its way

from hand to hand, my heart doing an odd, uneven rhythm in my chest. Name of mother: A. Barker. Occupation: domestic. Father: dash, dash, dash. A blank space where half a life should have been.

"Oh my," Cora breathed when it reached her. "That poor girl."

"So she really was pregnant," Kit said softly. "She had a baby."

"And then she comes back here, and there's suddenly an engagement announcement with William Lovell," Elodie murmured, eyes distant as she pieced it together. "No mention of a baby. No whisper. Just . . . respectability."

"An engagement to save face," Helen said quietly. "To make it all go away. As if it ever does."

The Lady of the Dunes had always been a story to me. A shiver. A warning. A ghost that haunted the shoreline and, supposedly, cursed my brother with bad luck and inconveniences and hearts that never quite healed right.

Right now, sitting in a circle of women with yarn in my lap and the smell of bergamot in the air, Alma Barker felt less like a ghost and more like a nineteen-year-old who had been terrified and in love and then forced to choose between her child and her reputation.

Selene flipped to another photocopy—the old engagement announcement we had already seen, brittle and yellowed.

"Do we know what happened to the child?" Harriet asked, voice low.

Selene shook her head. "Not yet. I checked for adoption records under Barker and Lovell in this county and the next two. Nothing that matches. Which doesn't mean the baby disappeared. Things went unrecorded all the time, especially if someone wanted them quiet."

"Or if the baby went to the father's family," Mom added. "Out of town. Out of sight."

The farmhand's face flared in my mind—the one in the old photograph, the one who looked unnervingly like Hayes if you squinted. Same jaw. Same eyes. Same stubborn tilt to his mouth.

"Has anyone considered . . ." I hesitated, then plunged ahead. "The farmhand. The one who looks like Hayes. Could he be the father?"

Elodie let out a low whistle. "That would track for our luck. Our cursed ancestor knocked up a ghost."

"She wasn't a ghost *yet*," Kit cut in, though her lips were pressed tight. "Maybe they were in love."

"The point is," Selene said, eyes back on the papers, "Alma had more at stake than anyone bothered to write down. She wasn't just a girl. She was a mother. She had something huge to lose. That changes the way we look at her story. She wasn't some vengeful sea witch or morose lover haunting a town for fun. She was someone who had her story taken away and rewritten by the men around her."

The words settled heavy and sure.

My fingers tightened around my needles, the yarn cutting into the soft flesh of my palm. I thought of Alma, pregnant belly, sent away to another county so nobody would see. I thought of her labor recorded on a single sheet of paper, no father listed, then her return with a ring and a smile that probably didn't reach her eyes.

A hidden pregnancy. A rushed engagement. A baby whose name no one bothered to say out loud in any of the records.

No wonder Alma couldn't rest. She had never gotten to tell her own story. It had been written over her in ink and whispers.

My own broken engagement slid into that space, uninvited. Greg's fingers clenched around mine at the fancy restaurants, the way his eyes would subtly slide over me as he looked for something better in the room. The way I had lied to everyone here for so long about how happy we were. I thought I was doing the best thing for the both of us.

Wes's mouth on mine flickered across my mind, hot and immediate. His hand on my cheek. His groan in my throat. The way I had kept that kiss secret, too, tucking it into the same place in my chest where all the other unspoken things lived.

Secrets had weight. They clung. They warped the shape of a life.

I looked down at the uneven row of stitches between my fingers and exhaled slowly.

"Poor Alma," I murmured. "Everyone else got to decide who she was."

Selene's gaze met mine over her knitting, sharp and knowing. "Not if we have anything to say about it," she said.

The yarn slid a little easier through my fingers on the next stitch.

In an attempt to lighten the suddenly sullen mood, Kit bounced her knee, the giant eggplant wobbling obscenely in her lap. "Speaking of the living," she said, eyes cutting to me, "what are you doing tonight?"

I blinked. "Uh . . . knitting and staring at my ceiling?"

Mom clucked her tongue as her head shook. "Absolutely not. You are too young and too pretty to sit in that miserable house every night like a recluse."

"It's not miserable," I protested automatically, then thought of his dented couch and winced. "It's . . . cozy adjacent."

"Great," Kit said. "You can tell yourself that after you

come out to the Lantern tonight. Drinks, dancing, poor decisions."

My stomach did a weird little flip. "The Lady's Lantern?"

"Is there another bar in Star Harbor?" she deadpanned. "Come on, city girl. You can wear something slutty. I'll even let you borrow my good lip gloss. We'll shake off this depressing mood."

Mom took a sip of her tea, eyes twinkling over the rim. "You should go, Clara. Get out. Let yourself have some fun."

Heat crept up my neck, stupid and telling. "I'll think about it," I said, which in Darling translation was already a yes.

Kit grinned like she knew it. "Perfect. I'll pick you up at eight."

## TWENTY-THREE

CLARA

GETTING ready took ten minutes and an embarrassing amount of overthinking.

I just stood in front of my suitcase and asked myself what version of me I wanted to be tonight.

The temporary roommate slinking around a neglected house in yesterday's pajamas? Nah.

The girl who'd gotten left at the altar in front of nearly everyone she knew? Hell no.

I wanted to be the woman who walked into a room and expected it to like her. I missed that version of myself and wasn't quite sure where I'd left her.

After a deep breath, I pulled on my favorite jeans—the ones that actually fit, hugging my hips without cutting off circulation—black boots with a little heel, and a thin knit top that dipped just enough at the neckline to feel feminine and flirty. My hair went down, waves finger-combed into something that looked intentionally tousled instead of slept on. A swipe of mascara. Lip gloss. Tiny hoops in my ears.

It wasn't too flashy, but a reminder to myself that I was still in here.

The house was quiet as I came down the stairs. It was the kind of winter evening hush that made every creak under my boots sound louder. Light spilled from the living room, warm against the dark.

Wes was on the floor in front of the couch, bent forward, his arms stretching toward his toes. His prosthetic leaned against the coffee table. He wore a pair of dark athletic shorts and a faded T-shirt that clung to his back, damp at the collar from a shower. The muscles in his shoulders flexed as he shifted his weight, the broad line of his back cutting clean against the soft, lived-in couch behind him. His hair was still a little wet, pushed back, a few pieces refusing to stay put.

He looked . . . settled. Focused. Like a man checking his range and not avoiding it.

For a second I just watched him—one hand on the banister, heart doing that stupid lift-and-drop thing in my chest. The stump where his leg used to be was bare, the skin pale and marked, and there was a slice of a second where my throat tightened for him.

Then his hands slid farther out, spine lengthening, the long line of his arms drawing my eye, and pity didn't stand a chance against the sheer, unfair reality of Wes Vaughn's body.

He glanced up at the sound of my foot on the last stair.

The stretch froze. His gaze dragged over me once, slow and unguarded, from boots to jeans to the low neckline of my top. Something dark and hot flickered in his eyes before he slammed the door on it.

"Going somewhere, Duchess?" His voice came out rough, a shade hoarser than usual as he turned his focus back to his stretch.

I pretended my stomach didn't flip at the nickname.

"Kit invited me out," I said, walking toward the kitchen for the illusion of purpose. "We're going to the Lantern tonight. Drinks, dancing, bad decisions. You should come."

His mouth curved, but it wasn't a real smile. "Yeah, no," he said flatly. "I don't dance anymore."

My face twisted as I turned back toward him. "Why not?"

He didn't answer right away. Just reached for the liner and started rolling it up, his fingers efficient and practiced. His jaw worked as he lifted the prosthetic and lined it up, balancing with one hand on the couch.

He shot me a look as he clicked it into place. "Take a wild guess."

My eyes dropped, uninvited, to his leg. To the way he concentrated on making sure the fit was right, the way his shoulders tensed like he was expecting it to fail him at any second.

"I meant," I said softly, "is it that you can't . . . or that you don't want to find out you still can?"

His head tipped, surprise flashing across his face before he covered it with a scoff. "Clara, come on. Nobody wants their toes annihilated by the guy with the metal leg. I trip, I go down, I take out half the dance floor."

"You didn't trip sledding," I pointed out. "You didn't fall. You just screamed like a little girl and then made out with me in a snowdrift."

His mouth tightened as his eyes flashed to mine. "Gliding on your ass down a hill is not the same as dancing."

"*Technically*, you were on a sled, not your ass," I said with a shrug. "And your balance was fine."

He shifted his weight onto the prosthetic, testing it, expression closing off. "A crowded bar is a lot," he said. "Noise, people, floors I don't trust. I'll pass."

The sting pricked quick and sharp—ridiculous, given that I'd invited him mostly on impulse—but it was there anyway. "I didn't say you had to go compete on *Dancing with the Stars*, Wes," I said lightly. "Just that you could come drink beer and bob your head like a normal person."

His eyes slid away, toward the TV that wasn't on. "I don't . . . do that anymore."

The hopelessness in those few words did something ugly and painful to my insides.

"Okay," I said, more firmly than I felt. I took a few steps back toward him, closing some of the distance. "New proposal."

He eyed me warily. "Those are rarely good."

"Two minutes," I said. "Right here. No crowd. No sticky floors. No strangers. If you hate it, I'll shut up and go twerk on strangers at the Lantern without you."

He huffed, like he was gearing up for a fight. "Clara—"

"Wes." I planted myself in front of him, close enough to see the faint shadow of stubble along his jaw. Close enough to smell soap and that faint woodsy note that had been driving me insane for days. "You survived sledding. You can survive swaying in your own living room."

His gaze dropped to my mouth before cutting away. The muscle in his jaw ticced. "This is a bad idea."

"So were most of my decisions in the last year." I grinned up at him and blinked innocently. "Didn't stop me."

Something that might have been a reluctant laugh flickered in his eyes.

I lifted a hand. "Come on. Two minutes. You can even count."

He stared at my outstretched fingers like they were a

test he hadn't studied for. Then he sighed, low and annoyed at himself, and took one step toward me.

"Two minutes," he said. "Then you leave me alone and go terrorize someone else."

I bit back a giddy laugh. "Deal."

He stepped even closer, careful, like he was approaching an edge. I reached for his left hand and guided it to my waist, right above my hip bone. His palm was warm and wide, fingers curling in reflex before he seemed to realize what he was doing and tried to loosen them.

The spark that shot through me at that little flex was ridiculous.

"Other hand," I said, offering mine with a wiggle of my fingers.

He took it, his grip a little too firm, like he was holding on for dear life.

"Okay," I murmured. "We're not doing a tango. Just . . . shift. Weight to the right. Then to the left. Most guys don't know how to do more than sway anyway."

He snorted. "Real inspiring imagery, Duchess."

"I'm not auditioning to be your dance coach," I said. "I'm just trying to prove your rhythm didn't get amputated."

His brow arched. "You're very confident for someone who can't knit a straight row."

"Harsh," I said, smiling despite myself. "Now move your feet."

His chest lifted on a breath. Then, slowly, he did.

We started small. Barely moving at all. His weight eased to one leg, then the other, the shift controlled and deliberate. I could feel every micro adjustment through his hand at my waist, the cautious give in his body, the way he kept his core locked, like he was still bracing for a fall.

"You're overthinking," I said, quietly breathing in the

scent at his neck. "It's just us, Wes. Nobody's judging you on your form."

His gaze flicked down, met mine. We were closer than I'd realized. Close enough to count the darker ring around his irises, the tiny scar at the edge of his eyebrow, and the faint hitch of his breath as his gaze locked onto mine.

"Easy for you to say," he murmured. "Your leg does what it's supposed to."

My heart pinched. "Your leg just got you down a hill and back up again," I said. "It's allowed to figure shit out. Same as the rest of you."

His mouth twitched, something soft and painful in his eyes. The stiffness in his shoulders eased a fraction as he rolled his shoulders back. His hand at my waist tightened, just a little, like he'd forgotten to be careful for one second.

We swayed.

A slow, quiet back-and-forth, the house dark and silent, the winter sky pressed against the windows. His prosthetic made the tiniest difference in the rhythm, just enough that I could feel it if I paid attention, a slightly heavier step, a careful recalibration, but it didn't make him clumsy.

It made him present.

"See?" I said, dropping my voice. "Everything still moves just fine, Vaughn."

"You're bossy as hell," he muttered.

"You like it," I shot back.

His lips curved into a real smile then—a quick, reluctant flash that gutted me.

Warmth pooled low in my stomach. The space between us shrank without either of us consciously deciding to close it. My chest brushed his with every shift. His thumb traced a small, absent-minded arc at my hip bone through my shirt, and my body lit up like he'd run a live wire against my skin.

This was too close. Too easy. Too dangerous.

*Two minutes. You promised.*

I let us sway for a few more heartbeats, memorizing the way he felt when he stopped fighting his own body. Then I cleared my throat and stepped back, gently sliding his hand off my waist.

"Time's up," I said, hoping my voice didn't sound as breathless as I felt. "See? Toes intact. Pride mostly intact. Rhythm confirmed."

He looked at me like he was still counting something only he could see. Then he shook his head, scoffing lightly. "Yeah, well. Add beer and twenty bodies in a room and we'll see how intact it stays."

"That's what walls are for," I said. "You find a corner, lean, sway. No one cares. They're too busy posting their drinks on Instagram."

He huffed, which was as close as he got to a laugh when he didn't want to give me one. "A crowded bar is a lot," he said again, more quietly. "Maybe next time."

The tiny sting came anyway, pricking the inside of my ribs. I pasted on a grin. "Fine. I'll just go dazzle the entire population of Star Harbor without you."

"Try not to get arrested," he said dryly.

I grabbed my coat from the hook and shrugged it on, stuffing my hands into the sleeves. "No promises."

At the door I paused and glanced back.

He was watching me, one hand rubbing absently at the seam where his prosthetic met his skin, the other hanging loose at his side. His face was neutral, but his eyes were not.

My heart kicked once, hard.

"Think about it," I said, voice softer. "The Lantern, I mean. Kit's dragging Hayes. It'll be loud and ridiculous. You two can complain about it together."

Something flickered across his expression at my brother's name, some kind of internal calculation. Then his mouth flattened. "Thanks for the invite," he said, which was clearly Wes-speak for *fuck no.*

I nodded and lifted a shoulder like it didn't matter. "Okay. Don't wait up for me."

"I won't," he said automatically.

We both knew he would.

I opened the door, winter air rushing in, sharp and clean. As I stepped out onto the porch, I could feel his gaze between my shoulder blades, hot and heavy, following me all the way to Kit's waiting car.

THE LANTERN WAS HUMMING when we walked in.

Warm light spilled over scuffed floors, catching on old ship wheels and brass lanterns hung along the walls. Somebody had strung fairy lights over the bar like constellations, and the smell of beer, fried food, and cheap citrus slices wrapped around us as we pushed through the door. A three-piece band was wedged into the corner—guitar, upright bass, and a guy with a fiddle who looked like he'd been born on that little stage. The music rolled across the room, something low and bluesy that made the windows shiver in their frames.

Out past the glass, the lake was a dark, restless shape, snow piled along the shore like the rim of a world.

Kit hooked her arm through mine and steered us toward a high-top near the back. Hayes trailed behind us, his sharp eyes assessing the room. He nodded toward the bar and was swallowed by the crowd.

Kit and I squeezed around a sticky table under a framed

newspaper clipping of the Lady of the Dunes. Kit jutted her chin toward the faded newspaper clipping over my shoulder. "Of course she had a secret baby. Women like that always have secret babies. It's practically a requirement."

Hayes walked up and set the drinks down with a clink—two ciders and something brown in a rocks glass for himself. "No father listed," Kit said, shaking her head. "That part just . . . makes me mad. What if he got to peace out of the story and she had to carry the whole scandal by herself?"

I wrapped my fingers around my glass, icy condensation slick under my palm. "That would have been peak small-town shame," I said. "Hide the girl. Hide the baby. Slap a ring on her finger and pretend the timeline math checks out. Or . . . maybe he didn't know?"

Hayes's panicked gaze flicked between our faces. "Did I miss something? Who's got a secret baby?"

Kit grinned like she was going to give him a hard time but chose mercy instead.

"The Lady," I offered. "All kinds of drama are shaking out. We think her engagement to William was to save face."

"Or to shut her up," Kit muttered, picking at the paper coaster. "Feels very on brand for the patriarchy."

The band slid into a new song, something faster that sent a little ripple through the crowd. I leaned into my brother. "We want to figure out who the father is . . . and what happened to the baby."

A chill walked over my skin that had nothing to do with the cold by the windows. "My money is on the farmhand," I said quietly.

*The one who looks exactly like you.*

Hayes patted a hand on the table. "Well, good luck with that." Our brother was dragged into a conversation with the table next to us, and I sighed in relief.

Kit shuddered theatrically before leaning in to whisper. "Seriously, every time I see that photo, I want to throw salt over my shoulder. Dude is Hayes with a sepia filter."

"Which means our family is likely tangled up in all this," I whispered back.

I took a sip of cider, the sweetness sitting heavy on my tongue. "So our brother might be a great-great-grandchild of the Lady's secret affair or the guy who ruined her life. No big deal."

Kit snorted. "Explains a lot about his curse, honestly. You'd be pissed, too, if your family tree started with a scandal and a cover-up."

The curse.

It hung between us even when we dressed it up as a joke. Hayes's endless streak of bad luck. Weird accidents and annoying inconveniences. The way the Lady's story spiraled through everything in this town like a thread nobody could quite pull free.

When Hayes turned back, we both straightened and pretended to be talking about *anything* else.

I took another sip, letting the cider burn a slow path down my throat, and tried—really tried—to focus on the band, on the chatter, on Kit waving at someone across the room like a human lighthouse.

It worked for about thirty seconds.

A guy in a flannel shirt and decent jeans stepped up to the table, all easy smiles and faint beer breath. I'd seen him around—maybe he worked at the hardware store or ran charters in the summer, but I couldn't place it. He was pleasantly handsome in a way that did absolutely nothing to my heart rate.

"Hey," he said, looking at me and then flicking an acknowledging nod at the other two. "I'm Nate."

Kit's eyes lit up like someone had just dropped a plot twist in her lap. "Nate, this is Clara," she said, far too innocently. "She was just saying how she needed to dance or she was going to combust."

"I literally wasn't," I protested.

Nate smiled, unfazed. "We should probably prevent spontaneous combustion, then." He held out a hand. "You want to?"

Hayes's brows went up before shaking his head. "I'm getting another drink." He slid off his stool and sauntered away.

"Go have fun." Kit laughed. "I'll guard your drink. And your honor."

I hesitated for half a breath.

I was here. I was dressed like a person who existed outside of sweatpants. I had spent an entire day trying not to replay a kiss with a man I technically had no business thinking about that way.

I could dance with someone who wasn't him.

"Sure," I said, sliding off the stool. "Why not."

Nate's palm was solid and a little rough as he led me toward the dance floor, weaving through tables and groups. The band shifted into something mid-tempo and swaying, couples already moving in that small-town way where everyone instinctively knew the steps, even if there weren't any.

He settled one hand at my waist, took my other in his, and started to move.

Technically, there was nothing wrong with it.

His hold was polite. Appropriate. Not too close, not too far. He smelled like bourbon and store-bought cologne, the kind that came in a gift set with a matching bodywash. His rhythm was decent.

It did absolutely nothing to me.

My body swayed because the music told it to. My feet moved because muscle memory kicked in. My mind, unfortunately, had no interest in staying here.

It slipped sideways, back to how it felt to dance with Wes in his quiet living room.

Nate's thumb brushed a vague pattern at the small of my back.

Wes's thumb had dragged slow and possessive along the waistband of my jeans, like he wanted to memorize every inch of skin between layers, like he wanted me closer even when there was no space left.

Nate's chest bumped mine lightly with each step, solid but forgettable.

Wes's chest had been a wall, heat and muscle and that familiar broadness I'd known for years compressed into a new, devastating arrangement. He had held me like he didn't want a single millimeter of distance. Like space between us was an insult.

"Am I stepping on you?" Nate asked, leaning in a little to be heard.

"Um." I blinked up at him. "No, sorry. You're good. I'm . . . a little out of practice."

He smiled, easy and kind. "You're doing fine."

*Fine.*

Wes hadn't made me feel fine.

Wes had swayed with me like I was the only thing in the world that made sense for a stolen handful of seconds. Like he'd forgotten about his leg, his fear, and the storm in his own head.

My throat tightened.

Nate twirled me lazily, one hand still in mine. I went with it, letting my body spin, letting my hair fan out, letting the room blur into fairy lights and faces. When I settled back into his frame, the contact felt . . . muted. Like turning down the volume on a song that should have been loud.

Somewhere near our table, Kit whooped, the sound bright and piercing through the din. She laughed, head tipped back, all teeth and reckless joy.

I wished I could drag my feelings into that brightness and leave them there.

Nate swayed to the music. "You're from here, right?"

"Kind of." I shrugged. "I grew up here, then left. Came back with my tail between my legs."

He chuckled. "Sounds like there's a story there."

A humorless laugh escaped my nose. "You have no idea," I muttered.

His hand pressed a little firmer at my waist. "Well, for what it's worth, you look like you belong here."

The words were nice. He was nice. The music was good, the bar was warm, the town was exactly itself.

My heart was such a traitor.

The song wound down. Nate loosened his hold and stepped back, still smiling. "Thanks," he said. "You want another drink?"

"I'm good," I said, because he deserved better than being my human control group. "Maybe later. I promised Kit I'd come rescue her if she flirted with the bartender again."

He laughed. "Fair enough. See you around?"

"Yeah," I said. "See you."

I slipped away before guilt could turn into pity on either of our faces, weaving back through the bodies to the safety of my sister.

At the table, Kit gave me a hopeful look. "Well?"

"He was nice," I said, grabbing my drink.

"Nice," she repeated with a groan. "Tragic."

My phone buzzed on the sticky tabletop.

WES

> How's the dazzling going? Anyone blinded yet or just mildly inconvenienced?

Heat pricked at the back of my neck. My lips tugged up before I could stop them, the smile sneaking out so fast I had to duck my head and pretend to study my cider.

"Who's that?" Kit singsonged.

"No one," I lied, thumbs already moving.

ME

> One guy survived the experience and can still see colors. I think I'm losing my touch.

Three dots appeared almost immediately.

WES

> Doubtful. Star Harbor just isn't ready for your full wattage yet.

My chest did a stupid little squeeze. I bit the inside of my cheek to keep from grinning like a teenager and locked my phone, tucking it under my palm before Kit could snatch it.

Out on the floor, couples swayed closer as the band slid into something slow and dirty. Hands skimmed hips. Heads tucked into necks. I watched a woman laugh as her partner spun her, trusting him completely to catch her.

My mind drifted back to Wes as he swayed with me in the dark like he wasn't sure he was allowed to enjoy it. To the tiny, careful way his hand had flexed at my waist when he'd forgotten to be afraid.

Maybe Hayes wasn't the only Darling who was cursed.

Maybe I was cursed too—cursed to want the one man in this town I absolutely, unequivocally should not.

A man who had my brother's trust.

A man who was still piecing himself back together.

A man whose kiss had somehow ruined every other touch.

Then it dawned on me, Wes's body worked just fine. It was his confidence that had taken the hit.

A reckless little thought whispered.

*If I could remind him he still knew how to move to music . . . what else could I remind him of?*

## TWENTY-FOUR

WES

THE LIVING ROOM was quiet enough that I could hear the heater hum. I was stretched out on the couch with the same book I'd been reading for an hour, my eyes sliding over sentences that refused to stick. Every time the clock flipped to a new minute, my gaze snagged there like it had a hook in it.

She was at the Lantern with half of Star Harbor, laughing at bad jokes and dancing on two good legs. I had considered texting Hayes, but the last thing I wanted to do was salivate over Clara while her brother watched me like a hawk.

One lie was hard enough to cover.

Besides, I'd already sent one idiotic text about how the dazzling was going, then sat there acting like I wasn't checking my phone every other page. So I kept pretending I was only awake because the couch was uncomfortable and the book was decent, not because the idea of her fumbling with the front lock alone in the dark made something low in my gut stay coiled and tight.

Headlights swept across the ceiling in a slow arc,

painting the walls in pale blue. A car door slammed outside, muffled through the snow. My hand stilled on the page, my pulse kicking up as boots hit the front steps and the door-knob rattled.

The front door swung open on a rush of cold air and noise—the low thump of some distant bass still vibrating in her bones, the soft smack of her boots against the mat as she kicked snow off them.

"Shit," Clara muttered under her breath, wobbling a little as she toed one boot free. The other followed with a damp squeak.

Kit's headlights were already disappearing down the road through the front window, a streak of white fading into the dark.

My thumb sat in the crease of my book, holding the same page I'd been pretending to read for a solid fifteen minutes. The words blurred as she stepped into the living room.

Her cheeks were flushed, high and bright, from either dancing or the wind off the lake. Maybe both. Her hair had gone a little wild, the waves looser now, and a few strands escaped to brush her jaw. Her outfit looked just as good as when she'd left—those jeans that hugged her curves like they had a personal stake in it, the soft top that dipped at her collarbone, a faint shimmer at her mouth where she'd reapplied gloss at some point.

It should not have been legal for one person to look that good in my doorway.

"You're still up?" she asked, one brow lifting as she leaned down to drop her keys into the bowl.

"I was finishing a chapter," I lied, the book suddenly heavy in my hand.

She wrestled out of her coat, shoulders twisting, hair

catching on the collar until she huffed and yanked it loose. Her smell hit me as she tossed her coat over the back of the armchair—bar air and winter, the faint salt of sweat under her perfume. My fingers tightened around the paperback.

*Some asshole had put his hands on her.*

It shouldn't have bothered me. That was what people did at a bar—pressed close on sticky floors, slid palms down backs, leaned into each other when the band got loud. Some faceless guy had been where my hands had been earlier, and even just thinking about it made a low, unfamiliar growl curl in my chest.

I had no claim. No right. No anything.

"So how was it?" I asked, aiming for neutral and landing somewhere closer to anger.

Her mouth curved as she walked farther into the room. "Loud. Sticky. Full of bad decisions in progress," she said. "So, you know. The usual good time."

She stopped near the end of the couch, her fingers tangled in the hem of her shirt. A little crease formed between her brows. She swallowed hard and planted both hands on her hips.

"Okay," she said after a heartbeat, exhale coming out in a rush. "So . . . just hear me out before you tell me I'm insane."

My shoulders went tight. "That's . . . never a reassuring opener."

Her laugh was quick and nervous. She took one more step toward me, close enough now that I could see the smudge of mascara at the corner of her eye, the way her pulse fluttered in her throat.

"You know how you keep acting like your life is over?" she said. "Like you don't dance, you don't go out, you don't flirt, you definitely don't do anything fun that involves another human body?"

"That's a sweeping generalization," I muttered as I rose.

"It's also true." Her eyes slid to meet mine. "You haven't lost your body, Wes. You lost your mojo. There's a difference."

Heat climbed the back of my neck. "Jesus, Clara."

"I'm serious," she pressed on. "You keep acting like this . . ." Her hand gestured vaguely at my leg, my couch, my entire existence. "Means you have to retire from . . . all of that. From touching. From letting anyone touch you. From sex. Which is bullshit, by the way."

Every word landed like a tap to a bruise I tried not to think about. My jaw clenched.

"What exactly are you proposing?" I asked, even though some desperate, half-starved part of me already knew.

Her lips parted, tongue darting out to wet the bottom one. That tiny movement punched straight through my stomach.

"I'm proposing," she said slowly, like she was picking her way across thin ice, "that you need . . . a safe space to figure out how your body works now. What feels good. What doesn't. Where the limits are and where they aren't."

A hollow laugh scraped my throat. "Kind of hard to book lab time for that."

Her chin lifted a fraction. "You don't need a lab." She swallowed as her hands opened. "You have me."

The room tilted, just a hair.

I frowned. "What?"

She took another step closer, until the toe of her foot bumped the edge of the rug. Her scent wrapped around me, skin washed clean with cold air, the softer scent underneath that was just her.

"I mean," she rushed on, words tumbling faster now, "I'm here. I'm not a stranger. You trust me. Mostly." Her mouth hitched. "We're already . . . doing this weird roommate emotional PT thing. It wouldn't be that big of a stretch to . . . expand the syllabus."

"Syllabus," I repeated, because my brain had temporarily forgotten what language was.

"It's like PT," she said, eyes bright, hands flying as she talked. "Except way more fun. We figure out what positions work with your leg, which ones don't, how you like to move now, what feels good, what you need. No pressure. No audience. No expectations you have to live up to except your own."

My cock hardened so fast it hurt.

Images slammed into me, sharp and visceral—Clara straddling my lap on this couch, fingers in my hair, my hands gripping her thighs while she rode me. Another of her knees bracketing my hips in that damn bed upstairs I'd barely started sleeping in again. Clara bent over the kitchen counter, cheek pressed to the cool surface, my hand fisted in her hair as I sank into her from behind, testing how deep I could go.

I shifted, praying she couldn't see how obvious my physical reaction was.

"Clara," I said, voice rough, but she was already barreling ahead, nerves sharpening her words.

"You'd get to practice," she said, cheeks flushing deeper now. "Without worrying you're going to disappoint somebody or freak them out or have to explain every single thing in your head. You don't have to fake confidence for me. You don't have to pretend you're fine with angles or speed or whatever else your brain is screaming about. We just . . . figure it out together."

Her throat worked on a swallow. For a second the bravado slipped and I could see the nerves trembling under it.

"It's like friends," she finished quietly, mouth curving into a grin. "Friends with some really good benefits."

Silence stretched between us, thick as steam.

Her eyes stayed on my face, searching, and she braced. Like she fully expected me to laugh or tell her she'd lost her mind, like she was already rehearsing how to pretend it didn't matter when I did.

My body had its own opinion.

Heat poured through me, low and heavy, pooling where I could do exactly nothing about it except breathe and try not to shift too much. Every place I'd touched her earlier in the snow felt vivid again—the curve of her ass under my hands, the soft drag of her tongue against mine, the way she'd moaned into my mouth when I'd pulled her down harder.

She was offering me all of that on purpose this time. No accident. No adrenaline excuse. No *we tripped and fell into a kiss*.

"Fuck," I breathed, the word leaving me before I could stop it.

Her fingers laced. "Is that a . . . good *fuck* or a bad *fuck*?"

My laugh came out broken. "Complicated."

My best friend's words dug in under my ribs like barbs. He trusted me. Hell, he looked at me like I was still the guy he'd grown up with, not the half-built version limping around my own life.

"You want me to use you as . . . practice?" I slowly dragged my gaze back to her, because looking away felt dangerous for different reasons. "To test-drive my fucked-up sex life on you?"

Her nose scrunched. "That is truly the worst phrasing I have ever heard."

"That's what you said," I shot back, even though we both knew it wasn't.

Not exactly.

"I said," she corrected, voice firming, "that you deserve to know your body isn't broken. That you're allowed to want things. That a bad thing happened to you, and it does not get to take this too." Her jaw set. "If I can help you remember what it feels like to want something without panicking, then . . . yeah. I want to do that."

My heart hammered so hard it hurt. My eyes narrowed. "What's in it for you?"

Her eyes flicked to my rock-hard dick and up again as she bit back a smile. "I think we both know the answer to that."

Cocky bravado filled my chest. At least that small part of me wasn't completely dead. I cleared my throat. "You realize this isn't going to be tidy. This doesn't stay in some neat 'lesson' box once we cross that line."

"I'm a grown woman, Wes." Her eyes flashed. "I know how sex works. I also know how not having it fucks with people's heads. We could set parameters. Rules. No falling in love. No grand gestures. No getting weird if we're in the same room as my family."

The laugh that tore out of me was closer to a choke. "You think it's that simple?"

She hesitated, just for a second, then lifted her chin. "I think you need a win. I think I can give you one. I think we're both adults who are attracted to each other, and pretending we're not is getting ridiculous."

The honesty of it hit me harder than any tease she could have thrown.

She was right. She was wrong. She was everything in between.

No falling in love.

My gaze slid over her without my permission—the stubborn line of her jaw, the spark in her eyes, the mouth I already knew tasted like cinnamon and trouble when I let myself have it. My chest ached, a deep, slow throb that had nothing to do with lust.

"You're asking me," I said quietly, "to take the one person in this town I have absolutely no business touching and make her the solution to every nightmare my brain has about my body."

Her voice softened. "I'm asking you to let me help you remember you're still *you*."

Something in my chest cracked.

Phantom pain flared low and mean, the nerves in my thigh spitting static into nothing. My hand twitched against my knee. Panic flickered at the edges—images of losing balance, of my leg giving out mid-thrust, of lying there humiliated, of her seeing all of it, not the fantasy but the failure.

My dick did not care about any of that. It was already at full attention, heavy and aching against my zipper, screaming its own answer.

"Wes," she said, barely above a whisper now. "Say something."

I looked at her. Really looked.

Flushed from cold and dancing, hair a little wild, vulnerability written in the tight set of her mouth. Every inch of her alive, right here in my living room, offering herself up like she didn't know what that did to me.

My tongue felt thick. My thoughts tangled on themselves.

*Yes* burned on the back of my teeth.

*No* sat there, too, heavy with every reason I didn't deserve this.

The book slid out of my hand and thudded softly onto the cushion beside me.

I still hadn't answered.

"No."

The word scraped out of me, heavy and rough. Her face flickered, like someone had cut the power for half a second.

"I mean—" My throat worked, useless. "I don't think that's a good idea."

There it was. Clean. Cowardly.

She went very still.

For one bare heartbeat everything she was feeling showed—hope cracking right down the middle, confusion rushing in behind it. Then her features rearranged themselves with brutal efficiency, expression smoothing out like she'd ironed it flat.

"Right." She nodded once, eyes dropping to somewhere over my shoulder. "Obviously. It was just an idea."

Her hand shoved in her pocket, then came out again like she needed something to do with her hands. A thin little smile tugged at her mouth, all edges and no heat.

"Forget I said anything," she added, voice going bright in a way that made my chest hurt. "Blame the cider."

I hated that I could hear the crack under the joke.

"Clara—" I started, reaching for something I couldn't even name.

She was already pulling back, putting space between us one careful step at a time. "It's fine, Wes," she said, not quite looking at me. "Seriously. I'm going to go wash the bar off me and try not to die of humiliation."

The laugh she tacked on was weightless and wrong.

She turned toward the stairs. The sway of her hair, the line of her shoulders, the stiff set of her spine—all of it pulled away from me. At the bottom step, she paused just long enough to toss "Good night, Wes" over her shoulder, like it cost her nothing.

"Good night," I managed.

Her feet thudded softly on the stairs, that familiar rhythm climbing higher, then fading. A door clicked shut down the hall, quiet as a pin falling.

The silence that rushed in after her was vicious.

My body still ached with want, cock hard and heavy, skin buzzing with the memory of her pressed against me in the snow and again when we danced. Every cell I owned was screaming that I had just told the one woman I actually wanted that I did not want her.

Regret hit so fast I almost swayed.

*You fucking idiot.*

The words echoed in my skull, sharp and accurate. She had offered me trust and heat and a way back into a part of myself I missed so much it made me mean. I had thrown up a wall and told her no because the alternative scared the shit out of me.

Relief slid under the regret like oil—thin, ugly, and immediate. No pressure. No test I could fail. No chance of her watching my leg buckle or my body short-circuit and realizing I was every worst-case scenario I already believed about myself.

Shame rose right on its heels.

She had heard exactly what I had not meant to say: not *I am scared*, not *I do not deserve you*, not *your brother trusts me with you and I am already hanging on by a thread.*

Just no.

No to her. No to the plan. No to the possibility that any of this could be something other than pain.

Upstairs, the pipes creaked as water started in the bathroom. The sound crawled over my skin, a reminder that she was up there, stripping off that bar air, cheeks probably still pink from dancing, washing away a night I had just managed to make worse.

My hand clenched on the couch cushion until my knuckles ached.

Every part of me felt wrong.

Silence pressed in on me from all sides.

My pulse still hammered from the conversation, too fast and uneven, like my body was trying to outrun the words I'd already said.

*No.*

The look on her face replayed, over and over, like a bad highlight reel. That tiny flinch. The way her eyes had gone bright and flat at the same time. The brittle joke she'd wrapped around herself like armor because I'd been too much of a coward to wrap anything else around her.

With a shake of my head, I gripped the banister and hauled myself up the stairs without another thought. Her door was halfway down the hall, light leaking in a thin line at the bottom.

The shower was off and her room had gone quiet. I could hear the faintest sounds from inside—drawers shifting, the soft drag of feet on the floor. My brain supplied an image I had no business entertaining: Clara wrapped in nothing but a towel, cheeks pink from hot water, hair damp and curling at the ends, lips still wet and waiting.

Heat punched low in my gut, sharp enough to tighten my grip on the jamb as I stopped in front of her door.

This was a bad idea. All of it. I was about to knock on

the door of my best friend's little sister, the woman living in my house, the woman I had turned down three minutes ago while my entire body screamed yes.

I had no speech prepared, no neat, grown-up explanation. Just the bone-deep knowledge that letting her go to sleep believing she'd embarrassed herself alone was not an option I could live with.

My hand lifted and my knuckles met wood in two hard knocks, the sound echoing down the narrow hallway.

"Clara," I said, voice rough, closer to a growl than anything reasonable.

My fist settled against the door, every nerve strung tight.

"Clara, open the door."

## WES

She yelped on the other side of the door—a quick, startled sound—followed by the scuff of bare feet on hardwood.

The door opened halfway, and Clara stood there in nothing but a towel.

Her hair was wet and wavy, darker at the ends where it dripped onto the terry cloth. Cheeks flushed, skin pink from hot water, collarbones gleaming in the soft light from her bedside lamp. The towel was knotted between her breasts, barely hanging on, leaving her shoulders naked and a long, dangerous stretch of thigh visible where the edge wrapped and overlapped.

My brain short-circuited.

Every sensible thing I'd come up here to say scattered like sawdust in a fan. All that was left was the fact that Clara Darling was half naked in front of me and looking at me like she hadn't expected me to actually be on the other side of that knock.

Her gaze flicked over my face and paused. The corner of her mouth tilted, small and surprised.

"Your reading glasses are still on," she said softly.

My hand flew up on reflex, fingers bumping the frame. Of all the things I was suddenly aware of—the quick punch of my heartbeat, the stretch of towel over her chest, the drop of water sliding down the inside of her arm—that was what she went for.

"Right," I muttered. "Forgot."

I started to take them off, heat crawling up the back of my neck. She moved faster, lifting her hand and wrapping her fingers around my wrist.

"No," she said, eyes on mine. "I like them."

The words were simple. Nothing more than a preference, but they landed like a live wire.

For months I'd seen the glasses as one more reminder that my body wasn't quite working like it used to. More proof that things were wearing out, falling apart, needing help. She was looking at them like they were . . . something else. Like they did something to her that she liked.

A flicker of confidence I hadn't felt in too long kicked in my chest, small and stunned. Maybe she was into this version of me. Not the blueprint of the guy I'd been, but the one standing here with a metal leg, a scarred brain, and stupid reading glasses halfway down his nose.

I swallowed, pulse pounding where her fingers circled my wrist.

"Clara." My voice scraped like gravel. "Can I . . . come in? We should talk."

A shadow crossed her expression—caution, uncertainty, the echo of me saying no downstairs. Her grip loosened, but she didn't move away.

I thought she was going to shut the door in my face. Then she exhaled, long and slow, and stepped back, giving me room.

"Yeah," she murmured, tightening her hand on the knot of the towel. "Okay. Come in."

I crossed the threshold into her room, my heart hammering, and shut the door behind me with a soft click. Suddenly the room felt a lot smaller.

Her lamp cast everything in warm gold—bed neatly made, pajamas tossed over the chair. She stood a few steps away, one hand clutching the knot of her towel, the other hovering uselessly at her side like it was looking for somewhere safe to land.

I stayed near the door at first. The wood was solid at my back, something to lean on while my brain tried to remember how to do this the right way.

"So," she said quietly, gaze flicking up to mine, then away. "You decided to come yell at me about my life choices or . . . ?"

A humorless breath left my chest. "No," I said. "I came to apologize."

Her fingers tightened on the towel. "You already said good night."

"Clara." Her name came out rough and annoyed. I dragged a hand over my jaw, trying to scrape together words that didn't sound like excuses. "What I said downstairs? That wasn't because I didn't want you."

Her eyes snapped back to mine, wide and searching. The air between us tipped.

"Wanting you isn't my problem," I forced out. "It's . . . everything after."

Silence settled, heavy and waiting.

I pushed off the door and took a slow, uneven step toward her. Her throat worked on a swallow, but she didn't move back.

"I was a dick," I said. "Mostly because my brain was

melting out my ears. Also because the list of things I am currently terrified of is long and pathetic."

Her mouth curved at the edges. "You aren't pathetic."

"You'd be surprised." My laugh came out low and frayed. I shifted my weight, the prosthetic a familiar pressure. "I have spent an impressive amount of time thinking about every way my body could fail me in bed. Leg gives out. Balance goes to shit. Phantom pain flares at the wrong second. I go numb or too sensitive or nowhere at all. You could see the not-fantasy version of sex with me and realize you signed up for a horror show instead of a highlight reel."

Her expression softened in a way that made it hard to breathe. No flinching or pity. Just a steady, clear look.

"Wes," she said quietly. "I am not afraid of the not-fantasy version of you."

I looked away, toward the window where the night pressed close and the snow outside glowed faintly. "You should be," I muttered. "I am."

She took a breath, slow and measured. "Then that's what this was about," she said. "What I was trying to offer."

I glanced at her. She stood a little straighter, shoulders rolling back despite the fact that she was wearing nothing but a towel.

"You keep framing this like a performance," she said. "Like you have to show up already knowing the choreography, already hitting every mark, or you'll get booed offstage." Her brows drew together. "This isn't an audition, Wes. This is practice. For you. With someone who already knows you're a stubborn ass and wants to be here anyway."

Heat flickered in my chest at the same time embarrassment crawled up the back of my neck.

She took a careful step closer. The towel shifted with

her, exposing another inch of thigh before she hitched it up again.

"I meant it," she went on, voice softer but steady. "I want to help you figure out what works now. What feels good. Where the limits are and where they aren't. Not for some hypothetical future woman you're going to date someday. For you. So you know your body isn't the enemy."

My jaw clenched. The quiet in her tone cut deeper than any lecture could have.

"We go at your pace," she said. "We stop when you say stop. We laugh if something's awkward. We try again or we don't. You're in control the whole time, okay? Not your fear. Not the accident. You."

The accident landed between us like a ghost. I swallowed hard.

"You really think it's that simple?" I asked.

"No." Her mouth twitched. "I think it's going to be messy and weird and probably a little hilarious. I also think it could be really, really good." Her gaze held mine. "Think of it as . . . a series. Lessons. Only as far as you want to go."

My body already knew exactly how far it wanted to go. Right up against the wall of this room, into that bed, down every road I hadn't let myself consider for months.

"They say exposure therapy works," I tried to joke. "Set me loose in the deep end, see if I drown."

"This isn't throwing you in the deep end," she said. "This is stepping into the shallow end together and letting you decide if and when we go deeper." Her throat bobbed. "It's not charity, Wes."

My head jerked up at that.

"It's not pity. It's not me doing a good deed." She took a breath, eyes dropping briefly to my mouth before returning to my eyes. Her voice dropped. "I want this too."

Her words hung there, vibrating.

Then she let go of the knot. The towel slid. It loosened around her chest and whispered down her body in one clean line, pooling at her feet in a small, defeated heap of white terry cloth.

My lungs stopped working.

Clara stood in front of me, bare and unashamed, skin still flushed from the shower. My gaze dragged over her in slow, helpless passes, as if my eyes had their own gravity and she was the only thing they recognized.

Water still clung to her collarbone, beading along the delicate notch before sliding down to the swell of her breasts. Her nipples were tight and flushed, pretty and obscene at the same time, and all I could think about was how they would feel against my tongue. She was all contrast —strong thighs and generous hips, soft skin over quiet muscle, the kind of body that looked made for being touched and held and ruined in the best possible way.

My gaze caught on the slick shine between her legs, and my lungs forgot how to work. Every possessive, filthy thought I'd tried to choke down roared back all at once—*on your knees, taste her, make her fall apart on your tongue until she forgets her own name.* Underneath it, threaded through the heat, was something that scared me more than the wanting did.

Reverence.

A bone-deep ache that had nothing to do with my cock and everything to do with the fact that she had given me this, had stood there naked and unashamed and offered herself like she trusted me not to break her.

Lust pushed at my ribs, hot and wild, begging me to close the distance. Tenderness pressed just as hard from the inside, slow and steady, whispering that if I touched her now, there would be no pretending this was just practice, no going back to clean lines and careful rules.

My cock throbbed so hard it bordered on painful. Every fear I had was still there, still hissing in the back of my mind, but it was drowned out by one loud, brutal truth: I wanted her so much it scared me.

She shifted her weight, bare toes curling briefly in the towel at her feet. Her chin lifted a fraction, like she was bracing for impact.

"This is not me just being kind," she said quietly. "This is me wanting you. Like this. Now. Knowing exactly who you are and what you've been through and what might happen." Her fingers flexed at her sides. "You can say no. I'll survive the mortification. But don't tell me I don't want this."

The reservoir in my chest cracked.

Hayes's voice thundered in the background—*I trust you*—followed by every worst-case scenario my brain could conjure. Phantom pain flared low, a warning shot across my nerves. My pulse pounded in my ears.

She was standing there anyway. Choosing me anyway.

"Clara," I said, and the sound of her name in that small room felt like something I should be on my knees for. I stepped closer, slow, giving myself time to back out and failing spectacularly at taking it. "You know if we do this, it doesn't go back in the box, right? There's no version where we pretend this is some clinical experiment in my sex life. I am not that guy."

"I am very clear on what kind of guy you are," she said, a flicker of heat flashing in her eyes. "That's why I asked you."

I stopped in front of her, close enough now that I could feel the warmth coming off her skin, close enough that one more step would put my chest within reach of her hands.

"This is probably," I said slowly, "the worst idea I have ever had."

Her mouth curved, soft and sure. "Mine too."

My quiet laugh came out hoarse. I let my gaze drag over her one more time, because there was no universe where I was not going to burn this into my memory. Every line, every curve, every inch of her—brave enough to stand there and say *I want you* when I had done absolutely nothing to deserve that kind of gift.

My fear was still here. My loyalty to Hayes was still here. The noise in my head was still here.

The desire was louder.

I lifted my hand, fingers trembling just slightly, and touched a strand of damp hair where it clung to her shoulder, letting it slide over my knuckles.

"Okay," I said, the word landing in my gut like a promise. "Yes."

Her breath caught.

"Yes?" she whispered.

"Yes to you," I clarified, because if we were going to do this, she deserved every ounce of clarity I had. "Yes to this. Yes to . . . lessons. Yes to going as slow as I need to and probably faster than I should. Yes to fucking up and laughing about it instead of going back into my cave and pretending I'm already dead."

Relief and heat flashed across her face so fast it nearly knocked me over.

"Okay," she said, voice shaking just a little. "Okay."

I swallowed, my thumb brushing the damp skin at her shoulder, glasses sliding down my nose as I looked at her like she was the first good decision I'd made in too damn long.

"Then teach me, Duchess," I murmured. "Show me where we start."

"Okay," Clara said slowly, like she was lining something up in her mind. "Then we need rules."

I huffed out a laugh. "That sounds ominous as hell."

Her mouth curved, nervous and determined. I still couldn't believe how confident she was, standing naked in front of me.

"Ground rules," she corrected. "So you don't bolt. So I don't cry. So nobody gets murdered at Thanksgiving."

"Strong opening," I muttered.

She ignored me, which I realized was becoming a theme. "Rule one," she said, lifting a finger. "We do not talk about this to anyone. Not my sisters, not the bros at Nerd Night, definitely not Hayes. This stays between us."

My stomach clenched at my best friend's name. "Yeah," I said roughly. "That one I can get behind."

"Rule two," she went on. "Either one of us can call a halt. For any reason. Or no reason. No guilt. No 'sorry I ruined the mood.' We just . . . stop."

The tightness in my chest loosened a notch. "Deal."

Her eyes flicked over my face, like she was checking for signs I'd spook if she pushed any further. "Rule three is more like . . . a suggestion," she said. "For tonight, I think we should start with you not touching me."

Every muscle in my body went to high alert. "That's a fucked-up suggestion," I said hoarsely.

Her lips twitched. "You said you were worried about going too fast, about your body freaking out or your brain short-circuiting." She lifted a shoulder. "So maybe tonight is about your voice. You stay where you are. I listen. You tell me what to do. What you want to see. What you want me to feel."

Heat punched low and brutal.

"You want me to just stand here and watch you?" My voice sounded like it had been dragged over gravel.

Color rose in her cheeks. "I want you to have control without worrying about balance or phantom pain or whether your leg's going to behave. You get to stay put. You get to call the shots. You get to actually see what looking at me does to you." Her throat bobbed. "If you hate it, we stop. If it works, then we decide where to go next."

Control without physical risk. The hottest thing I could imagine and the most terrifying.

My jaw clenched so hard it ached. I could almost feel the line we were standing on—safe on one side, everything else on the other. My hands itched to touch her, to drag her in, to find out every way this new version of my body could still make her fall apart. The same hands were already curling into fists at the idea of reaching and somehow failing.

Her eyes softened like she could see the war playing out in real time. "Lesson one," she said, a faint, crooked smile tugging at her mouth as she planted her hands on her hips. "Just your voice. No touching. No promises beyond that."

It should not have made me harder. Somehow it did.

I swallowed. "You're really okay with that?"

"Wes." She stepped back toward the space by the bed, the lamp glow gilding every line of her bare body. "You have no idea how okay I am with that."

My control slipped.

"Lesson one," I repeated, more to myself than her. "You do what I say. I stay over here."

Her gaze dipped briefly to the obvious problem pressing

against my sweats, then back up again, eyes darker now. "Tell me where you want me," she murmured. "You're in charge."

Those were words I hadn't trusted myself with in months.

I dragged in a breath, forcing my shoulders down, hands loose at my sides. "Stay by the bed," I said, voice low. "Right where you are."

She nodded once and planted her feet, chin tipped up, eyes never leaving mine. "Now what?" she asked.

I let my gaze drop, slow and deliberate, to the curve of her breasts, the line of her ribs, the soft slope of her stomach.

"Start at your throat," I said, the words feeling strange and right in my mouth. "Use your hand. Slow."

Her fingers flexed against her thigh, then lifted.

She started at the hollow of her throat, a slow drag that made the tendons in her neck flex. She skimmed over her collarbone, tracing its edge like she was learning herself in a new language, then slid lower to the swell of her breasts. The touch was barely there, more suggestion than pressure, but her breath hitched like she'd yanked a plug out of a socket.

Goose bumps followed in the wake of her hand. Her nipples tightened, pebbling under her own palm, and the smallest sound caught in her throat. I felt every micro-reaction like it was wired into me—the flutter of her stomach, the way her shoulders eased back a fraction, the way her lips parted on a shaky exhale as if she'd surprised herself with how good her own touch could be.

"Do you remember the feel of a woman's body?" she asked, voice breathy and teasing as her palm slid lower.

My laugh came out wrecked. "I'm having a hard time

thinking about anything except you lately," I admitted. "It's a real problem."

She smiled, shaky but pleased, and the sound that slipped out of her—half laugh, half exhale—loosened something that had been cinched tight in my chest.

"Good," she murmured. "Then this should help."

She dragged her hand down the center of her chest, over the curve of one breast, thumb brushing across already-tight skin. Her nipples peaked in response.

My mouth went dry. My hands curled into fists to keep from closing the distance between us.

"Slower," I said, surprised by the rough command in my own voice. "You're rushing it."

Her gaze snapped to mine, pupils blown wide. "Yes, sir," she whispered, and my cock jerked so hard I had to shift my weight.

She followed my words like a script.

"On the bed," I commanded.

Clara stepped backward until her legs hit the bed. She lowered herself and leaned back on her arms, toes facing me.

"Knees apart." I licked my lips. "Show me that pretty pussy, Duchess."

Her breathing changed first.

It went from steady to uneven, chest rising faster, then catching. A faint tremor ran down her arms. Her hips shifted, just a little, chasing her own touch. Her cheeks flushed deeper, a pink that spread down her neck, across her chest as her knees dropped open.

"Eyes on me," I said without thinking.

They snapped back up immediately.

*God help me, I love that look.*

"You're okay?" I asked, because if I didn't keep some

kind of check on myself, I was going to cross the room and wreck every rule we'd just set.

"I'm . . ." Her voice broke on a small sound, half gasp, half sigh. "I'm definitely okay."

"Drag your fingers lower," I told her, breath catching. "Not too fast. Take your time and stay right there." When she reached her clit, I smiled. "Less," I said, my voice rough. "Ease up and just . . . make slow circles." My cock throbbed as I watched Clara tease her swollen clit. "Yeah. Like that."

Clara moaned as she touched herself. Her thighs tightened around her hand, and her free hand gripped the bed.

My heart pounded in my throat. I'd done a lot of things with a lot of confidence in my life, but nothing had ever felt quite like this—standing there, fully clothed, while the most beautiful woman I'd ever seen undid herself one breath at a time because I told her to.

My palm itched to touch her. My fingers twitched at my sides.

"Wes," she whispered, my name frayed at the edges. "Please."

She didn't say for what. Didn't have to. "One finger. Then two." I watched as Clara's fingers disappeared inside her. I knew for a fact mine would feel better. My thick fingers would stretch her open in a way she wouldn't forget.

"Please," she breathed.

Her begging was my undoing.

My mind flickered through every filthy thing I wanted instead of this distance: my hand replacing hers, my mouth between her thighs, her knees bracketing my hips as she moved over me, testing what my leg could handle while I held her exactly where I wanted her and sank deep.

The line between what I was seeing and what I was imagining blurred so hard I felt dizzy.

Her body tensed, caught between movements, heart-beat visible in the hollow of her throat. Her lips parted on another quiet, choked little sound that went straight through me.

Something in me snapped.

Heat ripped through my body, fast and brutal. My muscles locked, breath stuttering as everything I'd been holding back punched free all at once. My vision went white around the edges.

I came, hard and humiliatingly fast, the sharp, undeniable release slamming into me before I could do a damn thing to stop it.

My hand hit the wall behind me to keep my knees from buckling. My pulse thundered in my ears. Shame and pleasure tangled together in a mess I didn't have words for.

Across from me, Clara was breathing hard, skin flushed and glowing, her hand still between her thighs, eyes wide and dark as they locked on mine.

I was wrecked. She was wrecked. Every line we'd drawn felt thinner than paper.

And for the first time in a long time, even wrapped in the embarrassment of losing control, I felt something under it that I hadn't expected.

*Alive.*

My breathing was a mess, rough and uneven, like I'd just sprinted instead of standing frozen against a wall while she remained on display for me.

The front of my sweats was damp and humiliating, my pride in tatters, but none of it could compete with the sight of her. Clara lay there, knees apart, flushed and soaked, chest lifting in shallow pulls. Every inch of her was soft curves and sharp edges, holy and obscene all at once.

I couldn't stop staring at her mouth. At her thighs. At

the slick, unmistakable evidence of what I'd just done to her without laying a single hand on her.

Something in her gaze shifted as she watched me—taking in my wrecked breathing, the death grip I had on the doorframe, the way my hips had jerked just once when I lost it. Her lips curved, slow and dangerous, like she'd just figured out the answer to a question she hadn't wanted to ask out loud.

She tilted her head, eyes dark and soft and a little wicked.

"Did you want a taste?" she asked.

# TWENTY-SIX

## CLARA

My legs were still trembling.

Knees spread, towel somewhere in a sad little heap on the floor. My chest heaved like I'd sprinted up the dunes. My hand was still between my thighs, slick and shaking, fingers frozen mid-movement.

*Did you want a taste?*

The sentence hung in the air between us. Like I could actually see the shape of it, hovering over the bed, impossible to drag back into my mouth.

*Oh god, maybe that was too far.*

*Please, please say yes.*

Both thoughts slammed into each other in my chest, colliding hard enough to make me a little dizzy.

Across the room, Wes was plastered to the wall like he'd been nailed there. One hand braced against the doorjamb, knuckles white. His jaw clenched so tight I could see the muscle jumping. The damp, dark patch on the front of his sweats left very little to the imagination.

He looked wrecked. Turned on. Humiliated. Like he

was equal parts furious with his body and stunned by what it had just done.

I couldn't tell if I wanted to apologize or crawl across the bed to him.

His gaze dragged over me—my bare thighs, my hand, the flushed pink of my chest—and something in his expression changed. The shame didn't vanish, exactly, but it shifted, making room for something darker, hotter.

He swallowed, throat working. When he finally spoke, his voice came out low and rough edged. "You have no idea how much I do."

Heat shot up my spine, sharp and electric. My fingers tightened on the comforter.

The rules we'd made—the safe little box labeled *lesson* —felt flimsy now, like tissue paper. This was not theoretical. This was me offering him more than a show. This was him admitting he wanted it.

"I meant it," I heard myself say, voice quieter than I intended. "You don't have to just watch."

His eyes flicked to my hand still resting high on my thigh, then back to my face. "Clara," he rasped. I could tell he was worried about his leg, how he would position himself, because kneeling was out of the question.

I pushed a breath out and sat up, trying to steady the wild fluttering in my chest. "We can have you lying back," I said, choosing each word. "Where you're not fighting gravity. Your body already knows how to be okay there. No balance. No falling."

His gaze searched mine, like he was looking for the trap.

"Then," I continued, pulse thudding in my ears as I rose to my knees, "you let me come to you."

Something raw flashed across his face. Hope, maybe. Hunger. Fear. All of it tangled together in one hit.

The only sound in the room was our breathing.

Then he pushed off the door with a small, decisive nod. His limp was more pronounced after everything that had happened, but his steps were steady, each one measured. He crossed to the bed and eased down on it like he'd practiced this a hundred times, testing the mattress, shifting his leg until he found a position that didn't make anything in his face tighten.

He settled onto his back, head against my pillows, broad shoulders sinking into my comforter, glasses still slightly crooked, chest moving in slow, deliberate breaths.

"Here," he said, looking up at me, voice a quiet challenge. "This work for you, Duchess?"

My thighs clenched. Every part of me screamed *yes*.

I made room for him, every inch of my skin aware of his eyes. The distance from the headboard to the foot of the bed had never felt longer. I moved anyway—on my knees, careful and deliberate.

One step closer to him. One step deeper into whatever this was.

"Yeah," I said, my voice coming out much steadier than I felt. "This works for me."

Wes pushed himself higher, his shoulders sinking into my pillows like he'd been there a hundred times instead of never. He shifted his leg, testing the angle, adjusting the prosthetic with small, efficient movements until his face didn't tighten. He could have taken it off. We both knew that. The fact that he chose not to told me exactly how much he trusted it right now—and how not-ready he was to be that bare with me yet.

That was fine. One thing at a time.

I moved beside him, the mattress dipping under my weight. My hand found his chest on instinct, palm flattening over the warm spread of muscle there. His T-shirt was soft under my fingers, the hard, steady thud of his heartbeat against my palm making my own heartbeat race faster.

"You good?" I asked quietly.

His mouth kicked up, the tension in his jaw easing just enough to let something wicked through. "Definitely more than good," he said, voice low and strained. "Get over here."

Heat pooled low in my belly as my pussy clenched in anticipation.

I shifted, aware of every inch of my own skin, of how completely bare I was while he watched me. It felt like undressing all over again, except this time there was no towel to drop. Just me, flushed and open and fully visible to the one man in this town I absolutely shouldn't want.

My fingers slid from his chest to his shoulder as I swung one leg over him, careful not to knee him in the ribs. First my knee landed by his side, then the other, bracketing his shoulders. The position was clumsy and intimate all at once, my thighs hovering over his chest, his heat rising up to meet the cool air on my skin.

My pulse roared in my ears. This was somehow more vulnerable than standing naked by the bed. There was nowhere to hide from his gaze, nothing between us but trust and a whole lot of bad decisions.

I hovered, muscles trembling, hands on the headboard to steady myself. I removed his glasses and set them on the bed beside us. "Tell me if this is too much," I said, breathless. "If I'm too heavy or—"

"Clara." His voice cut through my spiral, rough and utterly sure. His hands slid up to my hips, fingers curling in like he'd been waiting his whole life for this grip. He looked up at me from beneath his lashes, pupils blown wide, reverent and filthy all at once. "You're perfect," he said. "Now sit on my fucking face."

Something in my spine melted.

Trust won out over fear. I exhaled, slow and shaking, and let my weight settle back, his hands tightening on my hips to guide me exactly where he wanted me.

The first brush of his mouth on me shorted out my whole nervous system.

Heat, pressure, a devastating kind of focus—like he'd zeroed in on the exact center of me and decided that was the only thing in the world worth paying attention to. Everything went white noise. My hearing narrowed to the thud of my own heartbeat in my ears, the rasp of my breath, the low moan he made against me like he was the one being relieved of something.

My fingers clamped around the headboard, knuckles aching. My thighs wanted to snap shut on instinct, every muscle going tight and boneless at the same time.

*Oh.*

This was not tentative. There was no careful testing of the water, no awkward fumbling like he was trying to remember how anything worked. Whatever Wes doubted about his body, his instincts about me were sharp as a knife.

He moved like a man who had done this before and done it well—and like it mattered to him that I would remember this for the rest of my life.

I tried to tell myself this was good. This was what I wanted for him. A win. Proof to shove in the face of that ugly voice in his head that whispered every time he looked at his leg. He got to be steady here, strong, absolutely in control of what I was feeling.

*Helping him,* I reminded myself as another shock rolled through me. *I'm helping him.*

That fiction lasted about three seconds.

"Wes," I gasped, his name catching on a breath that wasn't fully formed. The noise that came out of me didn't sound like mine. It was too raw, too high. I groped for words, for direction, for anything that sounded like I was the one steering this. "That . . . oh my god, yes. Right there, don't—"

He made a low, satisfied noise, the vibration of it shooting straight through me.

Stubble rasped against tender skin, a rough counterpoint to the heat of his mouth. His fingers tightened on my hips every time I moaned, holding me in place when my body wanted to bolt and chase the feeling at the same time. There was something devastating in the way he held me—firm and grounding, like no matter how hard I shook, he wasn't going anywhere, and at the same time like he was devouring me, like he'd been starving and I was the first real meal in months.

"Tell me if it's too much," he managed against my skin, voice rough and muffled.

"More," I heard myself say, the word torn out of me on a broken little sob. "Please."

The desperation in my own voice shocked me almost as much as how fast he answered it, adjusting in ways that made everything worse and better all at once.

His hold on my thighs tightened, dragging me closer. "There you go," he murmured against me. "Ride my face. Use me. Let me feel you come on my mouth."

Coherent thought started to fray.

*Fuck, his confidence.*

Whatever he questioned about stairs and hills and dance floors, he did not question this. I could feel it in every deliberate movement. He knew exactly what he was doing to me, and he liked it—liked the way my breath hitched, liked the way I kept reaching for something to hold on to and only found him.

A sound tore out of me, half laugh and half sob. My thighs were shaking now, muscles trembling with effort. I let one hand slip, sinking into his hair. The strands were thick and soft under my fingers, his head angling into my touch like he wanted more of that too.

I tried to hold back. I really did. This was supposed to be a lesson, a first step, not me losing my mind on his face like some cautionary tale about mixing unresolved feelings with sex homework.

Then he moaned, low and rough, like he was enjoying this just as much as I was, and my last scrap of restraint snapped.

My hips started to move on their own, tiny helpless rolls that chased whatever he was giving me. He tightened his grip, guiding me, and the combination of him holding me there and letting me move wrecked whatever was left of my composure.

"Wes," I choked out, every muscle going tight as a wire. "I—I can't—"

Everything inside me cinched tight at once. My thighs shook, my spine bowing as heat coiled sharp and bright, then snapped. A broken sound tore out of me—half sob, half his name—as the world narrowed to the rush of release rolling through me in helpless waves.

I pitched forward, catching myself with one hand on the wall above the headboard, the other still buried in his hair. My thighs quivered around his head, breath sawing in and out like I'd just sprinted the length of the beach.

He eased up slowly, one last maddeningly gentle pass of his tongue that sent aftershocks skittering through me. His hands loosened on my hips, sliding up to steady my waist instead, holding me there while I remembered how to exist in my own body again.

*Holy. Shit.*

Every man before him felt like an echo—all suggestion and no resonance. Wes Vaughn had just taken my carefully constructed ideas about sex and blown them straight to hell, all without moving from one spot on the bed. That man didn't just put up with eating pussy, he reveled in it.

I'd made my offer thinking I was going to help him get his mojo back.

Right now, shaking and half draped over the headboard, I was pretty sure he'd just erased everyone who'd come before him like they'd never existed at all.

Carefully, I forced my knees to unlock.

Every muscle in my body felt like it had been unplugged and plugged back in sideways. I eased my weight off him an inch at a time, my shaky thighs protesting as I shifted. The last thing I wanted was to slide wrong and grind down on his leg.

"I've got you," Wes murmured, voice rough.

His hands slid from my hips to my waist, steadying, guiding. He helped me turn, helped me find the mattress, helped me settle beside him instead of collapsing like a stunned rag doll. My back hit the sheets, and I stared up at the ceiling, chest rising too fast, lungs doing a terrible job pretending they remembered how to work.

"You okay?" he asked.

A shaky laugh hiccuped out of me. "I'm not entirely sure I remember my own name."

One corner of his mouth kicked up. There was still moisture glinting at his jaw, his hair a little mussed from my fingers. The sight sent a fresh, traitorous flush sweeping over my skin.

"Clara," he said, like it was an answer, not a question. "There. Now you remember."

I let out a wobbly breath. "Show-off."

We just looked at each other, the air between us thick and quiet. Then he shifted, reaching blindly until his fingers found the fallen towel on the floor.

"C'mere," he said softly.

He sat up, bracing one hand behind him, and pulled me gently toward his lap. The bravado from a few minutes ago was gone; what was left was careful and almost shy. He used the towel to wipe between my thighs with a tenderness that made my throat go tight, his touch slow and unhurried, like he had all the time in the world.

"Sorry," he muttered, gaze flicking up once to meet mine. "I just . . . want you comfortable."

"You just melted my spine," I said, dazed. "Comfortable is relative at this point."

He huffed out a laugh, the sound low and pleased. When he was satisfied, he tossed the towel back onto the floor and pushed off the bed, moving with that familiar care he kept pretending I didn't notice. He crossed to the dresser like he'd done it a hundred times, opened the top drawer, and rummaged until he found an old T-shirt.

"Arms," he said.

He slipped the shirt over my head, careful not to tangle it with my hair, then tugged it down over my hips with a little pat.

"Very glam," I said. "Real seduction wear."

His eyes warmed. "Trust me," he said. "I'll be remembering the way you look in my T-shirt for a very long time."

My heart did a slow, dangerous roll.

He sat at the edge of the bed, close enough that our knees brushed, and dragged a hand over his face. For the first time since this started, he looked a little shell-shocked too.

"You okay?" I asked, because it felt like the only question that mattered.

He let his hand fall, fingers drumming once against his thigh. "Yeah," he said slowly. "I . . . yes."

A beat passed. Then he slanted me a look that was almost disbelieving.

"I didn't think about it," he said.

"Think about what?" I asked.

"My leg." His gaze dropped briefly to where the prosthetic stretched under his sweats, then came back to my face. "I didn't think about my balance. Or pain. Or what could go wrong. Not once. The whole time, the only thing in my head was you."

Something hot pricked behind my eyes.

"Well," I said, trying for light and missing, "you seemed pretty dialed in on the task at hand."

His mouth twitched. "Lesson two seemed to require focus."

I snorted. "Overachieving is what it was."

"Guess I had a good teacher," he murmured.

The compliment slid under my ribs and settled there, warm and heavy. We'd called this practice, framed it as work, but there was nothing clinical about the way he'd just taken my body apart like it was the only test that had ever mattered.

Pride swelled in my chest, sharp enough to hurt. Not pride in myself—though my ego was not exactly suffering— but in him. In the way he'd moved without second-guessing. In the way his hands had gripped my thighs like he trusted his own strength again. In the way he'd dragged a groan out of me and looked up like he'd just remembered his favorite language.

He hadn't been a broken man with a compromised body. He'd been a man who knew exactly how to worship a woman and had been starving for the chance.

It was dangerous how much that made me love him.

I flinched internally as soon as the word surfaced, shoving it back down so fast my brain rattled. Not love. Not that. We had rules. It was literally the *first one.*

He sobered, eyes searching my face. "We should call it for tonight."

A flicker of panic went through me before he added, quickly, "We should both probably get some rest."

Relief and disappointment collided in my chest.

"Yeah," I said. "Sounds good."

His fingers brushed my hand, slow and hesitant, as if asking permission. I turned mine over and let our palms press together. Somehow the simple contact felt more intimate than his mouth between my legs had. There was nothing to hide behind here. No shock, no urgency. Just two people on a bed, holding hands like teenagers.

"I'll . . . let you get cleaned up," I said, swallowing. "Or, you know, changed."

A flush crept up his neck, faint but there. "Probably a good idea," he muttered.

We just sat there for another long, quiet moment, our hands linked, breaths gradually settling in sync. The heater kicked on again down the hall. Snow tapped lightly at the window. Inside, everything felt unnaturally still.

"Thank you," he said finally.

I blinked. "For what? Hovering while you demonstrated your many talents?"

"For . . ." He shook his head, searching for words. "For letting me feel like myself again. For a few minutes."

The ache in my chest expanded, big and bright and terrifying.

"You are yourself," I said quietly. "Even when you forget."

His thumb stroked once across the back of my hand, almost absently. Then he let go, fingers slipping away with a reluctance I felt all the way down my spine.

"I'll, uh . . ." He cleared his throat and rose carefully from the bed. "I'll see you in the morning."

He took a few steps backward, toward the door, as if turning his back on me might break whatever spell we'd woven. At the threshold he paused and looked back, expression unreadable in the half-light.

"Sweet dreams, Clara," he said softly.

The door clicked shut behind him.

For a long time, I didn't move.

The room was dark except for the little pool of light from my lamp. My body still hummed, a slow, deep thrum under my skin, every nerve aware of what had just happened and who had done it to me. The sheets smelled faintly like my shampoo and his soap and something new we'd made between them.

I flopped back, staring at the ceiling, a dazed smile tugging at my mouth.

Then, beneath the floaty, postorgasmic haze, the stone of fear made itself known—a small, dense weight settling low in my ribs. This started as a way to build Wes's confidence. Confidence to be the man he used to be . . . with *other women*. A tiny pang of nausea rolled through me.

Now I couldn't stand the idea.

If this was just the beginning, I was in so much more trouble than I'd thought.

## TWENTY-SEVEN

WES

By the time the sky went dark enough to press against the windows, the house felt different.

Lighter. Or maybe that was just me.

My leg barely twinged as I moved around the kitchen, wallet and keys in one hand, the other braced on the counter more out of habit than necessity. Phantom pain that usually sat in the background like white noise had gone quiet, replaced by something else buzzing under my skin.

Every time my brain slipped, it went right back to last night.

Clara's thighs trembling around my head. Her fingers in my hair, tight and desperate as she rode my face. The way her whole body had gone tight and then loose all at once when she came, my name broken open on her tongue. The dazed, stunned little smile afterward when I'd gently wiped her down with a towel.

*Lesson two, my ass.* It was a highlight reel I had no business replaying as many times as I had today.

I'd gotten hard twice just thinking about it.

The weirdest part was what didn't come after. No crash

into shame. No mental replay of every worst-case scenario. Just that one simple, stunned thought circling like a hawk.

*I made her feel that good.*

Clara's footsteps sounded behind me as she crossed to the counter, bare feet, loose T-shirt, tiny shorts that should have been illegal inside my house. She popped open the fridge, grabbed the bowl of grapes, and used her hip to nudge the door shut. When she turned toward me, she'd already shoved two grapes into her mouth, cheeks puffed out like a chipmunk.

"Hi," she managed around them, cheeks rounding, eyes going a little wide like she'd only just remembered exactly what my mouth had been doing the last time we were face-to-face like this.

Heat crawled up my neck. "Hey," I said, and my voice came out low and dark.

She chewed quickly, hand cupped under her chin in case anything betrayed her. A blush rose in two pink flags on her cheeks, climbing toward her ears. It matched the one burning under my skin.

Her gaze flicked over me—the jeans, the hoodie, the keys in my hand. "Nerd Night?" she asked, like it was the most normal question in the world.

I huffed out a small laugh. "Yeah," I said. "Figured I should remind them I'm not actually a ghost."

Her mouth curved, soft and a little shy. "Tell Hayes I say hi," she said. "And try not to let Brody bully you into a character death this time."

"Unlikely," I muttered. "He's been trying to kill me since middle school. Dice just give him new ideas."

She grinned around another grape, and something in my chest did an alarming, unfamiliar thing—lifted, instead of sinking.

We'd spent the whole day orbiting each other in this new, careful gravity—brushes in the hallway, shared coffee, a couple of "you good?" check-ins that carried about twelve more questions underneath. No awkward apologies. No pretending last night hadn't happened. Just . . . awareness. More heat under the surface.

For the first time in too long, the idea of leaving the house didn't feel like work. It felt like proof. That I wasn't sliding back into the cave. That things could shift in both directions.

"Don't wait up," I said, twisting the cap off my water.

She tilted her head, eyes bright. "Liar," she said lightly.

She wasn't wrong. I was already planning to text her when the game inevitably went off the rails.

I pocketed my keys, leg steady as I crossed to the door. The familiar weight of my prosthetic felt . . . right tonight. Not like a warning label. Like a piece of me that had carried me through something hard and was still here.

The cold hit my face as I stepped onto the porch, breath fogging on the exhale. For once, the tightness in my chest had nothing to do with dread.

I locked the door behind me, glanced once at the warm rectangle of light where I knew she was still standing with that damn bowl of grapes, and headed for the truck.

THE CONDOMS WERE on the back wall under a flickering strip of fluorescent lights that made everything look slightly more tragic than it needed to.

I stood there, hands on my hips, staring at three shelves' worth of latex like they were an exam I hadn't studied for.

*What the hell am I doing?*

The answer arrived immediately, dry and unhelpful. *You know exactly why you're here, jackass.*

My gaze drifted over the options. Ribbed. Ultra-thin. Ecologically responsible. Size variations that made my ego twitch in three different directions at once. Boxes of three, ten, twenty-four.

Realistic. Optimistic. Former me on a good weekend.

My mouth curved despite myself.

There was a weird, fizzy feeling under my ribs, like the first beer on an empty stomach. Picking up condoms again felt . . . dangerous. Stupid. *Hopeful.* Like the kind of errand a guy with a future ran, not the half-busted version of me who used to avoid his own reflection.

Grief slid in under the fizz, quick and sharp.

I picked up a box, thumb brushing over the edge. I hadn't needed these since before the accident. Before hospital rooms and rehab and learning how to walk again one ugly step at a time. Before my sex life had been filed under "theoretical" instead of "probable reality."

My thumb tapped the cardboard, rhythm speeding up with my pulse. I could see Clara in my mind without even trying—her knees bracketing my shoulders, taste and heat and the way she'd begged for me. The idea of being inside her instead of just in my own head made my cock stir behind my fly.

Yeah. This was happening.

I reached for a second box, debated, and settled on one.

*Be real, man. Maybe aim for not humiliating yourself before you buy in bulk.*

"Wes?"

The sound of my name sliced through the aisle so hard my soul did a full record scratch.

I whipped around.

Hayes stood at the end of the row, shoulders filling the space between two sad displays of beef jerky and lip gloss. Work jeans, worn flannel, hair damp from a quick shower, a six-pack dangling from one hand and a bag of pretzels from the other. Every inch of him screamed cursed small-town leading man, right down to the expression that was half amused, half tired.

"Yeah. Hey," he muttered, giving the display a resigned pat.

As he stepped forward, his shoulder brushed a cardboard stand advertising some jerky sale. The whole thing leaned, wobbled, and then half collapsed behind him in a slow-motion slide of meat sticks.

My brain screamed. *Hide the condoms, hide the condoms, for the love of all things, hide the fucking condoms.*

My hand shot out sideways. I grabbed the first thing my fingers hit on the lower shelf and yanked it into view as I slid the condom box behind a stack of discount cold medicine.

I looked down.

Tampons.

Perfect.

I turned back, boxing out the rest of the shelf with my body like I was defending the lane in a fourth-quarter game.

He startled, swore under his breath, and righted the display with the air of a man who had absolutely expected that to happen.

Hayes's eyes scanned the aisle, landing suspiciously on the array of condoms and lube over my shoulder. "What's up?"

"Hey," I said, half strangled, holding up the box between us. "Clara texted. Emergency run."

Relief flashed in his face so fast it made my chest twist.

"Dang," he said, huffing out a laugh. "She's already got you running errands? Thought she'd at least wait a couple of months before breaking you in."

*Buddy, you have absolutely no idea.*

I snorted, trying to look like a man who regularly bought feminine hygiene products and absolutely not like a man who had just ditched condoms because his best friend had walked up. "Figured I'd help out," I said.

His gaze flicked down to the box in my hand. His frown deepened. "She uses the purple ones," he said, nodding toward a different shelf. "Same brand, different box. She once gave me a twenty-minute speech on why it matters."

I stared at him. "You know your sister's tampon preferences?"

"I have four sisters," he said flatly. "I know more about cycles than most ob-gyns. Do her a favor and grab the other ones or I'll never hear the end of it."

My throat constricted. "Right," I said, clearing it. "Wouldn't want to screw that up."

I turned back, shoved the wrong box back into its spot, and grabbed the one with the purple stripe he'd indicated. My pulse thudded in my ears as I did my best to look like a man entirely focused on absorbency instead of trying to mentally map how fast I could circle back to the condom aisle before closing.

Hayes shifted the pretzels to his other hand and jerked his head toward the register. "You heading to Brody's?"

"Of course," I said. "Figured I'd roll some dice, let him accuse me of cheating, the usual."

"Good." He sounded like he meant it. "It's good to get out of that house sometimes. Clara's already worried enough."

A huff of a laugh escaped me. "She told you that?"

"She tells me plenty." Fondness softened his features. "Half of it is about how much of a pain in the ass you are."

Warmth pricked along the inside of my ribs. "Keeps life exciting."

We walked toward the front together, fluorescent hum overhead, the linoleum squeaking under our boots. The place smelled like coffee that had been on too long and cheap aftershave. A teenage cashier with a nose ring and earbuds glanced up when we approached, expression flat with the boredom of youth.

Hayes dumped his beer and pretzels on the counter. I added my very important box of definitely-for-Clara tampons. The kid beeped everything through without blinking.

We paid and stepped out into the cold, plastic bags crinkling in our hands. The air hit my face, clean and sharp, clearing away some of the static in my head.

"Seriously," Hayes said as we crossed the cracked lot toward our trucks. "Thanks for doing stuff like this for her. She'll act like you're annoying, but . . ." He shrugged. "You know."

Hayes shook his head, the weight of big-brother worry sitting on his shoulders in a way I recognized too well.

"She needs somebody solid right now," he finished.

A laugh tried to claw its way out of my chest and die at the same time. Solid was not the word I would have picked for a guy who had come in his own pants watching that same sister touch herself the night before.

"Yeah," I said quietly. "I got her."

He nodded once, satisfied. "See you over there."

He headed for his truck, beer knocking against his leg. I stood there, bag hanging from my hand, guilt and something hotter tangling under my sternum.

~

Brody's dining room table looked like a small war had broken out on it.

Dice everywhere. Graph paper. A map in dry-erase marker that made absolutely no sense to anyone but Austin, with arrows and little X's and skulls scattered around a hand-drawn keep. Empty beer bottles, a bowl of pretzels, somebody's abandoned sweatshirt slung over the back of a chair.

"Still can't believe you almost ate it on the driveway," Cal was saying, shuffling a deck of spell cards and teasing Hayes. "It wasn't even a real hill, man."

Hayes flipped him off and reached for the pretzels. "Black ice is an equal-opportunity assassin."

"Sure," Brody said, lining up minis. "But only you would manage to almost concuss yourself." Brody pointed at Hayes. "Besides, I salted the sidewalk, so don't come for me."

My mouth twitched.

It hit me a second later that I was actually glad to be here.

The noise didn't feel like sandpaper on my nerves tonight. The scrape of chairs, the clatter of dice in the tray, the argument about whether our half-elf ranger could seduce the NPC stablehand again—it all landed like background music instead of overload. My leg was stretched out under the table, prosthetic braced, and I shifted without thinking about who was watching.

"You're up, Vaughn," Austin said, tapping the map where my character's mini figurine stood at the mouth of a cave. "Horse of the Damned or whatever you named him needs to pick a direction."

"Midnight," I corrected, because some things mattered. "And he's not damned. He's misunderstood."

"Just roll." Brody chuckled.

I shook the dice in my hand. The plastic clicked together in a familiar rhythm, grounding me in a way nothing else did.

Halfway through the roll, my phone buzzed in my pocket.

I caught it with my other hand, thumb flicking the screen under the edge of the table.

CLARA

> Why did my brother text me that I can thank him for the "perfect tampons"?

Heat crawled up my neck. A laugh tried to sneak out of my chest.

My thumbs moved before my brain could overthink it.

ME

> I'll explain later, but basically I panicked and had to roll with it.

Three dots appeared. Disappeared. Appeared again.

CLARA

> You're ridiculous. Thank you for the right kind anyway.

The little knot inside my chest loosened. I stuffed the phone back in my pocket, mouth fighting a smile.

"Text from work?" Hayes asked, tone casual as he reached for his d20 dice.

My face stayed neutral, but I could feel the amusement tugging at the edges. "Just Clara checking I didn't die on the stairs," I said.

"See?" Austin said. "Full-time live-in nurse. You're basically a Hallmark movie."

"Pretty sure Hallmark skips the part where she rolls her eyes and tells me to stop being such a baby," I said.

The table laughed. Hayes shook his head, but there was something thoughtful in his eyes, like he was turning the words over.

Game night rolled on.

We argued about spell slots and rations. Brody cursed when we walked right into a trap he'd been telegraphing for three sessions. Hayes's character did something spectacularly stupid that somehow worked out for everyone. It felt like old times in a way that made my soul ache a little—same guys, same table, same noise, except my leg didn't feel like a spotlight and my brain wasn't trying to drag me out of my own skin.

Underneath all of it, a thin thread tugged—a steady awareness that I was living two lives now. One at this table, rolling dice and talking shit. One back at the house, teaching my hands to stay off my roommate while my mouth did everything else.

Eventually the pizza boxes were empty, the beer was gone, and people started peeling off with clapped shoulders and shouted promises to "definitely read my spells before next time."

I shrugged on my jacket.

"You heading out too?" Hayes asked, grabbing his keys from the hook by the door.

"Yeah." I stretched, feeling the tug in my thigh in a way that was more information than pain. "Early PT tomorrow. My therapist will have my ass if I show up half asleep."

We stepped out onto the porch together. The night air was sharp and cold, breath coming out in white puffs.

Across the street, somebody's porch light buzzed, haloed in a cloud of fine winter air.

For a second it was easy. Just me and my best friend, standing side by side like we had a hundred times before everything changed.

"You seem . . . better," Hayes said.

The way he said it wasn't casual. It was careful.

I forced a shrug. "Good hair day."

He snorted. "Yeah, that must be it."

His hand slid into his jacket pocket. The other fiddled with his keys, metal chiming softly. "I mean it," he added, eyes on the dark street instead of my face. "It's been a long time. Tonight you actually yelled at Cal for trying to seduce an innkeeper with his charisma score again. That felt like the old you."

A huff of a laugh slipped out. "He deserved it," I said. "Guy keeps thinking he's the main character just because he's young and cocky."

Something eased in his shoulders, but I knew that look. The one that meant he was lining up a question and trying to figure out how to ask it without stepping on a land mine.

Hayes huffed a laugh, then sobered. He turned his head, studying me for a long beat, the way he used to when we were kids and he was trying to see if I was really okay after some dumb stunt.

"I really am glad she's staying with you," he said.

Something in my throat locked.

He rolled the keys between his fingers. "I'm not going to do the whole 'hurt my sister and I bury you under the barn' speech," he went on. "You know who she is. Just know that Clara feels everything big." His jaw tightened, the muscle jumping once. "So if things ever get . . . complicated . . . just don't forget she's Clara. Be kind."

The words rang like a struck bell between us.

My brain threw up every image it had stored in the last twenty-four hours—her naked in front of me, the tremor in her thighs as she came on my face, the way she had looked at me afterward like I was something more than a broken man getting some practice in.

There was no version of this where I could look him in the eye and promise nothing would ever happen. Not only had that ship sailed, but it had set fire to the dock behind it.

"I'd never hurt her on purpose," I said.

It was the only honest thing I could offer. My voice came out quiet and sincere. "Not in a way I can help."

Hayes's shoulders dropped. He nodded once, like that was the answer he'd been sifting for.

"I know," he said. "That's why I trust you."

He stepped off the porch toward his truck, then immediately caught the corner of his hoodie on Brody's side mirror. The fabric snagged with a sharp rip.

"Motherfucker," he muttered, yanking it free to reveal a fresh tear along the hem.

I shook my head, half exasperated, half fond, watching him stalk around the hood like the mirror had personally insulted him. Hayes Darling—cursed by ghosts, gravity, and the entire concept of inanimate objects.

My chest felt heavier as I walked to my own truck. Hayes's words rode shotgun all the way home, a low, steady weight I couldn't shake.

The house was dark when I stepped inside. My keys hit the bowl by the door with a clatter that echoed. My leg ached in that dull, familiar way from too much sitting and not enough stretching, so I rolled my shoulders, flexed my knee, and headed for the kitchen.

Cold light spilled over the floor when I opened the

fridge. I reached for a bottle of water, hand landing on the shelf, then froze.

The list on the door had grown again.

Clara's handwriting wove through mine in different colors of marker, looping and crowded, like we'd both kept reaching for rules because it felt easier than admitting how many we'd already broken. I let my gaze drag down the page.

**Rule #1: No pity parties.**
**Rule #2: No sponge baths.**
**Rule #3: No random guys in the house (per the landlord).**
**Rule #4: Landlord must attend his own PT.**
**Rule #5: Tenant reserves the right to eat ice cream for dinner without judgment.**
**Rule #6: Knock like you mean it.**
**Rule #7: No hostile workplace signage.**
**Rule #8: The one who cooks doesn't do the dishes.**

My mouth twitched when I hit Rule #9.

**Rule #9: No making out in the snow.**

She'd drawn a thick, black X through the *No*, the word obliterated under the ink. *Making out in the snow* stared back at me like a confession.

Lower down, fresh additions:

**Rule #10: Lessons stay behind closed doors.**
**Rule #11: Either one of us can call a halt. No guilt. No apologies.**

My throat went tight.

We'd joked, that first night, about the big one. The catchall. *No falling in love.* She'd tossed it out like a joke, and I'd laughed like it was obvious. Like it was something you could just stick on a fridge and brute-force into existence with sheer will and permanent marker.

It wasn't there.

Not crossed out. Not squeezed in at the bottom. Just . . . nonexistent.

The bottle of water sweated under my hand. The fridge hummed quietly, stubbornly doing its job while my stomach dropped for a reason that had nothing to do with hunger.

I told myself she'd forgotten to write it this time. That she'd been in a hurry, that she'd run out of room, that it was still understood even if it wasn't spelled out in black ink.

I let my forehead rest against the cool metal, eyes closed, the chill seeping into my skin. The list blurred in my mind, a mess of lines and promises we kept pretending would keep us safe.

We had rules for everything except the one thing I seemed completely incapable of stopping.

The truth slipped in anyway, slow and inevitable.

That rule didn't belong on the fridge because, for me, it was already broken.

## TWENTY-EIGHT

## CLARA

THE SALSA DISH between us was already half empty, a casualty of nerves and salt cravings, when I realized Wes hadn't scanned the door in the last five minutes.

He had done it when we walked in—subtle sweep of the room, clocking the exits, the knot of people at the bar, the kid running laps between tables—but once we slid into the booth at La Casita, his shoulders had settled. Not loose, exactly, but not locked in that braced-for-impact way I'd gotten used to seeing.

Now he sat opposite me, left leg stretched under the table, prosthetic braced along the underside of the booth. The overhead lights were warm, catching on the dark hair at his forearms where his T-shirt sleeves hugged his biceps. It was just a faded Army tee and those worn jeans he lived in, but his arms rested on the table in a way that made the corded muscles impossible to ignore.

His hand curled around his glass, fingers dwarfing it, veins standing out in sharp lines. I had to force myself not to follow one of them with my gaze, imagining the drag of my fingertip from his wrist to his knuckles. I remembered how those hands had been wrapped around my hips, holding me steady while he—

I shoved a tortilla chip in my mouth before my brain could finish that sentence.

"So." Wes tipped his chin at me, sharp blue eyes steady. "How's the photo shoot going?"

A sigh slipped out of me before I could stop it. "You mean the grand winter bridal circus?" I scooped more salsa like I was arming myself. "It's . . . a lot. Elodie's thrilled, which is great, but our makeup artist bailed for a better-paying gig in Traverse City, I'm still waiting on two dress designers to confirm, the photographer is a genius *and* a diva, and Michigan weather is threatening to snowpoca-lypse all over the schedule."

His mouth twitched like he was fighting a smile. "Snow could be . . . pretty?"

The knot between my shoulders loosened a fraction, and I smiled. "It could be gorgeous. But less so if my hair ends up in a wet, limp mess and my lips turn blue. I'll look like a wet dog."

"That's impossible. You always look beautiful." His gaze stayed on me, not wandering, not glazing over before he cleared his throat and his eyes sliced away. "You got the farm and the inn locked down, right? You can always use them as backup space if it dumps six feet of snow."

I dipped my chip, trying to hide the blush that had crept onto my cheeks. I was talking with my hands as my vision came to life in my mind. "Even if the weather isn't great, we'll lean into it. Winter brides. Cozy knits. Champagne in snowdrifts. Frostbite as a wedding favor."

He huffed. "Sounds like you have it all figured out."

"It's a gift." I shrugged.

He picked up another chip and broke it in half. "You're going to kill it, Duchess."

The way he said it—simple, certain, like he was stating the weather—made my throat feel tight. Greg and my friends in the city had always treated my modeling with patient amusement, like I was playing dress-up on my way to a real life. Wes Vaughn was sitting in a Mexican restaurant asking follow-up questions about weather contingencies and logistics like my career was not only real, but *important*.

My heart did a slow, traitorous roll in my chest.

"You know the only hole in my plan?" I said, because feelings were terrifying and deflection was my favorite sport. "I still need a groom."

His hand stilled halfway to the salsa. "A what?"

"A groom," I repeated. "You know, for bridal photos. It's kind of depressing to have a woman in a wedding dress gazing lovingly at . . . a barn door." A playful snort escaped my nose.

His jaw worked. "You're hiring some guy to—what—hold you in fake snow while you stare at him for hours?"

My eyebrows bounced. "And kiss."

His nostrils flared, and I erupted in a fit of giggles, reaching across the table to grip his forearm. "Relax, caveman. There's usually no kissing, and even when there is, it's more like a robotic peck than a passionate make-out session."

He grumbled something that sounded a lot like *better fucking be*, but I couldn't be sure. The bristle in his voice warmed my cheeks in a way the salsa never could have. Jealousy looked good on him.

Dangerous. Hot.

"Unless you're volunteering," I said lightly, as if my

heart hadn't just tried to climb into my throat. "You'd look very dashing in a tux. The broody, contractor groom. It's a whole vibe."

He grumbled again and shook his head. "Leave my ugly mug out of it."

My brows shot up. "First of all: rude. Second of all, your face would sell more photos than my entire catalog combined."

His ears went a little pink. "The idea of standing in front of a camera right now makes me want to crawl out of my skin. Hard fucking pass."

My chest squeezed. I wanted to tell him he was the most compelling thing in any room, whether he was in front of a lens or not. I actually liked the idea of his face in the photos, because the image of a future without that face in it made my stomach drop.

Instead of ruminating, I popped another chip and shrugged like it was no big deal. "Fine. We'll hire some poor unsuspecting idiot and make him stand in the snow all day. He'll probably cry."

"That I would pay to see," Wes said, a real smile breaking across his face, bright and quick. Lines fanned at the corners of his eyes. I wanted to reach across the table and smooth my thumb over them, memorize them with my hands.

Under the table, our knees brushed, and neither of us moved away.

Our plates arrived—tacos for me, something with enough meat and cheese to qualify as a structural challenge for him. I launched into describing the rest of the shoot, the dress silhouettes, how Elodie had offered to let us use the goats for a few fun shots. Somewhere between the carnitas and the churros, the conversation slid sideways into easier territory.

"So the Nerd Night campaign is almost over?" I asked, licking a line of salsa from my thumb. His gaze followed the motion before he blinked and reached for his fork.

"Couple more sessions." He chased a piece of steak around his plate. "We're down two horses and one wizard, which feels about right for this group."

"Tragic." I bit into a taco, talking around it like a gremlin. "What happens when it's over? Group therapy? Grief counseling?"

"Brody floated the idea of a new game. Crokinole, I think it's called? I don't fucking know." Wes shrugged, then rolled his shoulder like it was still a new motion. "I'd be lying if I said I wasn't going to miss it. Game night is . . . nice. Having somewhere to be that isn't PT or my sad living room."

Something soft flickered in his eyes at the admission. He poked at his rice. "Softball starts up in a couple of months. They're already making noise about the rec league. No idea what that looks like for me now. Maybe I'll be the bat boy. Or the team mascot."

The casual tone didn't hide the way his mouth tightened around the words.

I set my taco down and nudged his plate back toward him, but he absentmindedly pushed it away. "You can see where you're at when the time comes," I said. "You surprised yourself on that hill. Might surprise yourself on the field too."

His gaze lifted to mine, something like gratitude flickering there. "You're very annoying when you're optimistic."

"Thank you." I stole one of his chips and popped it in my mouth.

He rolled his eyes, grabbed another chip, and deliberately pushed the basket closer to my side of the table.

It felt easy in a way that scared me. The loop of conversation, the little touches, the way he made sure I ate when I forgot. People laughed around us, clinking glasses, a server's tray wobbling past. Across the room, a couple shared a plate of nachos, heads bent together over some private joke.

I could see us like that so easily it hurt.

Every time Wes laughed—that rare, low sound that came from deep in his chest—my body remembered his mouth between my thighs, the way he had coaxed pleasure from places I hadn't realized I'd stopped trusting. Anticipation thrummed under my skin, hot and insistent. Tonight hovered at the edge of my thoughts like a live current. *Lesson three.* His body inside mine instead of just his voice in my ear.

I had to drag myself back to the table so I didn't melt into a puddle in the salsa.

"You still with me, Duchess?" he asked, one brow arched.

Heat rushed to my face. "Absolutely. Just thinking about . . . makeup artists and weather reports," I lied poorly.

His mouth curved, unconvinced but not pushing. "Those must be some very interesting weather reports."

*You have no idea.*

I forced a grin and picked up my taco again. "Trust me. Lake effect is riveting."

We finished eating in that companionable quiet that happens only with people who know where all your bodies are buried. He flagged the server for the check before I could reach for my wallet, giving me a look that said we would argue about it later and he would still win.

"Let's go home." Wes's chin dipped toward the exit.

My chest squeezed at the casual way he said *home*.

When we stepped out onto the sidewalk, the evening air hit my face, cold enough to sting. The street was a ribbon of slush and light, cars inching past, someone's dog trotting by in a ridiculous sweater.

Wes fell into step beside me without seeming to think about it. Then, automatically, he shifted—one smooth, unconscious move that put his body between me and the curb. His shoulder brushed mine as we walked toward the truck, the outside edge of his arm catching the wind instead of me.

It was nothing. A small, protective tilt of his body. A habit he'd probably picked up a decade ago and never thought twice about.

My chest went hot and achy anyway.

This was what it would be like, my brain whispered. This was what it already was.

## TWENTY-NINE

CLARA

Snow squeaked under my boots as I stepped inside, the blast of heat from the vents a welcome reprieve. I bent to kick off my shoes, my cheeks still warm from La Casita's salsa and from the way Wes had watched me over the table like I was more interesting than the entire laminated menu.

I had one heel half out of my boot when the door clicked shut behind us.

Before I could straighten, his fingers circled my wrist. Gentle and sure.

I looked up just as he turned me.

My back met the inside of the door with a soft thud. Wes crowded in, all worn flannel and clean soap and winter air, his gaze dropping to my mouth like he'd been holding himself together by sheer force of will.

Then he kissed me.

There was nothing careful about it. His mouth was hot and hungry, teeth catching my lower lip in a way that stole the breath from my lungs. His hands bracketed my hips, thumbs digging in just enough to make my knees wobble. Every inch of him was solid against me, his thigh pressed between mine, the steady anchor of his prosthetic making it feel like the door and his body were the only things keeping me upright.

A broken sound slipped out of me, half gasp, half *yes*.

He pulled back an inch, his breath rough against my lips. "I've been waiting to do that all damn night," he said, voice shredded.

Heat shot straight through me, low and sharp. This wasn't a lesson. This was not a clinical, scheduled exercise. This was a man who had sat across from me in a vinyl booth, pretending to care about salsa choices while his mind was already here.

Any thought I had about rules or pacing evaporated.

My fingers fisted in the front of his shirt, and I dragged him back down, kissing him like I'd been just as useless at waiting. His mouth opened under mine with a quiet, wrecked groan, one hand sliding up my spine, into my hair, tugging just enough to tilt my head the way he wanted it. I pressed closer, chest to chest, hips rolling in a slow, helpless grind that had nothing to do with strategy and everything to do with the anticipation of what could come next.

The prosthetic didn't matter. The accident didn't matter. There was just his tongue stroking into my mouth, his palm curving over my ass, the way my body reacted like it had been primed for this very moment.

*Yes, yes, yes* thrummed through my veins, tangled right up with a wild flash of *we have rules and I do not care about a single one of them.*

We broke apart on the same ragged breath.

He rested his forehead against mine, eyes closed, like he needed to recalibrate his entire nervous system. His chest rose and fell against mine, not entirely steady.

"Your brother," he said eventually, voice still rough, "is

the ultimate cockblock, you know that? I couldn't even buy condoms without him materializing out of nowhere."

I blinked, and then the picture hit: Wes in the aisle of a store and Hayes appearing like a cursed jack-in-the-box. Laughter punched out of me, bright and breathless.

"Good thing I trust absolutely no one with my sex life but myself," I managed.

He drew back just enough to see my face. "What does that mean?"

My heart hammered. Nerves and giddy anticipation collided as I slid my hand into my purse, fingers closing around cardboard.

I pulled out the economy-size box and held it up between us like a rabbit out of a hat. "Ta-da."

His brows shot up.

"You got the big box," he said, a low, pleased rumble that stroked over every raw place inside me as his hips pushed into me.

Heat crawled up my neck. I forced my chin up anyway. "Optimism looks good on you, Vaughn," I said. "I thought I'd try it too."

Something loosened in his face. Old Wes flickered through—the one who would have made a filthy joke and backed it up, the one who walked into a room like he knew exactly what he could do with his body. It mixed with the new version of him, the one still relearning his edges, and the combination nearly knocked my knees out.

The joke settled between us, softer at the edges, like we both recognized what we were actually doing here. This wasn't just optimism. It was intent. Choice.

I let my hand drop and pressed the box between our palms. Step by step, I tugged him deeper into the house, away from the door, away from the chance of anyone seeing us framed in the entry like a confession.

"Are you ready for lesson three?" I asked, my voice not nearly as steady as I wanted it to be.

His grip tightened around my hand. When he looked at me, there was nothing teasing in his eyes. Only heat. Only want. Only a kind of raw gratitude that scared the hell out of me because it felt an awful lot like trust.

"Lesson three," he echoed, the words more promise than joke. "I want all of you tonight, Clara."

Upstairs, Wes's room felt smaller than usual, like the air had thickened the second we crossed the threshold. The lamp on his nightstand threw gold over the bed, the dresser, the long mirror propped in the corner and a sturdy wooden chair that would be perfect for what I had planned.

He closed the door with a soft click, and we just stood there, facing each other in the warm pool of light, the rest of the house falling away.

"So," I said, my voice coming out softer than I intended. "Game plan?"

With a shake of his head, he said, "Missionary's out." His gaze flicked between my eyes. "Without two good knees, I can't really get"—he cleared his throat—"leverage."

I nodded, silently letting him know I understood, though my cheeks flamed.

"Standing's still iffy," he admitted. "If things go sideways, I'd rather not take us both out."

I huffed a shaky laugh. "Fair. No concussions on lesson three." I tipped my chin toward the chair. "Sitting might work."

"A chair is solid." He tapped it with his knuckles. "Foot planted. Back supported. Low risk of me face-planting into the dresser. Very dignified."

"Sexy *and* practical." My heart squeezed. "I like it."

The corner of his mouth twitched. "Yeah?"

"Yeah," I said, and meant it. He wasn't less of a man because he thought about stability and the physics of his prosthetic. He was more himself. More careful, more deliberate.

More Wes.

We stepped closer at the same time, some invisible tether pulling us in. He stopped an arm's length away, chest rising, eyes dark.

"Strip for me," he said, voice rough as gravel.

Heat shot straight through me.

I met his gaze and held it, letting myself bask in the sheer hunger there. "Yes, sir," I murmured, because apparently my mouth wanted to get me in trouble.

His jaw flexed. "Clara."

I reached for the hem of my sweater, fingers suddenly not as steady as I wanted them to be. The cotton slid up my stomach, cool air kissing my skin as I pulled it over my head and dropped it to the floor. His eyes tracked the movement like he couldn't have looked away if the house caught fire.

I took my time with the rest, because it felt like the only power I had over how wildly my heart was beating. Jeans button, zipper, the slow tug of denim over my hips. His gaze followed every inch, knuckles whitening on the back of the chair as I shimmied them down my thighs.

By the time I stood in front of him completely bare, my skin felt too tight for my body. My pulse thudded in my ears. He was breathing harder, eyes blown and hungry, like I was both a miracle and a problem he fully intended to solve.

His hands flexed on the chair before moving in front of it. "Jesus, Duchess."

The nickname rolled over me like a touch.

"Your turn," I said, stepping closer until I stood right in front of him. My fingers found the hem of his shirt, the soft cotton stretched over the expanse of his chest.

"Is this okay?" I asked, checking in one last time.

He nodded once, jerky. "Yeah."

I lifted the shirt, inch by inch, revealing a strip of warm skin, the trail of hair, the carved muscles of his stomach. Scars cut across the planes of him—white lines, a map of what he'd survived. My throat went tight as I tugged the shirt over his head and tossed it aside.

He went still under my hands, like he wasn't sure what to do with being looked at. I let my palms skate slowly over his shoulders, down his chest, following the curve of muscle and bone, making no effort to hide how much I liked what I saw.

"This is ridiculous," I whispered, because it was either that or burst into flames. "You're offensively hot."

A startled laugh punched out of him, some of the tension leaching from his shoulders.

I slid my fingers to his waistband, popping the button, easing the zipper down. The thick bulge straining against the fabric made my pulse spike. I worked the denim over his hips, careful of the liner at his thigh, careful not to tug anything that would yank him out of his head and back into fear.

He caught my wrists.

For a beat, we froze there—him half out of his jeans, me bent close enough to feel his breath on the top of my head, the room holding its air.

His hand felt tight around my wrist, not harsh, just . . . hesitant.

I straightened, following the tension up his arm until

our eyes met. There it was. The line. Not the sexy one we'd been toeing all night. The real one. The moment where he either let me see all of himself or put the mask back on.

"I want *all* of you, Wes," I said quietly. "Not just the parts you think are easy to look at."

Something flickered—pain, disbelief, a little bit of anger at whatever part of his brain insisted that couldn't be true. It all moved behind his eyes, then slowly, finally, his grip loosened.

He let go.

"Okay," he said, voice hoarse. "All of it, then."

We pushed his jeans down together, working them over his prosthetic with a weird chorus of grunts and laughter when they caught on the edge.

I took in his leg and the rest of him. My fingertips skimmed the socket and the skin around it without flinching. I took my time cataloging all of him with open desire. Wes was tense, but his breathing relaxed when he realized I wasn't pitying him—I was turned on.

When he finally stepped free of the denim, he was just . . . Wes. All broad shoulders and corded muscle and long lines, the familiar and the new knitted into something that made my chest ache. His prosthetic caught the lamplight, metal and carbon and proof that his body had broken and healed in new ways . . . and he still sat down in that chair like a king.

He scooted back, legs spread, bare feet solid on the floor. The condom box waited on the nightstand, an unspoken promise.

Wes's hand stilled at his prosthetic. The room seemed to hold its breath with me as he loosened the liner, fingers working the familiar catches. I stepped back to give him room.

When he finally eased the prosthetic off, setting it carefully beside the chair, something in my chest cracked wide open. The stump of his thigh was pale and scarred, tender in a way he never let anyone see, and for a heartbeat I was terrified he'd mistake my silence for pity instead of what it was—pure, aching desire.

It was an honor to see him so vulnerable.

I stepped closer and slid my palm over his bare thigh, above the place where bone and skin ended. "There you are," I murmured, because it felt wrong to pretend this wasn't part of him. His shoulders dropped a fraction, some tight, invisible thing unspooling as he let me look, really look, at all of him.

I picked up his prosthetic and walked it to rest safely beside the bed.

"I'm good," he said, more to himself than to me as I turned to him.

He leaned back, hands braced on the arms of the chair, his gaze raking over me from toes to throat. When his eyes met mine again, something darker had settled there.

Old Wes. New Wes. All layered into one man who looked like he'd happily devour me whole.

"Now get on your knees and crawl," he said quietly.

Heat flashed through me so fast my breath hitched.

There was no cruelty in it, no edge of mockery. Just a low, thick want and a trust that I understood the difference.

"Yes," I whispered, my knees softening as I sank to the floor.

I started forward, slow on purpose. Each movement rolled through my hips, a lazy sway I could feel in the looseness of my spine and the drag of my hair over my shoulders. My palms slid across the hardwood, then the edge of the rug, then the last strip of floor between us. Every few crawled inches, I glanced up through my lashes just to watch what it did to him.

His breathing went rough almost immediately. The muscles in his forearms stood out, tendons tight as his hands flexed on the arms of the chair like he was fighting the urge to reach for me. His gaze burned over every inch of skin like I was something he'd been starving for.

By the time I reached him, his knuckles were white on the chair arms. I slid my hands up his shin, over his knee, and along the thick muscles of his thighs. His breath hissed out when I skimmed higher, the sound punching straight between my ribs.

I rose slowly, uncoiling over him, letting my body brush his, skin to skin, until I was straddling his lap, knees braced on either side of his hips.

"You're going to kill me," he murmured, eyes searching my face like he was trying to memorize it.

"That would be a tragic time for your luck to run out," I said, even as my hands shook a little reaching for the nightstand.

The condom box was cool against my palm. I flipped it open, plucked one from the foil, and tore it carefully. His gaze didn't leave my face, but his breath went a little ragged when my hand slid down to him.

He was hard and hot in my grip, a solid, undeniable answer to every doubt he'd ever had about his body.

His jaw clenched as I unrolled it down the length of him. It was a heady thrill to see him fully ready for me.

When I was done, I settled my hands on his shoulders, the tendons there tight under my fingers. His palms slid up my thighs, over my hips, fingers curving around my waist like they belonged there.

"Last chance to downgrade to advanced cuddling," I said, trying to make my voice light and failing.

"Not a fucking chance," he breathed.

I shifted my weight, lifted just enough, and reached between us to guide him. The head of him nudged against me, and my lungs forgot what to do. His hand slid between my thighs, teasing my pussy.

"*Fuck*," he growled. "You're so fucking wet."

I hissed at his words and lined the head of his cock at my entrance. We both stilled.

His eyes locked on mine, wide and dark and a little scared.

"You okay?" he asked.

I nodded, throat too tight for words. "You?"

His hands tightened on my waist. "Ask me again when I can think."

I sank down, inch by devastating inch, every nerve ending lighting up.

Achingly slowly he filled me.

I sank down further, feeling every new stretch as my body opened around him. Heat climbed my throat, my head tipping back as the fullness built, rich and overwhelming. His fingers clamped down on my hips, the grip bordering on bruising, like he was anchoring both of us to the moment.

Our breaths stuttered in the same broken rhythm—mine on every downward slide, his on every helpless thrust up to meet me—until I finally took all of him, hips flush to his. For a second we just stayed there, locked together, chests heaving, foreheads almost touching, sharing the same thin slice of air while our bodies learned the feel of being completely, irreversibly connected.

He let out a low, guttural sound that I felt all the way through my spine. His head tipped back, jaw clenched, then snapped forward again like he refused to miss a single second of this.

"Holy shit," he rasped. "Clara."

"That good, huh?" My voice shook.

His fingers flexed, hauling me a fraction closer. "You have no idea."

We found a rhythm the way we'd found everything so far—with a little awkwardness, a lot of communication, and more want than sense.

At first I was hyperaware of every adjustment he made with his leg—the way his foot pushed into the floor, how he shifted his hips to keep everything aligned. I checked in constantly.

"Here okay?" I asked, rocking my hips forward, grinding my clit against the base of his cock.

"Yeah," he grunted. "Right there."

"What about this?" I angled differently, feeling the drag of him in a new place that made stars burst behind my eyes.

His grip tightened. "Jesus, Duchess. Yeah. That. Don't you dare stop doing that."

His answers got less verbal as we went, more hands than words. He started guiding me without thinking about it, tilting my hips, slowing me with a squeeze of his fingers when he needed to breathe, urging me faster when he wanted more. Filth slipped out between gritted teeth.

"Look at you," he rasped when I leaned back, bracing my hands on his chest. "Riding me like you were made for it."

Heat pooled low and heavy. My cheeks burned, but there was no way in hell I was looking away from him.

Somewhere in the motion, I stopped tracking what was "best" for his injury and started memorizing little things about him instead. The way his eyes went half lidded right before a groan broke free. The angle that dragged a curse out of him and had his nails scraping down my back. The way his chest hitched when I leaned in, hands in his hair, and kissed him while my body moved over his.

A sharp ache bloomed in my chest mid-thrust, sudden and terrifying.

*I could do this forever,* whispered something traitorous and true.

With him. Only him.

I cupped his face, pulled his mouth up to mine, and kissed him like that thought hadn't just shifted my entire axis. His lips were hot and sure, tongue stroking into my mouth in a rhythm that matched the slow roll of his hips up into me.

He broke away on a ragged breath, forehead pressed to mine, voice raw against my lips. "You have no idea what you're giving me back."

Emotion punched through the heat. Tears pricked, unexpected and fierce.

"I think I do," I managed. I hoped he didn't notice the wobble in my voice.

The tension coiled tighter, lower, my muscles trembling with the effort of holding on. His hands were everywhere— hips, waist, up my back, in my hair—pulling me in, anchoring me to him.

"Clara," he groaned, voice breaking on my name. "I can feel you—"

"Wes," I gasped, the world narrowing to the drag, the heat, the way everything inside me clenched and climbed and begged. "I'm—"

That last word dissolved into a sound I couldn't have identified if my life depended on it.

The pleasure hit like a snapped wire. My whole body

went tight around him first—thighs locking at his hips, spine arching, every muscle strung to breaking—before something inside me finally let go and broke wide open. I clung to his shoulders, nails digging into his skin as I rode it out, his name tearing from my throat on a ragged gasp while wave after wave rolled through me, hot and blinding and so intense it felt like relief.

He followed me over the edge, a half second behind, his whole body going tight beneath mine. His arms banded around me, hauling me against his chest as he groaned into my neck, the sound low and broken and so grateful it made my eyes sting.

We stayed like that for a long moment—tangled, shaking, breathing each other's air. His heart hammered against my ribs. My thighs trembled on either side of his hips. His injured leg didn't flinch. It didn't seem to exist for him at all except as something that had done exactly what he needed it to do.

Eventually, my muscles gave up and I slumped against him, cheek pressed to his shoulder. He smoothed a hand down my spine, slow and steady, like he wasn't sure whether he was soothing me or himself.

I could have stayed there forever.

"Hey," he murmured into my hair after a while, voice rough but soft. "You okay?"

I let out a laugh that shook. "Define *okay*."

He huffed against my temple. "Not dead, not mad, can still feel your legs?"

"Barely," I said. "But in a good way."

He held me tighter, like he could squeeze the words into something more permanent.

The thought of this being a lesson for *him* felt ridiculous.

There was nothing clinical about the way he'd looked at me. Nothing casual about the way my heart had nearly broken open when he said I was giving him something back. This had not been practice. It was sex, yes—hot and messy and consuming—but there had been something threaded through every touch, every kiss.

*A life,* whispered the part of me I didn't let anyone see. *This is what a life with him would feel like.*

I wanted it with a bone-deep ferocity that scared the hell out of me.

I pressed my face into his neck, breathing him in, trying to memorize the exact mix of soap and skin and sweat—of safety and danger and home.

Somewhere along the way, our lesson had stopped being about his body and started becoming something else entirely.

My heart was in so much more trouble than I'd ever planned for.

## THIRTY

Clara stepped out of the bathroom in one of my T-shirts, rubbing a towel through her damp hair.

The sight hit harder than anything that had happened in the last hour, and that included having her come apart in my lap.

The shirt hung halfway down her thighs, neck stretched just enough that one bare shoulder showed. Her legs were pink from the shower, toes curling against the rug like she wasn't sure where to stand. She had wiped off her makeup, leaving nothing but freckles and flushed cheeks and those big doe eyes that had no business looking that soft in my room.

She hovered in the doorway, hand on the frame, like she was waiting for me to point her back down the hall. I was propped against the headboard, leg stretched out and waiting for her to finish.

I'd spent the time she was in the shower figuring out exactly how to say what I wanted. "You should stay." I cleared my throat. "If you want."

Her fingers tightened on the doorframe. Surprise flickered across her face, fast and sharp, followed by something that looked a lot like hope trying very hard not to be obvious.

"You sure?" she asked. It came out lighter than it had any right to. "You might wake up and regret voluntarily sharing a bed with a notorious blanket thief."

The fact she needed to ask did something twisty to my insides.

"I'll risk it," I said as I pulled the comforter back. "Stay."

She searched my face for another second, but crossed the room and climbed in on what could so easily become her side of the bed, careful of where my leg was, moving like she'd been doing this for years instead of minutes.

The mattress dipped under her weight, soothing in a way that scared the hell out of me.

She settled with her head on my shoulder, one arm draped across my stomach, her knee hooking gently over my thigh. Her hair smelled like my shampoo, warm and clean, wrapping around me when she shifted. I slid my arm around her automatically, my palm fitting in at the small of her back. The move felt effortless and enormous all at once.

I let my hand drift in slow circles over her hip, fingers drawing patterns across her skin. Contentment and terror ran neck and neck in my veins. I had no idea what this was anymore, only that the idea of her getting up and walking down the hall suddenly felt like someone standing and leaving halfway through a sentence.

She shifted, tucking closer, and something bright caught the lamplight.

The engagement ring flashed against my chest, the diamond throwing little shards of light onto the sheets.

I went still.

There it was. The past, gleaming on her finger in my

bed. A promise made to someone else, in another life, catching the light between us.

Her gaze followed mine.

She froze, then winced. "Right," she muttered, voice too bright. "That."

She pulled her hand back like it had burned her and tugged at the ring, twisting it off in one rough motion. It slid free, leaving a faint indentation on her skin. She held it between two fingers for a heartbeat, then huffed out a short, brittle laugh.

"I don't even know why I'm still wearing it," she said with a huff, aiming for casual and dismissive.

She reached blindly toward the nightstand, like she was ready to drop it in a drawer and pretend it had never existed.

"Hey," I said quietly.

My fingers closed around her wrist before she could let it clatter away like pocket change. Her hand hovered between us, ring glinting in the lamp glow.

"I know why." The words dragged out of a place I didn't visit often. I curled her hand into my chest. "You're mourning a life that doesn't exist anymore."

Her eyes snapped to mine.

Every shield she had went down. All the jokes, the deflections, the breezy bravado. Gone. What was left was a woman who looked like someone had yanked the floor out from under her and told her to make it look pretty.

Her throat worked. "I built my entire life around a lie," she whispered. "Not because I wanted Greg the way you're supposed to want your future husband, but because it was a *plan*. A direction. A way to be useful. To fix something for someone." Her mouth twisted. "Turns out you can't build your life on a lie and expect it not to collapse. I feel so stupid."

I eased the ring out of her fingers and set it gently on the nightstand, not in the drawer, not flung away. Just there. A fact. Something that had existed and ended.

"You lost a map," I said. "Doesn't mean you're lost."

She made a small, choked noise that might have been a laugh if there hadn't been that much grief under it. "Some days I feel pretty lost," she whispered. "Everybody else seems to have their lives at least directionally correct. Marriage, kids, jobs that make sense. I had . . . this whole thing drawn out in my head. Where I'd live an exciting career." Her fingers curled into me. "Now I'm back in my hometown, living in my brother's best friend's spare room, starting over."

My chest tightened.

She hummed. "I just can't shake this ridiculous feeling that maybe I can do it on my own. Maybe I never needed him or his money in the first place."

"It's not ridiculous." I slid my thumb over her knuckles, slow and steady. "And for the record," I said, "your brother's best friend's spare room has been significantly improved by your presence."

She let out a breath. "I just thought I had a plan."

"I know what it's like," I said. "When your plans get shot to hell in one afternoon."

The ceiling suddenly felt very close. I stared up at it anyway, because looking at her while I said this felt like too much and not enough at the same time.

"I thought I had everything figured out." My jaw clenched. "Then I woke up in a hospital bed with half a leg and a brain that couldn't make sense of anything."

Her grip on me tightened.

"I gave up on myself," I said, voice flattening on the edges of the words. "Told myself I was 'adjusting.' What I was really doing was hiding. Let the couch downstairs become home base. I told myself it was because it was easier, closer to the door, better for the leg. Some nights that was true." I swallowed. "Some nights it wasn't."

She went very still against me. "What do you mean?"

I drew in a breath and let it out slowly.

"I crashed on the couch because the idea of being up here made my chest lock up. It's too far from exits. Too far from help. Too many steps between me and getting out if something went wrong. I didn't trust my body not to betray me. Leg fail, phantom pain hit, smoke alarm going off for some bullshit reason—whatever it was, my brain ran a highlight reel of me stuck up here like a turtle on its back."

Silence pressed in, thick and listening.

"I hated that feeling," I admitted. "Hated that I could barely handle my own damn staircase. So I told myself the couch was more comfortable. Anything except saying out loud that the second floor of my own house felt like a trap."

The words sat there, ugly and true.

Clara's hand moved up, slow and sure, until her palm rested warm and flat over my heart.

"You're not trapped up here," she said softly. "Not with me."

It was such a small sentence. It slid under my ribs like a blade.

I covered her hand with mine, pressing it there a little harder than I meant to. "I know," I said, and the thing was, I did. "That's the messed-up part. Ever since you moved in, the upstairs has felt less like enemy territory."

My mouth twisted. "It's easier to come up here when I

know I'm not alone with it. With all of it." I cleared my throat. "I feel safer knowing you're down the hall."

Her breath caught.

She shifted, turning her face enough to look up at me. Her eyes were glossy, lashes wet, but there was steel under it. The good kind. The kind she turned on herself and everyone she loved when she decided something mattered.

"So I'm your emotional support person now," she said, voice wobbling just a little. "Your human security blanket."

"You're a very loud security blanket," I muttered.

She huffed out a watery laugh and pressed closer, sliding her bare hand up until it curved against my jaw. I leaned into it without meaning to.

"That's me," she said. "Cozy, bossy, great hair."

"That is accurate," I said.

I bent my head and pressed a kiss to the top of her hair, letting my lips rest there for a second longer than was strictly casual. Her fingers flexed against my chest in response, like she felt the line we were crossing and decided to step over it anyway.

Her gaze stayed locked on the discarded ring. "You know, if I ever do it again," she whispered, "it'll be because it's right. I don't care if it's a gum wrapper. I just want it to feel like me."

The discarded diamond sat on the nightstand now, a small circle of gold catching a sliver of lamplight.

Not on her hand. Not on her.

I swallowed past the gravel in my throat. "I just need you to know that I'm not someone you need to fix."

"I have never thought that, even for a second." Her big eyes met mine. "I'm glad you're finally figuring that out for yourself."

Clara curled in closer, fitting herself against me like

she'd been designed for that exact space. Her bare fingers spread over my sternum, tucked under my palm. Her legs tangled with mine beneath the sheets, her foot brushing the sensitive skin of my calf before settling.

We had rules on the fridge for everything except this growing feeling I couldn't ignore.

I didn't say *I love you.*

The words sat heavy on the back of my tongue, untested and huge. What I did admit, just for myself, staring up at the ceiling while her breaths evened out against my skin, was that this—her in my bed, my shirt on her body, our lives braided together in the quiet between midnight and morning—was what love felt like for me.

Darkness settled, soft and private. My thumb kept tracing slow lines on her arm long after I felt her muscles loosen, after her breaths turned into soft, steady pulls of air against my chest.

She fell asleep first, warm and solid and real in my arms.

I stayed awake a little longer, listening to the heater hum and the faint whistle of wind against the window. For the first time in longer than I could remember, lying in my own bed upstairs, I didn't feel like a man waiting for something to go wrong.

I didn't feel broken.

I felt free.

## THIRTY-ONE

I'D ALMOST FORGOTTEN how good it felt to get ready for something that wasn't a disaster.

My curling iron sat on the bathroom counter, cord snaked across the sink. I watched my reflection as another strand slid off the barrel and fell into a soft wave against my shoulder. I was no longer a runaway bride or the small-town girl returning home with her tail between her legs. I was simply a woman with a job. Someone who finally had a plan.

My jeans were clean, my sweater was soft and neutral enough to look intentional, and my makeup was perfect.

A mug appeared on the edge of the vanity in the mirror.

"Big plans today, Duchess?"

Wes leaned in the doorway, one shoulder propped against the frame like the house had been built specifically to give him something to smolder against. His hair was still damp from his shower and a little dark at the temples. The worn Henley he wore did obscene things to his chest and arms.

Coffee steam curled up in front of his face, carrying the

smell of dark roast and the tiniest, sweetest hint of vanilla creamer. He'd made it the way I liked it without asking.

Again.

I set the curling iron down and reached for the mug. "A few errands. I'll be starting at the farm," I said, blowing across the surface. "I've got to take measurements, finalize a few locations with Elodie and Cal, double-check power outlets and load-in paths." I shot him a wink in the mirror. "It's real glamorous stuff."

His mouth tipped. "Sounds pretty fancy to me."

I took a grateful sip and hummed as the coffee slid across my tongue. "I'm also trying to convince the weather to cooperate so no one gets hypothermia. All in a day's work."

He watched me for another beat, that lazy, quiet attention wrapping around my shoulders like a blanket. The bathroom had never felt so small.

"I'll drive you," he said, like it was the most obvious thing in the world. "You'll freeze your ass off carrying the gear on your own."

The mug hovered halfway to my mouth.

He usually said things like *Have fun* or *Don't die* and then retreated to his room or the safe end of the couch. Turning down invitations was practically his part-time job.

Volunteering was *new*.

"You don't have to," I said carefully.

He shrugged, his muscles shifting under cotton. "Roads are clear. Farm's not far." His gaze flicked over my shoulder to the curling iron, the notebook already half stuffed in my bag. "Besides, I can see Cal and catch up for a minute while I see you in action."

A fizzy little thought tried to uncurl in my chest. Maybe he wanted to see my world up close.

I swallowed it down with another sip of coffee. "Sounds good," I said, turning back to the mirror so he wouldn't see my grin. "You can be my assistant."

"I'll add it to my résumé," he muttered, but there was a warmth in his voice that hadn't been there a month ago.

SNOW PILED in soft drifts along the fence line at Star Harbor Family Farm, the inn sitting tall and moody against the pale sky. In the distance, the barn's blue siding glowed like a postcard. Everywhere I looked, my brain snapped into framing and exposure and the bone-deep itch to make something beautiful out of all this cold.

Wes parked near the side entrance of the inn and killed the engine. When we stepped out, our breath puffed white, the air crisp enough to sting my nose.

"Well, time for my butt to freeze off just like you predicted," I said, hitching my tote bag higher on my shoulder.

Wes's gaze dropped to my ass. "It would be a tragic loss," he replied, locking the truck. "Humanity will mourn."

The front steps creaked under our boots as we climbed, the old wood dusted with fresh powder. Inside, the inn smelled like coffee and cinnamon and the faint lemon of wood cleaner. Light poured through the front windows, washing over the polished floors and the Christmas garland still wound along the banister.

"Clara!" Elodie appeared from behind the front desk, cheeks flushed, braid looped over one shoulder. Her gaze flicked to Wes, and her smile went knowing. "You brought muscle."

"He insisted," I said, ignoring the way my stomach fluttered at the word. "I'm just here to boss everyone around."

Wes lifted a hand, half wave, half salute. "Contractor slash pack mule, reporting for duty."

"Perfect," Elodie said. "You can start by telling us where we're all going to die of OSHA violations."

My sister said something to Helen, who was working behind the desk before she wound her way around the desk and stood in front of us.

I pulled out my notebook, pen already uncapped. "Okay. So. I'm thinking we do the 'first look' by the old oak. If we get snow, the branches will look like a fairy tale. If we don't, we lean into the whole moody, winter-light vibe." I pointed toward the wide windows framing the field. "Ceremony-inspired shots in front of the tree line. Then the bride framed in the barn doors for that 'rustic but make it editorial' moment . . ."

Words poured out of me as I walked them through it— the path from the inn to the barn, a few shots along the fence line, the angle of the late-afternoon light, the quick-change plan if temperatures plummeted and we all started losing toes. Every sentence made my chest feel a little bigger, like my lungs finally had room.

"Backup plan," I added, scribbling in the margin. "If it's too cold or windy, we pull everyone inside and pivot to cozy, firelight shots by the hearth inside the restaurant. Maybe a champagne tower on that sideboard if I can keep Kit from knocking it over."

Elodie laughed. "I can wrangle Kit. Anything else?"

"There will be plenty of opportunities to highlight the inn and the farm for you too." I flipped to the page where my shot list was annotated with stars and arrows and the occasional panicked all-caps note. "The photographers and designers are booked. All I need is a guy willing to fake-propose in twenty-degree weather. I swear, this time everyone knows it's pretend from the start. In fact, it'll be my lowest-drama almost-wedding ever."

The joke slipped out before I could stop it. My eyes wanted to follow it straight to Wes. I forced them to stay on the paper.

He stood a few feet away, hands in the pockets of his jacket, watching me with that focused contractor gaze that had nothing to do with studs and joists and everything to do with me. No glassy eyes, no polite smile. He looked like he was actually picturing every frame, every angle, the same way I was.

"Are those stairs slick?" he asked, nodding toward the wide staircase up to the inn's upper-level rooms. "Will you be in heels?"

"Only for a couple of shots," I said. "I'll have someone on spotter duty."

"If we get one thaw-and-freeze before then, that path out to the pines is an accident waiting to happen," he added, moving toward the window. "We'll want to put salt down before you haul anyone out there in a ball gown or dress shoes."

Instead of rolling my eyes, I wrote it down. "See? This is why I bring a contractor. You think of all the ways we could die while I'm distracted by the pretty."

He snorted. "Teamwork."

It hit me, inexplicably hard, how different this was from sitting across a table from Greg while he nodded through my ramblings and glanced at his phone. Wes wasn't humoring me. He was building on it. He was putting his hands and experience under the fragile little scaffolding of my ideas and quietly shoring them up

Elodie was called away by the phone. I walked Wes toward the back door, notebook balanced on top of my tape measure.

"You know, I am accepting applications for a handsome groom," I said lightly as we stepped outside again, snow glare sharp enough to make me squint. "The job description includes 'looking hot in a tux' and 'doesn't mind frostbite.'"

His jaw ticced, barely there. "Nah," he muttered. "The last thing you need is me clomping around in the background of your perfect shots." The words were rough and self-deprecating. Wes turned to face me. "But whoever you get to stand in better keep his hands to himself."

The flicker of something darker underneath—the flash of his eyes at the thought of anyone else's hands on me in a suit and a staged kiss—lit me up in places I didn't want to examine too closely.

I pretended to write down something important so I could hide the way my mouth wanted to smile too much.

I didn't want some random guy either. The treacherous voice writhed in my belly. I wanted him in those photos.

But I slammed a door on it.

In the cold, we made a loop of the property, the barn looming blue and bright against the cliffs and snow. My phone was out, snapping reference photos of everything— how the path curved, how the light hit the inn's stained-glass windows, the way the pines made a natural aisle if you framed them just right.

Wes walked beside me, boots crunching, hands gesturing as he pointed out where the snow drifted deepest, the cleanest lines for power cords, the best place to stash portable heaters without ruining the aesthetic.

"Run your cables along here," he said, toe nudging the

edge of the path near the fence. "Tape them down or you're going to have a bridesmaid doing a full face-plant."

"Noted." I scribbled another reminder. "No maiming the pretend wedding party."

We rounded the corner toward the barn's side entrance, where the snow had been packed down by deliveries and Cal's determined shoveling. I stepped where I thought the ground was solid, my weight hitting a sleek patch of black ice instead.

My feet went out. My notebook flew.

Before my brain could even register the slip, Wes's hand shot out. Fingers clamped around my forearm. He steadied and pulled. My body jolted forward into his chest instead of backward onto my ass, the cold replaced by the sudden, ridiculous warmth of being flush against him.

"Easy," he said, voice low near my ear. "I've got you."

My laugh puffed out white into the space between us. "You really are committed to this lawsuit-prevention bit."

"You're not allowed to break anything before your big debut," he said. His hand slid from my arm down to my fingers, giving them a quick squeeze.

His palm was rough and warm, dwarfing mine, grounding me in a way that had nothing to do with ice and everything to do with the last few weeks in that house. I squeezed back, just once, then forced myself to release him before I got too attached to the feel of our hands fitting together.

Snow glittered around us, quiet and bright. The inn's windows reflected a smaller version of us on the glass—two figures in the cold, moving in the same direction.

*This,* I thought, as we started walking again, notebook retrieved, fingers still tingling.

*This* was what it would be like if we were just . . . together. No lessons, no secrets, no rules on the fridge.

Just us, showing up places as an *us*.

THE DRIVE back from the farm was one long, contented hum.

My notebook sat open in my lap, full of scribbles and arrows and terrible sketches. Wes's hand rested loose on the wheel, the other draped over the console, fingers drumming to some low classic rock station he'd turned on.

"Heading home?" he asked when the turn for Main Street came up. "Unless you need to stop anywhere."

"Um, the Crooked Spine," I said, chewing on my pen cap. "I wanted to grab a book. I can run in—"

"I'll come in," he said, like it was nothing as his shoulder lifted. "I could use coffee."

I blinked at him.

Old Wes would have dropped me at the curb with a grunt and gone back to his solitude. This version of him turned on his blinker, eased us into a parking space in front of the bookshop, and killed the engine like willingly entering a crowded public space was no big deal.

Something warm and gooey swelled under my ribs.

Inside, the bell over the door jingled, and the Crooked Spine's familiar moody vibes wrapped around us—shelves crammed with books, mismatched chairs, the hiss of the espresso machine, the smell of coffee and sugar and paper.

Selene was tucked into a corner with a paperback, Winnie curled beside her on a fat armchair, reading a picture book upside down and narrating absolutely none of the actual words.

Selene's eyes flicked up. Her brows shot toward her hairline when she saw Wes behind me. "Well, well," she murmured as I leaned in to kiss her cheek. "Look who left his cave."

"Field trip," I whispered back. "Try not to spook him."

She smirked and squeezed my hand. "Give me five minutes later. We found something weird in the archives."

"Ominous," I said as a tingle raced up my spine. "I love it. Tell me now."

Winnie lunged up to hug me around the waist. "Aunt Clara, Aunt Clara, Aunt Clara, I read three whole books today," she announced.

"Upside down?" I asked.

"Yeah," she said proudly.

"Genius behavior," I said solemnly. "I'm terrified of your superpowers."

Wes peeled off toward the counter with a little salute, already pulling his wallet from his back pocket. I watched him long enough to see him order two coffees without looking at the floor or the door, then forced myself toward the back hallway.

Selene had a folder already on the table in the little reading nook—printer paper, copies of old records, the latest chapter in our ridiculous hobby.

"So," she said, flipping to a new page. "Remember how we were hunting for Alma's baby?"

"Very distinctly," I said. "Mysterious small human, big scandal, all roads lead to Hayes looking like a cursed farmhand. What's up?"

She tapped a highlighted line. "There *was* a mention of a Barker baby in a census," she said. "But here's the kicker . . . it's not listed under Alma, but her *brother*."

My face scrunched. "Her brother had a secret baby?"

"Maybe," she said. "This mystery baby appears out of nowhere, but again . . . no mother and no birth record that I can find. So either he had a kid out of wedlock and we haven't found the right records or . . . something else happened that we haven't put together yet. It's thin, but it's . . . weird."

"Everything about this town is weird," I muttered, scanning the photocopy. The black-and-white type blurred a little. "So the Lady wasn't the only one with secrets."

"Apparently not." Selene sighed. "It's probably nothing. Or everything. I don't know yet."

It pinged something uneasy and electric in my chest—lines on a family tree we still didn't understand, legacies of shame and bad luck echoing forward.

Hayes. The curse. The farmhand's face.

I shook it off, scribbled a note in the margin, and promised I'd look again at the photos later. Ghosts could wait.

Real life—with a very-much-alive man at the front of the store—was calling. I hugged Selene and playfully flipped the end of Winnie's braid.

When I stepped back into the main room, I spotted him instantly.

Wes sat on a plush couch near a low shelf of oversize books, shoulders relaxed, glasses on. The frames had slid a little down his nose while he thumbed through a coffee-table book full of stormy landscapes and blurred, beautiful brides in long trains.

His thumb dragged slowly down the edge of a page, brows drawn in that intent way that meant he was actually interested, not just pretending. The sight of him—big, solid, a little rumpled from the day, wearing his reading glasses in my favorite place—made me fall even harder for him.

He glanced up as I neared and gave a small, crooked smile that hit me right in the knees. "They've got half your shot list in here," he said, nodding at the open spread. "Look."

He shifted sideways on the battered leather couch so I could sit, giving me that familiar little pocket of space that had somehow become mine without either of us agreeing to it. I sank down beside him and leaned in.

The photo he'd stopped on was a bride framed in a barn doorway—snow falling in a soft blur, twinkle lights behind her, the hem of her dress dusted in white.

"Okay, that's rude," I said. "That's exactly what I saw in my head. Down to the weirdly impractical no-coat thing."

"I thought so," he said. "See the way the light's behind her? You could fake that with your fairy lights and a couple of heaters. Just don't let Cal plug everything into one outlet or he'll blow half the county."

I laughed. "Noted. Divide and conquer the power strip."

We flipped to another page. This one was all golden fields and storm skies, the kind of moody drama Elodie secretly loved.

"I want the farm shoot to feel like this," I said, tapping a photo where the bride looked like she was about to walk into a hurricane and grin her way through it.

"Then it will," he said, like weather and budgets and logistics weren't a thing. "You'll have the barn, the inn, all those trees. It'll look better than this by the time you're done with it."

The certainty in his voice did that thing to my chest again, like someone was slowly turning a crank and stretching it wider. He didn't say *if*. He didn't say *try*. He said it confidently like it was a fact.

I shifted, turning so my knee bumped his thigh, the book balanced across both our laps. "Someday I'd love a space that looks like this," I heard myself say. "Big windows, white walls, racks of dresses. A corner for lookbooks. A storage area where I pretend I don't shove everything into one closet before clients come over."

"You need a studio," he said.

"Yeah." My cheeks heated, like I'd said something outlandish instead of the most basic creative dream. "Somewhere that's all mine. Not somebody's garage or borrowed barn. I won't always be in front of the camera."

He watched me for a beat, eyes softer behind the black frames. "You'll have it," he said simply.

The words landed like a stone dropped into deep water —small and quiet at the surface, ripples spreading everywhere underneath.

*You'll have it.*

He didn't try to temper it or joke it away. Just set it between us like a promise he didn't even realize he was making.

Ridiculous questions pressed at the back of my throat. *Will you be there? Will you help me pick paint colors? Will you build impractical storage cabinets and complain about them the whole time?*

I swallowed all of them down and smiled instead. "From your mouth to the universe's ears," I said lightly. "Maybe if I post enough behind-the-scenes shots, a studio will manifest itself."

"I'll build it," he said. "Whenever you're ready."

Warmth fizzed through me as my throat tightened. "Deal."

Time slipped away.

We drifted from bridal spreads to travel books to a

collection of vintage ads that made us both snort-laugh. He told me about the Nerd Night campaign—how their horses kept nearly dying and Brody kept looting cursed objects—and I offered my very serious professional opinion that their characters needed more capes and tighter leather pants.

Winnie barreled over at one point, backpack on, Selene shrugging into her coat behind her.

"Are you and Wes on a date?" she asked, blunt as only a kid can be, eyes flicking between us and our shared book and the two empty coffee cups on the table.

"Kind of."

"Uh, no," I said, my words stumbling over his, entirely too fast. Heat shot into my cheeks so fast it was dizzying. "We're just hanging out."

Wes smiled into his last sip of coffee as Selene's eyes widened.

Winnie considered this, then nodded sagely. "Okay. It just looks like a date," she said. "Bye!"

She skipped away before I could respond. Selene mouthed *We'll talk later* and waggled her eyebrows as she herded her daughter toward the door.

I stared at the page in front of me without seeing any of it.

*Kind of? What does that even mean?*

We look like a couple.

We felt like one too—sharing a couch, trading quiet jokes, him refilling my coffee when I got distracted, his thigh pressed along mine like it lived there.

Dangerous. It was all so dangerously easy.

When I checked the time on my phone, I nearly dropped it. "We've been here an hour," I groaned. "This was supposed to be a ten-minute stop."

"Guess we got distracted," Wes said, bumping my shoulder with his.

My eyes narrowed on him. "What did you mean by *kind of?*"

Wes's eyes sparkled with a playful glint. "Caught that, did you?"

I bit back a smile. He was frustrating when he was moody, but when he was playful? Downright infuriating.

"We should talk about this." I crossed my arms, pouting because I was reeling and he was smiling at me with that cocky grin that melted my insides.

He snorted as he stood and held out my coat. "Whenever you're ready, Duchess."

I shook my head and stood. We pulled on our coats and stepped back out into Star Harbor.

Dusk had slid in while we weren't watching. The snowbanks along the street glowed blue in the fading light, streetlamps flicking on one by one, little halos of gold fuzzing the edges of our breath as it puffed into the air.

Wes automatically eased to the outside of the sidewalk, between me and the street, just like he had once before. Some old reflex of his—protective and unthinking.

This time I didn't joke about it.

I just slid my hand into the crook of his arm, fingers hooking lightly around his biceps. He glanced down, then back up, a warm smile flickering across his face. Whatever he saw in mine seemed to answer it. His arm relaxed a fraction, his hand brushing against my hip with every step.

My throat went tight. *If this is what our ordinary looks like, I want it. I want Tuesday coffee runs and farm visits and him walking me down Main Street like it's the most normal thing in the world.*

Inside the truck, our hands collided over the center

console when I reached for the heater. My instinct was to pull back or make a joke, but Wes did neither.

He turned his palm instead, catching my fingers and lacing them with his. His warm, wide hand, calluses against my knuckles, and his thumb pressing once against my pulse like he was testing it.

He held on for a beat, eyes on the windshield, then let go to put the truck in drive.

The engine rumbled to life. Snow crunched under the tires as we pulled away from the curb. The cab filled with that easy, humming quiet that settled in only when you were full—of food, of coffee, of words, of feelings you weren't quite ready to unwrap.

I leaned my head back against the seat and watched Main Street slide by in soft blurs of light, the ghost of his touch still tingling in my fingers.

We were just running errands and drinking coffee and talking about nothing.

My whole body knew better.

This wasn't practice anymore. It was a life, threaded through a Tuesday in a half-empty bookstore, and for one blindingly stupid, beautiful day, I let myself believe it might actually be ours.

## THIRTY-TWO

WES

THE LIGHT in my room had gone soft and gold, slicing through the curtains in thin, lazy stripes. For the first time in a long time, morning didn't feel like something I had to survive.

It was something I got to keep.

Clara was warm and solid in front of me, back pressed to my chest, her hair a messy curtain against my throat. My hand rested low on her stomach, fingers splayed over soft skin, the curve of her hip tucked against my pelvis like we'd been made to slot together that way. Every muscle in my body hummed with the pleasant, used ache of the night before and the quieter, sweeter ache from the day we'd had yesterday—farm, books, her hand in the crook of my arm like it belonged there.

She shifted, a sleepy wiggle that dragged her ass along my already half-hard cock. A little sound left her, not quite a moan, not quite a sigh, and every thought I'd been pretending to have about coffee or logistics evaporated.

"Morning," she murmured, voice rough with sleep.

"Morning, Duchess." My mouth found the line of her

shoulder, pressing a slow kiss there, then another. Her skin tasted like sleep and my soap and something that felt a hell of a lot like hope.

I slid my hand lower, fingers easing between her thighs. Heat met me instantly, slick and ready, like her body had been waiting for mine to catch up. She shivered, hips tipping back into me.

"Wes," she breathed, already folding into my touch.

I let my cock nudge along the curve of her ass, the angle easier like this, my leg braced just right behind hers. A few weeks ago, the idea of moving this much in bed would have tied my brain into knots. This morning, I knew exactly where to plant my good foot, where to sink my weight, how far I could pull her in.

"Tell me if anything's off," I murmured against her neck, lining myself up. "If I'm too much. Too deep. Anything."

"Pretty sure the only problem is not enough," she said, voice shaky, a smile tucked into it as she reached forward and grabbed a condom from the pile on the nightstand.

I made quick work of getting it on before nestling against her. Lying side by side I eased into Clara, pushing in slowly as I let the heat of her close around me. The slow stretch was perfect agony. I adjusted my leg and gripped her hip to keep us steady. Her quiet gasps matched mine as I bottomed out.

She took me like she had been built for it, fingers clutching at the sheets, little broken sounds catching in her throat. I kept one arm snug around her waist, holding her back against me, the other braced on the mattress. My body remembered the groove from the last few nights, muscles learning that it was allowed to want, allowed to move, allowed to take.

"Jesus, Clara," I rasped, fucking into her in slow, careful strokes that went just a little deeper every time she pushed back. "You feel like . . . hell, you're fucking perfect."

Her hand clawed back to grab my hip, nails biting into my skin. "Say that again," she whispered.

I kissed the hinge of her jaw, breath stuttering. "You heard me," I said, words rough as gravel. "This"—another thrust, her shuddering around me—"you in my bed, in my arms, taking me like this . . . this feels like home."

She made a sound that went straight through my chest, half sob, half moan of pleasure. I lost myself in it for a while —her heat, the sunlight striping our bodies, the quiet creak of the bed and the soft slap of skin as I fucked into her tight little cunt. Every time she whispered my name, something inside me stitched back together.

When she tightened around me and came, I followed, burying my face in her neck, breathing her in while every nerve in my body lit up and burned clean. The world narrowed to the feel of her, the pulse of her, the way her hand found mine and tangled our fingers as we shook it out together.

Eventually the tremors eased. I slipped out of her and eased onto my back, dragging her with me until she sprawled half across my chest, hair everywhere, cheeks flushed, lips kiss-bruised. Her leg hooked over mine, the weight of her thigh resting over the remains of my leg like it was the most natural thing in the world.

My heart pounded, not from exertion and not from fear —just from the sheer, stupid fact that I got to have this.

That she was here. That I was here.

*She's my girl. This is our morning.*

I didn't say it out loud, because saying it felt like

tempting fate. Holding it close felt like the only prayer I'd ever really meant.

Instead, I tipped my head and pressed a slow kiss to her hairline, then another to the crown of her head. "You okay?" I asked quietly. "Not secretly regretting your life choices?"

She huffed a laugh against my chest. "Pretty sure that was the opposite of regret."

My hand traced lazy circles on her bare shoulder, knuckles skimming over soft skin. The words I didn't say lined up behind my teeth anyway, stubborn and insistent.

*I am completely in love with you.*

It sat there, hot and terrifying, so I kept my mouth busy with other things. "You're going to ruin me, you know that?" I said instead, voice low. "I can't remember what it felt like to wake up and not want you like this."

Her fingers toyed with the hair on my chest, drawing aimless patterns. "Tragic," she murmured with a laugh. "Guess you're stuck with me."

"Yeah," I said, throat tight. "Guess I am."

We lay there in the kind of quiet that didn't ask for anything. Sunlight shifted up the wall. Somewhere downstairs, the heater kicked on with a low hum.

After a while she tipped her chin up, studying my face. "What's on the agenda for today?"

I dragged my palm down her spine, letting my hand settle at the small of her back. "I was thinking about heading by the restaurant," I said slowly. "Check out the second-floor framing. Something looked off yesterday when Austin showed me the pics. I want eyes on it."

Her whole expression lit, pride softening her mouth. "Look at you," she said, warmth threading through the tease. "Out in the world, terrorizing unsuspecting employees. They're going to be happy to see you out there."

The hit of it landed hard in my chest. She wasn't talking to the guy who once lived on the couch and pretended the stairs didn't exist. She was talking to the man who ran sites, who climbed ladders, who made decisions that held up walls. The man who brought beautiful buildings to life.

She saw me as the guy I used to be. The man I desperately wanted to *be* again.

"Yeah, well," I muttered, trying to sound casual as my heart did a slow lurch. "Somebody's gotta make sure they don't cheap out on my beams."

She smiled against my chest, then pressed a quick kiss there, right over my heart. "They're lucky to have you," she said. "I am too."

That last line sat with me long after she slid out of bed to hunt for my T-shirt and hijack the bathroom. I watched her move around my room like she belonged in it—her lotion on my dresser, her makeup bag on the bathroom sink, her ringless hand shoving her hair into some kind of ponytail that was going to fall out in an hour.

By the time I was dressed, the decision was made.

I pulled on my work jacket, the one that still smelled faintly of sawdust and cold air, and grabbed my keys from the bowl. My leg felt steady under me, with any phantom pain a low, manageable buzz. My hand brushed the fridge where our stupid list of rules hung, the ink a little smudged from hands and time.

This wasn't just about lumber or framing. It was proof.

Proof I wasn't just the guy on the couch anymore. Proof I could walk a site again. Proof I could be a man who took care of things, of people, of *her*.

I squeezed the keys in my fist and glanced once toward the staircase. Upstairs, Clara hummed off-key in the bathroom, and I headed for the door.

*I've got this.*

~

CAL'S new restaurant looked almost finished from the outside.

My truck tires crunched over packed snow as I pulled in, the cold bright enough to make my teeth ache. I killed the engine, sat for half a second with my hands on the wheel, and then shoved the door open before I could think too hard about it.

The air knifed into my lungs, clean and sharp. I forced my shoulders back and walked across the cleared path like I owned it.

Because I used to. Because I needed to.

The blue barn hulled up against the winter sky, big windows already framed in, fresh siding buttoned up tight. Through the rolled-back doors, the main floor was a maze of mostly complete walls and defined spaces now—future bar gleaming with new lumber, booth platforms framed out, kitchen rough-ins tucked behind sheets of plastic. Above it, though, the second floor was still bones and echoes, the skeleton of offices and storage rooms taking shape in raw studs and open joists.

A couple of the guys glanced up from the sawhorses. One of the laborers straightened, lifting a hand. "Hey, boss."

Heads turned. A few more nods, a couple of quick, surprised looks that they tried to smooth out. I heard my name ripple through the half-built space—*shit, he's here*—as nail guns popped in the background.

Austin stepped out from behind a stack of drywall, clipboard in one hand, tape measure hooked at his hip, and a beanie yanked down over his ears.

"You picked a cold-ass day to come play foreman." He grinned and held out a hand.

Something warm and sharp slid under my ribs. This was who I used to be. Not the guy counting ceiling cracks from a couch groove.

"Somebody's gotta make sure you idiots aren't half-assing my plans," I shot back.

We met in the middle and exchanged a quick handshake before Austin pulled me into a one-armed guy hug that jostled my shoulder more than anything. My leg took the weight without complaint. The phantom pain that had haunted the morning was quiet, a low hum instead of a siren.

Austin flipped his clipboard up. "We're framing out the second-floor dining and checking the stringers," he said, nodding toward the interior. "Stairs are roughed in. They're ugly as sin right now, but they'll hold."

Through the open maw of the barn, I could see the skeleton of the staircase—bare treads, open risers, no rail, angling up into the half-built second floor. Fresh snow clung to the work boots lined up by the entrance, melted into a sheen along the plywood where guys had tromped in and out.

"I'm going to take a look up top." I nodded toward the staircase.

Austin hesitated, eyes flicking from my face to my leg and back. "You sure?" he said. "It's slick as shit up there from the melt. I can bring the plans down if you just want—"

"What, you think I forgot how stairs work?" I hooked a brow, forcing my mouth into something like a smirk.

He huffed out a reluctant laugh, still not fully sold. "Sounds good, boss."

"Let's go." I motioned forward. "You can show me your ugly-ass stringers."

The truth was, I needed this more than I needed the oxygen in my lungs. Clara's voice from the morning ran on a loop in my head—*Look at you, boss man*—and made me smile.

Austin thumped up the stairs first, boots leaving damp prints. I followed.

The first step was solid. My good foot landed neatly on the tread. The prosthetic came down with a hollow thunk on the next, the socket biting around my stump in a way I'd learned to ignore as we climbed.

Each tread had just the slightest film of moisture where snow had melted and refrozen. Not enough to see, just enough to feel in the faint slip of rubber.

An air compressor kicked on somewhere downstairs with a low, grinding roar. Nail guns popped in short bursts, sharp and staccato. It wasn't the same sound as mortar fire, not exactly, but my nervous system had never mastered nuance.

A warning zap of phantom pain shot through the end of my thigh, nerves misfiring in the empty space. I gritted my teeth and kept going.

*Not here. Not now. You're fine. One step at a time.*

Austin glanced back over his shoulder. "We're reinforcing this corner," he said, pointing, oblivious to the way my hands had tightened into fists. "Once the joists are—"

A two-by-four slipped from someone's grip below and hit the concrete with a crack like a gunshot.

My body reacted before my brain could remind it we were inside a barn in Michigan and not halfway around the world.

My shoulders flinched. My good foot jerked. The prosthetic, mid-step, came down a few inches off where I'd aimed it—right onto a slick patch where the melting snow had turned the plywood dark.

The rubber sole slid.

For one hideous half second, I was suspended between steps, weight pitched wrong, good leg scrambling for something solid that wasn't there.

Then gravity won.

My knee slammed into the tread, pain detonating up my thigh. My hip met the sharp corner of wood a heartbeat later with a jolt that rattled my teeth. My palm skidded out on the damp plywood when I tried to catch myself, skin scraping. The socket dug into raw nerves as the prosthetic twisted at an angle it had no business being in.

Breath punched out of me. The world narrowed to the burn in my stump and the humiliating fact that I was suddenly on my ass on a half-built staircase, staring at my own boots.

"Shit," Austin snapped. I heard the scramble of his boots coming back down. "Wes. Hold up, stay still—"

"I'm fine," I tried to say, but it came out thin and wrecked.

I planted my good foot, grabbed a stair, and tried to haul myself up.

The prosthetic foot skidded again, shooting out on the slick plywood. The angle was all wrong. With no rail and nothing to brace against, there was nowhere solid for it to push. Every time I shifted, pain knifed through the stump, sharp and electric.

My good thigh started to shake from the effort of trying to do it all.

"Boss, don't," one of the guys called from below. Boots

clattered as more of them hustled over. "Just hold on a second."

Voices crowded the space, too close, echoing off unfinished walls.

"Careful, man—"

"Get his arm—"

"Watch the leg—"

"Fuck, is he okay?"

Austin dropped onto the tread beside me. "Hey," he said, steady and calm, palms up like I was a spooked horse. "Hey, look at me."

I was very aware of the fact that my chest was heaving like I'd just sprinted, that my hands were trembling where they gripped the wood.

"I've got it," I ground out, trying again to lever myself up. My prosthetic slid with a useless little squeak and slammed back into the edge of the step. The jolt shot straight into the socket. My vision went white at the edges.

"Jesus, Wes," Austin said quietly. "You don't. Not like this."

Hands closed under my arms, trying to help. Someone's fingers brushed the metal of the prosthetic, trying to steady it.

"Don't move, man," another voice urged from somewhere above or below. "You're gonna hurt yourself worse."

Down on the floor, someone said the words that gutted me clean.

"He shouldn't be up there."

The words weren't cruel or mocking. Just honest. The kind of thing a guy says when he's worried about liability and the fact that his boss might crack his skull open on a jobsite.

It landed like a punch right under my ribs.

*He shouldn't be up there.*

*He doesn't belong on his own site anymore.*

Austin blew out a breath, then let his hand drop to the socket carefully. "Okay," he said, voice firm. "I think the best plan is getting the leg off, yeah? Then we'll get you down slowly."

Humiliation scorched hot across my face. "I can—"

"Or," Austin cut in, "you let me help you so you don't eat another stair. You have to pick one."

The crew had gone quiet. I could feel them hovering on the stairs, on the landing, radiating a mix of concern and not wanting to make it worse.

My fingers dug into the tread until my knuckles ached. Every worst-case scenario I'd ever played in my head about something like this happening—this exactly, this helpless, stupid scramble in front of my own crew—lined up with military precision.

I forced my hand away from my sides and reached for the leg.

Unlocking the prosthetic up here, with an audience, was ten times harder than doing it in my bedroom. My fingers fumbled. The sweat that had broken out across my neck made my grip clumsy.

The socket finally loosened. I eased the leg off, every inch sending fire through the raw skin at the end of my thigh. I had to clamp my jaw shut so I didn't make a sound.

"Got it," one of the guys said too brightly from below when Austin passed the prosthetic down. There was an awkward shuffle as he caught it. "I'll, uh . . . put this some-where safe."

Like it was a posthole digger or a damn drill.

I stared at the spot where the leg had been, at my jeans

wrinkling around nothing. The air on my stump felt cold and exposed, even through the denim.

Austin slung my arm over his shoulders in one practiced movement. "All right, man," he said. "Nice and easy."

Someone braced at my other side, ready to catch.

We started the descent.

With no prosthetic to balance me, every step was a lopsided, graceless negotiation—good foot down, pause, adjust. My thigh burned. My hip throbbed where it had hit. My pride lay in pieces on the plywood.

"Should we call somebody?" a voice floated up from below. "Like—clinic? Or—"

"We're not calling anyone," I bit out. "I'm fine."

Nobody argued, which somehow made it worse.

By the time we reached ground level, my shirt was sticking to my back with sweat. They eased me onto a stack of plywood sheets near the open barn doors.

Austin pressed a water bottle into my hand. "Here," he said. "You're white as a sheet."

I unscrewed the cap with shaking fingers and took a swallow I barely tasted. Around us, hammers had started up again in a half-hearted way, the rhythm wrong, the easy banter from earlier gone.

"Next time we keep the boss on ground level, yeah?" one of the guys said, trying to lighten it.

A few soft chuckles, nobody meeting my eyes for more than a second. No one was laughing at me. Everyone was being decent, kind even.

But the comment and pitying glances dug in deeper than if they'd pointed and snickered.

Austin crouched eye level in front of me, forearms braced on his knees. "You hurt anywhere that needs more than ice and ibuprofen?" he asked. "Be honest."

My stump pulsed in time with my heartbeat. My hip would blossom into a spectacular bruise by tonight. My good leg was still vibrating from the effort of hauling more than its share.

My dignity felt like someone had taken a sledgehammer to it.

"I'm fine," I said again, the words ragged.

He studied my face for a long beat and didn't call me on the lie. "I'll grab your leg," he said instead. "We'll get you settled in your truck. You can sit a minute and see if you want me to drive you to urgent care."

"I said I'm fine." The snap in my voice made a couple of guys glance over.

Austin's jaw flexed. "You're getting in the truck either way," he said quietly. "We're done doing stair gymnastics for the day."

He pushed to his feet and went to retrieve the prosthetic, leaving me sitting on a stack of lumber like another piece of misplaced material.

I stared at my hands wrapped around the water bottle, at the faint tremor in them I couldn't blame on the cold. The sounds of the job—the saws, the muffled music from a radio in the corner, the shuffle of boots—blurred together.

This site was supposed to be proof that I was still the man I'd been. Instead, it had done the one thing I'd been dreading most.

It had exposed me.

I wasn't a leader, I was a hazard.

## THIRTY-THREE

WES

Austin got me as far as the truck before my self-respect finally crawled out of whatever hole it had been hiding in.

The prosthetic was back on, liner hastily adjusted, pain still snarling around the stump. Every step across the packed gravel lot felt wrong, the angle off, the rhythm shot to hell. Austin stayed glued to my side, one hand light on my elbow like he was trying to offer support without making it obvious.

"Last chance," he said when we reached the driver's side, breath puffing in the cold. "I can drive you. Swing back and grab my truck later."

"I've got it." My voice came out thinner than I wanted.

His mouth pressed into a line. "You don't look like you've got it."

"Then lie to me and say I do," I muttered, popping the door. The movement tugged something ugly in my thigh, but I swallowed it down.

He didn't move away. "Text me when you're home, yeah?"

I hauled myself up into the driver's seat, jaw clenched,

every muscle screaming for me to pretend this was no big deal. The door shut with more force than necessary, cutting off the winter light and the sight of Austin standing there, worry all over his face before he turned and returned to work.

Silence snapped into place.

I just sat there, both hands braced on the wheel, heart racing like I'd sprinted a mile. The truck cab felt too small, air thick and stale. My leg throbbed in brutal pulses, each one sending a spike of static up through my hip and along my spine.

*Breathe in. Breathe out.*

Nothing listened.

My hands were shaking with a traitorous tremble in my fingers as they tightened on the leather.

"Stop," I whispered, to myself or my nerves or the whole damn situation, I didn't know.

The sting behind my eyes hit without warning. One second I was gritting my teeth, the next my vision blurred at the edges, heat burning up from somewhere deep in my chest.

*Not here.*

*You do not cry in the truck like a goddamn kid.*

I sucked in a breath that scraped my throat raw and blinked hard, willing it back. A hot tear escaped anyway, tracking down over skin that had gone too cold.

"Fuck," I bit out, swiping it away with the heel of my hand. The movement jolted my leg and pain flared. Another tear slid free, then another, like my body had decided to double down just to spite me.

I bowed my head until my forehead hit the steering wheel, breath sawing in and out of my lungs, shoulders tight enough that it hurt to breathe.

*You thought you were back, didn't you?*

The thought came fast and vicious.

*You thought you were that guy again. Boss man. Walking the site. Climbing stairs like it was nothing.*

I saw them in my head, crystal clear: the crew crowding the landing, hands under my arms, someone grabbing the metal, the careful way they'd eased me down like I was a crate of glass. Austin's voice talking too calmly, like he was trying not to spook a wild animal.

*They had to peel you off the floor.*

*They had to take your leg off in front of everyone because you were deadweight with it on.*

I squeezed my eyes shut. The image of my prosthetic being handed down the stairs like a misplaced tool turned my stomach. Faulty equipment. Boss's leg is busted, toss it to the side.

A humorless laugh scraped out of me, more breath than sound.

*You couldn't even get up one flight without turning into a team project.*

Clara's face flashed up next. Her smile over the table at La Casita. The way her bedroom eyes had gone bright and proud when I'd told her I was going to the site. *Look at you, boss man.*

She deserved that guy. The one she thought she was looking at.

Not the one who sat on a half-built staircase while his crew disassembled him so he wouldn't fall on his face.

My grip on the wheel tightened until my knuckles ached.

She walked away from a life where her entire job was propping up a man. She lost herself trying to hold someone else together. How could I hand her a fresh version of the same goddamn thing and call it love?

*Love.*

That was what this had started to feel like. Her in my bed. Her in my truck. Her hand in mine at the farm, in town. A day of errands and coffee and plans that had tasted suspiciously like a future.

*You really believed it, didn't you?* whispered the cruelest part of my brain. *One good day and you started thinking you were whole.*

My throat closed up.

Tears burned and spilled over, hot and unwanted, blurring the view of the half-plowed lot and the skeletal frame of the building outside. I swiped at them again, angry at myself for not getting a lid on it faster.

*Maybe you can fake it in the kitchen, on a chair, in bed with the lights low.*

*Out there? On stairs and plywood and steel?*

*You're a liability. A hazard your own guys have to plan around.*

Clara deserved a man who didn't need to be peeled off plywood in front of his employees. The mere thought of it was a nail driven straight through my chest.

My vision narrowed to the arc of the dashboard, the curve of my hands, the faint tremor that wouldn't stop. I took one more shuddering breath, tried to cram everything back into the box it had clawed its way out of. It didn't fit. Not really. But I got it shut enough to function.

"Enough," I muttered.

My fingers found the ignition, turned the key. The engine rumbled to life beneath me, familiar and grounding in a way my own body no longer was. I shoved the truck into gear and pulled out of the lot, my world narrowed to the line of the road and the tight, punishing band around my ribs.

I drove toward home with my jaw clenched and my vision tunneling and chest in a vise, clinging to the one clear thought that cut through the noise.

I had dared to believe I was whole again.

The universe had made damn sure I remembered exactly what I was instead.

THE HOUSE WAS warm when I walked in, heat licking at my cheeks in a way that felt undeserved.

I forced my gait into something that looked like normal as I crossed the threshold, my keys biting into my palm. The stump burned where the socket rubbed wrong, and every step sent a little shock up my spine.

I pretended like it was nothing.

Clara sat at the kitchen table, laptop open and a scatter of books and printed reference photos spread around her. Late light from the window caught the loose pieces of her hair, turning them copper at the edges. She looked up the second the door shut, that easy, instinctive smile blooming before she had any idea what she was about to walk into.

"Hey, you," she said, voice warm enough to slide right under my ribs. Her gaze swept over me, soft and appreciative in a way that used to make me stand taller. "How was your day, handsome?"

The words landed like gravel in my throat.

*Handsome.* The guy who had sat on his ass on a half-built staircase while his crew untangled him from his own leg. The guy who broke down and cried in his truck because stairs were too much to ask.

My jaw clenched.

"Fine." The word came out flat and sharp at the edges.

I dropped my keys into the bowl by the door harder than I meant to. The metal hit ceramic with a loud crack that made us both flinch. Something in my hip twinged at the twist. I swallowed the sound that wanted to come out.

She straightened slowly, the smile slipping a notch as she took me in more closely. Her brows pinched, worry lighting up behind her eyes before I could dodge it.

"You okay?" she asked. "You look—"

"Long day," I cut in, already angling my body past the table toward the living room. "I'm going to sit down."

The tightness in my voice was evident, even to my own ears.

A chair scraped behind me. Her footsteps followed, light and stubborn. By the time I lowered myself onto the couch, she was there, arms folded around herself like she was resisting the urge to reach for me.

"Wes," she said quietly. "Talk to me. Did something happen at the site?"

The question made my skin crawl.

The upstairs landing flashed behind my eyes—plywood, hands under my arms, the murmur of *He shouldn't be up there.* Shame rose like heat, thick and suffocating. Her concern felt less like a hand offered and more like a spotlight pinned between my shoulder blades.

I latched onto irritation because it was easier to hold than fear.

"Not everything is a crisis I need to unpack with you, Clara." The sentence snapped out before I could soften it.

Her head jerked back a fraction, like I'd reached out and physically pushed her. Hurt flared across her face, quick and unguarded, before something cooler slid in to cover it.

"Wow," she said, a brittle little laugh escaping as she raised her palms. "Okay. I didn't realize asking if you're okay was micromanaging now."

Guilt punched hard in my gut. The right move would have been to back up, to apologize, to tell her the truth instead of bleeding all over her with half of it.

"I'm tired," I ground out, staring at some point over her shoulder because looking her in the eye felt dangerous. "That's it. You don't have to fix it."

The second the words were out, I wanted them back.

*You fucking asshole. She isn't your triage nurse. She isn't the enemy.*

Her mouth pressed into a hard line. Color climbed her throat, high and hot, like anger was the only thing holding back something worse.

"I wasn't trying to fix it," she said, voice too even to be anything but forced. "I was trying to be your person for thirty goddamn seconds."

That one landed square in the center of my chest.

My leg pulsed in time with my heartbeat. I shoved my fingers against the aching muscle above the socket like pressure on the pain would stall out all of it.

"I'm going to ice my leg," I said, doubling down because running away was the only thing I seemed to be good at. "I'll be fine."

Her eyes went shiny for a heartbeat, then cleared in that eerie way I'd seen once before—on a front porch with a dress bag over her shoulder and a life unraveling behind her.

"Right," she said coolly. "Great. I'll get out of your way, then."

She turned on her heel and walked back to the table, spine straight, shoulders tight. The slight tremor in her hands as she picked up a stack of photos was the only tell she hadn't gone completely numb.

The room felt colder just from the space she put between us.

I sank back into the couch cushions like my bones had turned to lead, staring at the blank TV screen, listening to the soft, careful sounds of her stacking books instead of the easy, looping hum we'd had the last few days.

My leg hurt. My ego hurt worse.

I dragged a hand over my face. The crack I'd just put in us felt small on the surface.

Deep down, it was already starting to split wide open and bleed.

The knock came sharp and no-nonsense.

My jaw clenched. Every part of me wanted to sink deeper into the couch and pretend I wasn't home, let whoever it was stand on an empty porch and call it a day.

From the kitchen, cabinet doors clicked shut a little louder than necessary. "You expecting someone?" Clara called.

My leg protested as I pushed to my feet. "No," I muttered.

Hayes stood on the step in his work jacket and a sweat-dark baseball cap, jaw tight, eyes already checking me for damage. He swept me once, head to toe, taking in the stiffness of my stance, the way I'd braced a hand on the jamb without thinking.

"Austin called," he said by way of hello. "Said you took a spill. You okay?"

A spill. Like I'd tripped over a curb, not eaten shit on a

half-finished staircase and had to get disassembled in front of my crew.

My skin crawled.

"I'm fine," I said, stepping back to let him in.

He snorted under his breath but came inside, stomping snow off his boots on the mat. "You don't look fine."

His gaze pinned me in place.

"So." He sighed, and his hand gently slapped his side. "What happened?"

"Wet stair," I said. "Bad footing. I went down. The end."

His eyes narrowed. "You hurt?"

"Bruised." I rolled my shoulder like it proved something. "Nothing's broken."

He blew out a breath, some of the tightness leaving his shoulders. "Good. Don't do that shit, man." His mouth hitched, but there wasn't much humor in it. "We don't get to lose you. My mom would haunt my ass for eternity."

The punch of that landed in the usual spot and hurt in familiar ways.

Then he added, almost offhand, but not really, "Clara would lose her damn mind if you did real damage."

That one detonated somewhere new.

Clara, on my porch hauling in too much luggage, her face determined as she ripped off the ring. Clara, in my bed this morning, breathy and soft and all in. Clara, at my table an hour ago, asking how my day was like she had a right to know, like she really was my person.

I swallowed and it felt like gravel.

Clara appeared, arms crossed over her chest, shoulders squared like armor.

"So I didn't imagine it," she said. "Something *did*

happen." Her eyes found mine, sharp and scared and already building a case. "You fell?"

Humiliation surged hot and choking. Being witnessed by one of them had been bad enough. Both at once felt like being pinned to a dartboard.

"I said I'm fine," I snapped. "Everyone can stop hovering."

Clara took one step closer, her gaze never leaving my face. "You are not fine," she said. "Why didn't you call me?"

*Because I didn't want you to hear me stutter through it. Because I didn't want you to see the leg come off in the middle of my failure. Because I didn't want you to have proof of exactly how bad of a bet I truly am.*

"Because I didn't feel like giving a blow-by-blow to my live-in safety committee," I said instead, the shitty line sliding out slick and sharp.

It hit its mark. Her mouth went tight, eyes going glassy for half a heartbeat before steel dropped in behind them.

Hayes straightened and stepped in. "Hey," he snapped, voice cutting through the room like a whip. "Don't fucking talk to her like that."

I flinched. Shame spiked so fast I almost stepped back.

He was right. That was the worst part. He was right, and the truth crawled over my skin, that I was standing in my own living room lashing out at the one person who had done nothing but show up for me.

Clara shook her head, a quick, sharp movement, then looked back at her brother. "I can take care of myself," she said, steady. "If he has something to say to me, I can take it."

Her focus whipped back to me, eyes flaring as her chin lifted in defiance. "So say it. Stop snapping at everyone and tell me what's actually going on."

The room closed in. Walls, windows, the weight of their

attention. Fight-or-flight roared in my veins, that familiar rush of panic.

*I need out. I need air.*

There was a third option. The one I knew best.

*Burn it down before anyone else can.*

Hayes's gaze flicked between us, reading the pressure build. He blew out a breath and stood, hands up in a loose I'm-not-fighting-you gesture.

"You two should talk," he said. "I'm not refereeing this."

On his way past me, he jabbed a finger lightly at my chest. "But not like that again. I mean it."

I nodded once, which was pathetic considering the words that had already left my mouth. It was the best I had.

The door shut behind him with a soft click that sounded louder than the knock had.

The house felt huge and too small at the same time.

Silence stretched. Clara watched me from across the room, arms still wrapped around herself like she was the only thing holding her together.

"So," she said finally, voice low and shaking just enough to give her away. "You fell. You scared everyone. And now your solution is to treat me like *I'm* the problem?"

I stared at the floor for a beat, then lifted my head. There wasn't anywhere else to look that didn't have her in it.

"I went up to the second floor," I said, words coming out flat. "My leg slipped. I went down and couldn't get my footing to get back up without help."

Venom clung to every syllable, all of it aimed directly at myself.

Her expression softened immediately, like someone had opened a window. She took a step closer, anger bleeding into something worse.

"I'm sorry that happened," she said. "That sounds terrifying. Why didn't you call me?"

The question went straight through whatever flimsy armor I had left.

*Because then it would have been real in your eyes too. Because I can live with them seeing me as pathetic, but I cannot live with you thinking it.*

"Because this"—I gestured between us, hand slicing the air—"is exactly why today happened."

She reeled like I'd shoved her. "What are you talking about?"

"I got cocky," I ground out. "I started believing I was . . . fixed. Normal. Like I could just stroll into a site and be the guy I used to be." I laughed once, humorless and sharp. "Joke's on me, I guess."

Her chin lifted. "No. That's on wet stairs and gravity. That's it."

"You already built one life around taking care of someone else's shit," I said, the words tearing their way out. "You stood up there in a dress and realized you'd signed up to be the emotional support wife, not a partner."

Color drained from her face. "That's not what this is."

"Isn't it?" The snarl scraped my throat raw. "I can't even walk up a set of stairs without needing three guys and a fucking incident report. Today proved exactly what I've been trying not to say out loud: I am not a safe bet, Clara. Not for you. Not for anyone."

She took another step toward me, close enough that I could see the shimmer in her eyes, the fine tremble in her mouth. "You fell," she said again, desperate for me to listen. "That's all. You're allowed to have a bad day. That doesn't erase everything we're building."

Her hand hovered near my chest, fingers curling like

she wanted to touch me and didn't know if she was allowed anymore.

"I get to choose this," she said, voice rough. "I get to choose you."

The hope in that sentence hurt worse than the fall.

"You think love or choice or whatever the hell you're calling this today is going to matter when you're dragging my ass off the floor in ten years?" My voice shook, but I couldn't stop. "When every room we walk into, you're scanning stairs and exits and wondering if today's the day my body fails me again?"

I swallowed hard, tasted blood and regret and couldn't tell them apart.

Her first tears slipped free, tracking hot down her cheeks. She didn't bother wiping them.

"That's not fair," she whispered.

"Your brother trusted me with you," I said, Hayes's face flashing behind my eyes, that mix of worry and faith that had no business being aimed at me. "Today was proof he shouldn't. I'm one bad day away from wrecking everything I touch."

She shook her head hard enough that her hair swung. "That's not what happened."

"The fuck it didn't."

Silence pressed at the edges. If I stopped talking, I knew what would happen. I'd cave. I'd let her talk me down off this ledge, curl around her like nothing had cracked, and then we'd both be standing there next time the leg gave out with fewer exits and even more to lose.

"You wanted to help me figure out my body again," I said, going for the throat. "Mission accomplished. I can get off. I can fake being normal a little better now. You don't need to keep doing this."

Her face crumpled. It was like watching a building collapse in slow motion.

"Is that really what you think this is?" she asked, voice breaking but sharp. "That I'm still here for practice? For rehab?"

My mouth opened. The truth crouched right there.

*No. I think you're here because for some reason you picked me, and if I let you stay, I will ruin you.*

"Yes," I said instead.

The word dropped between us like an executioner's axe.

She stared at me, long enough that I felt every stutter of my heartbeat. Then she nodded, once, like a verdict.

"Got it," she whispered. "Message received."

She stepped back. Each inch might as well have been a mile.

"If you decide you want to stop punishing yourself long enough to tell me the truth," she said, voice low and lethal, "you know where my room is."

She swallowed, eyes shining and furious and heartbreakingly done.

"Until then," she added, quieter, "I'm done begging you to let me in."

She turned and walked up the staircase, her shoulders squared like she was holding herself together by pure stubbornness. I heard her close the door a moment later. She hadn't slammed it, just shut it with a quiet, final click that echoed louder than any shouting match we could have had.

The house went still.

I stayed where I was, breathing like I'd just run sprints instead of tearing my own life in half with a handful of sentences.

My leg throbbed in time with my pulse, phantom pain

spiderwebbing through my thigh, but it barely made a dent in the ache sitting square in my chest.

Eventually, gravity dragged me down. I sank onto the couch, elbows on my knees, hands hanging uselessly between them. The TV stared back at me, black and blank.

She had given me every out. Every chance to tell her the truth.

I'd chosen the version that hurt us both, because it was the only one that made sense with the story my brain refused to stop telling: that I was a walking hazard, a wreck in progress, a problem to be managed, not a man to be loved but pitied.

Every time I reached for something good, I turned it into collateral damage.

I leaned back, head hitting the cushion, eyes burning as the ceiling fuzzed in and out of focus.

I had dared to believe I was whole again, and the universe had reminded me exactly where I stood.

Punishment for wanting too much settled into my bones like wet concrete, heavy and cold, setting hard around the shape of a man who had just proved his worst fears right.

## THIRTY-FOUR

CLARA

I HADN'T SLEPT MUCH.

I knew he hadn't either. I was painfully aware of his movements across the hall—the soft thud of his footsteps on the hardwood, the shower turning on, then off again, like he couldn't quite settle in.

Wes had stayed in his room. I'd stayed in mine. The space between us felt bigger than the whole damn house.

I zipped the duffel and sighed.

It wasn't even that big. A week's worth of clothes, my toiletries, my laptop, and the overstuffed folder full of shot lists and contracts for the farm shoot. Half my closet still hung in place, my shoes still lined up underneath. My favorite sweatshirt draped over the back of the chair.

I wasn't emptying my life into a suitcase, but I was drawing a line.

I wrapped my fingers around the strap, testing the weight. It dug into the pad of my palm, heavier than it had any right to be.

The thought made my throat close. I swallowed hard,

hitched the duffel onto my shoulder, and stepped into the hall.

The house was too quiet. No TV, no music from his phone. Just the low hum of the heater and the faint clink of ceramic from the kitchen.

Of course he was making coffee.

My heart lurched when I saw him at the counter, shoulders broad and familiar in a worn T-shirt, frowning at the coffee maker as it slowly brewed. Two mugs sat on the counter, side by side.

The sight of that second mug nearly undid me.

He heard the duffel bump the wall and turned. His gaze skimmed my face, dropped to the bag on my shoulder, then snapped back up again. Confusion flickered into something sharper, alarm tightening his features.

"Where are you going?" His voice came out rough with panic teasing at the edges.

My heart thudded so hard it felt like it might leave bruises. I tightened my grip on the strap until my fingers ached.

"I'm going to stay with Kit for a bit," I said, amazed at how steady my voice sounded. "Until after the shoot. Until I can figure everything out."

He took a step toward me, a small hitch in his movement betraying the lingering fallout from the fall he refused to talk about.

His jaw flexed. "You don't have to do that."

His words were instinctive, automatic reassurance. *You don't have to go. You don't have to change. You don't have to leave.*

I shifted the duffel higher on my shoulder and lifted my chin, forcing myself to really look at him—sleep-creased, unshaven, eyes bruised with exhaustion and something close to panic.

"That's the thing," I said softly. "I do."

The words burned all the way up. I let them sit between us, hot and undeniable, then took the breath I'd been avoiding since last night.

"I love you."

His whole body went still.

The air felt different after that—thicker somehow, charged. He stared at me like I'd just spoken in a language he didn't know he understood, like he'd heard the words and they'd hit bone.

I didn't look away. I wanted him to see all of it—the shake in my hands, the way my chest hurt, the fact that I meant every syllable.

"I love you, but I also love myself," I said, my voice quieter but no less clear. "I can't stay in a house where you choose your fear over both of us."

Something in his expression cracked. His mouth opened, then snapped closed again. He looked like he was reaching for a denial, an argument, an apology—*anything*—but whatever he found wasn't enough to make it past his throat.

"You're not a monster, Wes," I went on, because I needed him to hear that part too. "You're just scared. All the time. Of getting hurt. Of hurting me. Of not being enough."

I saw the flinch in his eyes even though his shoulders stayed rigid.

"I understand that more than you know," I said. "I have built my life around someone who struggled to accept himself before."

Greg's face flashed in my mind—the tight, brittle smile, the way his shoulders had always looked like they were carrying something heavy he couldn't put down. The realization at the altar that I was signing up to carry it with him forever.

I shook my head, eyes stinging, but I didn't let the tears fall. Not yet.

"I can't do it again," I whispered. My voice cracked. "I can't fix this for you."

Silence settled over the kitchen. The coffee machine gurgled in the background, oblivious.

He took another breath, like he might try again. "Clara—"

I shifted my grip on the duffel and took a step back, toward the door.

"You don't have to earn anything with me, Wes," I said, gentler now. "You just have to show up as you. For us. Until you can do that, I have to go."

His eyes were wet, and he looked like he'd been hollowed out and didn't know what to do with the space.

"Clara, wait—*please*," he tried, the words breaking halfway out.

I held his gaze for one last second, letting him see it all—the love, the hurt, the line I was drawing in permanent marker.

"Goodbye, Wes," I said.

Then I opened the door before I could lose my nerve, stepped into the slap of cold air, and pulled it shut behind me.

The chill hit my cheeks, sharp enough to feel like punishment. I blinked hard, the duffel strap weighing down my shoulder as I descended the front steps and across the shoveled path to my car. My knuckles were white on the keys by the time I slid behind the wheel.

I didn't cry on the drive to Kit's. I kept my hands at ten

and two, breathing in and out, in and out, counting stop signs like they were the only thing keeping me from turning around.

By the time I climbed the stairs to her apartment, my eyes burned and my chest felt hollow. I shifted the duffel higher, lifted my fist, and knocked.

My knuckles stung. My eyes did too.

The further I drove away from Wes, the more broken I felt.

KIT YANKED the door open on the second knock, took one long look at me, and blew out a low whistle.

"You look like shit," she said, eyeing me. "Who are we murdering?"

A laugh scraped out of my throat, raw around the edges. "Hi to you too."

Her gaze dropped to the duffel clutched in my hand, then back up to my face. The joke slid off her expression like water. Protective little-sister mode slammed into place.

"What happened?" she asked, already stepping aside. "You know what, save it. Get in here. Shoes off, emotional baggage on."

The hallway behind her smelled like fried onions from the diner downstairs and someone's laundry detergent. Inside was all Kit: plants on every surface, a leaning gallery wall of thrift-store frames, a couch that had seen better decades. A mug with drying paintbrushes sat on the coffee table beside an empty ramen bowl and three different kinds of lip balm. My mind flipped back to all the houseplants I'd killed.

*Poor dead Phil would have thrived here.*

I toed my boots off, and my grip tightened on the duffel.

"Can I stay for a little while?" The words came out small and stilted.

Kit's eyebrows shot up, then pulled together. "Obviously," she said. She hooked two fingers in the duffel strap and dragged it inside, kicking the door shut behind me. "Couch. Now."

The cushions sagged under me, and I tucked my feet up. My arms wrapped around a throw pillow because I needed something to hold on to that wasn't my own rib cage.

Kit folded herself into the opposite corner, facing me, one knee bumping my thigh. "Okay," she said. "Start with why you're crying and work your way toward why you have luggage."

The laugh that burst out of me tilted straight into a sob. I pressed the heel of my hand to my sternum, like I could hold everything in place.

"We fought," I said. "Wes and I."

Kit's mouth flattened. "Okay, but last time we talked he was just your grumpy rehabilitation raccoon, and now you're on my couch with sad-girl energy and a go bag. Please fill in the middle."

Heat crawled up my neck. I stared down at the pillow seam between my fingers. "It wasn't just a fight," I admitted. "We've been more than roommates."

Her eyes went wide. "Define *more*."

My laugh came out thin. "We've been sleeping together."

There was a beat of stunned silence.

"Wes? Hayes's best friend Wes. Wes who we've known since we were kids. *Wes* Wes?" She blew out a breath. "I mean I get it. He's hot in that rugged, 'maybe my magical pussy can cure your depression' kind of way but . . . *holy shit.*"

I exhaled, trying to find a good place to begin. "It started as—" I broke off, wincing. "Okay, you have to promise not to make it weird."

Kit leaned in, eyes glittering. "Those are the exact words someone says right before it gets so weird. Give me the PG-13 version, because I am not emotionally prepared for full-penetration details before lunch."

"It started as sex lessons," I blurted. "For him. So he could figure out how the physical mechanics worked now. After the accident."

She just stared at me. "I'm sorry," she said slowly. "Sex. Lessons."

I groaned, dropping my head back against the cushion. "It wasn't like that. I wasn't grading him. He was scared. I offered. We made rules. It was supposed to be controlled and helpful and very . . . mature."

A slow, delighted smile curved her mouth. "You absolutely made a syllabus."

"I did not make a syllabus," I said, annoyed. "I maybe— it was an organized approach."

Kit pressed a hand to her heart, desperately trying not to grin. "I'm so proud."

Ignoring her teasing, I told her about watching his confidence come back in stuttering pieces. How it had felt to be the safe place he could practice wanting again. How somewhere along the way, practice had stopped being the right word and I had fallen stupidly, quietly, all the way in love with my grumpy, injured, ridiculous roommate.

Then I told her about the jobsite. About the stairs and the slick wood and the way his leg had gone out from under him. The crew, the humiliation, Austin calling Hayes. The way Wes had come home vibrating with shame and turned it on me because it was an emotional overload from already turning it on himself. The words he'd thrown between us like a barricade: lessons, practice, faking being normal.

Saying it out loud made my chest ache all over again.

"I told him I loved him," I finished, voice fraying. "And then I told him I loved myself too. Then I picked up a bag and walked out."

Silence settled between us, thick and stunned.

Kit stared at me for a long beat, her jaw tight. She did not, miraculously, say *I told you so* or *men are trash* or a single thing about how I should have kept my distance from a situation that complicated.

She simply exhaled. Hard.

"I swear to god," she muttered, "emotionally unavailable men should come with warning labels."

A wet laugh hiccuped out of me. "He did have one," I said. "It was just written in sarcasm and trauma and posted on the refrigerator."

"Yeah, well, I want it printed on a forehead next time so we can all see it from space." She bumped her shoulder into mine. "For what it's worth, I think you did the right thing."

"It feels like shit," I said.

"Right things sometimes do," she answered, because she was annoying and usually correct.

My nose started to run. I sniffed, patted my pockets for tissue, and came up empty. With a groan, I dug into the duffel instead, pawing past leggings, a bundled hoodie, and my toiletry bag. My fingers knocked against something small and hard at the bottom.

*Of course.*

I wrapped my hand around the velvet box and pulled it out like a magician producing a very inconvenient rabbit.

"I'm a mess," I muttered, throat burning again. I popped the lid open, caught one glimpse of the diamond glaring up at me like a floodlight, and snapped it shut so fast the hinge clicked. The box landed on the coffee table with a dull thunk.

Kit's eyes went sharp. "Is that—"

"Greg's," I said. "Well. Mine. Whatever."

She reached for it without asking, flipped it open, and slid the ring onto her finger. It dwarfed her hand, the stone catching every bit of weak winter light sneaking through the blinds.

"Damn," she said reverently. "You could signal ships with this. Are we sure this isn't actually a weapon?"

Despite everything, a reluctant laugh shook loose. "You should see it under church lighting. It basically started a small sun."

She wiggled her fingers, watching the diamond flash. "What are you going to do with it?"

That was the question that had been tapping on the inside of my skull for weeks.

"I keep thinking I should give it back," I said slowly. "To Greg. Like it's . . . evidence. Proof I'm still tethered to a life I walked away from." Emotion rose sharp and hot in my throat. "Like as long as I have it, some part of me is still standing in a dress at the front of that chapel, waiting to be rescued from my own bad decisions."

Kit snorted so violently the ring almost flew off. She caught it and shoved it back into place, scowling at me.

"Absolutely not," she said. "Fuck no. That is your time-and-trauma tax. If you give it back, I will never speak to you again."

A laugh escaped me. "You're so dramatic."

"Correct." She slid the ring off, dropped it back into the

box, and shut it with a snap. "He lied to you. You tried to martyr yourself into being the world's saddest supportive wife. Then you detonated your life to stop doing that. The least you get out of that disaster is market value to start over."

"I don't even want to look at it," I said. "I can't wear it. I can't shove it in a drawer. It's too much . . . everything." I rubbed the empty place on my finger, remembering how heavy it had felt, how wrong. "It's not even something I would have picked."

Kit's expression softened. "Okay," she said. "So we agree we're not giving it back. Next option: Convert it."

"Convert it into what?" I asked, even though somewhere between my ribs, an answer was already stirring.

"Into something you actually want," she said simply. "Pawn it, sell it, make a necklace, whatever. Turn it into a thing that belongs to you instead of a ghost of bad decisions past."

The idea flared up inside me, bright and terrifying.

"I could," I said, heartbeat loud in my ears. "Maybe. Sell it and use the money for a studio. There's that empty storefront by the Crooked Spine."

Kit's eyes lit. "The one with the big front window and the awful green carpet?"

I snorted. "Yeah. The carpet looks like it's seen some things."

"It's perfect," she said, grin going soft at the edges. "You do like a fixer-upper. Very on brand, Clara Darling."

Hope and fear tangled in my chest. "I don't know if it's enough," I said. "Or if anyone would actually book me enough to pay rent, or if I'd just end up crying in a room with terrible flooring and a very expensive mistake."

Kit shrugged one shoulder. "That's a later problem.

Right now, all you have to do is admit that there is a version of your future where your name is on a lease and not on someone else's to-do list."

My eyes stung again, for an entirely different reason. "It feels right," I whispered. "In a way that makes me want to throw up."

"Congratulations," she said with a shrug. "Maybe that's how you know it's a real desire and not just something someone else told you to want."

She pushed to her feet, scooping up the ring box and setting it carefully next to a stack of padded mailers on the tiny table by the kitchen. Then she grabbed a scrap of lace from the back of a chair and started stuffing it into an envelope.

I swiped under my eyes with the cuff of my sweater. "What are you doing?"

"Working," she said. "Unlike some of us, I don't have a rich ex-fiancé's diamond to liquidate yet."

She taped the envelope shut and reached for a sheet of address labels. That was when I noticed what exactly had disappeared into the white padded rectangle.

My eyes narrowed. "Did you just put underwear in that?"

Kit didn't even look up. "Sure did. Do you know how much money I'm making from this?"

Horror and fascination warred in my chest. "Please elaborate immediately."

She grinned. "Say hello to your sister's thriving niche enterprise. Men on the internet will pay truly stupid amounts of money for nicely packaged lingerie."

I stared. "Are you selling used underwear online?"

"Relax," she said, rolling her eyes as she slapped a label on. "It's not that bad." She paused. "Technically, yes, but if it makes you feel better, it's not to a bunch of creeps. It's only one creep. Some guy paid extra to be the only person who gets my goods." She waggled her eyebrows.

My jaw dropped. "Kit, that is . . . disturbing. What if he tries to find you?"

She waved a hand. "Do not yuck my yum. I have bills to pay, Clara. Also, I use a PO box and a fake name. The only way this man is finding me is if the USPS goes rogue, and frankly they have enough on their plate."

A shocked laugh burst out of me. "Our mother would die."

"Our mother thinks I make all my money on Etsy and freelance painting gigs," she said serenely. "Which is also *technically* true. Everyone wins."

She dropped back onto the couch, leaving the labeled envelope and the ring box side by side on the table. Past and future. Disaster and possibility.

"Okay," she said, nudging my knee with hers again. "Game plan. Gaudy ring becomes studio, eventually. You crash here as long as you need. I will provide carbs and questionable streaming choices. That part is easy."

Her eyes gentled. "But what are you going to do about Wes?"

The question landed in my chest like a stone dropped down a wishing well, sinking until I couldn't see the bottom.

"I don't know," I said. The admission came out on a breath that shook.

Tears welled again, less explosive this time and more like something worn-out giving way. "I don't know how to love a man who can't even love himself," I whispered. "Not without disappearing again. Not without contorting myself into whatever shape makes it easier for him. I promised myself I wouldn't do that."

Kit's arm came around me, tugging me in until my head rested against her shoulder. She pressed her cheek to my hair, voice low and fierce.

"Then don't," she said. "You are allowed to love him from over here. But don't climb into the hole with him. If he wants you, he can crawl out."

My throat closed. I nodded, because words felt dangerous.

"And if he doesn't," she added, squeezing me, "then we swap out that hideous green carpet and hang your name in the biggest window on Main Street as a daily reminder to him of what he lost. We can build you something that is yours. With or without him."

I let my eyes close, listening to the hum of the fridge and the muffled music from the shop downstairs. I could still feel Wes somewhere under my skin, like a bruise I kept pushing on. I still loved him. That wasn't going anywhere.

The difference was, for the first time, I could imagine loving him without erasing myself to do it.

I could see a studio with bad flooring and beautiful light. I could see my name on the door in pretty lettering. I could see a version of me who chose herself, even when it hurt.

For now, that version of me was the only thing keeping my heart from splitting clean in two.

## THIRTY-FIVE

## WES

I STARED at the door like it might crack open and rewind the last ten minutes if I glared hard enough.

It didn't. Obviously.

The house was stupidly quiet. No Clara humming under her breath in the kitchen. No soft pad of her feet on the stairs. Just the tick of the heater, the faint rattle of the vent, and the echo of the door closing behind her playing on a loop in my skull.

It felt like she'd taken the center of the place with her. Like the walls were still here, the furniture still in the same spots, my boots still by the mat—but the gravity was gone.

*I love you.*

The words hit first. They always did.

*I love you. I also love myself. I can't stay in a house where you choose your fear over both of us.*

My jaw clenched until it hurt. I could still see her, duffel strap biting into her shoulder, eyes bright and steady and so damn sure.

She told you exactly what she needed.

You picked fear anyway

She asked you to show up. You ran.

I dragged a hand over my face, palm scraping against stubble. The living room blurred at the edges—same couch, same coffee table, same stack of mail on the console. Same life I'd been pacing circles around for months.

Except it wasn't the same. Not really.

I could see myself in the reflection of the dark TV screen—broad shoulders, bad leg, haunted eyes. The guy who had slept on the couch because stairs felt like enemies. The guy who'd timed showers to when someone else was home, just in case. The guy who'd let the house go quiet and stale because the alternative was letting anybody see how far he'd fallen.

Then Clara had walked in with her boxes and her rules and her ridiculous optimism and, somehow, breathing hadn't felt like a chore anymore.

And I'd still managed to drive her out.

My feet carried me to the kitchen without checking in with my brain. Habit. Muscle memory.

I opened the cabinet without thinking. The good bourbon sat where it always did, amber and patient, promising quiet in a glass. I curled my fingers around the neck of the bottle, thumb rubbing over the label.

I could pour some into my coffee.

Or skip the coffee and just go straight for the hard reset. A couple of big swallows, let everything fuzz at the edges until her voice didn't sound so clear. Until my body stopped remembering the exact weight of her curled against me in my bed. Until my chest didn't feel like someone had wedged a fist behind my ribs and just . . . left it there.

My grip tightened.

I set the bottle back down and shut the cabinet hard enough that the door rattled.

The sound cracked through the quiet, sharp and ugly. It didn't make me feel better. It didn't do anything except prove, once again, that I could make noise and still be a coward.

If I was going to hurt, I was going to know exactly why. I didn't want to drink her into a blur. I wanted every second of this to sting.

I leaned back against the counter, leg throbbing deep in the socket, and stared at nothing.

The old script kicked in, automatic as breathing.

You flew too close to the sun, Vaughn. Thought you were back. Thought you could be that guy again. The one who took stairs without thinking. The one who walked a jobsite without turning into a safety hazard. The one who could stand next to a woman like Clara and not drag her down with him.

Look how that turned out.

A different thought shoved in, quieter but meaner.

*No, that's not it.*

The universe didn't shove you. You did this part on your own.

You swung the hammer. It just watched.

My throat went tight. I pushed away from the counter and limped into the living room, dropped down onto the couch like my strings had been cut.

The leg hummed with that bone-deep ache that meant I'd overdone it. My stump burned where it met the socket, a raw reminder of plywood stairs and rough hands and the worst seconds of my year.

I could feel the spiral opening up under me, familiar as the grooves on my palm.

Clara, laughing with some faceless guy who didn't have to think about where his foot landed.

Clara, planning shoots and hanging her name on a studio window while I sat here counting pills and pretending jobsites didn't scare the shit out of me.

Clara, with a partner who didn't need a contingency plan every time they left the house.

I dug my fingers into my thighs, nails biting through denim, like I could anchor myself to the present.

The house felt smaller by the second. The air heavier. Every corner held some ghost of her—a mug on the counter, a blanket tossed over the arm of the couch, a sticky note on the fridge with her loopy handwriting telling me to buy more coffee.

Sitting here was just letting the tide pull me under.

I lurched up too fast. The socket protested, a sharp jab up my thigh, and I grunted, catching myself on the back of the couch. The edges of my vision went gray.

Then I focused on the key bowl by the door.

My hand moved before my brain could talk me out of it. Keys jingled in my fist, cool metal biting my palm.

From the outside, it probably looked like I was doing something reasonable. Going after her. Trying to fix what I'd broken.

I wasn't that noble.

I just knew if I stayed in this house one more minute, surrounded by the shape of her without the reality, I was going to crawl back into every old version of myself she'd spent weeks trying to drag me out of.

I yanked the door open, stepped into the cold, and let it close behind me.

I didn't point the truck toward Kit's place.

My hands were already turning the wheel toward the one person who'd been there for the first wreckage and might—if I didn't screw it up—help me figure out what the hell to do with the second.

I SAT THERE with my hands on the wheel, staring at the familiar front steps, the dent in the railing we'd put there moving a couch in five years ago.

I could turn around. Go home. Crawl back into the pit I'd dug in my living room.

Instead, I killed the engine and hauled myself out of the truck.

The cold slapped my face awake. Gravel crunched under my boot as I limped up the path, leg a steady throb. My knuckles were stupidly tight when I knocked.

The door swung open a second later.

Hayes stood there in a faded Star Harbor hoodie and sweats, hair shoved back like he'd had his hands in it. His brows shot up when he registered it was me on his porch.

"Uh," he said. "Hey."

My throat felt like sandpaper. "I'm here to say I'm sorry," I managed.

The words landed between us with a dull thud. Something in his shoulders eased, tension sliding down a notch. He took one step back and crooked two fingers in a "get in here" gesture.

"Then don't just stand there like a lost puppy," he said. "It's freezing."

Warm air hit me when I stepped inside—coffee, laundry detergent, whatever he'd cooked recently.

He nudged the door shut with his heel and jerked his chin toward the couch. I lowered myself onto the end. He took the armchair opposite, forearms braced on his knees.

Up close, I could see the crease between his brows. Worry, not anger, and somehow that was worse.

"I shouldn't have snapped at you," I said, staring at my hands. "Or her. You were right—about not talking to her like that. I crossed a line and I'm sorry."

The admission scraped its way out, rough and reluctant. It was still the truth.

Hayes let out a low breath, rubbing a thumb along the line of his jaw. "You were scared and in pain," he said. "It's still not an excuse, but I get it."

He tipped his head, eyes narrowing just a little. "Did you happen to apologize to her, or am I getting the exclusive premiere?"

A humorless sound huffed out of me. "She left before I could."

Something flickered behind his eyes. "Yeah," he said quietly. "I don't blame her."

Hayes was always a protective older brother. Honestly, I knew he was giving me a break because of our friendship. Instead of piling on, he just watched me, giving me enough silence to hang myself or spit it out.

"When I went out to the site, I figured I'd . . . you know. Be the boss for five minutes." I told him my version of everything that happened. Enough that my chest felt tight all over again.

Hayes didn't interrupt or crack a joke when I paused. My friend watched me with that steady, infuriatingly patient look he'd been perfecting since we were teenagers. When I finally ran out of words, he sat back, palms rubbing once down his thighs.

"Okay," he said.

I stared at him. "Okay?"

"You fell," he said, like it was the simplest thing in the

world. "It sucked. You scared everybody." He lifted a shoulder. "That's not proof you're broken, Wes. That's proof you've got a crew that gives a damn."

The words hit like they were bouncing off armor I didn't remember putting on. I shook my head. "It didn't feel like that."

"I know it didn't," he said. "But how it felt and what it was are not the same thing."

I looked away, jaw clenching, because the worst part was that I could see his angle and some traitorous part of me wanted to believe it.

"I'm a grown man," I said. "I used to take stairs without thinking about it. Now I'm an OSHA hazard who needs a spotter every time he wants a different view."

His mouth twitched. "You're very dramatic when you're spiraling, you know that?"

I let out a breath that was almost a laugh, then scrubbed my hands over my face.

Hayes slouched farther back in the chair, one ankle over his knee, his socked foot bouncing once. "So," he said mildly. "Clara walked out with a bag."

The words dropped like a brick in my stomach.

"What did you do?" he asked.

I let my hands fall. Met his gaze because I owed him at least that much. "What I always do," I said. "I panicked and lit everything on fire."

His jaw tightened. "Define everything."

I gave him the outline and nothing more. Told him I'd come home loaded with shame and fear, and instead of letting it sit in my own rib cage, I'd lobbed it at the closest target. How Clara had tried to get me to talk, and I'd taken her concern and twisted it into control. How we'd gone from roommates to friends to something . . . more.

I didn't give him specifics, but it was enough.

By the time I finished, Hayes's eyes were closed, his thumb and forefinger pressing into the bridge of his nose like he was staving off a headache.

"Jesus, man," he said quietly.

"Yeah," I said. "I fucked up."

He opened his eyes and looked right at me, no buffer, no joke. "You're in love with her."

I swallowed it. It tasted like battery acid.

"See the thing is—" I started, then stopped, because that was bullshit, and we both knew it.

Hayes's brows went up the smallest fraction, *really?* written all over his face.

"You forget I've known you almost as long as I've known her," he said. "I watched you watch her, even when we were kids. I've watched you watch her the last few months. It *is* that simple."

Something in my chest gave. The hairline crack I'd been pretending wasn't there finally spiderwebbed across the surface.

I stared at the ground. My voice came out low.

"Yeah," I said. "I'm in love with her."

The words didn't fix anything. They didn't magically unstitch what I'd torn. They just sat there, heavy and real and long overdue.

Hayes blew out a breath, shoulders dropping a notch. "Okay," he said again, but this time it sounded different. "Good. Step one, we're being honest."

He leaned forward, elbows on his knees. "I didn't ask you to look out for her because you're perfect," he went on. "News flash, none of us are. I asked you because you're kind. Because even when you're being a cocky asshole, you've always shown up for the people you care about."

Guilt twisted low in my gut.

"But you don't protect someone by pretending you don't give a shit," he said, voice sharpening. "You protect her by actually doing the work so you don't bleed all over her every time you get scared."

I flinched. "That's not what I'm trying to do."

"I know it's not what you're trying to do," he said. "But it is what you're doing."

Silence stretched until I felt it between my shoulder blades.

"She didn't leave because you fell, man," Hayes said finally, softer. "She left because you chose your fear and then used it as a weapon on her."

The line landed like a fist under my ribs because it was too close to the thing I hadn't wanted to say out loud.

My fingers dug into my thighs. "What if this is just who I am now?" I asked before I could stop myself. "The guy who goes down on stairs and takes everyone with him. The guy who freaks out and says the one thing that hurts most. What if I keep doing this? To her. To you. To everyone."

Hayes watched me, eyes dark and steady. "Then you figure out how not to be that guy," he said simply.

I huffed out a breath. "What if I break her?" The words felt like they were being dragged over gravel on the way out. "Again."

"You already hurt her," he said. "That's done. Now you decide if that's the story you stick with, or if it's the chapter before you finally pull your head out of your ass."

I let my head tip back against the couch cushion, eyes burning, throat thick. The idea of doing anything felt impossible and necessary in the same breath.

Hayes's voice came again, quieter. "You don't have to earn her. She already picked you. But if you want to keep her, you can't keep pretending this is just about your leg. You gotta deal with the rest of it too."

*The rest of it.*

My entire life I had dealt with difficult things the same way—stuff it in a box and never think about it again. My time in the military, losing my sister, the way my parents practically died alongside her. The way any future that involved someone else felt like a lie I didn't deserve to tell.

I swallowed hard, pulse drumming in my ears.

"For the record," Hayes said, sitting back again, "I still trust you with her. More than most people on the planet. I just need *you* to start trusting you with her."

I let out a rough laugh that didn't feel like amusement at all.

He shrugged. "Go big or go home, man."

I stared at him. I had come to my best friend expecting —maybe even wanting—to be told I was right to push her away. That I was too dangerous. Too broken. That he understood why I'd done it.

Instead, he'd handed the responsibility right back to me and called it what it was.

Fear. Not fate.

"Okay," I said finally, the word tasting like gravel. "Say I don't want to be this guy anymore."

Hayes's mouth curved, this quick, fierce grin that looked a little like relief.

For the first time since Clara closed the door behind her, the idea of doing something different didn't feel like an insult. It felt like the smallest, scariest possible mercy.

I stared at the spot on the wall above his shoulder, at the weird dent in the drywall from the time we'd tried to hang a shelf after too many beers. My mouth was dry. My pulse wouldn't settle.

"Okay," I said again, slower this time. My hands flexed on my thighs. I forced the next words out before I could talk myself out of them.

"I have a plan to unfuck this." I huffed out a breath. "My head. My leg. All of it."

Hayes's eyes softened in a way that made my chest hurt. "Good," he said simply. "That's a solid start."

"This isn't . . ." I swallowed. "It isn't just for her."

His brows tipped up.

"I want her back," I said, throat tight. "Fuck, I can't breathe without her, but even if she never walks through that door again, I can't keep living like this. I won't. I'm tired of being at war with my own body. My own brain. I'm tired of being the guy who nukes everything good because he's scared."

Saying it out loud felt like peeling skin, but it was also the truth.

Hayes nodded once, like he'd been waiting to hear exactly that. "Then do it for you first," he said. "The rest can come after."

It didn't feel like some big triumphant moment. There was no swelling music, no sudden lightness. It was more like standing at the bottom of another staircase, looking up, knowing exactly how far there was to fall if I screwed it up again.

Only this time, I wasn't pretending I could do it alone. My best friend was there with me.

I blew out a slow breath, shoulders sagging. "Therapy is a start, but it's not enough."

Hayes tilted his head. "No?"

I shook my head. "No. I know exactly what I need to do if I want any shot at getting her back."

## THIRTY-SIX

CLARA

The wind knifed straight through my coat the second I stepped out of the car, breath puffing white in front of me. My arms were full—a camera bag digging into one shoulder, garment bags piled over the other, a clipboard wedged against my ribs—and I just stood there in the packed snow of Star Harbor Family Farm's parking lot, heart thudding for reasons that had nothing to do with the cold.

It had been a week since I walked out of Wes's house with a duffel and a shaking voice.

Seven days of pretending the lumpy couch at Kit's was a fun sister sleepover and not an emotional evacuation point. Seven days of trying not to think about the jewelry store envelope folded into the back pocket of my camera bag with an appraisal and an obscene number attached to the ring I had every intention of selling. Seven days of smiling in town while feeling the weight of small-town stares slide over me—curious, sympathetic, nosy in that way Star Harbor had perfected.

"Clara!" Cal called. "You're here—good. We're running about fifteen minutes behind on florals."

Right. Work. I had work.

I smiled at Cal as he helped me off-load the wedding dresses. "I've got you all set up in the cottage. Plenty of room to get ready."

I was so grateful for him. I'd promised him and Elodie that I would make the farm shine, and I had every intention of delivering. "Thanks. I'm going to pop over and make sure no one needs anything, and then I'll start getting myself together."

He nodded, and I squared my shoulders against the wind before starting toward the big blue barn.

The place looked like the inside of a snow globe someone had shaken a little too hard. The white trim peeked out behind the trees, and the dull gray-blue water of an icy Lake Michigan made the blue pop against the Western Michigan sky. The barn doors were propped open, strings of twinkle lights already glowing against dark wood even though it was barely early afternoon. Elodie's touch was everywhere—vintage lanterns on barrels, crates stacked with folded blankets, a chalkboard sign that read WINTER WEDDING SHOOT in her feminine looping script.

Inside, it was controlled chaos. Buckets of flowers on a folding table. The photographer's light stands, gear cases, and the faint hiss of a space heater working overtime.

"Florals over here, please," I called automatically, weaving through bodies to the center of the barn. "No, a little closer to the doors so we get the light through them. Twinkle lights higher—we'll start at the oak, then move to the barn doors."

Hands moved. People adjusted. Someone shoved a clipboard into my free hand.

"I think this is yours," they said, already hurrying away.

I took a breath and let the rhythm of it steady me. Shot

list. Timeline. Problem-solving. It was easier to focus on logistics than on the hollow ache under my breastbone.

"Big day." Elodie's voice came from behind me, warm and familiar.

I turned as she wrapped me in a quick, tight hug that smelled like cinnamon and cold air. Her cheeks were pink from the wind, hair tucked up under a knit hat, clipboard of her own half-tucked against her chest.

"You holding up okay?" she asked, leaning back to search my face.

"Great." I pasted on a smile that didn't feel entirely fake. "Busy is good." I exhaled and leaned in to tell her the truth. "I'll be okay."

Her mouth flattened a little, revealing exactly how much worried big-sister energy she'd been expending. "Well," she said, patting my arm, "if it turns out you're not, you know where the good whiskey is. In the meantime, this place has never looked better."

Pride flickered under my ribs, bumping against the hurt. "Thanks. I think the florist is having a meltdown about the temperature, but it really did all come together."

Elodie laughed and moved off to wrangle vendors. I stepped toward the open doors, fingers tightening on my clipboard as a gentle gust of wind cut through the barn and made the lights sway.

A low murmur of voices floated from near the entrance. I caught just enough as I walked past to set my teeth on edge.

"That's the Darling girl, right? The one from the almost-wedding?"

"Can you imagine? I'd never look at a bouquet again."

Their voices dropped when they realized I was within

earshot. I kept walking, spine straight, cheeks burning under the winter air. Clipboard, camera, shot list. Nothing else was their business. Not today.

"Clara?" Mara, my photographer, waved me over from where she was adjusting a lens. Her dark hair was stuffed under a beanie, breath fogging the air. "Question. Do you want me to grab some groom shots before things get crazy, or . . ."

My brain stuttered. "Groom shots?"

"Yeah," she said slowly, like she was checking to make sure she hadn't hallucinated something. "I thought I saw a guy in a tux heading toward the back path a minute ago. Maybe I'm losing it. Anyway, do you have a model lined up? I can start with details and landscape if not."

The words slid over me but didn't stick. Some stand-in Elodie had wrangled at the last second, probably. Maybe Cal or Hayes, conscripted against their will. The thought made me chuckle.

I shook my head. "No groom on this one. We'll start with solo bridal shots. The dresses and the farm are the stars today."

"Cool." Mara gave me a look I couldn't quite read—confusion, maybe, or curiosity—but she just nodded. "Works for me. I'll get some establishing shots around the property and meet you by the inn when you're ready?"

"Perfect. I'll text you." I checked my watch, then the light spilling in through the barn doors. We were on schedule. On paper, everything was exactly where it needed to be. "Text me first, if you need anything."

She headed out into the snow, camera already lifted, her assistant trailing behind with a bag of lenses. People swirled around me—florist, caterer, Elodie's staff, Cal hauling something heavy—but I felt weirdly separate from all of it, like I was directing a play from just offstage.

I took one more steadying breath, tucked the clipboard under my arm, and turned toward the cottage nestled next to the inn.

*Time to make myself look like the kind of bride who didn't have a heart that felt like a bruise.*

I crossed the packed path between the barn and house, snow squeaking under my boots, cold biting at my bare fingers where they clutched my camera bag strap. From the outside, it probably looked perfect—the barn, the wreaths, the lights, the woman in charge of making it all look like magic.

If I kept moving, maybe I could almost believe it.

I STOOD in the renovated cottage, mostly put together, while winter light poured in through the big front window and turned everything soft around the edges. My hair fell in loose waves, one side pinned back with a comb of pearls and tiny crystal sprigs. My makeup was the kind I only ever gave other people—fierce and soft at the same time, liner sharp enough to cut and blush warm enough to make me look like I hadn't spent the last week crying into Kit's couch cushions.

The dress was a work of art. Winter-white lace sleeves hugged my arms, sheer and delicate, the pattern crawling over my skin like frost on glass. The bodice dipped low in the back, a clean, elegant swoop that met a skirt that spilled out from my hips like fog over snow—layers of tulle and satin floating around my legs when I shifted.

"Hold still," Elodie murmured behind me.

I caught her eye in the mirror as she tugged the zipper up, fingers sure and gentle. The satin hugged my ribs and settled into place with a quiet, final little whisper.

For a heartbeat another dress hovered over this one. Stiff bodice. Too-tight lace. A chapel full of people holding their breath while I ran through two equally mortifying options: stay and be humiliated or run.

My stomach flipped, and I breathed through it.

I could barely remember that woman anymore.

I met my own gaze in the glass. There were nerves there, sure, but there was something else too—something steadier. I'd put a wedding dress on again. I'd stepped into it on purpose, knowing exactly what it meant and what it didn't.

One day it would be real. One day I would marry someone who actually wanted to stand beside me. For a half second I saw it too clearly—Wes at the end of an aisle, grumpy and gorgeous, eyes soft just for me.

The ache that followed was so sharp I had to swallow around it.

"Hey." Elodie's reflection leaned in, fingers fussing with a curl near my temple. "If anyone pisses you off today, just remember you're wearing enough skirt to hide a body."

A startled laugh punched out of me. "Good to know."

She smiled at me in the mirror, wise and kind. "You look beautiful, Clara. And not just in the *good for my marketing* kind of way. You're a vision."

I blinked hard and turned the emotion into a smirk. "It's just work," I said. "We're selling the dream, remember? No actual grooms were harmed in the making of this content."

"If you say so." Her tone suggested she didn't entirely

buy it, but she squeezed my shoulders anyway. "Cal's waiting."

A knock sounded on the door. "Ready, ladies?" Cal's voice floated in, followed by his head. He gave a low whistle when he saw me. "Damn, Clara. You're going to break the internet."

"Please don't let me fall on my face," I said, gathering the skirt. "That's all I ask."

"Not on my watch." He tipped an invisible cap and disappeared again.

Elodie helped to gather up the layers of skirt so I could shuffle forward without tripping. We made it outside in a rustle of fabric and nervous laughter. At the side door, the cold hit my bare back in a shocking rush, stealing my breath. Elodie grabbed a wool blanket, tugging it over my shoulders to fight the frigid temperatures.

The side-by-side idled just off the path, engine rumbling, a little plume of exhaust curling into the air. Cal sat in the driver's seat, gloved hands on the wheel, his expression a mix of professional calm and boyish excitement.

"Your chariot awaits," he called.

I scooped the skirt up with both hands, bunched it against my thighs, and carefully climbed into the passenger seat. Layers of tulle puffed everywhere. Elodie did a last-minute tuck-and-fluff so I wasn't sitting entirely on a small mountain of dress.

"Text me if you need anything," she said, stepping back. There was something in her eyes I couldn't name. Hope, maybe. Or just the kind of faith that made you build a whole business on other people's vows.

I nodded, throat tight. "We're going to make the farm look incredible. I promise."

Cal shifted into gear and eased us forward, tires crunching over the packed snow. The wind found every gap in the blanket, sneaking under lace and tulle, raising goose bumps along my arms. I wrapped one hand around the roll bar, the other still clutching the front of the wool, and I tried to let the focus settle over me.

We'd start with wide shots at the oak—long lines of branches overhead, my skirt spread over the snow, a bouquet of winter greens in my hands. Then closer—hands on bark, veil catching peeks of golden light. I ran through the sequence in my head like a checklist.

The anticipation made my stomach lurch, like I'd gone over a too-fast hill in a car.

Today was about work. About proving—to myself, to everyone—that I could build something beautiful out of all the poor decisions I'd made in my life.

The inn fell away behind us. Dunes rolled out on one side, water crashing below, snow lying in uneven drifts where the wind had pushed it. The old oak rose at the far edge of the property, a dark silhouette against the pale-pink sky, its bare branches reaching wide like arms waiting for an embrace.

Cal eased off the gas as we crested the little rise in the terrain leading up to it.

"Okay," he said, voice a little different. "Don't freak out."

My pulse stumbled. "What?"

He didn't answer right away. The side-by-side rolled the last few feet, engine rumbling low.

I looked up.

The oak came into full view.

Bare branches were laced with fresh strands of twinkle lights, with snow packed into a rough aisle leading up to the trunk. My brain automatically cataloged the details: gorgeous soft lighting, a decent path, a slightly crooked lantern on the left that I'd fix before we shot.

Then my eyes found the man standing under the branches, and everything else went fuzzy.

## THIRTY-SEVEN

Wes.

In a tuxedo.

I blinked. He was just . . . there. Black jacket, white shirt, dark tie, large broad shoulders filling out the fabric like it had been tailored for him alone. A breeze off the lake ruffled his hair. Late-afternoon light cut along the strong line of his jaw, and my eyes burned. He was solid and strong and waiting.

My brain tried to reject the image as some kind of stress-induced hallucination. Wes did not do crowds or attention. He certainly did not do cameras. Wes did not put on formal wear and stand under a decorated tree on purpose.

My heart took off at a dead sprint.

Cal cut the engine, and the sudden quiet made the blood rushing in my ears louder.

I was still staring when he lifted his chin, his mouth curving into a soft, devastating grin.

"Guess the groom problem sorted itself out." Cal winked as he climbed out of the ATV and made his way over to my side.

A hysterical bubble of something—laughter, maybe, or a sob—hit the back of my throat. "That's Wes."

"I know who it is." Cal smiled. His eyes were kind and uncharacteristically twinkly. "You good?"

That was an impossible question.

"No," I said honestly. "Yes. I don't know."

His boots crunched in the snow as he tried to tame the skirt of my dress. When he offered me his hand, I clung to it like it was the only stable thing in a world that had suddenly tilted.

The skirt of the dress fought me, layers of tulle and lace catching on the edge of the side-by-side. Cal untangled me with careful patience. Once I was upright, he squeezed my fingers.

"You got this," he murmured. "I'll hang back."

Then he stepped away, retreating toward the photographer, who was staring between me and Wes with a wide smile. She lifted her camera.

I could feel everyone watching. Cal joined Elodie, who stood off to the side, by the barn. Some staff were near the path, a couple of curious farmhands pretending to check on something. The whole scene shimmered like a movie set: snow glowing blue white, lights in the oak tree blinking steadily, breath fogging in the cold.

I was frozen in place.

Wes's gaze found mine, like maybe it had never really left, and the rest of the world dropped out of focus. His shoulders squared. His expression shifted, and his lips formed a determined line. He stepped toward me.

"Clara," he said, just loud enough to carry.

My name in his voice did something awful and wonderful to my rib cage.

His feet took one step. Then another. I moved forward,

drawn to him by an invisible tether. The dress rustled around my legs. Halfway down the makeshift aisle, the slow, careful walk turned into something else. My body chose for me.

I ran.

The skirt bunched in my hands, lace fluttering around my boots as I closed the distance in a rush of cold air and thudding heartbeat. I heard the photographer's shutter pick up speed, quick, stunned clicks like distant applause.

I barreled to a stop right in front of him, breathless and shaky and so full I might crack.

Up close, the tux was even more obscene. The jacket hugged his frame, the white shirt made his tan skin glow, and his eyes—bright and earnest—were pinned on me like there was no one else in the county.

"Hi," he said quietly.

Tears stung my eyes. "You're in a tux."

One corner of his mouth lifted, not quite a smile. "I noticed."

"What are you doing here?" The question came out as a whisper. "Wes, there are eyeballs everywhere . . . and a camera."

"I know." His gaze flicked past me for a heartbeat, to the crew, the inn, the wide, watching world. When his eyes returned to mine, they were steady. "I'll survive."

I huffed out something like a disbelieving laugh. "That's your bar now?"

"No," he said. His throat worked, and when he went on, his voice was rough as his hand found my arm. "My bar is you."

The photographer's shutter kept clicking—soft, constant—but the rest of the farm fell away. It was just him and me and the huge, beautiful oak tree.

"I started therapy," he said. The words tumbled out in a rush, like if he didn't say them now, they'd choke him. "For my head, not my leg. I should've done it a long time ago. Hayes has been trying to shove me in that direction for months. It took you walking out with a bag for me to finally listen."

My lungs forgot how to work.

"You—you're seeing someone?" I asked.

He nodded. "Some guy in Outtatowner. Twice a week, for now. I sit in a chair and say horrible, true things instead of letting them eat me alive in the dark."

One of my hands had curled in the front of his jacket without me realizing it. I could feel his heart pounding under my palm.

"Wes . . ."

"I also joined a group for amputees. For now I'm still sitting in the back and watching, but . . . I'm going. I needed you to know," he said, talking over his name like the words were a dam he'd finally blown open. "That when you said you loved yourself enough to leave, I heard you. I didn't like it. I hated every second of it. I still do. But you were right. I've been choosing fear over both of us. I forgot what it was like to choose myself, and then I blamed every fear I had on the leg like it was doing all the work."

His voice dropped. "It wasn't. It was me." His blue eyes lifted to meet mine. "I'm doing the work for myself as much as I am for you. It's important that you know that."

Wind tugged at a piece of my hair, and I shivered, more from his words than any cold. He reached up and smoothed it back automatically, fingers shaking just a little.

"I don't want to be that man," he said. "I don't want to be the guy who makes you do all the emotional heavy lifting while I hide behind worst-case scenarios. I love you, Clara."

His words hit harder than the cold, harder than the humiliation of the chapel, harder than the slam of my own front door when I'd walked out of his house. A tear slipped free.

"This isn't me being noble," he added, eyes earnest. "This isn't 'go live your best life and I'll brood from a distance.' I'm telling you I'm in love with you. Fully, stupidly terrified and in love with you. I want you in my mornings and my bad days and my building sites and whatever comes after that awful green carpet."

A startled laugh caught in my chest. "You know about the storefront?"

His eyes warmed. "You told Kit. Kit told everyone she ran into. This town loves a story, Duchess."

"That's . . . horrifying."

"Good for me, though." His mouth tipped into a quick, crooked smile. "Otherwise I wouldn't know you're thinking about a studio. That you might sell a ring you never really wanted to get one that fits the life you actually do."

My throat tightened. "I'm excited for what comes next."

"I know." His hand slipped down, catching mine. His fingers were warm around my cold ones. "That's yours to choose. Where you put it. What you call it. How big your windows are. I just—"

He stopped and took a breath, like he needed to steady the words.

"I just want a chance to stand next to you in it," he said. "Not as something you have to prop up, but as a partner. As the guy who bids your build-out at full price like any other client and then sneaks in on weekends to fix the trim because he can't keep his hands off your space."

My eyes burned for a whole new reason.

"Wes . . ."

"You said once," he went on, softer now, "that you'd marry the right person with a gum wrapper before you ever put on another ring that felt like someone else's life."

I froze.

That had been a throwaway line in the quiet comfort of his arms, the gaudy ring glinting accusingly from the bedside table. I could hardly believe he remembered.

"I did," I said. My voice came out barely audible.

He swallowed. "I'm not asking you to marry me," he said. "Not yet, at least. I am asking you to let me prove that I deserve to be your man."

He reached into the inside pocket of his tux jacket, fingers fumbling, and pulled out something small and silver.

A gum wrapper. Folded and twisted into a tiny, imperfect ring.

All I could do was stare. The foil caught the twinkle lights overhead, bright and ridiculous and charmingly beautiful.

"This is not a metaphor for how much money I have," he said quickly, a cheeky huff of a laugh escaping. "When you're ready, I'll walk into a jeweler and buy something that needs its own insurance policy, but that's not the point. You said you wanted something that felt like you. Once you know how serious I am about showing up for you, we'll talk."

I grinned at this charming, confident version of Wes that stood in front of me.

The cameras were clicking nonstop now. My eyes blurred, turning the whole world into soft halos of light around the man in front of me.

"This is all I have today," he said, voice shaking. "A promise and a gum wrapper. I'll keep doing the work."

He looked at me, eyes clear and sure in a way that made my own heart ache.

"Will you let me stand next to you?" he asked. "In these photos. In that studio with the terrible carpet. In whatever life you choose. Scared, if I have to be. But here. Really here."

Air rushed back into my lungs on a shaky inhale.

I thought about the chapel and the dress and the way I'd stood there waiting for someone else to tell me who I was. I thought about his stairs and his fall and the way he'd used his fear as armor until it had pierced both of us. I thought about Kit's couch and the empty storefront on Main and my name on glass.

Mostly I thought about the man in front of me, hands trembling around a gum-wrapper ring because he was trying so hard to meet me where I'd drawn the line.

My chest hurt in that sharp, stretching way that meant something inside it was making room.

"Yes," I whispered, and then louder, so there was no way he could miss it: "Yes, Wes. I love you."

His eyes closed like he was taking the words all the way in. When they opened again, his gaze was bright and damp and so full I had to bite my lip.

A startled laugh broke out of him. Relief. Wonder. Something wild and young.

He slid the gum-wrapper ring over my knuckle with ridiculous care. The foil was cool and a little crinkly against my skin. It settled crookedly at the base of my finger, catching the oak's twinkle lights and throwing them back in tiny flashes.

It weighed virtually nothing.

It felt like everything.

I stepped closer until the front of my dress brushed his

legs. My free hand slid up his chest, over the crisp line of his lapel, to the warm skin at the back of his neck.

"I'm not asking you to never be scared," I said. "I'm asking you to let me be there when you are. We do it together, or we don't do it at all."

His breath hitched. "Together," he said.

"Good," I whispered. "Because they're definitely taking pictures right now."

A wet laugh choked out of both of us.

"Then let's give them a show," he said, and then his mouth was on mine.

The world narrowed to the press of his lips, the slide of his hand around my waist, the way he hauled me in like he was afraid I might disappear if he didn't hold on tight enough. I kissed him back, fingers in his hair, gum-wrapper ring digging lightly into his neck. A camera clicked in a rapid-fire staccato somewhere beyond us.

Someone whooped. It sounded suspiciously like Kit. Another cheer rose near the barn—Elodie, probably, because she lived for a good romantic spectacle.

Snow crunched under his shoes as he shifted to balance us both. The oak lights glowed above us. My dress fanned out around our feet in a ridiculous circle of lace and tulle.

For the first time in a long time, I didn't feel like I was standing in the middle of someone else's picture.

I felt like I was exactly where I was supposed to be.

Kissing my ridiculous, stubborn, strong man under an old oak tree, a gum wrapper sparkling on my finger, the shutter catching frame after frame of the moment we finally chose the same future.

Ours.

# EPILOGUE

### Wes

By the time the last of the frost burned off the fields at Star Harbor Family Farm, Clara's name was splashed across a Main Street window.

Painted in looping gold script across the glass was *Darling Studio*. In smaller block letters underneath: Lifestyle & Event Design.

I stood on the sidewalk across from it, hands in my pockets like I was just another guy killing time, and tried not to stare like a creep. Fresh paint framed the glass, clean and bright where that god-awful green carpet used to glare through like mold. Now the floor inside was hardwood, soft and warm, catching the light from the big front window.

She'd filled it with her: white walls, trailing plants in mismatched pots, a garment rack with dresses and veils, a little sitting area with two cream chairs and a tiny brass table that looked like it had come from some fancy antique place instead of a Star Harbor yard sale. Framed photos from the farm shoot lined one wall—snow and twinkle lights, Levi and a group of his friends laughing by a bonfire —and right in the middle, in pride of place, there we were under the oak. Her in lace, me in a tux, mid-kiss while snow fell around us.

Cars were jammed into every spot up and down Main. Kids ran past with ice cream from the shop on the corner, sugar high and wild. Someone had tied balloons to the lamppost, yellow and white, bumping together in the breeze. A chalkboard leaned against the brick under her window:

## GRAND OPENING! COME IN & LET'S PLAN SOMETHING BEAUTIFUL. — CD

It hit me, fast and hard, that six months ago all of this had been ugly carpet and dusty walls and a FOR LEASE sign nobody looked twice at. That six months before that, I'd been barely scraping by, convinced winter was the only season left for me.

I just hadn't had the sense to recognize what was standing in front of me with bright eyes and a messy bun.

The glass door swung open, and Clara stepped out, ponytail high today, sundress brushing her thighs, a little gold name tag pinned above her heart. She was already talking to Elodie, laughing, cheeks flushed. She looked happy.

I was never going to get used to that—seeing her happy and knowing I hadn't just survived long enough to witness it, but had actually helped build the space that held it.

"Stop lurking and get your ass inside," Hayes muttered over my shoulder.

I snorted and bumped him with my elbow. "You're late," I said.

He huffed out an annoyed laugh and held up a yellow piece of paper. "Parking ticket. Can you believe that shit?"

Inside, the place hummed. Bodies everywhere. Somebody had dragged the door open and propped it so the warm air could roll in, bringing the smell of pavement and distant lake water. Soft music played from a speaker hidden somewhere, the kind of acoustic playlist Clara liked that made everything feel like the montage part of a movie.

Elodie and Cal were front and center by the little refreshment table, Elodie fixing a tray of Cal's freshly baked tarts. When she was satisfied, she stepped back with her hands on her hips. "Perfect." She turned toward her little sister. "Consider this your welcome to the Star Harbor business-owner coven."

Clara laughed, eyes bright. "Amazing, I hope I'm qualified."

Cal set a big mason jar of flowers—peonies and whatever else Elodie had cut from the farm that morning—on the counter I'd built. He caught my eye and tipped his chin in a quiet, approving nod. I didn't need the words. The look was enough.

"Uncle Wes!" Winnie barreled into my side, almost taking me out at the knee. She latched onto my leg like a koala. "You came! Aunt Clara's place looks like a princess house."

"Good thing she's the princess and not me," I said, prying her off before she did actual damage to my hamstring. "I don't have a single dress for it."

Selene smiled and mouthed *sorry* over Winnie's shoulder. I simply smiled and shook my head.

"Congrats," she said, pulling Clara into a hug. "Now I get to say I knew you before you were the most in-demand planner in the county."

"Please start that rumor," Clara said, crossing her fingers and holding them in the air. "Manifest that shit."

When Winnie's eyes went wide and flashed to her mom, it was Clara's turn to look sheepish.

Hayes slid by me to wrap an arm around Clara's shoulders, squeezing like he might never stop. "Always knew you'd find your way."

She blinked hard and smiled up at him, and the knot in my chest loosened at the sight of them. I'd spent a lot of years trying to pretend I wasn't part of this family. As it turned out, all I'd been doing was making it harder on myself.

Somebody I didn't know ran a hand along the custom counter, whistling low. "This thing is gorgeous. Where'd you get it?"

Clara pointed straight at me. "Ask him. He's the reason the whole place didn't collapse when I ripped out that nightmare carpet."

A little heat crawled up the back of my neck. Compliments still sat weird on my skin, but they didn't itch quite as much as they used to.

The guy—a local teacher, maybe, that I'd seen at the grocery store—stuck out his hand. "You do client work?"

"Depends on the client," I said, then sharpened my mouth into something like a smile. "But yeah. I do."

His grip was firm, respectful, not pitying. My leg was bare in shorts, carbon and metal catching the light. For the first time in a long time, I didn't have the itch to pull fabric over it or find a table to sit behind.

The prosthetic was a steady and welcomed part of me, familiar now instead of foreign. I'd spent a lot of hours in my therapist's office talking about exactly that—the difference between hiding and healing. It still pissed me off that he was usually right.

Across the room, Clara caught my eye.

She was in her element and completely out of her depth at the same time—laughing with Elodie; answering questions from the owner of the bakery, who wanted to book her services; keeping mental track of the food table and the sign-up sheet and the trash can without missing a beat.

The thing that wrecked me was that she looked steady. She wasn't performing or pretending. She was simply herself. Clara had taken an engagement ring that used to feel like a shackle and turned it into walls and windows and a sign with her name on it.

And she'd done the same thing to me—taken all the jagged pieces and helped me build something out of them instead of just dodging the sharp edges.

Clara broke away from the little knot of people, weaving through the crowd toward me. Her dress skimmed her thighs, and I itched to feel her smooth skin.

She stopped in front of me, close enough that I could smell her perfume under the scent of coffee and sugar. Her smile tilted, soft and private at the edges.

"How's it looking from the contractor's perspective?" she asked. "Anything out of plumb?"

"That sign's crooked," I teased.

She bumped my shoulder, eyes laughing. "Such a shit stirrer."

"Everything looks good," I said quietly, taking a breath of her hair. "Especially you."

Her throat moved as she swallowed. With all of Star Harbor pressing in around us, it felt like it was just the two of us in an empty shell of a building again—her with a wild idea, me with a toolbox and a dozen ideas I couldn't wait to try.

Clara sighed and leaned her head on my shoulder. "I couldn't have done it without you, ya know."

I shook my head. "You'd have ripped up that carpet with your bare hands and charmed half this town to help if you needed to. You'd have been fine."

She tipped her head, studying me. "Maybe." Her smile widened. "But I'm really glad I didn't have to."

Winnie was spinning in a circle and talking about fairies. Elodie's happy laugh floated across the air as she listened to Cal's son Levi tell a story. Hayes stole another mini tart and popped it into his mouth in one bite. The studio filled up with voices and the scrape of shoes and the kind of easy, messy noise I'd once thought was gone from my life for good.

I slid my hand into Clara's, just long enough to feel her fingers squeeze back before she turned to greet the next curious person.

It was a future I hadn't dared to let myself picture.

And her. Always her.

The door swung open hard enough to rattle the bell, and Brody stepped in, arms wrapped around a massive vintage mirror, gilt frame and all, like he'd wrestled it away from an old lady or a haunted house.

"Delivery for Ms. Darling," he grunted. "If I walk into one more door with this thing, I'm billing you hazard pay."

"Careful," Clara called, half laughing, half horrified. "If you break it, that's seven years of bad luck on my insurance policy. What is this?"

He pivoted sideways, barely missing a hanging plant. He set it down and exhaled, placing his hands on his hips. He jerked his head toward Kit. "This one insisted on picking it up from the side of the road. She said, and I quote: 'If you don't do this for me, I am cutting off your balls.'"

Kit popped out from behind his frame with a grin. "Men are too easy."

He adjusted his grip and shot her a lazy grin over the top of the frame. "Always a pleasure to serve you, Kitten."

Kit visibly gagged at the ridiculous nickname. "Call me that again and I'm tilting this thing so it only reflects your receding hairline."

Brody barked out a laugh, but his hand shot up to his hair anyway.

Kit snorted and winked at Clara. "What did I tell you? *Easy.*"

Brody's eyes simmered with annoyance, and something else lingered beneath the surface.

*Oh. Oh shit. I know that look. That man is absolutely doomed.*

"I need a drink." Brody scanned the room until he locked eyes with Cal and headed in his direction.

Clara pressed her lips together, clearly trying not to smile before pulling Kit into a tight hug.

The afternoon blurred into a steady stream of people: neighbors, old classmates, business owners from every corner of town. They flipped through her lookbooks, signed up for consultations, hugged her like she'd just come home from a war instead of finally stepping into the life she should've had all along.

I moved where she needed me—refilling the punch bowl, grabbing extra folding chairs, fixing the loose screw on the bathroom door when it squeaked too loud. Mostly I hovered by the back wall, watching her work the room with that mix of nerves and competence that wrecked me every time.

She glanced over once, across the heads and the sound and the mess, and our eyes met. She grinned—wide and real—and the whole damn studio sharpened around her.

*My woman.*

My mind wandered to the ring that was waiting for her at home. I didn't want our engagement to overshadow her big day, so it could wait, but I was crawling out of my skin. I couldn't wait to ask her to marry me. To make her officially *mine.*

Eventually, the tide started to ebb.

Elodie rounded up Cal and Levi, herding them toward the door.

"Come on, you two," she said. "If we don't leave now, I'm going to start reorganizing her supply closet, and then none of us will make it out alive."

Levi dragged his feet, eyes still on the mirror. "Can I drive?" he asked Cal hopefully.

"Sure can, kid," Cal said, digging out his keys and tossing them to his son.

Austin tucked a sleepy Winnie against his chest while Selene hugged her sisters.

"Say bye to Aunt Clara," Selene murmured.

Winnie lifted her head, hair sticking up, and waved a floppy hand. "Bye, Aunt Clara. Your princess house is the best."

"Thanks, bug," Clara said, kissing her forehead. "Come visit me and boss me around soon, okay?"

Kit and Brody were last, of course. She shrugged into a denim jacket; he held the door open with his hip, already mid–eye roll.

"I'm not watching anything with dolls," Kit said. "Or clowns. Or creepy children."

"So . . . none of the classics," Brody said. "Got it."

"Stop trying to trick me into having nightmares," she shot back. "We're getting Thai, and we're watching something with absolutely zero murder."

He shook his head like he was annoyed, but I saw how he couldn't take his eyes off her. Seemed like I wasn't the only one who was going to have the *sorry dude, I kind of fell for your sister* talk with Hayes.

"Lock the door behind us!" Kit called over her shoulder, adding an incredibly unsubtle eyebrow wiggle in Clara's direction.

The bell jingled as the door shut. Then it was quiet.

We both exhaled. Balloons bobbed gently near the ceiling. The last of the flowers sat in mismatched vases on every surface. The playlist had looped into something soft and slow.

Clara stood in the middle of it all, barefoot now, heels kicked off under the counter, her dress a little wrinkled, lipstick worn down to a soft stain. She turned in a slow circle, taking it in like she couldn't quite believe it was real.

"Hey," I said, coming to stand beside her.

She looked up at me, eyes tired and shining and completely, utterly happy.

"Hey," she answered.

Clara flipped the little sign on the door to CLOSED and turned the dead bolt with a soft click.

The studio fell quieter in that way spaces do when they're suddenly meant only for two. The overhead lights were off, just the front lamp and the fairy lights along the back wall glowed, bouncing off the mirror Brody had delivered.

She moved through the room on bare feet, doing one last pointless lap—straightening a hanger on the garment rack, nudging a frame a millimeter to the left, fingertips brushing over the new hardwood where that crime-scene green carpet used to be. Her hair was down now, swinging against her shoulders, her dress doing things to my brain I still wasn't fully equipped to handle.

I leaned back against the custom counter I'd built, hands braced on the edge, and watched her with that slow, hungry warmth I still couldn't quite believe I was allowed to feel.

"You did it," I said, because there wasn't a better sentence in the world for this moment. "You did all of this."

She looked over, eyes catching the light, and the smile that spread across her face hit me dead center.

"We did it," she corrected, crossing the floor. She stepped between my knees like she'd been built for that space, arms looping around my neck. "You built half this place, after all."

I caught her wrist, turned it, and pressed my mouth to the inside, right over the flutter of her pulse. "You're the one who decided what to grow from it," I murmured. "I just brought the tools."

Her breath hitched.

Then she was closer, all soft curves and quiet strength, nudging me back against the counter. My hands slid up from her waist, palms finding warm skin. She shivered, a little full-body tremor that had nothing to do with the faint draft under the door.

"Hi," she whispered.

"Hi," I answered, and kissed her.

Our kiss was slow at first—no rush, no edge. Just the easy slide of her mouth on mine, the familiar tease of her tongue, the way her fingers tightened in the hair at the back of my neck like she never intended to let go again.

I broke away just enough to breathe, forehead resting against hers, trying to get my heartbeat to level.

For so long, my life had felt stuck in one long winter. Numb. Gray. Every part of me frozen in place, convinced that wanting anything more was just an invitation for the next storm to rip it away.

As it turned out, I hadn't been broken at all.

Just buried.

Clara brushed her nose against mine, smiling like she could feel the thought. "You're looking at me like you're having *dirty* thoughts," she teased.

"Oh, I am," I said. My hands slid lower, fingers tightening at the curve of her ass, pulling her flush against me so she could feel exactly what kind of mood I was in. "Starting with you on this counter."

Her laugh spilled out, warm and breathless. "Bold design choice, Vaughn. How mad do you think my landlord would be if we christened the studio before my first official client?"

I kissed the corner of her mouth. "Depends," I said. "What did you have in mind?"

She arched a brow, eyes going dark. "I was thinking we start with that counter you're so proud of and see if it survives quality control."

The sound that came out of me was half groan, half prayer.

I gripped her hips, dragging her even closer, my voice dropping to the place that always made her breath catch. "I was thinking the same thing," I said. "Only this time, Duchess, I'm going to teach *you* a thing or two."

Heat flashed across her face, down her throat. She

reached past me, fingers finding the switch on the standing lamp, and flicked it off. The studio dipped into a softer darkness, lit only by the streetlamp outside and the fairy lights stretching across the ceiling, casting us in a warm, secret glow.

"In that case," she murmured, hands already bunching in the hem of my shirt, "you better hope your craftsmanship is as good as you think, because I fully intend to test every inch of this counter."

"Yeah?" My voice scraped out, desperate for her.

"Mm-hmm." She tugged my shirt up, knuckles skimming my skin, and smiled that wicked little smile that had fueled far too many late-night fantasies when we'd still been dancing around each other. "Show me all the ways you can use me up."

I caught her mouth with mine before she could say anything else that might actually kill me.

Her back met the edge of the counter, hips fitting into my hands like they'd been made for it. She hooked a leg around my waist, dragging me in, kissing me deeper, harder, like this was the only language we were ever meant to speak.

I wasn't thinking about anything but her. My body was just my body—strong and steady and exactly where I wanted to be.

Exactly where I chose to be.

Her fingers slid up my spine, nails grazing my skin, and she sighed into my mouth, that soft, wrecked sound I'd do anything to keep earning for the rest of my life.

I smiled against her lips, dizzy with it all—the studio, the fairy lights, the woman in my arms who'd walked away instead of letting me drown, then let me earn my way back.

My woman.

My future.

My second chance, standing here in a place we'd built together.

"Clara," I whispered, just to taste her name.

She looked up at me, eyes shining, and that was it. That was the moment I knew there wasn't a damn thing left of the man who'd chosen fear over her.

"I love you," I said, simple and sure, like a fact. Like gravity.

Her fingers curled in my shirt, tugging me down into another kiss that left no room for doubt.

"Good," she breathed against my mouth. "Because I love you too."

I laughed, low and stunned and completely gone, and kissed her back while the town I loved hummed outside and wrapped around us like a promise.

I had thought the accident stole any chance I had for happiness, so I'd turned cold. Turns out, beneath the frost, a whole new, incredible life had been quietly getting ready to grow.

*Clara* had been there the whole time—waiting.

And this time, I wasn't going to waste a single second of it.

~

Need more Wes & Clara?
Read a very special bonus scene here:
https://www.lenahendrix.com/clara-and-wes-bonus-scene-landing-page/

**I never meant to accidentally date my brother's best friend.**

Brody Shepard has been Star Harbor's golden boy for as long as I can remember. Decorated police officer and all-around sexiest man alive, it's taken *years* to get over my girlhood crush.

Trouble is, my brother Hayes might *actually* be cursed. The ghost stories in our small town run wild, but there's no denying that when it comes to epic bad luck, my brother wins the prize. It's why I was determined to set him up with the perfect woman.

For that, I needed Brody's help. Together, we could increase my brother's happiness and prove to him that he isn't really cursed. But all our spying and conspiring meant late night talks, dinner reservations to check on him, and a few too many accidental touches.

***Touches that start to feel a little too real.***

I know better than to fall for Brody's cocky charm, smoldering looks, and affable humor. Besides, he'd never cross that line with me . . . right?

But the more we work together, the more lines are crossed and boundaries blurred. Our lifelong friendship started to change. Now we're both making excuses to spend time together. Whispered secrets turn into secret touches.

Soon, I learn all too quickly that the girlhood fantasy I'd thought I'd cut down just might be *in full bloom*.

Pre-order BOOK 4 in the Star Harbor Series, ***In Full Bloom***, on Amazon!

# ACKNOWLEDGMENTS

As always, I have to start with you. My readers are the best in the whole world. I am so eternally grateful for each and every one of you! Thank your for believing in me and my stories. I love you!

Kathryn, without your insights into the world of amputees and recovery, this book would not have happened. Thank you for letting me into your group and allowing me to run through various scenarios with you. Because of you, Wes was allowed to be a fully rounded individual and I am so grateful.

Anna, you have the coolest job in the world. Thank you for answering my twelve billion questions about bridal modeling and all of the logistics. While I knew jobs like this existed, you made it feel so chic and it was PERFECT for Clara. I'm so happy our friendship has continued to grow and I can't wait for our next girl date!

Page, thank you for your endless creative ideas and thoughtful leadership. I was positively giddy to hear how much you loved Wes & Clara's story! Your feedback and faith in me is something I will always cherish.

Another huge thank you to my cover designer Cat for seeing my vision and creating the most gorgeous, cohesive covers. Somehow you outdo yourself every time!

To my beta readers Trinity and Ashley, thank you for always taking the time to provide amazing feedback. Every time I'm excited to see the parts that were your favorites. You push me to be a better writer every time.

I cannot thank Dawn and James enough for outstanding editing and help with creating the slowest burn I've ever written! Your insights and guidance means more than I could ever say and I am thrilled with how healing this journey was.

To Jess & the entire SDLA team - thank you for all you have done to get my stories in the hands of as many readers as possible. You are the dream-come-true makers and I am so grateful to have you on my team.

To Kandi, Corinne, Elsie, Catherine, and the rest of my incredible writer friends–without our sprint session, plotting chats, and your general encouragement, writing would be a sad and lonely job. I love our unhinged text threads, random voice memos, and the gentle reminders that the characters that live in our heads are, unfortunately, fictional. You're the best friends a gal could have.

# LENA HENDRIX

*Reader Group*

hot-as-sin small town romance

Want to connect? Come hang out with the Hendrix Heartthrobs on Facebook to laugh & chat with Lena! Special sneak peeks, announcements, exclusive content, & general shenanigans all happen there.

Come join us!

# ABOUT THE AUTHOR

Lena Hendrix is a *USA Today* and Amazon Top 5 Bestselling contemporary romance author living in the Midwest. Her love for romance stared with sneaking racy Harlequin paperbacks and now she writes her own hot-as-sin small town romance novels. Lena has a soft spot for strong alphas with marshmallow insides, heroines who clap back, and sizzling tension. Her novels pack in small town heart with a whole lotta heat.

When she's not writing or devouring new novels, you can find her hiking, camping, fishing, and sipping a spicy margarita!

Want to hang out? Find Lena on Tiktok or IG!

**Star Harbor**

Chasing the Sun

When We Fall

Beneath the Frost

In Full Bloom

**The Sullivans**

One Look

One Touch

One Chance

One Night

One Taste (prequel novella)

**The Kings**

Just This Once

Just My Luck

Just Between Us

Just Like That

Just Say Yes

**Redemption Ranch**

The Badge

The Alias

The Rebel

The Target

**Chikalu Falls**

Finding You

Keeping You

Protecting You

Choosing You (origin novella)